To Jeanette

PIPER

A Last Score Spin Off

K.L. SHANDWICK

Love

K L Shandwick

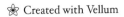 Created with Vellum

ACKNOWLEDGMENTS

Editor: Andie.M. Long Editing & Proofreading
Cover Design: by Francessca Wingfield
Cover Images: Anuki @ A.Chumburidze Photography and K.L.
Shandwick

Cover Model: Joseph Wareham

Beta Readers: Elmarie Pieterse, Sarah Lintott, Donna Trippi Salzano

Proofreader: Lisa Perkins, Sue Noyes

PROLOGUE

*P*iper

You only get one life. Period. Living it the way you want comes down to how willing and able you are to make it happen. You have to want something enough for it to become a need.

What I desperately wanted, I craved so much; it became living matter inside me. Every day it continually gnawed away at my gut, creating a feeling of driven angst inside.

Life hadn't been easy so far, but then again, I'd never known anyone who didn't have rough patches in life. Personally, I never truly lived until I came to Dignity House.

Before then I had merely existed. Since that time I had become a survivor with an innate knowledge deeply embedded in my brain from my time at home. Back then I felt lucky to survive—and felt I was meant for nothing more.

Unafraid at the thought of hard work, I had strived for my place in this world and with the incredible opportunity fate had thrown into my lap, my new life was definitely all about change.

For this I owed a debt of gratitude to the memory of my mom to live my life exactly how I wanted, regardless of how others thought it should be lived, and to make sure I used my freedom to make my own decisions.

If I'd known having guts would have led me this far, I'd have pushed my mom sooner... harder. Then again, maybe if we had found the courage to leave at any other time, I would not have landed as soundly on my feet as I did.

Never in a million light years did I think for one minute the pendulum of hope I had clung to would have swung me in the direction of Gibson and Chloe Barclay.

Growing up in a hostile environment full of verbal, emotional, and physical abuse, was infinitely oppressive. Colin, my mother's partner, reserved the right to his sole opinion and ruled us with fear; but fate intervened in the guise of a simple pamphlet offering help, and now my life could not be more different.

Loved and cherished, my life since then has been full of privilege and rights, where freedom of expression is not only encouraged but expected.

Every last one of the people who watch over me are protective and caring and expect nothing in return. Teaching me how to treat one another with respect, to value myself, and helping me learn to value the opinions of others. Most importantly, they taught me how to respect and protect myself.

Knowing me well became part of my problem because it gave me the challenge to convince those I valued and loved that I was mostly healed and more than capable of striking out on my own.

For the majority of the time I stayed with the Barclays I was quiet —still shy in some ways—and if I'm honest, a little mindful of the world I had grown into. But as time went on, I learned to open up when surrounded by the people I trusted, or the time when I could care less who stood in judgment—when I sang.

Mom always said the more you practiced something the less feared it would be, and I had begun to see her point when it became certain the only way I would overcome fear would be to face my insecurities and fight them.

"If you were mine. I wouldn't be happy to let you go out there on your own," Simon voiced, in his lazy dulcet tone. I scowled with narrowed eyes because he had supported what Gibson had said.

Obviously, I knew this reaction would be a possibility. Who was I kidding? I was sure Gibson had felt it was a slap in the face I had chosen to go with a small indie record label instead of the vision he had in his head for me.

It wasn't that I was being rebellious or anything. Most people would have paid a fortune to have a seasoned rock star on their side, and I more than most should have been a people pleaser where Gibson was concerned. Why? Because Gibson was my hero.

When he agreed to be my legal guardian prior to my eighteenth birthday I was speechless, lost in mourning, and eternally grateful. There were no words to describe how much love was stored in his huge soft heart, hidden behind his tough exterior.

Since then, he'd done all and anything he could think of for me, making sure my life ran as smooth and stress free as was humanly possible. Until this.

Fighting the rising anxiety, I watched a tight line immediately form across Gibson's mouth and my chest tightened. I knew before I voiced my choice he wouldn't be happy with the decision I had made.

One glance and I knew he was majorly pissed. Anger radiated from his tense upper body toward Simon instead of at me. Gibson had missed the point that Simon's comment was in agreement with what he, himself, had said.

"Keep the fuck out of it. She's not yours, and never will be," he snapped back. Fragile nerves still at play inside me made my body jump at his raised tone and I stared anxiously as he gave Simon a dark pointed glare.

Cocking his head to one side, Gibson looked toward me, winced and frowned. My heart ached at the sad expression on his face. Noting my stiffened frame, his eyes softened, and he breathed in deeply before he sighed. "Sorry," he muttered, running his fingers through his hair.

None of what was happening between us was Simon's fault. It was Gibson's reaction to my future plans that had made Simon the target for his frustrations.

I knew Gibson thought he knew best... and even though I had

considered that maybe he did, I wasn't prepared to surrender to what Gibson had in mind for me and my career.

Although I called Gibson by name, he and I viewed each other as father and daughter since I had no other. Always ready with a hug and a chat, I'd usually felt safe and protected by him; but the edgy vibe he gave off was different whenever his bandmate Simon was around. I had no idea why.

Sometimes I wondered if Gibson felt threatened by Simon because I tended to agree with Simon more than I did with him. Then again, Gibson viewed my decisions from the perspective of a parent instead of a potential peer like Simon did.

My eyes glanced nervously between the two men and I wondered why Simon didn't argue back. Given he knew Gibson better than me, I knew he must have had his reasons. Instinct had taught me Gibson was nearing a meltdown when he had stopped shouting and sat in silence.

Glancing at Simon's impassive stance, I realized Simon thought if he said anything else there was a distinct possibility the situation would become more inflammatory.

Witnessing the quiet stand-off between the two men wasn't easy, and for the first time since my mom and I had sought sanctuary at Dignity I felt anxious in the company of a man.

Eventually, Gibson braced his hands on the table, pushed his kitchen chair back and stared directly into my eyes. I steeled myself in defense as adrenaline pumped through me in anticipation of what he had to say.

Quietly, he stood and ran both hands through his hair again before dropping them to his thighs with a helpless slap. A long sigh relaxed his shoulders like he felt defeated and he turned away from me.

Shaking his head, he strode over to the refrigerator and yanked hard on the door handle. My eyes darted to Simon who was watching him, before he stole a secret glance in my direction. With a wry smirk he raised his eyebrow in a 'what's with him' kind of way.

Feeling shy, I rolled my eyes, my heart pumping rapidly in my chest —part with anxiety and part excitement from staring at Simon—when he flashed me a sexy smile and winked. Instantly, my heart flipped over and I took a second to relish in how handsome he was.

Allowing my eyes to tick over his face, a shot of euphoria rushed through me, leaving me shaky and my thoughts little muddled after our innocent little non-verbal secret conversation.

When I realized I was still staring, I noted his eyes were locked in a gaze neither of us appeared willing to break. Something about the way he looked at me had changed.

Electricity shot through my body right to my core and left me breathless. Then I wondered if I had imagined the whole thing.

Another attack of shyness gripped me, and I was instantly self-conscious of his scrutiny. *Now you're just being stupid, Piper.*

Cross with myself, I sat waiting for Gibson to speak, to break our gaze which was becoming uncomfortable. The thrill of what I was imagining passing between Simon and I, left me buzzing as I continued to be mesmerized by the look in his eyes.

When I could no longer stand it, I lowered my gaze. Fortunately, the glass of wine I had been drinking earlier was still half full. Taking it between my hands, I focused intently on my glass like it was suddenly the most fascinating liquid in the world as I fought to hide the effect our encounter was having on me.

In truth, I had a big 'thing' for Simon McLennan, Gibson's band-mate from M3rCy. It was obviously a 'stupid' thing because not only was he twelve years older and the most stunningly handsome, sexy as sin guy in the world, he had also been linked to most of the beautiful, high profile, and influential women in the world of celebrity.

There wasn't the slightest possibility a man like him would be remotely interested in anything I had to offer. *Jesus, Piper get a grip. So, what he smiled and winked. How many women have dropped their panties for him with that move?*

I swore that given my limited experience of boys, I was prone to foolish ideas about exploring my sexuality with someone like Simon. I scoffed at the thought, and both Gibson and Simon's eyes darted toward me. When I said nothing, another silence stretched between us all.

Ever since I'd lived with Gibson and Chloe, Simon had been a regular visitor to their home. It felt odd he had chosen to spend so much time with Gibson, but not having a girlfriend, I expected he felt at a loose end sometimes.

It suited me to have him around, and I was surprised at how kind, caring, and patient he and Gibson were at helping me cultivate an original sound, and encouraging me when I said I wanted to make a career of it.

Most aspiring singers would have given all that they had for the incredible opportunity to learn from the very best.

Gibson Barclay and Simon McLennan from M3rCy were my very own captive audience at home. However, sometimes, it had felt like a curse on the occasions one or the other of them ripped apart what I was most proud of.

Ultimately, I accepted their advice in regard to my music because they knew infinitely more about being paid to make music than me.

Trading secrets for success, Gibson and Simon had given me most of the tools necessary to succeed in my quest for a sustainable career in the music business.

From kindergarten to date, it was the one skill I had paid particular attention to, and it had been my saving grace in the darkest of times.

A wave of bittersweet memories of my mom's sad life reminded me how that bastard Colin took her music away to control her, but it hadn't prevented her from instilling a love of music in me, and I was prepared as I'd ever be to put my music to the test.

Trusting Gibson Barclay had been a huge gamble because I'd been left terrified of men. Yet as huge and powerful as Gibson was, I trusted him and Chloe much quicker than I ever expected I would. As time passed, I knew Gibson was the one man who would never fail me.

From that point, he had my utmost respect. I owed the man my life. It was the main reason I wanted his blessing and understanding as to why I had decided not to take his offer when I knew all he ultimately wanted was the very best for me.

Being on the right side of Gibson's protection sometimes came at a price. Like my relationship with Simon.

At first, I thought when Gibson interjected in our conversations it was cute; like he was a tad jealous of Simon growing close to me. I almost told him once I loved him as a father figure and Simon would never be his competition.

One night prior to another visit from Simon, my view on things changed when I accidently overheard Gibson telling Chloe she had to watch Simon around me. I was only two steps away from being within their sights and I stopped in my tracks.

Tuning in to Gibson's clipped tone I heard him say, "I fucking hate it." There was a pause in the conversation. "You know what he's like, darlin'. He destroys women," he scoffed. "It pains me to say it, and I love the guy to death, but I'll kill the fucker if he makes a move on her."

"Gibson, stop it. You're overreacting. Calm down, or you'll give yourself an ulcer," Chloe said in a flat tone, "And keep your voice down, Piper will hear you," she added, more urgently.

"Keep my voice down? What the fuck? I'd rather she was clued in." I heard his heavy feet pacing and imagined how annoyed he would look doing that, "Trust me he'd have that pretty little peach flat on her back and be balls deep inside her before she knew what was happening, given half a chance."

My jaw dropped, and I covered my mouth with my hand as my heart banged in my chest. Even though no name was mentioned, I instinctively knew he was talking about Simon with regards to me.

Hearing him talk in such crude terms shocked me to my core. Hurt and embarrassed, I continued to eavesdrop as Chloe and Gibson discussed whether I was a virgin. I felt mortified to hear them talk about intimate details concerning me. He then asked Chloe to warn me off Simon and guys like him.

"I've seen first-hand how he treats women and trust me he's fucking barbaric." Shock jolted my heart at Gibson's description of his friend; the words he used were horrible. "He's a horny asshole with low morals, and I hate her being around him," he continued in his gravelly voice that barely contained his anger.

Even though I had done nothing wrong, I felt ashamed at his words. Dread settled in my belly. *How can I face any of them knowing what Gibson thinks?*

How am I supposed to behave casually around the two men I had placed my trust in, given Gibson's assessment of what Simon is?

From my perspective, I wasn't the only one fantasizing about Simon. Gibson was talking nonsense. I figured he had to be.

How could he believe a worldly man like Simon would have the slightest interest in me? The plain, small-town girl who had been brought up in restricted circumstances? *I sure as hell didn't.*

At twenty years of age, I knew there were certain life skills and rights of passage I had totally skipped. I knew this made me seriously deficient with social situations and the opposite sex, but I was only twenty and figured I had plenty of time to catch up.

At the same time, I had an abundance of experience I would have given anything to forget; like how to survive living with domestic violence, or which coffin to bury a mom in.

Nevertheless, I knew enough to know the attention Simon had given me with regards to my music and day-to-day conversation was innocent, and at that moment in time I felt Gibson had read far too much into the situation with Simon and me.

Still, even though I was sure there was no way I'd attract a hard rock womanizer like Gibson's bandmate, just knowing Gibson was suspicious made me self-conscious and much less open in expressing my opinions.

Simon *was* seriously hot. The guy oozed sex appeal, charm, and charisma, without even opening his mouth. Naturally flirtatious and magnetic, I became fascinated by him from the moment I set eyes on him in the flesh. I hid it well.

Despite our age gap and different backgrounds, I had always enjoyed how he had treated me as an equal and that meant everything to a girl like me.

The part I enjoyed a little less was his ability to turn me on with a wink or his smile. It was laughable to think for one minute I'd captured the interest of a sexy rock star. As far as I was concerned, Gibson knew a lot about life, but I thought he was way off about this.

At thirty-two years old, Simon McLennan had a much more sophisticated palate for women than a sexually backward girl of twenty. It was insane to imagine an experienced, broad-minded guy like him would even look at an ordinary female like me.

CHAPTER ONE

*A*lthough I loved Gibson, Chloe, and Melody, with all that I was; I became worried Gibson's thoughts might disrupt the beautiful friendships Simon had with his bandmates.

This point made me glad I was leaving because the last thing I would ever have wanted was a twenty-year friendship between Gibson and Simon to dissolve around an argument about me.

Besides, apart from the Simon thing, I had already decided the longer I stayed cocooned by Gibson and Chloe, the less incentive I'd have to take control of my own destiny, and it was for this reason I became more determined to try to make it on my own.

Being with the Barclays had given me a second chance at life and by a stroke of luck someone believed in me enough to take a risk on my music. Best of all, the label that came through knew nothing about me or the connections I had.

Sitting down heavily in his chair again, Gibson shook his head. "Excuse me, baby girl, but I'm having a hell of a time trying to wrap my mind around why you'd throw over a sweet-loaded deal with an incredible record label, to sign with a relatively unknown one on a shoe-string budget. Do you know how many demos pass through Sly Records' hands every month?"

I eyed him with concern, taking in the unmistakable hurt in his eyes and wondered if he felt I was rejecting all the support he and Chloe had given me since my mom passed the year before.

It wasn't as if I'd dismissed his record company's offer to sign me, out of hand. It was more a case of if I made it, I would never know whether it was because of Gibson's connections or if I had succeeded on my own.

"No, I have no idea how many demos; but I imagine thousands considering Sly Records are one of the biggest and most prestigious record companies on either side of the Atlantic Ocean. I don't doubt I'm taking a hit by not having access to their massive social media platform."

The scowl Gibson wore made my heart ache. "Please... don't be hurt. This isn't personal. It doesn't mean I'm questioning your judgment or ignoring what this could mean for me. All I'm asking is for you to see things from my perspective."

"You're twenty years old, Piper." He sighed, moving directly in front of me. Still tense, he moved his head from side to side in a vain effort to release some tension. "What perspective? What do you know about the music business? How do you think you're going to survive out there peddling your music every day without the right people behind you?"

"You did it." I retorted before I could engage the brake on my mouth.

"I did, and I was so damned lucky to catch a break but let me tell you it was fucking tough. You know how many nights we went without food? Playing dive bars for peanuts or a bed for the night? At least I had bandmates who constantly had my back. Who do you have? What happens if you get in with the wrong kind?"

"I hear your concerns. Don't think I haven't considered all this. I've gone without food too, Gibson. I know what it all means. Thanks to Otto, the owner of Gravity, I'll be able to feed myself. They're paying me a living wage on account while I record."

Watching Gibson think I was making the wrong decision and perhaps thinking I had no further need for him almost killed me.

"And I'd like to think I still had you guys to advise me with the day-to-day stuff or do the ties that bind us together get severed the moment I walk out your door?" I sighed, and my eyes softened when I looked at the startled hurt in Gibson's eyes.

"Sorry. We're both saying things neither of us means," I offered.

Watching the new worry flit through his eyes almost killed me. The last thing I ever wanted to do was let him down, but I figured if we didn't settle all we had inside, it would fester and eat away at our relationship, longer term.

"Are you saying unless I choose what you want me to do, instead of what my gut tells me is the right course, you'll no longer back me?" I winced at how ungrateful I sounded. It felt like an insolent thing to say. I desperately wanted him to know I wasn't trying to be ungrateful. Gibson was the only father figure I had ever truly trusted... loved.

Seconds ticked by as he stared me down, his eyes narrowing and returning to normal as thoughts passed through his mind, until he glanced at Simon then returned his gaze back on me. My heart beat faster than I'd ever felt it before and I wondered for a moment if I had pushed him too far.

For a moment I had wanted to take the words back, but they were out there. *He's so mad with me.* Slowly, he placed his huge hands palm down on the table beside me, splayed his thick fingers wide and studied them.

My eyes were immediately transfixed on them because those were the same strong, gentle hands that had rubbed my back or hugged me tight when I was distressed. Gibson had used them to help me believe I wasn't alone in the world.

A poignant memory reminded me of the way he always comforted me because his hands were the only man's touch I had accepted as being safe in the desperate days after my mother's death.

"Please," I begged and the knot in my stomach twisted tighter again. "I really don't want us to fight about this. You think I don't know your way would be my guarantee for success? How easy it would be to roll up somewhere as Gibson Barclay's daughter and expect red carpet treatment? Success would be a given. I know this, but can't you see how important it is for me to do this on my own?"

"But you're not on your own. Not as long as there is breath in my body." Relief washed through me that no matter what, he wasn't willing to give up on me, but his low abrupt tone barely disguised the rising temper he was fighting hard to suppress. His admission was said with such fierce determination my heart ached for disappointing him.

Gibson continued to watch me closely, biting his bottom lip in frustration and attempting to roll the tension off his shoulders. I closed my eyes briefly because I could hardly bear to see the effect my disagreeing had on him.

A wave of guilt swelled from inside, forming a lump in my throat. The sting of salty tears burned as they rose past it and even though I swallowed roughly, I wasn't quick enough to stem their flow as they filled my eyes to the brim.

Never before had I tested the certainty of Gibson's statement to be there always. He and Chloe had opened their door to me in my time of need and he had grown to love me like his own.

Again, I wondered how my life had dealt me the best of pleasure and the worst pain anyone could imagine, in one single year... how fate had given me this unimaginable yet true second chance to rewrite my future.

Stilling quietly, a flashback came to mind of the night my mom and I had arrived at Dignity—the safe house that Gibson had funded, but his wife Chloe had set up as a refuge for victims of domestic violence.

From the second we stepped over the threshold of Dignity, I instinctively knew we'd finally escaped the violent, controlling clutches, of my mom's long-standing partner, Colin.

The way Chloe and her team took care of us gave us time to breathe and taught me it was the beginning of a brighter future.

The one thing I never expected was the devastating news that my mom's time to breathe was extremely limited and her future was about to end abruptly.

We had no idea she was sick when we ran out on Colin that day. The only thing we'd known for certain was it was our one chance for a new start and we'd taken it.

Little did we know then, that my future would be secured in the most unlikely way. How could I have predicted that Gibson Barclay, a rock star with a shady past with women; and his beautiful wife, herself a survivor of domestic violence, Chloe, would be waiting to save me?

Being childless back then, Chloe and Gibson agreed to take care of me, allowing my mother to die in peace, and I came to be the ward in the care of the biggest rock star the world had ever known.

Gibson and Chloe saved me not just from poverty but from being just another isolated victim of domestic violence and an outcast from collateral damage of a cancerous disease.

Turning my mind back to Gibson, I noted he had grave look on his face. I realized the silence had continued to stretch between us and wondered for a moment if I'd missed what he said, or if he was waiting for further debate from me.

"I know I'm not on my own," I said quickly picking up the thread of our conversation again. "And you'll never truly know how much I love you guys. I'm not doing this to hurt anyone, or to piss you off."

"Don't talk like that. Don't cuss, you're better than that," he scolded.

I drew in a sharp breath, let it out again and sighed. It eased the knot I felt deep within me.

"Look, I know Gravity isn't a big label and I know they have limited resources, but can't you see if I do this it will be against the odds? The same odds as you had."

"Sounds to me like the lady has already made up her mind, Gib." For a second I glanced nervously from Gibson to Simon and wondered if Gibson was going to lose his cool. If my belly had a knot before, it was nothing to the pain I felt when it squeezed tighter.

It was a brave but foolish move for Simon to stick his neck out and defend me when Gibson was so vehemently against my choice.

"You still fucking here?" Gibson barked, lifting his palms from near me and placing them close to Simon. I held my breath for a second and waited. After a few seconds, Gibson stood up from the chair and stretched his back.

Looking up at the ceiling, he took a deep breath and exhaled through his nostrils, bringing his head forward again. He held my gaze —which was pretty unnerving—then he narrowed his eyes. The weight of his direct stare hit me square in the chest like a brick. He hated what I wanted to do.

"I admire your principles, Piper, but this music business is so fucking tough... and it's riddled with people who either want to fuck you, fuck you over, or kick you the fuck out of the way."

I shrugged. "If there's one thing my childhood taught me, it's that I have smarts. I'm street smart, and I'm not my mom." My heart squeezed at the mention of her name. "Please give me your blessing because I'd rather work in a store earning an honest living, than make music the way someone wants me to because of who I am to you."

Gibson regarded me with suspicion and I figured he saw how deadly serious I was. Asking him to trust my judgment wasn't easy, but I was confident enough to believe I could make it on my own.

Restraining himself from further comment, Simon stood and pulled his jacket from the back of the chair he'd been sitting on. When he shrugged himself into it, his jerky movements did nothing to hide his frustration.

"Right, I'm out of here before we clash. Good luck convincing him, Piper, but I've not got all night to watch this soap opera play out," he said, barely hiding his anger. "I've got things to do and people to see." Without saying anything further, Simon shoved his chair back, excused himself with a small salute and headed for the door.

CHAPTER TWO

*O*nce Simon had gone, Gibson walked around the table and pulled out the chair next to me. Spinning it around, he sat, leaning his forearms on the back of it. Extending his hand, he waited for me to take it. When I slipped my hand into his, he clasped his large thick fingers around it and slowly shook his head.

"I swore on your mama's death bed I'd take care of you," he said, speaking the truth. "You've either got so much confidence in your ability as a singer, or you're fucking crazy not to take the free ride you're being offered." I sighed. We were going around in circles.

"See. Even you're saying it. A free ride. I don't want to be Gibson Barclay's adopted orphan when my voice hits the airwaves. I want to be known as Piper, the smoking hot new discovery with the voice that makes men hard when they hear it and women envious of that fact."

As soon as the words fell out of my mouth I cringed. It was a joke Simon had said to me once when he wanted more provocation in my performance. Gibson had pushed me to the point of frustration where I'd blurted out the one thing that was supposed to remain unsaid, and in my mind.

Roaring loudly with laughter, he crumpled up, his body doubling over the chair in a fit of raucous laughter. Chloe ran into the kitchen to see what had happened.

"What's going on? What's so funny?" she asked, looking first at me then to Gibson, for the answer.

Gibson wound his laughter down save for a few light chuckles, wiped the tears that had sprung to his eyes with his cuff, and nodded in my direction but still addressed Chloe.

"Tell her what you said to me," he urged, chuckling again to himself as he stroked down his abdomen.

Mortified I'd uttered something so ridiculous, my lips twisted and I gave her a wry smirk as I saw Chloe fold her arms indicating she was waiting patiently for me to comply.

Oh, I knew he thought I'd blush and get flustered because I hadn't really meant to say what I did aloud. It was all his fault I'd made such a stupid statement in the first place when he had pushed me into a corner with his silly little questions.

Glancing at Gibson, I drew him the stink eye when I saw how amused he was and no matter what we'd been arguing about before there was something in the way he looked at me that made me giggle uncontrollably too.

Gesticulating with his hand in a winding motion Gibson told me to get on with it as he continued to laugh somewhat breathlessly by then, so I took a deep breath and prepared to humiliate myself.

Considering I knew I'd meet a lot worse than Gibson if I went out on my own, I called his bluff and rose to his challenge if for no other reason than to show him I meant what I said.

"We've been talking about my decision to go with Gravity as a recording label. I don't have to tell you the resistance I've met from Gibson about my choice to do this, Chloe," I began. She nodded and glared at Gibson because they'd obviously had words about this in private and I knew Chloe had backed me on this.

"Anyway, he was telling me yet again how much easier it would be for me as a singer if I went on Syd's books and I put him straight when I said I want to be known as Piper, the smoking hot new discovery with the voice that makes men hard to hear it and women envious of that fact."

Glancing quickly from Gibson, who I had addressed, and back to Chloe, I saw her chew on her smile. Nodding slowly, she looked like she was pretending to consider what I'd said as she fought to compose herself. Wandering over to Gibson's side she placed her petite little hands on his shoulders.

"With an answer like that, I'd say Piper's got this, Gibson." He gave her a look like he could easily have committed murder and she sighed. "Maybe it's time to show Piper your support and consider that she's thought long and hard about what she wants and how she wants to do it? You weren't exactly the kind of guy to take advice from others in the early days and look where it got you." She bent to kiss him on the lips. *Way to go, Chloe.*

"Thanks for the backup, Chloe," he muttered in an acid-tone laced with sarcasm. "What is it with the women in this house using their sexuality to get what they want?" he asked, sounding like the wounded party.

"That's not what's happening here, baby. What's happening is you trying to use yours because you want to protect this innocent little female here. Or am I reading you wrongly?"

"Is it a crime I want to protect her? If so, then yeah that's true, I am. You've heard the saying, 'It's a jungle out there'. The music business is like being on safari covered in ketchup, waiting for the deadliest predators known to man to strike," he replied.

"Please let me do this, Gibson," I begged. "I promise I'll keep you up to speed and consult you whenever I have the slightest hesitation about something. I'm not above taking advice, but I really want an honest shot at this on my ability, not because of who you are."

Standing upright from the chair, he slung his leg clear of it to meet the other and pulled me up out of my seat. "First hint of anyone doing you over, and I'm all in, you hear? I know you think you got this, but I'm always gonna do what I think is right to keep you safe... don't forget I promised your mama," he reminded me again.

This time when he mentioned my mom I lost all the fight within me and hugged him tight. Finally, I had his reluctant approval to strike out on my own, but with Gibson's protective nature I knew I may have won the battle, but I guessed I was far from winning the war.

Six weeks later, Gibson had had time to absorb me leaving, and I closed the heavy metal reinforced door on my new penthouse apartment. Gibson, Chloe, and Melody—Gibson's daughter from a one-night-stand eight years before—had only just left, and as soon as I heard the soft click of the lock, I turned my back, leaned against the cool metal and let out a deep sigh of relief.

Moving out was harder than I envisioned. Chloe wept openly, and it was clear I meant a lot to her. My heart ached for inflicting misery on all of them by going to live in Santa Monica on my own.

Melody clung to my body like I was facing an executioner and she was never going to see me again, while Gibson had checked and double-checked the window locks, alarms, and reset the alarm entry codes again so that the guys who had undertaken the re-model couldn't regain entry.

Purchasing the top-floor apartment in a high-end block overlooking the beach was incredibly extravagant, but Gibson insisted the gated community property was necessary in the event I became known. I took his comment as a mark of confidence in me, but in truth Gibson always left very little to chance.

From the ten-minute journey to the studio, to how my essential groceries would be delivered, his team had ensured my transition to my new living arrangements would feel as smooth as possible.

Earlier that day he'd taken delivery of a shiny red mid-ranged SUV with full breakdown and valet services and handed the keys to me as a 'house warming' gift.

I was overwhelmed by the Barclays' generosity. In my mind, their kindness only made me thirstier for success because I wanted to pay them back.

"It's all yours," Gibson said, smiling affectionately as he held out the keys after attaching the spare car fob to the apartment keys. Overcome with emotion, I felt awkward about accepting everything.

"It's a loan. I'm gonna pay you back someday, just watch me," I replied, meaning every single word. Gibson immediately pulled me into his chest and wrapped his arms tightly around me, then placed his chin on my head.

"Sweetheart, we love you. There's no charge. You owe us nothing except to have the best of everything life offers you. Choose wisely, think long and hard, but be impulsive and spontaneous whenever you can. Have fun, be safe, and always remember we're more than blood."

For an alpha male who had a bark that could cut any man down to size, his gentle way with the women in his life made Gibson somewhat of a mystery. He had a heart of gold, but a tongue of the hardest leather when he was crossed. I knew I'd never want to be on the receiving end of that side of him.

Ruby, a close childhood friend of Chloe's, had a new job that had brought her to live just a couple of towns over from where my place was, and I promised to call her if I ever needed anyone urgently. Surprisingly enough, Chloe was a lot less uptight about my change in living conditions than Gibson was.

Then again, Gibson was a guy, and from what Chloe had told me there was an incident from when he was dating Chloe which had given him reason to be overly protective at times.

Deciding to move out had been the easy part. Moving all my possessions from home to my new apartment was the end of one emotional journey and the birth of another. Hanging my most precious gift—a silver-framed picture of my mom singing on stage—I spoke aloud softly and asked for her guidance over me.

This is what she had wanted for me. It was the new beginning we should both have had that I was taking on my own. Although I'd miss her for my whole life, I had finally come to terms with the trauma of my past, lived with the grief I had no control over, and I had the will to do better. What better testament to her life than to live the life my mom wanted for me, and to find my own personal identity.

Wandering over to the balcony, I slid the sliders open and stepped out onto the amazing little outside space with the wicker hanging chairs facing out toward the beach. I leaned slowly on the railing.

The huge amber Californian sun was low on the water, casting an image of burnt coppers and shades of silver and brown over the ocean.

My gaze wandered over to the multi-colored Ferris Wheel lights in the distance and my heart ached. I'd never ridden on one.

Standing up straight, I filled my lungs with the balmy evening air, and I couldn't describe the feeling that washed over me. I suppose that was because I'd never really recognized it before and I guessed it was the feeling of being safe and home.

Stepping inside, I made my way through to the master bedroom of my three bed, three bath, penthouse apartment. Although extravagant, I knew it was the Barclays' intention to visit regularly and therefore the size made sense.

Kneeling in front of the four huge boxes I had yet to unpack, my mind turned to little Melody, Gibson's daughter, who stayed at home with us every other week. It felt cruel to leave her because she was the one who had suffered the most change.

Gibson had no idea she existed until after they'd taken me on, but they loved her, and Melody took all of us in her stride. She had gained a whole new family, only to lose me from it a couple of years later.

~

By 8pm I had unpacked all my comforts of home and stamped my mark on the place with my own soft furnishings, small ornaments, and the precious vinyl record player the Barclays had given me.

Chloe and I had spent hours trolling through the thrift shops in the small towns close to their home in Colorado; making me a collection of albums from artists my mom had introduced me to.

Selecting an Eagles album, I showered to the apt tune of "Hotel California" then slid into some cotton shorts and a tank top before climbing into bed. It was only when I snuggled down on my side that my tears fell. I was sad for the life my mom had missed out on and I promised her in my prayers to make her, Gibson, Chloe, and Melody proud.

~

Several times in the night I woke with the searing heat and quickly realized living near the Pacific Ocean was going to take some acclimating after my time in the mountains. I even got up and showered to cool myself down, but when I woke in the morning with my cell vibrating, my hands felt wet when I picked up my phone.

"Good morning, baby. Did the move go all right?" Otto, the producer from Gravity asked.

"Yep, all settled in," I confirmed and found myself smiling sleepily at his upbeat tone.

"Want to meet me for lunch? I have a couple of sessional musicians I'd like to introduce you to."

Sitting up, my heart fluttered excitedly, and I was instantly fully alert.

"Sure. What time? Where? Do I need to bring anything with me?"

"Whoa. Cool your jets, baby. Breathe," he told me, chuckling down the line, and I shook my head.

Does anyone even say that anymore?

"Sorry, I'm just keen to get this going, you know?" I said, as I tried to tone my excitement down.

"Indeed, I can't wait to get that sexy-as-fuck voice of yours on a few tracks in the mixing room."

I grinned at the way he openly shared what he thought. All he'd had was one demo, and he'd called me minutes later. Inspired by my voice, he'd taken a shot on a total unknown when they only had funding for maybe three artists a year.

Otto's confidence and his small budget meant more to me than the millions Sly Records had at their fingertips.

The way I saw it, the smaller fish was willing to spend more of their budget on me. If that didn't express their belief in me I don't know what did.

"Want me to pick you up?"

"No," I said a little too quickly. I didn't want any of them to know about my connection to Gibson. For the best part of two years I had managed to keep out of sight. I was also afraid Colin may come to find me if I made it onto TV or some other form of media.

Some may have thought me mad, but I had gone to great pains to hide the rock royalty that surrounded me, to remain anonymous.

My determination was set in stone. I wanted to make it alone or not at all. If Otto knew where I lived, he'd surely know by the address alone that I had access to someone with money to burn.

Armed with the latest technology in my bells-and-whistles little car, I found the address of the sports bar they hung out at. It was right across the street from the studio.

I'd already been there once when I signed the contract and toured their facilities, but Jerry, one of Gibson's security guys, had come with me and pretended to be my dad. It felt daunting being back there on my own.

Noise from the rowdy sports bar could be heard in the car lot. The outside was packed bumper-to-bumper with trucks, cars, and SUVs.

Every spot was already in use. I had almost given up hope of parking, when a waitress came out, drove off in her old beat-up truck, and I managed to snag her space.

Grimacing at my hair when I looked in the mirror, I tried flattening it. My hair hated the humidity more than me. Heaving in a huge gulp of air, I reached for the door handle and muttered, "You got this, Piper."

The blazing hot sun seared into my skin as I hurried across the hot, dark-gray asphalt, as the stifling heat burned my nostrils and lungs when I breathed. Finally, I reached the covered porch doorway and stepped inside.

A blast of cold air from the air-con above the door felt most welcome, and I stood there a few seconds longer than I intended before I shoved my large sunglasses up on my head and tried to adjust to the dark, crowded surroundings of the noisy sports bar.

Glancing around, I noticed everyone was totally enthralled by the football game that was in progress and stepped up to the counter to see where Otto may be.

"ID?" I stared unblinking toward the balding hulk of a man

standing behind it and gave him an innocent smile. "I'm not drinking, just looking for someone—"

"I got her Randy" Otto said, as he approached me. His hand settled possessively on the middle of my back. "This is Piper, the fabulous singer I told you about. Piper, this is Randy. Be nice to him, his bar food will feed you most days. Don't want him spitting in your grub if you piss him off," he joked.

Turning to look at Otto, I wasn't too sure what to say. I mean I knew it was a joke, but when you've been where I'd been in my life, joking about someone fucking with my food wasn't funny to me.

"Isn't she lovely?" Otto asked, addressing Randy like I was his fresh newborn child, and fortunately for me he didn't tap into my awkward anxiety surrounding his earlier comment.

"Beautiful," Randy agreed. I felt myself blush at their scrutiny. "If she sings like you tell me she can, she's a real find."

"Can we not talk about me like I'm some classic car or something?" I asked, hiding my irritation behind my tone playful. It was embarrassing when Otto spoke about me like I was some commodity, but I felt I handled it fine.

"Sorry, baby, I'm just stoked you're here. Thanks for doing this afternoon. You're not too tired from your journey?"

"Nope, I'm fine. Dying to get started," I replied honestly.

"Okay, come meet the sessional guys I've found for you. Two of the guys I've used many times and I've got a pianist coming into the studio first thing tomorrow from Utah. He lands a bit later tonight, so he'll be here at 8am sharp.

Your sessions are 8am to 11am, and 2pm to 4pm. Another artist is recording outside your times with another producer. We run a tight ship but allowing others to use the studio gives us more in the bank for the artists on our label.

"Makes sense," I mumbled, calculating in my head I'd be expected to sing for five hours a day. I wasn't used to stretching my vocals for that amount of time and had followed Gibson's advice of a maximum of three hours a day.

Still, I figured with the break in between, plenty of fluids, and minimum conversation to rest in between I'd be fine. *Singing for two more hours a day would be fine.*

Leading me back to the large booth, he introduced me to Jeff, who he informed me was the lead guitarist on my tracks; and Grunt, my drummer for the album. I nodded my head, looking first to Jeff, who flashed me a welcoming smile, then to the deadpan face of Grunt. I couldn't help noticing they were like chalk and cheese.

Jeff was in smart but casual dress of a white linen shirt and cream, cropped Chino pants. Almost as young as me, I guessed him to be around twenty-three years old at the most. He was very attractive with his bright sky-blue eyes and shiny blond, shoulder-length hair. Taking in his strong physique and dark customary Californian golden tan, I smiled back.

Flashing me another perfect smile that reached his eyes, I was instantly taken with him because he radiated a friendly, laid back vibe. *Definitely a picture ad for the classically healthy-looking California beach boy.*

Grunt's appearance was entirely the opposite. His thin and weedy looking frame was slightly hunched as he held his beer in both hands. His bony fingers made his hands look older than the rest of him, although I'd have put him in his mid-forties at a guess.

Grunt's greeting was much less enthusiastic. He gave me a curt nod as he took his hand off his cold beer glass just long enough to grant me a small salute gesture with two fingers over his forehead and a small noise in the back of his throat, which explained the name he'd been given.

His welcoming attention drew my notice to his lank, thinning mousy-brown hair, with a small bald patch at his crown. Giving me a forced smile, he then yawned, and I tried hard not to dislike him.

I figured he probably thought of me as talentless bubble gum pop music wonder. That thought made me determined to impress him. My stomach tightened a little in his presence and I found myself trying not to do what I'd done with Jeff and judge him on first appearances alone.

"Well, hello," Jeff said, dismissing the fact that Grunt had nothing to say, and he gave me a wider grin as he stood from the booth to greet me properly. His friendly approach had a calming effect on my nerves and I sighed, realizing I had been holding my breath while being introduced.

Sliding my hand into his outstretched larger one, I felt genuine warmth at his touch. Our eyes connected, and I saw his pupils dilate when he looked at me. I wondered if mine did the same. His warm welcome meant everything to me and I immediately felt relaxed in his presence.

CHAPTER THREE

Otto gestured me into the booth and sat down beside me. I felt a little apprehensive but excited at the same time. Appearing pale, Otto looked like a man who spent no time in the sun. There were no outstanding features about him and he seemed so ordinary; almost nerdy of average height, medium build, with mid-brown hair, and brown eyes. The most notable thing about him was his old iconic ZZ Top t-shirt.

Glancing around the table at Jeff, Grunt, and myself, I'd never have described us as a dream team for setting my music career on fire. But that's the thing about music...it has the ability to bring out hidden talents in the least expected people.

When Otto became animated about the sessions and drilled into us how important punctuality was, I felt fortunate to have a manager to oversee everything because as a concession to Gibson I'd let him put me in touch with a mutual friend of his, Thomas.

The formal part of the meeting ended a couple hours later, when Grunt told us he had a gig that evening, got up, and left. The atmosphere around the table became far less intense from the second the bar door closed behind him.

"I know what you're thinking. He's an Oddball, right?" Jeff asked, his eyes sparkling mischievously when Otto left us at the table to grab some food menus.

Feeling my nose wrinkle despite my thoughts to keep my opinions to myself, I shrugged.

"Everyone's different. I try not to judge people without knowing them," I replied, taking care not to voice what I thought.

"Great answer. Very diplomatic. I don't blame you for being guarded. If I were in your shoes, I'd be the same. By rights that guy should be at the very top of his game. Missed out on several huge band spots in the nineties," Jeff said, and smirked ruefully.

Suddenly I had empathy for Grunt, still toiling so hard doing bar gigs after twenty years or so.

"I kid you not, Grunt has incredible talent on percussions." He shrugged helplessly, and I could feel his sincerity. "Unfortunately for him, he doesn't have the ability to present himself very well."

"That's so sad," I said, a wave of sympathy for the musician who had missed out because of his social awkwardness.

"It truly is. When you hear him play, you'll know what I mean," he advised me, plucking a small packet of brown sugar from the condiments box on the table.

"What about you?" I probed, clasping my hands together on the table.

"What about me?" he echoed my question back.

"I know you're a sessional artist at the studio, but have you auditioned for many bands?"

"Nope."

"No? Why not?"

"Too lazy," he replied and slumped down in his seat.

I hid a grin and raised an eyebrow, thinking he was toying with me. "And what happens when you get too old to be lazy?"

"That'll never happen," he replied eyeing me. Then he shrugged again and his facial expression was one of resignation. "I love my life, Piper. Not everyone needs aspirations to be more than they are," he replied flatly. *Huh?*

It was the least expected reply to a question I'd ever asked of anyone. I didn't know how to respond to it, so I said nothing. I blinked, my mind unable to form something else to say as I continued to watch him for any signs he was joking.

For someone who didn't appear much older than me, and who looked like God's gift to girls, I found it hard to believe he had no personal ambitions. I wasn't sure whether I should admire him or slap him in the face for his lack of drive and being so contented.

Until this point I had directed my sympathy toward Grunt who had tried all his life to be more, but now wondered if my pity should be aimed at Jeff, who at the tender age he was, didn't have it in him to aspire to be more.

An uncomfortable silence fell between us and I turned to look for Otto. Unfortunately he was deep in conversation with Randy, the barman, and I somehow knew he wasn't going to return to the table anytime soon.

Turning back to Jeff, I tried again, "Favorite bands?"

"No favorites. I'm pretty eclectic in my listening choices."

Jeez, the conversation is going south fast.

Just when I thought of excusing myself to seek refuge in the bathroom, he had a comeback.

"You? Who are your main music influences?"

Without hesitation I jumped straight in with my artistic heroines. "I loved listening to Motown as a kid, but my main influences have been everyone from Janis Joplin, Pink, and Mariah Carey, all the way back to Aretha Franklin and Barbra Streisand," I replied with enthusiasm.

Jeff looked thoughtful then nodded, "Hmm," he hummed, "I can see you're very eclectic in your listening choices as well." I was, but unlike him, I contributed my thoughts to the conversation.

Once a common thread was established between us, our communication was much more relaxed. When Otto came back to the table, and the conversation turned to bands they had recorded with in the past, I felt much more confident that Jeff's earlier remarks weren't that much of an issue.

I was impressed by the number of artists the small label had supported in the nine years Gravity had been in business. Otto spoke with such passion about them and I was convinced I'd made the right choice to launch my music career with them.

Four hours later, we said our goodnights, and I left the bar and headed home. During the journey, I thought about the album, and songs I was due to record.

Otto was in awe of how Thomas had managed to negotiate the amazing material for me to record. What he didn't know was Thomas had worked with Gibson and I during the previous few months to scout the most suitable material for me to use.

There were five songs written by other top drawer recording artists —two of my own, and four Gibson and I had collaborated on. These were credited as co-written by Paul Gibson, with any potential royalties going into a trust fund for Melody.

Entering the lobby of my apartment block, the superintendent called me over, handed me some mail and asked me to wait. Handing me a Styrofoam box, I frowned a questioning brow as I opened the envelope with it.

"Congratulations on your first day at work. We figured you'd be feeling pretty tired on your return, so we've ordered you dinner." My heart clenched because although being out on my own was what I had longed for, it struck me I had no one to share my day with.

A lump swelled in my throat and I quickly handed the super a ten-dollar bill in thanks, juggled the box between my body and arm, and made my way up to my apartment with tears brimming in my eyes. Suddenly, the full impact of being out on my own hit me hard and I pulled out my cell phone, swiped the screen, and called home.

"Hey, baby, how was your day?" Gibson asked, and I heard Chloe protesting in the background that she wanted to listen as well. A slow smile curved my lips because I felt loved.

"All right, you're on speakerphone and Chloe's right here." I felt far less lonely for knowing they were only one call away.

～

My second night of independent living was much like the first.

Stiflingly hot and sticky. No matter how high I cranked the air conditioning, I still felt hot. At one point I laid dog tired on the cool tiled floor in my bathroom and tried to sleep.

Eventually, I passed out through sheer exhaustion, and woke around two hours before it was time to get up, so I got into the shower to freshen up. From then on time dragged and my anticipation grew for getting to the studio. Every time I looked at my wristwatch it was only a few minutes from the last look.

I arrived at the studio early, with butterflies in my stomach and a racing heart. Facing the building, I stood staring at the tinted windows, adorned with their cursive writing, as nerves vibrated through every cell in my body.

Sucking in a breath to settle my nerves, I blew it out slowly. *This is where the magic happens.* I chuckled at the corny line in my head and dug deep to find my confidence. *Here goes.*

Self-belief was all I had. It was what I had clung to during my darkest days as I grew up in the suppressive and controlling environment Colin had made for us, but now it was time to prove to those who had taken a chance on me that I had what it took to succeed.

Entering the studio foyer, I had to press the intercom and wait for entry to the studio. It wasn't a big place, but security was tight due to the expensive equipment inside. Seconds after pressing the bell, the door buzzed and I heard it unlock.

As I pushed the door open, Jeff came out of the studio door to meet me.

"Ah, you made it. Ready to blow us away today?" he asked in a friendly tone.

"That's what I'm hoping," I said, toying with the shoulder strap of my oversized satchel as I kept my nerves in check.

His eyes held mine and his smile widened showing most of his pearly white teeth. *God, he's so good looking, it's distracting.* "After you," he gestured, sweeping his hand for me to enter before him. My heart fluttered in my chest and it had nothing at all to do with making music.

Suddenly I felt self-conscious and flattered from the slightest attention he'd given to me, but I convinced myself he was only being polite. I wasn't really used to being around guys apart from a couple in high school.

~

For the first hour of the day Otto introduced us to Wyatt, the piano player, and we listened to the tunes I had chosen to record. Otto made suggestions, and I learned Jeff and Grunt had been given prior access to familiarize themselves with them before I arrived.

Choosing the first song to record, Otto went with an upbeat number called, "Faces In Unfamiliar Places", written by an A-list music artist.

The song was about a girl who missed her train and ran into a café out of the rain. She then sees her boyfriend who she thought was out of town, walking with another girl.

Once in the booth, for some reason I felt more nervous and keen to impress my sessional musicians than I was Otto, and my nerves temporarily kicked in as soon as they started to play. However, after two false starts, I found my flow when the familiar music and my words centered me.

Jeff was right, Grunt was an incredible drummer. For someone who looked like he'd blow over in the wind, he had the most incredible speed, strength, and stamina. He also had vision and improvised on the percussion from the original score, producing a sound that took the song to a whole new level of sick.

Obviously, Otto had to run the final arrangement past the artist who penned it, to ensure we were able to use his version, but I was sure they'd admit the number was improved with a few tiny changes.

"Goose bumps, baby," Jeff mumbled and held out his arm. "The way you sang that made my heart pound. Look at the hair on my arms; your voice is electric," he said, staring at me like I'd grown a third eye. "You can't just sing, Piper, you're fucking fantastic," he added, looking amazed, then he turned to glance at Grunt. "Am I right, or what? That sound was fucking insane."

Grunt was soaking wet and was drying the sweat from his hands and drumsticks on a small sports towel when his head snapped up and he stared directly toward me. "Yeah, fucking ace," he said in a voice to rival Barry White's, a smooth old soul singer from the seventies.

It was the most animated I had seen him, and I grinned. His response probably meant more to me than anything Jeff had said before, because until that moment I'd never heard him say more than, 'Got a gig', in a monotone when he'd left the day before.

From that point on my nerves subsided, my voice loosened up as I relaxed, and by the end of the day we had a pretty perfect track of the first song for the album.

Otto informed me the first few tracks usually took a long time to nail because of the differences in interpretation, the musicians connecting with someone they weren't used to jamming with, and vocal pitch imperfections.

Time passed too fast and before I knew it, it was time for us to pack in for the day. It was fortunate that another band had the studio time because if that hadn't been the case, I'd have pushed myself harder and probably ruined my tone through straining my vocal chords.

I was almost at my car when I heard Jeff call out for me, and I turned to see him kicking the dirt on his way over to talk to me.

"Heading out to a house party for a few hours R&R. Want to come with? I could introduce you to a great crowd and you can maybe make a few friends since you're new in town."

My initial reaction was no. I didn't know him from a hole in the wall. Then again, he was now one of the team and I wondered if I'd appear standoffish if I didn't at least accept his hand in friendship.

"Sounds nice, but I'll follow you in my car because I'm still trying to find my way around and I'm dependent on my trusted satellite navigation to get me home safely." Really it was my way of ensuring I had a get-out strategy if he took me somewhere I wasn't that comfortable with.

Jeff looked thoughtful as he narrowed his eyes. He looked disappointed for a moment, but fortunately he didn't push the point.

Apart from my issues of trusting men, he rode a huge flashy motorbike. There was no way I felt I could have coped with the intimacy of clinging onto his back with my arms wrapped around him and my legs next to his.

"Suit yourself. I just have to make a quick stop along the way," he advised me as he cocked his leg over his machine and sat back on the wide leather seat with a spongy bounce. Kicking the bike stand away with his heel, he took the heavy weight underneath him and held the handlebars.

My eyes fell on his tanned outstretched muscular arms and I sighed. He looked like every girl's fantasy and could easily have passed for a movie star. The shiny bike only made him look more appealing.

My greedy gaze followed his every move and when he glanced up and flashed me a dimpled smile, I exhaled in a rush. With my heart fluttering in my chest, I clenched my thighs together because he was undoubtedly one of the most alluring men I'd seen since... whenever.

Stealing another glance, I admired the image he struck as a smoking-hot-looking guy with an immensely power-packed set of wheels between his muscle-toned legs. With its shiny chrome exhaust and trim, and black metallic body, it was a stunning piece of expensive machinery.

Normally I'd have said a motorbike like that was a 'babe magnet', but I doubted very much if Jeff had any need for such an accessory to pull women toward him.

Women aside, of course he'd have a ride like that. It suited him down to the ground.

Perhaps he had wealthy parents and with that kind of financial freedom he was happy to live a much simpler life than the one I had envisioned for myself? *Maybe I was hasty in judging Jeff's honesty.* I wondered if perhaps he felt he already had it all anyway.

An amused smile stretched my lips as I imagined what Gibson's caveman reaction would be had I acted irresponsibly and taken a ride from a relative stranger on his motorcycle. Gibson didn't have to worry on that score. I was as naturally guarded with my personal safety as he was.

In the past, Chloe had warned me about how I'd either have difficulty mistrusting men or trusting them too easily in the hope of feeling secure after the experiences I'd had, and this made me mindful of how alert I wanted to be in regards to this advice.

Sometimes I wondered if there would ever come a time when I would manage to shake my suspicious thoughts about relationships.

I'd half expected Jeff to protest at my caution regarding the transport but he didn't bat an eyelid when I insisted on taking my own wheels. Shrugging his shoulders, he asked me to follow him and took off down the street.

CHAPTER FOUR

On first impressions, I was less eager to meet his friends when Jeff drove me down a number of backstreets a few blocks from the studio.

With each block we traveled, the properties and general feel of the area became less desirable to hang around in.

When he finally stopped outside a single story property in a slum condition and in desperate need of a lick of paint, I was wary. Luckily, he didn't ask me to join him inside.

Shaking off the negative vibe the place gave me, I figured it was probably because I had lived in the lap of luxury for the previous two years and told myself it was probably a student rental or something.

Turning off my engine, I watched him climb off his motorbike and sighed again as he wandered over to me.

"Just gotta give some money to a buddy," he advised me. "Sit tight, I'll only be a minute," he added then turned and entered the house.

True to his word, he came out of the house again inside two minutes. When he left the house and headed toward me again, I noted he carried a small backpack.

"Do you mind giving these beers a ride for me?" Eyeing the small gymsack already on his back, I was happy to help.

A few minutes later, we pulled up in front of the tall wrought-iron electric gates of an imposing Tuscany-style mansion enclosed within a woodland estate. Again, I questioned my initial opinion of Jeff and work because it appeared he knew people in high places.

When he spoke into the intercom I heard a low electronic buzz and the gates jolted on their metal hinges before they slowly cracked open.

Waving for me to follow him, he drove around the back of the property where more than twenty vehicles were already parked. My eyes scanned up the walls and over the courtyard of the beautiful Tuscan home.

I stepped out of my car and walked over to Jeff who had already parked and gotten off his bike. He had turned to watch me with his backside lazily perched on his leather seat with one leg crossed over the other.

Conscious of his stare, my heart hammered with excitement when I caught his gaze in mine. He flashed a wicked grin and my knees buckled a little at the sight of it.

Watching him watch me made me anxious, and I felt so ill-prepared. Had I done the right thing agreeing to go with him? How did that make me look? What if he kissed me? What if he wanted more? *Oh, Lord. Stop it. You're reading into something that isn't there.*

As soon as I was close enough, he reached out and grabbed me by the hand. The effect of his touch on me was electric.

"Come on," he urged and turned, leading me down a pathway at the side of house. The way he held my hand firmly and tugged me behind him, anyone would have thought he had known me for years.

"What is this place? Who lives here?" I asked as he led me around a corner and toward a covered walkway. "Paradise", Coldplay's song, belted out at high volume and eventually we came to a set of smaller iron gates.

"Just a guy I've worked for a ton of times," He informed me, eyeing me. Then he smiled reassuringly. "Don't worry, he'll love you," he offered as if to reduce my uncertainty, before guiding me down a final walkway covered with overhanging lilac Wisteria and into a large outdoor quadrangle.

Most of the area had been designed for entertaining, with specific sections boasting a cocktail bar with bar staff, a temptingly inviting tiled swimming pool with three mosaic dolphins embedded at its center, and enough patio seating to put a beach-side café to shame.

My greedy eyes scanned the glamorous setting as beautiful people mingled around against the perfect backdrop bathed in rich aqua lighting, and my heart fluttered excitedly.

Everything was so new to me and once I had taken in the lively music and raucous laughter, I felt a different kind of excitement about my future, one possibly full of fun with friends.

"Know where Benton is?" Jeff asked a heavily set guy when he stopped at the third set of patio furniture nearest the sliders to the house.

"Kitchen," he replied, hardly giving him a second glance. Instead of going inside as I had expected, Jeff led me over to few young girls in bathing suits.

"Evening, ladies. This is my new friend, Piper," he beamed. "She's very new in town and doesn't know anyone. Do me a favor and keep her company. I need to catch up with Benton for a few minutes."

Piling on the charm, he winked, and the prettiest of the three girls rose to her feet. Without hesitating she stepped in to hug him and I figured Jeff was obviously close to her because his hands had immediately grasped at her waist and he kissed her softly on the mouth. "Hello, baby," he smiled again.

"When are *we* actually going to spend time together?" she asked, pouted and struck a seductive pose. She sifted her fingers through her hair after she pulled it to one side. Jeff obviously couldn't resist her exposed neck and leaned in to kiss it. The girl giggled and glanced back at him with hooded eyes.

"Soon, baby, soon... I promise, Miranda," he cooed, and I watched as he wrapped her around his little finger with one sentence before he stepped away and turned his attention to me. Even though I had gone there with him as friends his action toward her had made me feel slightly embarrassed.

"Give me ten minutes. I won't be long," he told me and winked as he walked away. He held Miranda's hand until she almost toppled over then she let him go.

The awkwardness of the situation made me feel like I shouldn't have been there. Feeling like Jeff had put me in this difficult situation, I diverted my gaze to a couple playing noisily in the pool with a beach ball as I tried to shake off the uneasy feeling about being abandoned with them.

My eyes flitted from Miranda to her friends and they all stared back at me like I was naked. *Has Jeff brought me here to make a point with Miranda?* From the interaction between them. It was clear she was far more interested in Jeff than he was in her.

Usually it took a great deal to rile me, but his rude behavior toward me left me feeling out of place and annoyed. *If this is how he treats girls, I'm surprised they hang around him at all.*

"What does friend mean?"

I glanced back at Miranda, who had asked me the question.

"You mean am I anything more? The answer is no. He's one of the sessional musicians on the album I'm cutting."

"Cutting an album? You mean CDs and downloads and shit?" she asked, bluntly to clarify.

"Yeah, if you put it like that, I suppose I am. I'm recording my first album at Gravity Record Label. I hope to release in the summer."

"No shit? How many record execs did you have to blow to get that gig?" I was taken aback by her crude bitchy implication, but regardless of what she said, it was clear she had made up her mind she didn't like me.

Even though she had fired the most insulting accusation my way, I kept my body language relaxed and flashed her a warm smile.

"You don't have to blow anything when they think you have real talent," I replied flatly. I owed those girls nothing. I had no problem in sounding smug because if she figured it was okay to suggest I'd stick some fat guy's genitals in my face to cut an album she was very much mistaken.

My estimate was that she was at least five years older than me and I guessed she thought she could intimidate me. I wasn't afraid of any woman and being young didn't mean I wasn't equipped to deal with girls like her. If she wanted a bitch fight she'd picked on the wrong person.

Miranda may have thought she was Queen of the Hill sitting there with all her girlfriends, but she was no match for the smart mouth I'd relied and survived on in my previous life. *Girls like these knew nothing about girls like me.*

From what I saw of Miranda with Jeff, she appeared clingy and insecure. But how Jeff treated her was nothing to do with me, and I wasn't about to shrink and roll over because she decided to vent her frustrations on me.

It was obvious she saw me as a threat, but when I challenged her remark, her snarky attitude toward me was quickly retracted.

"I'm only teasing," she told me as she forced a fake smile. I saw through it in a heartbeat and suddenly Miranda looked as uncomfortable being at the party as I had felt.

"Shall we start again?" I asked, offering an olive branch.

"No point, honey. Miranda's had her nose put out of joint. I'd say there are a lot of insanely jealous thoughts running through that pretty little head of hers because Doobie's turned up here with you. He's never taken her anywhere," the girl closest to her replied.

Cursing Jeff under my breath, I felt sick he'd brought me into this cesspool of hostility when it was billed as a place to make friends. There was no way I could ever be friends with people such as Miranda and her girlfriends.

Feeling awkward and alone, I hugged myself, drawing Miranda's eyes to what I was doing. I dropped my arms quickly by my sides and stared pointedly at her.

"Piper, my frustrated friend here can't fathom why she's opening her legs to Doobie when he does his Booty Call routine, yet he's only known you a day and you waltz right into his inner circle. Let me tell you girl, you may think your 'new friend' Jeff is being kind showing you around town, but I'd watch my back if I were you," the same girl offered as a warning.

"You're supposed to be my friend, Gayle," Miranda snapped, staring wide-eyed at her.

"And I am. I've been telling you for weeks, he's using you. Give it a week and you'll be on the subs bench. Doobie's not the kind of guy to offer anything to anyone unless there's something in it for him."

Glancing from each to the other, I wondered whether they were trying to screw with me for arriving with Jeff. I bunched my brow, and Gayle tipped her chin in the direction of the door.

"In the four years I've known Doobie, he has never brought anyone with him to his place of work, so she's got something the rest of us don't."

"Shut up, Gayle," Miranda snapped again, her eyes widening; this time as if her friend had said too much.

Gayle's jaw dropped, and she covered it with her hand. When I saw her body slump, I knew instinctively she'd made a mistake and run off at the mouth about something I'd yet to learn.

My radar for drama suddenly kicked in as I took in her body language and noted she toyed nervously with the string tie at one side of her bikini bottom.

Suspicious of Miranda's friend's comments and subsequent reaction, a new feeling of unease crept over me and I knew I'd obviously missed something. Confused, I glanced from one girl to the other before the third of the three stopped filing a perfectly shaped nail and sighed.

"Work? Doobie?" she questioned, holding her hand palm up as if a penny should drop with me at her hint. "My God, girl. You're as green as the grass. Grass, get it?" She looked smug as she glanced to her friends.

The others cackled with laughter and I took that as my cue to get the hell away from them. If Jeff thought for one minute I would have been friends with those bitches he was sadly mistaken.

"Obviously, I am, but no matter. Excuse me, ladies." *Fuck*. I turned my head and looked at the large patio doors leading into the house. There was no way I wanted to spend another minute in their company.

"I'm going to look for Jeff. I didn't intend on staying here long," I offered as I spun on my heel and walked in the direction of the house.

Relief washed through me the moment I made my escape and I inhaled a deep breath of fresh air to calm the irritation I felt about Jeff leaving me alone with them.

Stepping inside the huge living room, I noticed a couple of separate seating areas with couches full of people deep in conversation.

"Hello, baby," I turned and eyed someone who looked familiar and wondered if I'd seen him with Gibson. My gaze returned to pan the room looking for Jeff. "What's a nice girl like you doing in a place like this?"

Not even trying to hide the scoff that fell from my throat at the most clichéd pick-up-line in history, I rolled my eyes and snickered, then suddenly stopped.

Electricity ran through my body with both shock and excitement when I came face to face with Ronnie Silvers, the lead singer of Scripted Letters, a well-known rock band.

Shaking inside, I gave him a nervous smile as my mind froze at meeting one of my rock idols. Obviously, there was no one bigger than Gibson, but apart from being around the guys in M3rCy, Ronnie was the first bona fide rock star I had once followed.

Inside my head I screamed and had a fangirl moment right there, but on the outside, I had tried to remain indifferent.

"Uh, no. I mean... I'm new... here, in Santa Monica, I mean," I could have kicked myself for the lack of confidence in my voice and mostly monosyllabic babble as I tried to speak to him.

"New, huh?" he repeated, considering me for a moment as he checked me out more closely.

My face flushed under his watchful eye. "I'm not a groupie," I blurted and swallowed audibly as his eyes crawled back up from my feet to my face.

Ignoring my response like I hadn't spoken, he took a deep breath and tilted his head to one side. "So how did you find your way here... to Benton's place?" he asked gesturing at the room.

"Benton?" I was embarrassed to say I had no idea who he meant, and I earned another wide grin when he realized this.

For a moment I lost my focus and allowed myself to scan his attire of white t-shirt, blue suit vest, and grey denim jeans. Then I did what no woman in her right mind would do and inhaled his addictive cologne.

"What's that you're wearing?"

"My clothing?" he asked and chuckled as he held his arms out to display his attire.

"No, the cologne."

"Did you just smell me?" he asked, biting back a smile.

"Um, I guess," I admitted and blushed deeper.

He chuckled lightly then hid a smirk with his hand. "Not sure, it was a gift. Why?"

"I'd like to buy my dad some for Christmas," I responded, and cringed slightly at my downright fabrication, but I had committed to asking the name of it and I had to say something.

It was a lie; there's no way I'd have ever bought something that smelled so alluring for Gibson. Chloe would have lynched me. He had enough trouble fighting women off without the use of another 'babe magnet'.

Ronnie chuckled and threw his head back. "Ouch," he joked, then flashed me another warm smile. I took another moment to take in this was really happening because I had sung along to his music on the radio, and now he was standing right there in front of me.

I wanted to pinch myself because before we had escaped our life of purgatory, my only focus for every day had been to survive. The memories felt distant standing in the swanky house in California. *With my life changing the way it has could it get any more dreamlike?*

"Hello. Are you in there?" Ronnie's low mellow tone snapped me out of my trance.

Shaking my head quickly I gave him an awkward smile, "Sorry, yes, I was fangirling for a second," I replied truthfully, having been totally caught off guard.

"Good. I was beginning to think my cologne had paralyzed you," he said deadpan and took a slug of his drink.

His playful response made me giggle, and he eyed me still smiling, "So, Benton?"

"Who's Benton?" I asked again and searched his gorgeous features for the answer.

"You've heard of Drone Bird, right?" he quizzed, searching my face with a serious expression.

"The band? Sure, who hasn't? I'm not following," I added with a creased brow.

"Benton is the lead guitarist, Ton Mattison?"

"Ton? Benton is his real name? I'm in Ton Mattison's house?" My voice slid up an octave in shock. I wasn't sure how many more surprises I could have taken in one evening.

"Yep, and since you don't know him and you're new in town, I figure you haven't come alone. So... let me ask you again. Who did you come here with?"

"Jeff," I replied. Realizing I didn't know his surname, I felt stupid for mentioning him at all because I had already anticipated Ronnie's next question. *Why would someone like Ton Mattison know Jeff? Had he substituted for someone in his band before?*

"Jeff?" Ronnie asked, dragging me back to his question. The look he gave me told me he had no idea who I was talking about.

"It doesn't matter. He's just a guy who's one of the sessional musicians at my record label."

"Record label? You work at a record label? Doing what? Secretarial? Reception?"

Tensing defensively at his assumption I felt more than a little aggrieved. In an industry where we as artists were supposed to challenge expectations, he had answered in the same way most men would have done. In that moment I figured Ronnie saw me as just another pretty face.

"No. I'm recording an album." I stared directly into his eyes and saw the weight of my challenge staring back at me when his eyes widened and his brows shot up.

"Wow, really? Are you in a girl band?"

"Please." I pleaded, indignantly and saw my request register with him.

"I'm sorry. Forgive me, I just assumed,"

"Yeah, I guess I'll have a fight on my hands to be taken seriously." I shrugged.

From the moment I said I was ready to face the prejudices of the music business, his attitude shifted and we had a long, interesting discussion about current music influencers.

Ronnie even gave me some sound pointers about how to cut through some of the glass ceilings that still existed in the industry.

The conversation turned when he asked who my manager was, and the moment I mentioned Thomas Lyndsey by name he looked very impressed.

"Jesus, girl, what did you do to get him onside?"

Inside I panicked, and I couldn't think of a plausible story. It was the one thing I hadn't really thought about. How stupid was I to have thought I could pass off a manager like Thomas? The man hadn't taken on a new client in years.

"Oh, you know, I lucked out. It was a case of that six degrees of separation thing, you know? A friend of a friend of someone else told him to check me out and when he heard me he agreed to manage me."

"But you're with Gravity, you said? They're not a big outfit like the labels Tom is used to dealing with."

"Ah, that was all me. I wanted a small label because I felt it may take me some time to hone my craft and I preferred to do it in a setting that didn't pressure me to produce bubble-gum pop instead of quality.

"Oh to be young. I was like you once, the idealist... and poor."

"Well, I'm neither of those things," I replied. "I don't have great material wealth, but I have self-belief in what I can do. If I make it in the music business, it will be because I have what it takes."

It occurred to me that I'd been there for almost an hour and Jeff hadn't come back once to check up on me. "If you'll excuse me, I have to find my friend because I need to get myself home. I'm due in the studio first thing. It was fabulous to meet you, Ronnie, and I hope we cross paths again someday. I love what you do and I'm a fan of your work."

"Tell you what, Piper. You make that album and I'll buy it just to hear that talent you've been telling me about, then I'll look you up."

His response made me smile, and he reached out and put his hand on my back. "Go get 'em, girl, but stay away from these parties. They're a cesspool for corruption and they're full of predatory cock-suckers."

Hearing his description of his friend's get-together made me laugh.

I glanced around the room at the faces of the people he spoke about and noted a lot of them looked high or drunk, or both. Suddenly I recognized Jeff standing against a wall with a bottle of beer in his hand.

"Ah there's Jeff, got to run," I reiterated and shrugged my shoulders then turned and wandered over to stand beside him.

"Having fun? I see Ronnie Silvers was trying his luck with you."

"Not really. He was just keeping me company because the guy who brought me here dumped me on arrival."

"Sorry about that. I had a few things to take care of."

"Well, anyway, I need get going." Truth be told I was pretty annoyed he'd invited me all the way across town and then dumped me with strangers. "I've got an early start tomorrow. Don't worry, I'll see myself out," I informed him in a clipped tone and began to make my way back to the pool area to leave. Jeff made no attempt to follow me.

As I reached the sliders, I saw Ronnie wander over toward Jeff who pushed himself lazily off the wall to meet him. *Hmm, that's weird, I thought Ronnie had said he didn't know Jeff?*

I was glad I left when I did and arrived home just after 10pm. After following my evening routine, I slid into bed. The heat initially made me restless and my mind recapped the events of the party and how poorly Jeff had treated me until I eventually passed out.

CHAPTER FIVE

"*D*id you think you were clever dragging me along to that party?" I asked as I strode into the booth the following morning and interrupted Jeff tuning his guitar.

"What are you five? No one expects a guy to stay by their side at a social occasion or are you that insecure you needed hand holding?" he retorted back.

"What the fuck? Let me tell you if you had treated me the way you had treated that poor girl last night I'd have taken great delight in slapping you. I found you rude and ignorant and maybe I expected more of you than the way you behaved, but I'll know better in future."

Jeff put his guitar back on the stand and turned to look directly at me. "Look, I'm sorry. I had some business to take care of and I got caught up. A man has got to eat you know. What would you say if I offered you pizza when we're done to say sorry?"

When his eyes engaged with mine I thought he looked and sounded sorry for what had happened and sighed because I knew we still had to work together and the more harmonious our relationship the better for the album. I nodded.

"Fine, but I'll still need some convincing what you did was a one off."

Jeff smiled, "Hard to please...got it. I'll make it up to you."

Without replying I left the booth to grab some water before Otto took his seat to start our day.

～

"Come to spy on me?" I smiled affectionately at my manager, Thomas, when I stepped out of the recording room and stood by Otto at the mixing desk.

It was a surprise when he showed up forty minutes before the end of my afternoon session. Several times I looked in his direction and almost burst out laughing at how enthralled he looked watching me.

Eventually I had to sing with my eyes closed to prevent a fit of the giggles.

"Absolutely, and I make no apologies for that. I like to keep an eye on my client's progress to make sure you're staying on track to make me my fortune," he replied in a mock strict tone. "Seriously, I figured now you've had a couple of days to settle in, I'd make an effort and offer the poor struggling musician some dinner."

"Oh, I can always eat." I nodded, smiling warmly at his thoughtful gesture.

"Good, grab your shit and let's get out of here. I know a great little seafood restaurant on the Boulevard," he advised me as he picked up his heavy leather satchel and slung it over his shoulder.

"Tomorrow then?" Jeff interjected, and I suddenly remembered he'd invited me to dinner.

"Sorry," I shrugged, "This is business," I replied mimicking his excuse for leaving me hanging at the party. It felt good to put him back in his place.

Thomas eyed Jeff with suspicion but didn't say a word, then he placed his hand on my back and ushered me out toward his car. Again, I refused, telling Thomas I preferred to take my own and would follow him, because although I trusted Thomas, I needed my transport for the following day.

～

The restaurant wasn't fancy and with its kitsch decor it was perfectly in keeping with its beachside position.

Large, brightly colored metallic starfish, turtles, and delicately painted creatures of the sea donned the walls over a background of aqua blues and turquoise greens painted in large sweeping swirls.

Little silver metal buckets sat on the tables full of silverware and napkins, and the few other diners present were dressed mainly in casual shorts, swimmers and sarongs, or sundresses. It was the perfect place to lighten my mood and make me feel relaxed.

Thomas gestured for me to sit, so I slid into the booth where the waiter tended to us in a heartbeat. "Two iced teas and would you give us five minutes to check out the menu please?" Thomas ordered before the poor guy had opened his mouth to speak. My eyes immediately connected with the waiter. I sighed. I wasn't keen on Thomas' tone. It had felt highly dismissive when the poor guy was doing his job.

"Are all the men in California rude?" I asked as I struggled to keep my temper. "I mean, is it normal for people to have total disregard for others? Civility costs nothing."

My outburst may have appeared disproportionate but between Thomas' attitude toward Jeff and the waiter, and Jeff's behavior the night before, I wondered if this was normal life and perhaps I'd been overprotected during my time at home with the Barclays.

"I prefer to catch my breath before I choose my food," he informed me brusquely, carefully folding his cream linen jacket before placing it neatly on the seat beside him.

Plucking the menu from the small wooden menu holder, I began to study it carefully. From the side of my eye I noted the waiter on his way back with the drinks and promised myself if Thomas even dared to make another rude comment or be snippy toward him he'd get a taste of his own curt behavior from me.

I'd never seen him in this light before and even though I was deemed to know nothing about my craft as yet, my mom had taught me about speaking in kind and treating people with respect. Ironic since the guy she lived with never showed her an ounce of kindness in my presence.

Placing the drink napkins down he placed our drinks and I could see he was hesitant to ask again if he could take our order. Before Thomas could blow him out again, I engaged the waiter.

"So, I'm new here in town. If you were me what would you be ordering from the menu today?" I flashed him a warm smile and glanced over to Thomas like I was addressing them both.

"Fresh Calamari. Personally, I could eat buckets of the stuff. It's caught locally and out to the table in hours," he responded knowledgably, giving me a broad smile loaded with gratitude for smoothing his path with Thomas.

When Thomas didn't respond, I prompted him. "Should..." I glanced at the waiter's name, "Kyle start my order or are you ready as well? I'm starving," I added for effect.

"Two... I'll have the same," Thomas stated flatly without making eye contact with the waiter.

As soon as our server had gone out of earshot, I tackled him again. "I don't appreciate your attitude toward people. You are supposed to be representing me. If that's how you conduct yourself around people I'm not that sure you're the right person to do so. You weren't like this at all in front of Gibson. Was that all an act for him, or do you intend to try to be more approachable?"

At the risk of sounding pretentious, I tried to assert my position and Thomas almost cracked a smile. Then his face contorted as he struggled to hold it back. "I'm sorry. I had some news today that worried me and I'm not sure what to do with it."

Immediately my manner changed, and I felt empathetic and concerned for him since he was having a bad day. No one knew more than I did what it was like to worry about something and not be able to work out what to do.

"Would talking about it help?" For a few seconds he stared me straight in the eye and said nothing. For a moment I thought he hadn't heard me. *Does he think me too young to confide in?* That was a real possibility.

No one I knew, except perhaps Gibson, understood what it was like to feel misunderstood. *Maybe Thomas doesn't regard me as being old enough to have solutions to his problem.*

My heart sank, and I wondered if anyone would ever see past my age and accept that I had been through more in my short life than most people did in a lifetime, or if I'd have to wait until I reached a certain age to have added value.

"That would depend on whether you accepted my concerns as in your best interest," he admitted. He began to fiddle with the salt shaker, giving it his utmost attention.

"You're worried about me? Who could possibly have an issue with me when I've only been in Santa Monica for three days? Is it Otto? Isn't he happy with—"

"For fuck's sake, stop," he said, tiredly. "Breathe. Jesus, this is exactly why I was concerned about how to deal with the issue. This has nothing to do with Otto, but everything to do with your future. If you're smart you'll listen. If not, then we're going to be at loggerheads for the whole time you're down here. If you want me to treat you like an adult, then you are going to have to accept that whatever I say is in your best interests as your manager, not as a parent figure. I'm not your father."

"Then you'd do well to remember that. I'm not a child you have to treat to dinner to broach an issue. If something needs addressing then I'd appreciate if you'd just tell me."

Interrupting the conversation, Kyle pushed his way backward out of the kitchen and into the dining area, turned and walked toward us with our food. My appetite had all but gone.

"The party last night?" he said, deadpan.

Hiding my shock, I immediately thought I knew what had happened. "Gibson had me followed?"

"Of course not," he barked, giving me a pointed look as his lips pinched in frustration. "He knows nothing about this."

"You? You had me followed?"

"No. Stop jumping to conclusions," he huffed. "Listen. Why are you being so petulant? I've never seen you like this before."

"No one has ever had me followed before," I bit back, sitting back in my seat with my arms folded in defiance.

"You have no idea how lucky you've been. Can you imagine how I felt waking up five hours away from here to a call informing me you showed up at Ton Mattison's place last night with Doobie, his drug dealer?"

My jaw almost hit the table. "I did no such thing. I was there with…" *Fuck*. Initially I was in denial but suddenly it all made sense. "A drug dealer?" I said in a high-pitched voice. "I was invited to a party. Jeff's the sessional guitarist on the album and he invited me to hang out with him after the studio yesterday because I didn't know anyone."

"And he took you with him to deal," he replied. "Fortunately for you, Ronnie Silvers called to warn me. Doobie is pretty well known in celebrity circles. He's the local dealer to the stars. His clientele are actresses, rock stars, dancers, and musicians. Jeff as you call him is known as Doobie… didn't you hear them call him that? Ronnie told me when he realized you were with Doobie he warned him off… but that wasn't before Doobie had offered to hook you up with him."

My head pounded as I absorbed the revelation and wondered how I could have been so naïve and stupid. I didn't even challenge what he may have been doing. I definitely hadn't been thinking straight.

"Oh, Lord, how could I have been so stupid? I mean the place he took me to looked real fancy, and everyone looked affluent, dressed in expensive clothes or like they took great care of themselves. You know, groomed from head to toe, pearly white teeth, expensive jewelry. I feel like the biggest fool on the planet," I admitted quietly as I hung my head in shame.

"It's such a clusterfuck I considered calling Gibson about this. Doobie's way too smart for a young kid like you. He took you there with him last night because he wasn't sure about you. Now he thinks he has something on you. The only thing that saved you was you went there under your own steam and you didn't travel there with him. Can you imagine if you make it big and he suddenly started to tell everyone you used to run drugs with him?"

"Please don't tell, Gibson," I pleaded, then a thought almost made my heart stop. "Oh. My. God, the backpack."

"Backpack?"

"Yeah, he made a stop on the way to the house and put the backpack of beer in the back of my car."

"Fuck. Had you been stopped by the police…" Thomas's voice trailed off. I shuddered.

"You stay the fuck away from him outside the studio. He's sufficiently connected for a newbie like you not to rock the boat, but as soon as the album is complete you sever all contact."

"That doesn't seem fair. I did nothing wrong. I never passed drugs to anyone if there were any in that backpack." A knot formed in my stomach. "What about the other guy in the studio? Is he a drug dealer or addict too?"

"Who Grunt? Nope. Never done drugs, he's just an unfortunate. The way he looks has stopped him from being who he should have been."

"That's what Jeff said," I confirmed.

"At least he was honest about him. Grunt is a clean-living guy, but you need to know what you're up against. You owe Ronnie Silvers a big thank you. He's a friend of a friend like most well-connected people, but he actually had his PA track me down, and then rang me himself to warn you."

"Good to know he had my back," I agreed. Another feeling of relief washed through me. Shaking my head, I cringed. "And here I was thinking I was doing great and I almost fell at the first hurdle."

My anxiety rose at Gibson's likely reaction if Thomas told him what had happened to me. As early as it was into my independent living I had to accept the blame for my lack of judgment and naivety.

"Please don't tell Gibson and Chloe," I urged, "They have enough to worry about." When I heard myself plead, it reinforced that even though I was an adult I had people who cared for me and I knew how worried they would be if anything happened to me.

"I work for you, not Gibson," he stated flatly, "But I really need you to get your shit together and stay clear of Doobie, you got me?"

"Yeah, absolutely. I had no idea he was like that he looks so…"

"That's why he's successful," he said anticipating what I was going to say next. "He looks like a football jock, no one would ever tag him as a dealer."

My eyes widened in surprise because Thomas saw the same thing as I did about him, "Exactly! That's how I saw him."

"All right. Now here's the part you're not gonna like but I want you to agree to this. I'm thinking of getting you a minder."

"The fuck you're not." My response was instantaneous.

"Yep, according to Ronnie, Jeff is a master corrupter. He's already had two girls arrested as dealers in the past eighteen months by slipping his blow in their purses when there have been shakedowns at parties, and he's walked away as clean as a whistle."

"Does Otto know the shit Jeff pulls?" I asked, realizing Jeff would do whatever was necessary to protect himself.

"He's aware and Doobie's been warned never to bring anything to the studio. Fortunately for Otto he's got some heavy hitting contacts so that keeps Doobie contained just enough to stop him from pissing where he works."

When I thought back to the party, none of those other girls there had much on in the way of clothing and none had a purse and I was pretty much the only female that had one on me.

I couldn't bear to think about what could have happened if the cops had been called to that noisy party or if they had raided it. My guess is Jeff may have tried to offload what he had into my purse.

After Thomas had cleared the air with me he was much more relaxed, but the incident lingered in my mind and sat heavily in my stomach. I was glad when he left our waiter $200 in $50 bills and apologized for being curt.

As he drove me back to my car, he explained he was putting someone on call for any issues that arose, a minder of sorts—not to watch over me, but someone to call if I found myself in a difficult situation who would come to my assistance. He also made me promise never to take Jeff to my apartment. Like I'd have done that anyway after what I had learned.

CHAPTER SIX

After I had said goodnight to Thomas and climbed behind the wheel of my own car, I drove home but my concentration was poor as my mind wandered back to the interactions at the party.

Jeff being called Doobie should have been a big 'tell' for me. If only I had known what the slang nickname meant, and I shuddered at the thought he may well have used me as his mule to take the drugs to the party.

I'd never know for sure if that was the case because it never occurred to me to look in the backpack, but it taught me I'd never take responsibility for someone else's effects again unless it was someone I trusted like Gibson or Chloe.

By the time I arrived home, I felt far less confident about taking care of myself. I wondered if Gibson had been right about me needing his support. I had behaved so stubbornly about being independent and it had almost cost me my reputation and personal safety, not to mention the risk of a criminal record.

In a couple of days, I had gone from being thankful for my own space to feeling desperately lonely because the only person I could talk to about what had happened was Thomas. Since leaving high school in Colorado I'd had no one around to confide in.

Truth was, I had only attended high school in Colorado for the last few months due to the timing of seeking sanctuary out of state, at Dignity. I had made a few close friends but no one that I'd have confided in.

My thoughts turned to Simon, and I figured he'd keep anything I told him in confidence and then I wondered how he'd feel if I contacted him. Shaking that possibility off I resolved to guard myself more closely in future.

As soon as I got home, I headed for the shower and afterward spread a huge white bath sheet over the couch. Spreading my naked body out I lay buck naked and dripping wet and willed the rapidly rotating ceiling fan to dry me out and cool me down.

My idea had worked and as I gradually drifted off to sleep my cell buzzed interrupting my clearing mind. Reaching across, I swiped my phone off my coffee table and recognized Simon's number.

When I saw Simon's name, it had felt like fate or telepathy or some other strange force that he should have called me right then and my heart rate doubled at the thought of him contacting me.

The day before I left he had waited until Gibson was busy and grabbed my phone. Silently he punched his number in, dropped my cell back in my lap and winked.

It was later I realized he had called his own number from my phone. Now I realized he had done that to save my number instead of asking me for it.

"Hey, Princess, how's it going?"

"All right," I replied, sounding less enthusiastic than I had aimed for.

"Hey, what's wrong?" he asked, sounding concerned.

"It's... nothing," I replied hesitating. "I'm fine, just tired," I added quickly in my attempt to cover up my true thoughts.

"Nope, I know you better than that, Princess. What's the deal?"

"First, can you drop the princess, it makes me feel like I'm five years old?"

He chuckled. "But you are a princess, baby," he coaxed.

"Isn't that what you call your groupies when you can't remember their names?"

"Never, Princess. Personally, I use sugar," he informed me without a hint of shame and chuckled again.

"Ew." My reaction was immediate, "So do they call you Daddy?"

Simon cracked up laughing, "Ouch, and there she is my smart-mouthed little princess," he replied, playfully.

"I'm your little princess?" I sighed, "See what I mean? You make me sound like I'm five... eight at the most," I amended.

"No, you're my beautiful young adult princess," he told me.

"Now you just sound creepy," I chuckled.

"Not creepy just enthralled by you, honey."

My heart flipped over in my chest. *Did he just flirt with me?* "This conversation is embarrassing; did you want something?"

"Depends what you're offering."

I sat naked on my couch blinking. OMG, he *is* flirting with me. *I wouldn't know where to start to offer a man like you.*

"Let's start again. You called me remember?"

"I did," he confirmed decisively.

When he paused and said nothing else I thought the line had dropped. "Hello?"

"Hey, Princess," he replied, taking me literally and talking as if we'd just connected our call. I began giggling because it felt like a stupid conversation.

"Did you want something, Simon?" I asked again even though I was enjoying his playful side.

"I do. You," he replied, quickly. My heart stuttered, and I was sure I'd misheard him. I shook my head.

"What do you want with me?" I dared to ask as I lay naked on my couch smiling like a deranged chimpanzee.

"Tomorrow's the start of the weekend. Got any plans?" My heart pounded so hard the vein in my neck popped and my lips tingled at the possibilities his question held for me.

"Nothing yet, I've been here less than a week remember?"

"Exactly, and you know I live just up the coast from you? Want to come hang out with me?" His question almost made my tongue fall out of my mouth. Initially, I was flattered until I thought he was offering to spend time with me out of some sense of duty.

"Thanks, but I don't need a babysitter, Simon," I chided

"Well glad we cleared that up because I'd be shit at that job."

"Did Gibson put you up to this? Chloe? Thomas?" My mind raced as I began to think someone had asked him to keep an eye on me, or worse if Thomas had told him what had happened and Simon himself felt obliged to check up on me out of loyalty toward Gibson. I sighed, "I don't understand why you'd want to waste your time with me."

"Spending time with you could never be wasted. You're a very sweet, cool girl, Piper. If I didn't want to do it, I wouldn't have asked. What do you say?"

A buzz of electricity ran through me at the thought of spending time with him on my own. *What do I say? Seriously? Yes, Please?* "What did you have in mind?" I asked my voice sounding even and unfazed.

"Nothing fancy. Good food, chilling out with a few glasses of wine? I could send a car for you to come hang out at my beach house."

"At your place?" I could hardly speak for the tremors going on inside me at the thought of spending time with Simon on my own.

"Sure. In case you don't know this, I'm in a band. We're a little bit famous which means I can't really hang out with you on Santa Monica beach without being noticed."

My heart skipped a beat at his description because it was drastically understated about the attention he'd receive; a mini riot would have been more near the mark. Excitement coursed through me at his invitation. Like I even had to think about how to answer.

Sheer delight filled my head with notions of spending time with him, but at the back of my mind I couldn't help feeling it may have felt like his duty to him.

No matter what the reason I was flattered and even that was an understatement. Swamped constantly with invitations, Simon was never short of a place to be. I'd heard women beg on the phone during the times he'd spent at our home.

"So, what do you think?" Simon's low timbre cut into my thoughts.

"I guess... I mean I'd like that," I replied, trying not to let my excitement bubble over into my voice, despite me trying to talk myself down from cloud nine in my head.

"You could at least sound a little excited to spend some time with me," he added playfully.

I smiled so wide I felt the sides of my mouth tweak. *Holy fuck, am I excited*. "I am. It'll be nice. I'm looking forward to it," I admitted but without alluding to the silent happy dance going on inside my head.

"Princess, a note to ponder. Most women would be squealing with excitement if I brought them to my home."

"You want me to squeal?" I asked then realized what I'd said and cringed.

Simon chuckled softly, "Maybe. I'd definitely have fun making you squeal," he teased, in a comment loaded with sexual connotation. *Good Lord*. I had no smart mouthed comment to reply to that.

"Ah, but you forget I'm not most women," I replied as I tried to take us back to solid ground.

"Hmm, I guess you're not," he replied after he'd hummed like he had considered my point. "Okay tomorrow from your place, what time do you finish?"

"5pm."

"All right, a car will be waiting for you back at the apartment."

A female voice murmured softly in the background and my heart immediately sank. *What did you expect, Piper? Of course he has a woman there already. His invite is out of kindness that's all. What the hell did you expect?*

"Just coming," he muttered in a gentle tone to whoever she was then turned his attention back to me. "Gotta go. See you tomorrow, Princess."

When the call disconnected, I was left with the sound of the woman's velvety voice and felt infinitely less enthusiastic about visiting him than I had when the conversation had begun.

I sighed, the weekend would be interesting if nothing else. His house was only thirty minutes away from Santa Monica and if I got there and I was expected to play a third wheel, I could always head home again.

～

Coming face to face with Jeff and my last session of the week at the studio had filled me with dread, but it was clear he was kept in check by whatever Thomas and Otto had said. Jeff barely looked at me all day and I focused on the music which got me through.

At one point I had thought about challenging him, but the advice was to leave it to others, and thankfully the recording session went smoothly.

No one had prepared me about singing the same song for hours at a time. It was mentally draining. Otto made me feel better when he advised me we were ahead of schedule.

I was surprised to learn some seasoned bands don't crack an album for many months due to constant rejigging of scores and lyrics, or technical stuff.

At the end of the day, apart from Otto, I was the last to leave and when I did, I noted Jeff was waiting by my car. *Shit.*

Tensing on sight, my mood swiftly changed from one of accomplishment to anger as soon as I laid eyes on him. *Jeff may have taken advantage of me once, but it's what I do now that matters.*

"I never gave you drugs in the backpack you carried." His voice had an urgency about it.

"I never said you did." *Of course I didn't believe him because offering information I never asked for was a sure sign of guilt.* "I'm not interested, Jeff. Just do your job and leave me alone."

Jeff scoffed and place a hand at the back of his head. "Can we start again?"

"Nope. No second chances with this chick," I replied, in a clipped but decisive tone. I knew I sounded harsh, and that was my every intention.

"Aw come on, I made a mistake," he insisted.

"Which mistake would that be? Passing me off as your mule, or underestimating my connections? The real mistake was trying to take advantage of someone who had no idea you were dealing in drugs, without knowing I had connections with your buyer." I unlocked my car and slid into the seat. I was about to close the door when he caught it and held it open.

"Listen—"

"Take your fucking hands off my door or I'll sound the horn and bring Otto out here. Is that what you want? Now leave me the fuck alone, I have plans for the evening."

Anger flushed his face as his fist bunched at the end of the stiff arm by his side. Frustration radiated through him and he shoved the car door at me with the hand that held it. It swung shut so hard it rocked the car, the bang startling me, making me jump.

Jeff's behavior showed me yet another side to him, but thanks to the counselling, self-defense and coping strategies I'd been taught at Dignity, I felt better equipped to deal with him and his violent behavior. I knew how to handle his aggression. Never to show fear and act with total conviction.

My pulse raced as I sat and watched him stomp away. I sighed in relief and I thought he was heading to his motorcycle, but when he stopped about thirty yards away blocking my exit, I saw he was far from done trying to intimidate me. He made me furious by his effort to control and frighten me and I knew I had to deal decisively

Sticking my key in the ignition, I pressed my foot on the accelerator pedal and heard the car roar to life. Whenever I felt my personal safety was under threat, I had no hesitation in what I had to do.

Men like Jeff, who used women for their own gain were cowards. I'd lived with the master of them. Jeff may have thought he was stronger than me and physically he was for sure, but he had no idea who he was fucking with when it came to me facing a bully.

I slammed my foot on the gas to the floor, my other one on the brake. It was a move I had seen in a movie. Smoke rose from the exhaust, the tires screeched, and they began to burn rubber. Jeff threw his head back laughing at what he felt was my attempt to scare him. I wasn't attempting anything. I was as serious as a heart attack.

Sending what I felt was a definitive message for Jeff to back off had to be effective or I knew he'd be persistent, so with fear and determination fueling my decision I released the brake pedal. Shock registered on his face the moment he realized I wasn't messing with him.

Diving chest first into the dirt he called out, "Crazy bitch," as I sped past him with my heart in my mouth. *Yep, I am. So don't you dare fuck with me in future.* Without glancing back, I drove out of the car lot and onto the open road.

Physically shaking with nerves, I drove about four blocks down and pulled up to the side. Nausea burned at the back of my throat and I opened the door in the nick of time, vomiting onto the road beneath me.

After witnessing what my mom went through with Colin, I swore I wouldn't let someone threaten my freedom because he thought he was stronger or more ruthless than me and I had just proven to myself I meant it.

Consoling myself with that thought, I took another deep breath and let it out, hoping my actions would make Jeff think twice before he tried anything else to bring me down.

CHAPTER SEVEN

*A*rriving back home, I quickly showered, and slipped into a casual but feminine outfit of a loose-fitting, deep-red, off-the-shoulder top and some white Capri pants. Wanting to make an impression that I'd at least tried to look good, I reapplied my light makeup and headed out the door to meet the driver.

On the way to Simon's place, Melody rang me from Chloe's phone and we chatted about her day. It was obvious she missed me from what she had said, and I reassured her I'd get back to Colorado as soon as I could.

Putting me on speakerphone when her parents had joined her, we all chatted like we were around the kitchen table.

Gibson was pleased to hear Thomas had been to see me. I totally omitted why he'd made the journey, but I promised myself I'd tell him the whole story at some point, just another day.

All through the conversation I waited nervously for one of them to ask where I was headed. I'd already decided if they did, I'd answer honestly. My respect for all they had done wasn't going to be buried in lies.

Since the incident with Jeff, I had accepted Gibson's concerns were valid and knew from the start all he wanted to do was to protect me from getting hurt and because of this had any of them asked where I was going, I'd have been straight with them. Even if the friendship between Simon and I was a sore point for Gibson.

Fortunately, I caught a break when Gibson got a call on his own phone in the middle of our conversation, and left Chloe, Melody, and I, to conclude the call.

Slipping my phone into my purse, I stared out the window at the silver shimmering waves as the huge glowing moon cast a bright reflection on it, making the waves on the Pacific Ocean flow like mercury.

As we drove toward Simon, I felt apprehensive yet had no expectations for the time we'd spend together. *God, what if he found me boring? Immature? He didn't know me outside of the ranch.*

A knot formed in my stomach again and I wondered if our friendship could possibly be sustained now I wasn't living at home.

My stupid crush for him was my business, there was nothing I could do about that, but I knew I would hate it to come between the friendship that had developed between us.

My innocence was one thing. My lewd thoughts and feelings toward Simon were something else. But even with my very limited knowledge of men, he was definitely my fantasy man. When I caught sight of myself in the rear-view mirror, I barely recognized who I was from a little over two years before.

Everyone had to accept I'd get things wrong from time to time. It was how I'd learn from the experience that would get me where I needed to be. As long as those lessons weren't too drastic.

From the roadside, Simon's place was nothing like I had imagined it would be. Tall, whitewashed walls stretched either side of an imposing set of solid wooden gates.

Apart from alluding to a substantial property inside, there was no indication a famous rock star lived beyond the fortressed boundary.

Gazing out at the steep sweeping driveway with perfect landscaped gardens on either side, butterflies rose from deep in my belly.

The anticipation of seeing Simon felt almost too much. I knew it was crazy having a crush on him, but the heart doesn't care about age or other prejudices when something touches it in the way Simon touched mine.

Evenly spaced sprinklers twirled in perfect synchronicity as they sprayed fine misted fountains of cool water on the carefully manicured lawns. I shook my head in wonder. *Who would have thought Simon had such immaculate taste?*

As we pulled up in front of the entrance to Simon's home, my curious eyes scanned the front of the double story contemporary build with its floor-to-ceiling tinted glass; obviously designed to keep the sun out.

His house was almost a polar opposite of the homey lifestyle Gibson and Chloe lived in and it was expensive, chic, and luxurious.

My gaze fell to the huge glass door as it opened wide. I was caught totally off guard, my breath hitching as Simon, looking more appealing than ever, strode purposefully toward us. His usual sexy smile made my mouth dry as I perused his awesome hard body in his tightly stretched white t-shirt and low-rise dark-denim jeans. *Sweet Jesus.*

For a moment I struggled to even out my breathing as my pulse galloped uncontrollably, and I sucked in a long, deep breath as I fought to calm myself down.

Mirroring his friendly cue, I offered a warm smile in return as I did my best to hide the chaotic effect he had on my mind.

"Hello, Princess," he said, giving me his cocky, wide grin, as he offered an outstretched hand for me to take. Hearing the low gravelly tone, I realized I had almost swooned right there in front of him.

Instead, I remained speechless, not trusting my voice not to let him hear how displaced I felt and smiled affectionately back at him despite the 'Princess' reference.

I wiped my sweaty hand on my pants and slipped my small warm palm into his. Electricity coursed through me, leaving a buzz on my lips and fingertips and a warm glow staining my cheeks.

"Smooth trip out here?" he asked, leaning past me to close the car door. In doing so his hard, warm chest brushed my arm.

Immediately, his scent surrounded me as my head filled with an alluring cologne, spearmint chewing gum, and the smell that was him. I inhaled until my lungs couldn't take anymore.

"Hungry?" he asked and for a few seconds I had difficulty with the constant tiny excited vibrations running through me to answer him. I exhaled slowly and answered.

"A bit," I managed to squeak out as he led me by the hand through his front door and into a huge open plan living space.

Another silent squeal escaped in my head and I glanced briefly at our hands, mine small, smooth and delicate in comparison to his huge, strong veiny one. *Holy crap.*

Scrutinizing the décor as he led me into the center of the room, I was surprised by the impeccable contemporary taste.

Everywhere sported clean symmetrical lines with white and gray furniture which was complimented with the right amount of soft furnishings bringing splashes of color to match his carefully chosen artwork.

Styled for contemporary open-plan living, it was light and airy. The far wall sliders were completely retracted giving a feel of bringing the outside right into the room. Soft amber lighting cast a warm glow over the infinity pool which stretched into the black night beyond.

"Wow. This place is incredible," I remarked wide-eyed. Simon rewarded me with a shy smile.

"Thanks," he mumbled and looked around the room then back to me. His humble response made him even more attractive. "I had Stevie make us some ribs and corn bread, I know it's your favorite dinner," he added as I glanced nervously around the room.

Still in awe of my surroundings I let my eyes flit to the upper elevation and I wondered if someone else was present in the house. *Wait a minute. He knows ribs are my favorite? How did he remember that?*

"I figured you probably hadn't eaten any home-cooked food since you got to Santa Monica. Am I right?" He asked bringing my focus back on him.

"True... and ribs sound amazing," And amazingly messy. *What the hell? No chance of looking seductive eating those unless I was trying to impress a caveman... which Simon definitely wasn't.*

His food choice knocked the wind out of me and shattered any ideas I had of attempting to appear sophisticated during dinner. I had imagined myself holding a close conversation over a much less difficult meal.

"Love the outfit, Princess, very cute," he stated over his shoulder as he dropped my hand and wandered over to the oven. I stared down at my hand and missed his warm grip immediately.

Plates with ribs already on them were laid out. He added some corn bread then turned to face me. I felt myself blush when his eyes locked with mine and his compliment totally fucked with the look he gave me. *Cute as in childlike, or cute as in he liked it?*

Wrapping my arms around myself in a self-conscious act I covered up a little, but he had stopped looking at me when he addressed me casually again.

"Where do you want to eat? In here or out on the patio?" he enquired, appearing totally unaware of how awkward I suddenly was.

It was a no-brainer. The patio was darker, and I thought if I got any of the barbecue sauce on me it wouldn't be as apparent as it would look under the bright downlighters hanging over the dining room table.

"Patio sounds great," I replied as I wondered how I'd even eat them at all in his presence.

I didn't want Simon to see me as the kid Gibson took in, and I prayed he saw me for the young woman I was; but being in his home I had nothing to hide behind like I usually would have had back in Colorado.

Suddenly I felt totally inept as to how to conduct myself. It wasn't as if Simon was behaving any differently to normal. All the hang ups I felt were mine.

"Come on then before they get cold," he coaxed in a light, friendly voice as he held both round plates in his hands. Gesturing his head toward the patio area, he invited me to follow.

Once outside, he led me through the sultry night air to a huge, round glass dining table with a Lazy Susan at the center.

The patio seating area hadn't been visible from the inside. I tried to figure out why, then realized the patio extended beyond the building.

Once situated, Simon sat back in his chair, grabbed one of his ribs and took a large hungry chunk out of it. "Mm," he hummed in an exaggerated sound of enjoyment.

The noise immediately made my core pulse, and I stared fascinated as he chewed his first bite. "Oh, God," he groaned in ecstasy and I squeezed my thighs tightly, together. "Go on, dig in," he encouraged as he nodded toward the delicious, but messy looking food.

My focus was squarely on his cherry-red lips, visibly wet from his tongue, among his full beard and I just about managed to drag my eyes away from them to meet his gaze.

Drawing a deep breath, I swallowed roughly and resigned myself to knowing I'd look like a pig eating in front of him, but the smell from the barbecue sauce was ridiculously inviting.

My dilemma was very real as I shifted my gaze to my plate. My stomach betrayed me when it grumbled in protest as the delicious aroma assaulted my brain. Simon was spot on, they were my favorite food. Of all the times to remember what I liked, why did it have to be now?

The way he was devouring his meal made my mouth water. But I knew there was no way I'd walk away from the table without getting in a filthy state once I began to eat.

With an extraordinary amount of delicacy, I choose the smallest rib —if there is such a act as picking up a pork rib covered in gooey sauce delicately—and hesitated when it was level with my mouth.

Stretching my lips clear of the sauce, I dug my teeth into the pork and took several small nibbles of the succulent meat. "Mm." An involuntary moan of appreciation crept up from my chest because they tasted delicious and I hummed in appreciation just as he had moments before.

Simon grinned and shook his head. "Fuck," he muttered, chuckling to himself as his eyes darkened, and I frowned because I felt I'd obviously done something wrong.

I shrugged and said the first thing that came into my head. "Like my mom always said, 'You can't say meat without saying Mm'."

Reaching over toward me, he lifted his hand and swiped his coarse thumb pad across my lips then stuck it in his mouth. When he pulled it out, he licked his lips seductively and another wide grin sent a rod of delight straight between my thighs.

"What did you do that for?" The question was out before I had the chance to think about what I was saying. His unexpected intimate gesture had stolen my breath for a moment and my heart pounded wildly in my chest.

"What?" he asked, looking confused, but I thought I detected a playful tone. He certainly looked amused.

"The thing you just did with your thumb," I stated because when I'd seen Gibson do that to Chloe it had always looked intimate... like I shouldn't have been there. I may not have had a lot of personal experience of men, but I'd seen enough romance movies to be sure he'd crossed a line.

He shrugged. "There's only one thing better than the taste of barbecue sauce from a woman's lips," he said, ignoring the liberty he'd taken as he flashed me a cocky smile.

Picking up another rib he dug in like nothing had happened and using his teeth, ripped another large chunk of meat from it.

"But they were *my* lips," I replied, sounding utterly confused at where he was going with the conversation. For a few seconds I felt vulnerable, inept, unprepared for the move he had made, and unsure why he would have chosen to do that to me.

Was this how Simon really was? Is this why Gibson argued with him when he paid attention toward me? Up until that point I had never experienced anyone invading my personal space uninvited, outside of Colin's anger, the way Simon did.

"Exactly," he said, his eyes dropping to my mouth and suddenly I wasn't hungry any more. For a second I thought I was mistaken, then wondered if he was joking, then ultimately, I felt out of my depth.

I immediately felt uncomfortable and acted on instinct, challenging his comment.

"It's not okay for you to screw with my feelings, Simon. I'm here because I thought I could trust you, yet I'm barely inside your house and you think that gives you the right to take liberties with me?"

Simon's eyes went wide, like I'd shocked him by calling him out. He stopped eating, rib poised mid-air and stared at me, hard.

Holding his gaze, I was determined not to turn away from him because it had taken all of my courage to stand up to him.

Suddenly he threw his rib back onto the plate, the hollow bone clattering noisily and shattering the otherwise silent night air.

Sighing heavily, he looked apologetic and when he spoke it was in his low serious tone.

"Fuck. You're right. I'm sorry. That shouldn't have happened. I totally forgot myself with you... and of course you can trust me. I'd never hurt you, Piper."

"Is this how you treat all women?"

"Only the ones I'm attracted to," he replied, and I searched his face for a hint he was teasing me. When I saw none, I wasn't sure what to do with his new disclosure.

Deciding he was joking, I called him out again. "Don't fuck with my head. I've had enough of that for a lifetime. I may be young but that doesn't give you the right to poke fun at me." Pushing my chair away with the back of my knees I stood up and stared down at him as anger rose inside me.

"After the week I've had I'm not in the mood for games, Simon. I lived with the King of Mind Fucks and I don't appreciate you toying with me like this.

You're making me feel uncomfortable and frankly I expected more from you. Maybe I should go home?"

"Who says I'm playing games?" he asked throwing his arms wide. "Look, that thing I just did with my thumb? What can I say? It was completely spontaneous. I forgot who you were for a second."

I huffed out a breath. "Yeah? So, mistaking me for one of your groupies is supposed to make me feel less offended?" I snapped. Anger replaced the awkwardness of the situation.

Simon leaned over and plucked several small white napkins from a silver dispenser on the table. Silently he wiped each of his fingers one by one.

My eyes followed his hands until he'd finished, then looked back up into his. He shrugged then smoothed his closely groomed beard as he considered my question.

"That's not what I meant." He sighed flatly, all hint of humor gone from his voice. Glancing up at me he sighed, and I inhaled a deep breath as I tried to remain calm.

It would have been easy for me to call a cab and run away because I was so unfamiliar with the line of conversation, but this was the kind of issue I had to get past if I was going to take care of myself.

Simon took a bottle of wine from the cooler on the table and poured us both a drink. Grabbing his glass, he took a small swig and set it down.

"Look, Piper. I agree what I did was intimate and in hindsight I guess no one has ever done that before to you. I get how it must have looked, especially since you weren't through my door more than ten minutes before it happened but trust me when I say I didn't do it to take a liberty. If I'm honest I forgot myself. It kinda shocked me too, but it happened, and there's no use my pretending it didn't."

Getting out of his chair he wandered over to my side of the table, pulled out the cane dining chair next to me and turned it to face me.

Scooting my chair to face his, he eased me back down in it, then sat down himself. Tenderly, he slid his hands underneath mine and lifted both my hands in his.

If my heart had been cantering before, it went into a full on gallop the instant he closed his fingers and pressed them firmly against the back of my hands. Strangely, when I should have felt wary, a sense of calm settled within me.

For a few seconds he allowed the pause in the conversation to stretch between us. With eyes full of sincerity, I recognized the Simon I knew; the Simon I could trust.

The look of regret on his face appeared genuine, and he drew a small breath before delivering his honest smile. "Why do you think Gibson gets his balls in a stranglehold about us being alone sometimes?"

I shrugged. "From what you did a few minutes ago I'd say he doesn't trust you not to take advantage." The time for anything but straight talking had passed I felt.

Simon snickered and shook his head slowly, but never dropped eye-contact with me. "Piper, the last thing I wish to do is take advantage of you. Why is it so hard to believe that I can be a good man when it counts?"

"And that was you being a good man? Pulling that little stunt with—"

"That was a genuine slip, an accident; an absentminded mistake." His voice was laced with frustration and the fact someone with his reputation and experience bothered to deny anything actually gave him credit. "Trust me, Piper, if I could have a do-over I'd take it back in a heartbeat." I sighed. *Am I overreacting?*

"So where does that leave us?"

"I guess it leaves us starting again. Are you going to eat those ribs?" he asked nodding his head at the practically untouched food on my plate and giving us both the opportunity to skip past what he had done.

"They're hardly the kind of dish you serve up when you invite a woman to your home for dinner," I giggled, suddenly seeing the funny side of the start to our evening.

"Ah, well you see, I've never had a woman home for dinner before, but your comment is noted. Ribs are off the menu next time." My attention immediately flitted to the sultry female voice I'd heard the night before and my eyes narrowed in suspicion, but I continued to play along.

"There's going to be a next time?" My questioning brow was met with a wicked grin and I was glad we had managed to salvage the evening. More than that, I was proud I hadn't retreated into myself like I could easily have done.

"Definitely," he replied with another warm smile. My heart turned a somersault at his immediate reply.

CHAPTER EIGHT

"Should we abandon these and swap them out for wine and tapas, since I made such an ass of things?" Tapas were far easier to eat with more finesse.

"Sounds like a plan," I smiled, relieved that he was still intending to feed me. I was starving hungry by this point.

Tugging me up to stand, he dropped one hand to his side and took me into his kitchen by the other.

After pulling out a counter stool and ensuring I was seated, he pulled on the huge fridge door and lifted out a large sectional porcelain tray full of everything needed for a feast of tapas.

Stretching up, he pulled some crackers from a cupboard, flashing the most delectable small strip of toned, golden-tanned midriff with a smattering of fine hair, and I almost passed out from the strongest ache in my hands to run my fingertips across it.

When he turned sharply to face me, he caught me checking him out and a small not-so-secret smile played on his lips. Fortunately, he didn't comment, and carried the crackers and tapas to the couch facing the infinity pool.

Sliding down from the seat I followed him, and by the time I reached him he had placed the food on the low coffee table and turned stepping right into me.

"Whoa," he said sharply as his strong hands closed in a firm grip around my upper arms. When he steadied me, my eyes focused on his inviting full lips. His face was so close to mine I felt a sigh escape from his mouth.

Excitement and desire radiated through my veins when his warm breath ghosted over my cheek. *Oh, God. What you're doing to me.* I stifled a groan that threatened to escape from my throat and a rash of tiny goose bumps spread over my skin.

A pleasurable electric current ran from my toes right into my hair. "You okay? I didn't hurt you, did I?" he asked in concern as he took a step back to gauge my reaction.

"No. I'm fine, I never expected you—"

"Sometimes the best things happen unexpectedly," he replied, cutting across what I was about to say. His eyes narrowed in curiosity as they held mine just a fraction too long. I swallowed audibly and found his nearness powerful and unnerving.

For a few moments all I could feel was the disquiet his touch emitted within my body and the air became charged between us. His eyes dropped to my lips, and I swallowed nervously, this time willing him to kiss me, pleading silently with God to make it happen.

Dropping his hands from my arms he quickly stepped back and scratched his head. As quick as the air thickened between us, it was gone. Frustration passed through his eyes and an awkward silence developed until he sighed and stepped to the side.

"Sit. I'll grab the wine. White still okay? I hate red wine, it tastes like shit," he informed me as he reached into a chilled drinks cabinet over by the kitchen and pulled out an oversized bottle.

Grabbing two fresh wine glasses, he weaved his way back to where I sat and quickly poured us some new drinks. Passing me a large measure of wine, he sat back on his couch at an angle, one leg bent at the knee with it resting on the seat between us.

The piercing look he gave me felt suddenly different—intense— intimate... too intimate when his leg was only a few inches from mine.

I dropped my gaze until I realized I was staring right at the sizable bulge between his legs and my head snapped back up, my eyes meeting his again. I thought I saw him bite back another smile, but he never faltered in his conversation.

"So," he said in a soft encouraging tone, "Tell me what's been happening. How has your first week gone? Does it live up to your expectations?"

Thankful for his ordinary conversation we spoke for around an hour, ate the last scraps of food he'd brought out, and drank all of the wine. Gradually, I felt myself relax around him and I felt the warm familiar feeling I'd had with him back in Colorado.

After a while, I felt more than a little light-headed and realized I had drunk more than I ever had and felt a little woozy.

Unfortunately, this happened as the subject for our conversation turned to the sessional guys Otto was using. I was glad I was half drunk because it wasn't something I cared to talk about.

A couple of times I tried to digress, but Simon's focus on the musicians brought the conversation full circle and I mentioned how talented Grunt was. I was surprised when Simon told me he had watched a YouTube video of him when he had heard he was working with me.

Immediately following this the topic inevitably got on to Jeff, and I was stunned and disappointed when I realized Thomas had broken my confidence and told Simon about the incident.

"Ah, so this is the real reason why I'm here?" My heart sunk to my stomach in disappointment. *Jesus Simon's invitation is no more than a babysitting exercise.* I was livid. *Thomas is going to be sorry.*

My body stiffened in anger. If I hadn't been so drunk on the wine I'd have been mortified. To say I was pissed at being put on the spot both by Thomas and Simon was an understatement. The evening had turned out anything other than how I had envisioned it.

"No, Princess—"

"Will you stop with the fucking Princess, already?" I barked, cutting his protest off as I leaned forward and banged my stemmed glass down with a loud chink on the wooden table in front of me. It was a miracle it stayed in one piece.

"No, Piper. Listen. That's not the case. I was looking for an excuse to invite you out here when Thomas called me. And now that you're here it's something I had to mention. Apparently, this guy is a real slippery fucker. And naturally I feel protective of you."

"You're not my dad," I hissed.

"Thank fuck, I'm not," he added before he had a small chuckle to himself.

"Meaning?" I glared indignantly at him.

"I'd be in jail with the thoughts I've had about you in the last few months if that were the case."

His comment stole my breath and left me speechless. I swallowed roughly before taking a sharp gulp of air as I felt heat rise and my face redden. His directness left me feeling stunned.

"Jail? I don't understand," I replied and shook my head. *Now I'm definitely drunk to think he's attracted to me.* I'd never drunk that much before in my life.

"I've seen the way you look at me, Piper. You think I've been immune to the stolen glances and other little 'tells' you've emitted my way? I can see you're attracted to me." Embarrassed and muddled, I was lost for words, flustered beyond measure.

Oh, my, God he knows? For a moment I had no idea how to respond to him. My first thought was to deny it, but I figured that would only make me look immature.

Stalling for time, I grabbed my wine, drained the rest from the glass and swallowed nervously. Fighting how shy I suddenly felt, I gave him my best pointed stare.

"And how is that, exactly?" I snapped, changing from the pointed to an indignant stare.

Simon chuckled softly around the wine glass he held to his mouth. He sipped slowly on his wine with his curious eyes then leaned forward, toward me. Smiling flirtatiously, he asked, "Are you going to deny you're attracted to me?"

Christ, kill me now. I'm dying anyway.

When he called me out, I knew if I wanted to be taken seriously as an adult woman I had to answer honestly, even at the risk of being let down.

Inside my stomach rolled over and my heartbeat raced. *What's the worst that can happen if I admit my feelings? Rejection, that's what. Is he bringing this up to clear the air and shut me down in a kind and gentle manner?*

"That's a pretty stupid question to ask a young woman who's a fan of a band like M3rCy," I settled on saying, and sounded like I wasn't committing myself one way or the other. *Good recovery, Piper.*

"Don't do that. Don't make this about my job. I expected more than that from you. I'm not fucking with you, Piper," he said, sternly.

My heart stilled for a nanosecond. Glancing at his wine glass, he took another mouthful and my eyes were riveted to his lips around the rim of the glass. Placing it on the table, he sat back and leaned into the couch with his head resting on the backrest of it.

"Don't you think we've been around each other long enough for you to admit what you feel? We've grown pretty close. Tell me I've got it wrong, that what I've seen is my imagination, and this conversation stops right now." My whole body was gripped by nerves.

My gaze dropped to my lap, and I felt every emotion everyone who had paid close attention to me had probably seen before.

Inexperience, youth, and immaturity, but mostly fear of the rebuttal I was sure would follow any admission of wanting a man like Simon and what it would mean for our friendship. *I must be crazy to even have fantasized about Simon McLennan and me. He'd eat me alive, and I'd have no chance for recovery.*

I was so busy wigging out that in my temporary insanity I almost missed his confession. "This may come as a shock to you, Piper, and when I say this aloud I know I'm going to sound like some sick fuck because of your age, but I've been fighting some feelings of my own. Since the first time I saw you in fact; but trust me when I say I've never regarded you as a child. You're all woman to me."

Simon slipped his index finger under my chin and raised my head to look into my eyes. "I don't want to scare you by admitting this, but I'm not usually in the habit of flying back and forth to Colorado to visit my buddy Gibson. By the time we finish touring we're sick to fuck of each other, and I'm not the benevolent kind that wants to mentor budding singers the way I have with you."

My eyes darted across the room because his searing gaze felt too intense.

"Look at me, Piper," he coaxed in a gentle tone. I glanced back at him with a heart full of uncertainty. "Surely you must have picked up this vibe? I've waited two long years for the chance to tell you this. I tried to ignore, forget...I don't know what else, but I could never stay away."

Sitting motionless, mainly due to the wine, my mind grappled with what he had said to me. "You still living under Gibson's roof is the only thing that's stopped me from voicing my feelings. You have no idea how hard he warned me off and from his perspective I know he'd take great delight in disemboweling me if he knew I had invited you here and aired my feelings like this."

"I don't understand. What was it I did? How did you know?" I asked confused, because to my mind I had never done anything that was overly flirty or wore clothes that were provocative around him.

"Sometimes no matter how well we think we hide our feelings, the other person just knows. You may have thought you were careful, but you didn't consider whether I could read all the subtle signals you gave off."

Leaning forward, I shoved the plate I'd been using further into the center of the table to break the intensity of the moment between us then I sat back again. Avoiding his eyes, I looked down at my hands.

"Signals... what do you mean?" Inside, I felt both shame and anxiety radiate through me in equal measure when I thought that Gibson and Chloe may have noticed what Simon had obviously seen in my actions.

Oh, God, I should have known better. Both Gibson and Simon were used to women lusting after them and they were well versed at being hit on. Even though I had never made a conscious effort with Simon he still knew. Is it how I look at him? What is the difference between how I look at him to how I look at everyone else?

"Yeah, signals. The way you always touch your lips when I'm talking, and you're supposed to be listening. You're doing it now," he added, and I became conscious one of my hands had migrated and was stroking over my lips. I dropped my hand immediately to my lap, and he chuckled. *Shit.*

"Then there were all the times you carefully tucked your hair behind your ears or stroked your fingers across your cleavage when you wore those tiny white tank tops and brought attention to your tits." My eyes went wide with shock and I shook my head with my jaw open.

I had no idea where his comments were coming from, but as he had busted me with the lip thing I guessed I had done what he said.

"You're not going to tell me those long stares that have passed between us had no effect on you," he asked, one eyebrow raised in question? They had. They made me wet and I'd clenched my thighs together more times than I cared to remember. Remembering those feelings again made me embarrassed and hot all over again.

It was obvious Simon had paid close attention to me, and my body language had let me down. I could hardly deny the very specific gestures and figured the only course of action was to come clean.

Nothing had prepared me for this moment and for a few seconds I felt foolish, childlike, and almost convinced myself he'd laugh when I admitted the feelings I had for him. Eventually I figured I had no choice when I stared into his eyes. Simon could obviously read my thoughts.

CHAPTER NINE

"*B*ig deal, I have a crush on you. What girl doesn't have one?" I answered, sounding a little more impertinent than I had intended, but finally fronting him out for putting me on the spot.

"Good to know I'm not mistaken," he replied as he gave me another small smile and chuckled before he leaned across and tucked a strand of my hair behind my ear.

Instead of drawing back to his usual position, his hand cupped my cheek, and I was immediately out of my depth. I chuckled nervously, a new wave of shyness taking me way past my comfort zone. "Please don't... this is embarrassing, stupid—"

"What's embarrassing about being attracted to someone?" I didn't answer, and he sighed, looked puzzled and tried again.

"Come on, tell me what you're thinking?" his voice was gentle, encouraging, nurturing.

"Please..." I pleaded as my eyes ticked over his face. When they stopped and locked in his gaze, the intensity and weight of his piercing stare mesmerized me.

I thought if he could read me like he professed, he would have seen I had no words, my mind consumed fully by the tenderness in his gentle touch.

Another pause in the conversation told me he was being patient, but he wanted an answer. I sighed heavily then shrugged my shoulders, helpless for what else to say because the situation I had found myself in was bigger than I was prepared for. And when my silence continued it became clear to him I didn't want to respond.

Eventually, he sighed. "Want to know what I think?"

"I already know what you think," I snapped quickly, pulling away from him. Persisting for answers I didn't have was annoying me. "You don't have to say it. You're flattered and interested enough to mess around with me like this, but you're sure when I'm older I'll find a guy—"

"What the fuck? Really, Piper? Nope. That's not it at all. I won't say any of that. Didn't you listen to any of what I said to you before?" He stopped talking and stared pointedly again. "Now, do you want to hear what I have to say, or would you prefer to keep making your own shit up about what's in my head?"

The knot in my stomach tightened when I tried to hold his gaze. Simon reached over again and placed his large strong hand over both of mine resting in my lap. His action made me realize I was absent-mindedly wringing them together and my gaze fell to his soothing gesture.

"Hey. Stop. Please don't feel uncomfortable with me. You have no need to be nervous, Piper," he advised me in his soft quiet tone. It was all right for him to say that, but I'd never been confronted about my feelings before.

My eyes flicked to Simon's, and he held my gaze again as frustration flitted through his. Drawing in a sharp breath, he held it for a moment before letting it go. His eyes softened, and he shook his head.

Shifting his position, he shuffled closer. When he sat alongside me, his arm brushed mine and he left them touching, but his focus was straight ahead toward the pool. A small thrill ran through my body at how close we were. I felt the heat from his arm radiate onto mine.

"Piper, what I want to say isn't designed to embarrass you or make you feel uncomfortable. All I want to do is tell you how I feel about you. Gibson may see you as a young vulnerable girl and I get that, he's bound to think the way he does given the role he's taken on with you."

When he paused, I glanced over at him. Sitting quietly, he chewed the inside of his cheek in thought for a moment, as if mulling over what he had said.

I'll admit I may have been a little vulnerable, but I didn't want Simon to feel as if I was fragile.

"Gibson and I don't see eye to eye on this at all. What I'm trying to say is I'm not Gibson and I'm only gonna say this once," he sighed heavily and turned his head to look directly into my eyes, "What I'm trying to say is you matter to me."

Blinking rapidly, I stemmed the tears that immediately filled my eyes. My throat burned with a lump that had formed and I sat motionless unsure what the word 'matter' meant. Hearing he cared about me was overwhelming.

I'm so out of my depth. What should I say? For the first time in my life I felt incompetent and ignorant as to how to respond, like I hadn't earned his feelings.

Back home in high school I had fooled around with a boy a couple times, but I always stopped short of the home run. I wasn't ready, and I wasn't in love. *What a time to recognize just how socially backward I am with the opposite sex.*

There was one thing Gibson had said about Simon that I couldn't deny. He was very experienced with women. So experienced, the thought of me being anything to him appeared absurd, yet it appeared it was an unexpected reality.

My suspicious eyes studied his face for the truth. I'd seen him often enough when he yanked Gibson's chain about something, and I saw no trace he was lying or deriving pleasure from seeing me confused.

"I'm not fucking with you, Piper," he added like he'd read my thoughts.

"This is... I... we can't... I don't... I'm just a girl, Simon," I finally spat out helplessly when I'd changed my mind from the several alternatives I left unsaid, such as *This is ridiculous, I'm a virgin, we couldn't possibly do anything about this, Gibson would go crazy... he'd kill the both of us.* "How can you possibly be interested in someone like me?"

"Someone like you? Are you serious? How the fuck could I not be?

Look at you, Piper, you're perfect. Adorable. Why wouldn't I be interested? What is it about me you're afraid of?"

I shrugged, feeling lost for words.

"Yeah, you're younger, a lot younger than me, but you're a very beautiful woman nevertheless. If you need further convincing, I find you intelligent, smart as fuck as an artist, and I've never been drawn to anyone more. I know you're probably vulnerable and I want to get this right."

"Vulnerable? Do you see me as an easy target? A challenge? An innocent virgin? To be honest Simon, I don't know what to think... what you want with me... what this all means." I tossed my hands helplessly in front of me.

The air between us felt highly charged with an expectation on both sides. Simon's with the need to convince me of his attraction. And mine with doubt and suspicion. "I overheard Gibson talking to Chloe about you and I think he's right."

"Right? About what?"

"That you'd hurt me."

His hand moved to my hair, and he stroked it gently. "I'd die trying not to, sweetheart. Look, when Gibson told me what you were going through right before your mom passed I'll admit I felt sorry for you. But believe me, I know the difference between pity and lust. I hadn't even met you then. What I feel is as much of a revelation to me as it is to you. I never expected to feel how I did the first night I saw you."

I felt my face grow red and his eyes softened empathetically. "Trust me, baby. I tried hard to fight these feelings. I get hard in normal conversation with you and I can guess how it looks to everyone else, but I don't see a twenty-year-old girl. What I see is much more than that. I see a strong and ballsy, if a tad innocent, woman. You're beautiful, your voice gives me goose bumps and the way you move mesmerizes me."

My eyes ticked over his face because it felt incredulous he was attracted to me. "Gibson said he felt he had to protect me from you. Did you know that?"

"Sure, because I have a bad boy reputation as a player, right? Back in the day Gib's rep was much worse than mine. I get it—he thinks I'm out to tap you and that would be the end of it, but that's not what's going on in here." He slapped his chest hard with his palm.

"Forget what Gibson says or anyone else who'd have an opinion on this. Big deal, there's an age difference. Age is merely a number. Relationships are borne out of chemistry, attraction and common interests. It's the connection between two people that counts. Some of the strongest relationships have wide age gaps. What matters is how couples treat each other and how they feel... which incidentally has nothing what-the-fuck-so-ever to do with anyone else."

Simon placed his palm against my cheek once more and for the first time I felt comfortable with his touch. I leaned into it. His serious face brightened and he gave me his a sexy smile.

"Piper, I'm not going to act on my feelings right now other than to make it clear they're real. I only want you to know that despite what Gibson thinks will happen this isn't about me nailing you for the sake of it."

I felt my face flush. "This is..." I sighed, my inadequacies swamping me. "I never expected..." No matter how I tried, I had no idea what to tell him. How to respond.

"Shh. I know, sweetheart," he soothed, placing his finger across my lips to silence me. "I can see you feel overwhelmed. You don't have to worry, I have no expectations and I'm not gonna make a move on you unless I think you're giving me the go ahead, so you can relax."

Relief washed through me because although I craved more of his touch, his kiss and more, I needed time to get used to the idea of Simon being interested in me.

"As you saw earlier, my attempt at handling my feelings hasn't gone the way I expected either and the last thing I want is for you to feel coerced by anything. All I wanted you to know is I feel something between us too."

My chest felt tight because it was one thing to have schoolgirl butterflies and a crush that was going nowhere. To realize the potential I had with Simon to do things I neither felt ready or confident to do gave me a much greater challenge to mull over.

My sexual experience was practically ziltch, nada, zero. Entering into something with Simon was far from the schoolboy fumble behind the bleachers I'd experienced before. I didn't even have anyone I felt close enough to talk to about how to handle it. There was no way I could discuss it with Chloe for fear of her telling Gibson.

Most of the stuff I knew about sexual relationships came from Google and porn sites, but nothing could prepare me for how to respond to the real life feelings that ran through my body, that made my thighs squeeze, my core pulse, and my panties wet.

The sum extent of what I knew about the normal psychology of relationships, was that relationships should be between two people who had equal status and value, where no one wanted to control the other.

My thoughts turned again to Simon and all the unfamiliar feelings he awoke within me and the knot in my stomach twisted tighter than I ever knew it could.

"If you feel the same way and you want to explore what we've got, I'm ready whenever you are. I get it. I'm a much older guy with a record of sexual conquests. Truth be told that should make me a no-go area for any decent girl, but there's always that one girl a man is willing to change for. Take Gibson as case in point. You'd be hard pressed to find a more loyal and loving man to his wife than him."

Everything he said was true. I'd heard about Gibson's Legacy; read about it in fact: Google is a mine of information. His antics had made some shocking reading, but Simon was right, Gibson was nothing like the reputation that preceded his life with Chloe. Knowing how he was with his wife I saw for myself what the right woman could do for a man.

"Sorry, I should be better at dealing with this kind of... I've never been in..." my voice trailed off, then I looked at him and smiled. "I'm kinda out of my depth right now," I confessed.

"I figured that, and like I said, I won't put pressure on you, sweetheart. Shit, I never even imagined saying any of this today, then I went and swiped that sauce from your lips and made that crass remark about it."

I chuckled, seeing the funny side of it, "It could have been worse I suppose. If the table hadn't been so big you may well have sucked it off," I replied, then almost swallowed my tongue when I realized what

I said. I glanced nervously at him knowing there would be some kind of response to my comment.

"Shit, I really want that do-over now," he said, flirting back. I became conscious my body was reacting to every comment he made when my thighs squeezed together again.

"Is it me or is it too hot?" I asked fanning myself. I wasn't sure if it was the situation I had found myself in, the balmy night air or being near Simon that suddenly made the heat unbearable.

"We could take a swim if you want?" he offered.

"I didn't bring swimmers with me... I didn't think to."

"You can always skinny dip," he teased, his eyes darkening with lust at the thought.

Shaking my head shyly I replied, "Not sure I'm ready for that."

"I am," he replied and chuckled again, "I mean me... not that I'm not ready... aww shit, you've got me as tongue-tied as you are now," he teased and chuckled again.

"You could go in wearing your underwear," he suggested, and I stared at the beautiful cool pool as I considered his offer. "Don't overthink it, Piper, if you want to do something just do it." *It would be like wearing a bikini and he's seen me in those hundreds of times at home.*

Simon stood up and wandered over to the wine cooler again and pulled out another bottle. This one had a cork. After opening it with the corkscrew, he made his way back to the couch and filled our glasses again.

"Maybe another drink will make you feel loose enough to forget your inhibitions and help you feel more comfortable about being around me here."

"Are you trying to get me drunk to take advantage?" I probed, but my tone sounded playful.

"Piper, if that's what I wanted, I'd have been inside you the first day you arrived in Santa Monica," he said with conviction and I believed him.

I blushed at his blunt reply. "Sorry, that wasn't fair," I admitted.

"No, it's a fair question considering my reputation for having loose morals," he said without shame.

My heart clenched in response to his honesty and something shifted inside. "About that swim," I suggested, giving into the heat.

Simon's eyes glittered mischievously. "You're game?" I didn't miss the disbelief in his tone.

"Well since the temperature is at melting point and I'm all hot and sticky..." I replied and let my voice trail away, cringing when I realized the double meaning my choice or words had.

Simon's laugh was infectious, "Enough already," he scolded, chuckling as he stood and adjusted himself in his pants. My eyes fell to his groin before he turned, but he didn't notice and walked toward the pool.

"Drink up your wine, and I'll get us some towels from the pool house," he replied over his shoulder as I tried once again to contain my embarrassment.

CHAPTER TEN

Following Simon outside, I saw a light on in a pretty single story dwelling set back from the edge of the patio on the other side of the pool.

Bending, I trailed my hand across the surface of the cool water. The ripples shimmered in the disturbed surface by the light of the moon.

Glancing up in the direction of the pool house again, I noted Simon was still inside and wondered if I could get my clothes off and slide in the water unnoticed. It wasn't that I was ashamed of my body, I was just shy about him seeing me in my underwear.

My legs were sticky with perspiration from the humidity and my coordination was impaired from the wine. When I tried to pull down my Capri pants it wasn't as quick and easy as I had originally imagined in my head.

Continuing to struggle, my breath hitched when I saw Simon emerge from the darkness at the other side of the pool. I tried to move faster to free myself, but by the time he reached me, I still had one foot tangled in my pants and my bare ass showing in my thong as I lay on my side, pulling frantically at the material.

My foot came free just as Simon hovered over me, grinning. A soft chuckle escaped his lips. Scurrying to my feet, I jumped into the water and heard Simon laugh again right before the sound of the splash I made.

Initially the water stole my breath, the difference between temperature marked, but once I got used to it, I felt refreshed.

For a few seconds everything appeared calm, almost serene beneath the water then as I broke the surface and grabbed for the side I came face to face with Simon who had bent down at the edge like I had been and was testing the water. "How do you feel now?" he asked with a small smile.

Self-conscious? Shy? I thought.

"Wet," I replied, then groaned aloud because my attempt to be funny was loaded again with connotation.

Unable to help himself Simon made another flirty comment. "Hmm, sounds inviting... the pool I mean," he said in a low, seductive tone. I groaned, mortified at my comment and the innuendo implied in his response.

Embarrassed, I ducked my head under the water and swam to the bottom end of the pool. As my head broke the surface of the water I heard a small splash.

"Oh, goddammit, it feels cold," he said and grunted as he broke the surface near me and shivered. If I had thought Simon looked hot before, it was nothing to when he stood next to me with wet hair and small water droplets covering his forehead and eyelashes.

Unable to tear my eyes away I stared intensely, mesmerized by how beautiful he was by the moonlight.

Shaking off my daze I grinned. "It's refreshing once you get used to it," I argued and floated away on my back to make a little space from him. When I stopped and looked at him again, he was checking me out, his jaw slightly slack as his tongue tasted his bottom lip. When he knew I'd seen him, he cleared his throat.

"Fuck, it's harder being around you like this, than it seemed in my head," he admitted. "Maybe we need some music to take our minds off the temperature difference," he suggested, and I wondered if it was to take his mind off me.

"Sounds good," I agreed, because I felt the look he gave me was weighted with a level of intimacy I wasn't prepared for.

Maneuvering away from me, he swam in powerful strokes as his strong, athletic body made short work of covering the length of the pool. Reaching the edge, he placed his hands up on the side and hoisted himself clean out of the water in two fluid movements.

I gulped, feeling out of my depth again when I realized Simon was totally naked. It was hard work fighting my shyness, but that was nothing to how flustered I felt because I knew when Simon came back into the pool he'd be naked right next to me.

"Dreaming Out Loud" by One Republic suddenly filled the quiet and Simon threw a remote control he had in his hand onto a patio table, turned and immediately dived back into the pool. When he reached me he noted my awkward eye contact.

"What's the matter?"

"You might have kept your boxers on," I said honestly and cringed because I sounded like a prude.

"I would have, Piper, except I don't wear them. I did debate putting some swimmers on, but it would have meant going all the way back to the pool house. Nobody apart from Stevie and the guy who does the pool comes back here, and I never thought about it until after I'd stripped off."

"Ah, well this is awkward," I said.

"Why? Because you are sharing a pool with a naked man or because that naked man is me?"

"Both... no, you I suppose."

"Well I don't feel awkward because I got a good glimpse of your ass when you were struggling with your pants earlier, so we're kind of even," he replied playfully.

Flicking water at him, I lifted my hand to smack him and he caught my wrist with his hand and pulled me closer. The water was deeper than I was tall and I almost went under. I grabbed his shoulders to keep my head above it.

"Oh, I see, can't keep your hands off me, huh?" he teased in a murmur close to my ear. My heart skipped a beat at his playful tone. His breath warmed the shell of my ear, and I shivered when a thrill ran down my spine. His hands slid around my waist and my whole body tingled from the contact of his skin next to mine.

"Am I all right to hold you like this?" he asked, suddenly aware of my lack of experience. I cringed he'd had to ask, and I nodded, swallowed nervously and moved a hand from my waist and shifted my hair behind my shoulder.

"I got you, Piper. I'm not gonna do anything you're not comfortable with, honey," he said, feeling the tension I held in my body. "We're gonna take this real slow, okay?" he asked, softly.

As I shifted again in the water his huge palm landed on my back and he trailed a finger down each bone from the center of my spine to the string of my thong. A pang of desire shot through me and pulsed between my legs. *Oh, Lord, this is crazy.*

The tune "Hold My Hand" by Jess Glynne blared out and the upbeat number matched my racing heart.

"You got to tell me where the lines are and when you need space. My body wants to devour you, but my mind has got the brakes on hard. You understand what I'm saying?" I nodded, thankful for his caution and my gaze fell to his lips. "You want me to kiss you, sweetheart?" he asked in a low gentle tone, picking up on my unspoken gesture.

Holding me up with his arms tightened firmer around me, my feet were barely off the ground. For the first time that night I stared back with the confidence to nod my head, certain I never wanted anything more.

Instead of kissing my mouth like I had prepared myself for, Simon bent and kissed the crook of my neck. When a sharp zap of electricity radiated through me, I moaned. A small gasp of surprise came from my mouth as his lips moved over mine.

Simon drew me closer, his lips moving gently, and when his tongue slipped into my mouth, a thrill of excitement radiated through me. Losing all power to resist, my arms snaked around his neck as I lost myself in the moment.

By the time we broke the kiss, I had wrapped my leg around his.

Clinging to him, I buried my face in the crook of his neck and he shifted my leg further up his thigh. In turn I wrapped both of my legs around his waist like it was the most natural thing in the world, until my center met his hard, erect cock. I stilled, suddenly a little scared of how fast things were moving.

Tension gripped me for a second and I shocked myself at how natural everything felt in his arms and took a deep breath to calm my adrenaline fueled desires down. *Oh, sweet Jesus.*

Sensing my unease, Simon lifted his head away from me and looked into my eyes. "It's okay, baby. Nothing you don't want, remember? You want me to stop?" he said, encouraging me that if I was happy with what was happening then so was he.

"No l like it," I replied.

His careful questions were very timely and it gave me confidence to know, if I said no at any point, he'd respect my decision.

"You're doing great, baby. Look, I know your mind is probably full of uncertainty, but I'm determined to go at your pace, sweetheart. I get that no means no. I never expected us to have come this far tonight and any taste of you is a bonus, you got me?"

Heat rose to my face and I let out a shaky sigh. The inadequacy of my virginal position at the age of twenty was never more apparent in me as I stood in the pool with Simon. I sighed. Swallowing nervously, I reminded myself of how often I had dreamed of a moment like this.

Acutely aware of how close his face was I noted we were breathing the same air. It was intoxicating and powerful and found myself nodding.

When I looked into his lust-filled eyes, I believed him... trusted him, and it was the intensity and weight of his stare that finally freed my mind to take what I wanted.

That want and my curiosity outweighed any awkwardness of the few previous intimate moments we'd had. The burning desire inside me had been awakened, and I knew I wouldn't be satisfied until I took what I needed from him.

Leaning closer with my heart pounding, I pressed my lips to his, taking my first kiss, on my own terms, of any man.

Shifting his position, his arms shifted to my hips then slid slowly round to my butt and he cradled both cheeks in his hands. I felt weightless... between the buoyancy of the water and his support.

"Jesus Christ," he muttered, his mouth tearing free just long enough to say it before his passion grew.

As the kiss grew deeper, his hands gripped tighter, and he gently rolled my center over his hard cock. Before long, I found myself move in response. My nub aching with a pang of need so strong that shot a strong pulse into my core.

"Fuck," an urgent cuss mingled with his hot breath as he jostled me further up on his hips, then I heard him growl in frustration.

Next thing I knew we were on the move, heading toward the shallow end of the pool as his kisses grew in urgency and depth. His tongue lashed against mine as he pressed me closer.

I had never been kissed like the way Simon, kissed me. His kiss was laced with urgency, hunger, care and desire, but without the sloppy demands of the ones I had experienced from a teenage boy.

Our bodies positively vibrated with desire as he continued to kiss me slowly and I reveled in the feel of his soft warm lips in contrast to our cool skin from the pool water.

"Goddamn it," he muttered shakily under his breath as he broke the kiss. Easing me gently down his body, he slid me onto my feet. I whimpered at the loss of his arms around me, but before I could think his hands were back, this time, cupping my face as he bent to kiss me again.

Taking my mouth hungrily, a thrill of ecstasy shot through me when his hot wet tongue swept over my swollen lips and I parted my mouth, giving him entry. Holding my head, he moved it sensually as it filled with desire and the way he possessed me left me breathless for a moment.

My heart skipped a beat when he deepened the kiss and his cool hands slid back over my butt. A deeper more urgent wave of desire passed through me.

Suddenly I felt light-headed again and I sagged against him for support temporarily surrendering to all the new sensations flowing through my veins.

Losing his balance, Simon staggered backward and up against the side of the pool, pulling me along with him.

"Fuck, Piper, we gotta stop, baby," he muttered, a frustrated gruff tone in his voice. Dipping his head he groaned against my neck then pressed his lips back against mine, ignoring his own warning. He allowed his hands to glide sensually over my skin in all the right places.

When he pulled me closer against him, I felt how hard and turned on he was. For all my inexperience there was no denying the effect I had on him.

As the kiss became more heated, Simon broke it again and tenderly wound his hand in my hair. Tugging my head back he extended my neck.

Placing his lips seductively over my neck he muttered, "We need to get out, sweetheart. We've got to cool our jets, or I may not be able to stop myself from asking for more."

Gently, he pushed me away. The frustrated look in his eyes made me feel powerful that I had affected him as much as I had, and I felt a little put out by his restraint. I hadn't wanted to stop.

Kissing the top of my head, he turned me in the direction of the steps and led me out of his Roman shaped pool with one arm around my shoulder.

"A dip in the pool was supposed to cool us down, not set me on fire," he mused in frustration and shook his head as he chuckled. I glanced up, my eyes meeting his, and I felt my shyness return.

Disappointment tightened my chest and my body felt both weak and frustrated from all the cravings, desires, and unfamiliar emotions that ran through my body, and it ached for more.

As he left me by the edge of the pool and wandered over to grab the towels I realized they were bathrobes instead. When he bent down to pick these up I couldn't resist checking out his firm, lean body. As my eyes scanned down I caught a better glimpse of his cock and I swallowed, roughly.

Standing proud it bobbed in front of him at a forty-five-degree angle from his body. Suddenly a fresh wave of desire flowed through me, along with fear, panic and want in equal measures.

"Night Changes" came on the playlist by One Direction as I stood waiting for him to come back and I fought the urge to hide when he cast his wide curious eyes filled with desire all over my body.

Shaking off my attack of self-consciousness, I gave him a look of surprise when still naked, he dropped one bathrobe to the floor and held out the other for me to walk into.

"Thank you," I said, sounding shy.

Placing the robe regally over my shoulders, he pulled the lapels to the front and held them tightly together in his fist, trapping me inside as he placed another small kiss on my mouth.

"You are so damned adorable, Piper," he whispered, placing another kiss on my forehead. When he let go of my robe, he turned and treated me to a full display of his rippling muscles, firm glutes, and his strong back as he picked up his own.

Shrugging himself into it he tied the belt at the waist before turning toward me. I figured it was a deliberate move to save my blushes now we were up close to one another again.

I may have gotten Jeff wrong in my assessment of him, but I was certain I hadn't made the same mistake with Simon. He had been nothing but upfront in his intentions toward me. A man who was upfront and honest was far more important than someone who only treated me well to get what he wanted.

CHAPTER ELEVEN

*W*aking in a light and airy room, I squinted sleepily at the sun shining though some vertical blinds. The sound of gulls or geese and soft rolling waves jarred me up onto my elbows. My heartbeat picked up its pace when I remembered where I was.

Flopping back heavily on my pillow, I felt heat rise to my cheeks when I thought about what had happened the night before.

Glancing at the clock on the nightstand, I was amazed when it was already 9:30 am. I strained to listen for movement in the house and vaguely heard what I thought was Simon in the kitchen.

We'd both headed to bed almost immediately after leaving the pool and I was thankful for the space to think. Fortunately, the wine was still at play and when I lay down my concentration was centered on not throwing up instead of anything else, and I fell asleep almost straight away.

Once I had showered and washed my hair, I dug into my duffle and pulled out the spare denim shorts and small purple tank top I had stowed there for emergencies due to the Californian heat, because the outfit I had on the night before still lay by the side of the pool as far as I knew.

After a quick check in the mirror I had wished I hadn't, because in my attire with my braless top I looked less than elegant and more slutty than sexy.

My bra was still damp and stank of chlorine, so after I had a quick shower I had no choice but to suck it up and go downstairs to face Simon.

An attack of self-doubt gripped my stomach as I reached the top of the stairs. *What if what happened was all a mistake? What if he had regrets? Did Simon really want me or was I his only option last night?* My feet were moving regardless of the questions in my mind. *What else can I do? Hide in his guest bedroom all day?*

As I made my descent toward the kitchen, a slender, golden tanned female with platinum blonde hair came into view. She looked too comfortable behind Simon's counter as she swayed sexily to the radio.

My heart stopped for a beat and fear flowed through my veins because Simon had a woman in his house who looked perfectly at home. *What the fuck did you expect, Piper?* The first thought I had was to run back up the stairs, and I was about to turn away when I heard her speak.

"Hey. Sorry, I didn't see you there. Did I wake you?" I recognized the soft tone immediately as the woman I'd heard on the phone and I glanced back to the upper floor over my shoulder.

Looking toward her again, I was embarrassed Simon had put me in such a position. "No. I was awake," I said, giving her no more than necessary without being rude.

"Coffee?" she asked in a friendly tone and held up the glass pot of freshly made black liquid.

I shook my head, my nose turning at the smell. I hated coffee. "Got any orange juice?" I croaked, still feeling the remnants of wine which had left a seedy feeling in my stomach.

"Sure, just a sec," she replied and pulled open the fridge door. Pulling out a gallon carton she placed it in front of me and grabbed a pint glass from the cupboard. "Anything to eat or are you waiting for Simon to come back?" *Come back? Where did he go?*

Slowly, I poured the citrus liquid into the tall glass as I came to terms that he'd left me alone with another woman. When my glass was full, I screwed the lid back on and shoved the carton back in her direction.

"Thank you," I smiled, "Sorry, did you say Simon's not here?" I asked, bursting to ask who she was. What was more intriguing was she didn't appear to be fazed at all, by my presence in his home.

"Don't panic, he hasn't gone far. He's on the beach taking his morning run. He'll be back in..." she hesitated and looked at her wristwatch, "ten minutes if he's on his short run, which I guess is all he'll be fit for given that I found an empty wine bottle by his bed this morning," she added and snickered.

I felt my eyes widen as I sipped the orange juice.

When she made no effort to say who she was, I couldn't wait any longer. "I'm sorry we haven't been introduced. I'm Piper," After how Simon had behaved with me I didn't feel very friendly toward her. She was at home in his kitchen, and obviously comfortable around his possessions.

"Yep. That's right. I know all about you, honey," she replied not taking the hand I had offered and instead stuffed hers into some oven mitts. "Just a sec, I need to grab these," she informed me and turned to pull some perfectly baked pain au chocolat from the oven.

Dumping the trays on the gray granite countertop she slipped off the mitts, rinsed her hands and dried them. "Stevie," she offered, and I shook her hand. Dipping her knees slightly she looked quizzically into my eyes, "Aw fuck, he never told you about me, did he?" she asked.

Huh? My heart fell to my stomach as I chewed the side of my mouth. I narrowed my eyes in question. "Stevie McLennan, or Stephanie as the 'Olds' call me. I'm Simon's sister," she informed me, and my punctured heart instantly inflated again.

"Olds?" I asked, cursing Simon for leaving me to face the awkwardness of the moment. Never once had he spoken about a sister.

"Our parents. Since I was little, I've always hated my name. Not that Stephanie is a bad name, just my association with it. One great aunt and our grandma on my dad's side. They were kinda crinkly since I was a baby, so I always thought of it as an old-fashioned name, you feel me?" I grinned at her explanation and nodded. I knew people at school who had names that I thought of like that too.

"All right, since Simon has neglected to tell you about me, here goes. At twenty-four I'm Simon's famous foot model sister. I live in the house next door. Yep, Simon bought it for me... but it comes with conditions."

"Conditions?" I mused.

"When he's home I order his groceries and supplies, take care of the laundry deliveries, and manage the house maids who also do mine. Robbie, my guy, who's a voice-over actor, keeps the pool area maintained and manages the groundsmen. When Simon's away he has a realtor management company take care of everything."

Before I could ask what in the world a foot model was, Simon's voice cut into the conversation. "You forgot to tell her you also eat my food, drink my wine, and skinny dip in my pool when you think I'm not looking, and according to the CCTV, have the occasional sex romp on my patio with my pool guy."

"Are you fucking kidding me, you're spying on me? You've watched —" she asked, her eyes wide with shock as they darted around the room looking for cameras.

"Nope, but your reaction tells me I'm right on all counts," he replied with a smug grin. Stretching over the counter he swiped one of her pastries from the hot tray and stuffed it almost whole into his mouth.

It took me a second to connect that the pool guy was her partner and then I grinned. Simon finished his pastry, swiped the empty water bottle he'd been carrying and filled it up with fresh water from the fridge dispenser.

Stevie remained speechless as she shook her head with a smirk on her face while she transferred the remaining breakfast pastries to a large oval tub and sealed the lid.

Meanwhile Simon bit back a grin as he watched his sister gather her composure, then sucked down the water. Immediately my focus was on his long, tanned neck and I felt instantly thirsty as I watched him drink every drop.

A loud gasp escaped his throat when he withdrew the bottle and his eyes connected with mine. I smiled shyly, and he wandered around the counter to stand beside me.

"Sleep well?" he asked and leaned in, placing a small kiss with his cold wet lips on my temple. His gesture was all that it took to reignite my desire from the previous night.

"I did. Too much wine though," I replied and nodded toward the orange juice. As he stood so close, I became acutely aware of heat radiating from his sweaty body.

"I'm gonna grab a quick shower, then we'll eat and plan the day, all right?" I nodded again, too tongue-tied to speak and too dazed by his sexy sweaty appearance to think in words.

My eyes followed him until he disappeared from sight and I sighed before I turned and looked back at my juice. "Well, there's a first," Stevie muttered shaking her head as she folded a tablecloth and placed it on the counter.

"Excuse me?" I asked wondering what I'd missed.

"My big ugly brother is more than a little smitten, kitten," she teased, and I felt my face redden.

"Aw, honey. Sorry, I didn't mean to embarrass you." Hearing her instant retraction told me she knew she'd overstepped. "For the six years I've lived next door, I can honestly say *no one* comes here apart from the band and their other halves, my parents, and two of his old friends from school."

Stevie didn't have to spell out the significance of her statement, but I wondered if it was because of my connection to Gibson and Chloe that the exception to his rule had been made.

"Can I be frank with you, Piper?" *Oh, Lord here comes the lecture.*

"Of course."

"Up until the tail end of last year we all despaired of Simon. I felt ashamed of him because he was a pig in the way he treated women. A dog even. Every time I picked up a magazine, opened a newspaper, or searched online for something I cringed because of his behavior.

"It felt as if he was always in my face; him acting out some crude gesture or other for the cameras with some bimbo on his arm. 'Eye candy with air between their ears and zippers in their pussies' my mom said."

I frowned in distaste because I figured her build up was supposed to warn me off. Obviously, I knew all about his past, but I had never seen that side of Simon. With me he had always been gentle, respectful and caring.

In my head I began to formulate a speech to defend us because I figured I was about to get the 'he'll hurt you' or 'you're too young and naïve to know' lecture. They were the same issues I struggled with in my own mind when I thought of how everyone else would view us.

"All I'm going to say is I hope you make it together. Sure, you're young, but I've never seen him as centered as he's been this last year or so. He's really been getting his shit together. Clean living, no other women, and I had no idea what the change in him was due to until he told me you were coming to Santa Monica."

It came as a shock that she thought the reason for Simon's turn-around behavior was because of me. We were nothing but mentor and pupil in real terms... until our kiss in the pool.

Relief flowed through me because having an alliance like Simon's sister was important if our relationship did develop to more. I loved her for her open mind and lack of judgment about our differences already.

"At first, I thought it unusual for him to be so enthusiastic about helping you, but then I figured he most likely had grown up a little since Gibson had taken you on and decided it was time to give back. That was until he began to talk about you nonstop."

Watching how serious her expression was made me listen intently.

"One day it all clicked, and I knew he'd developed strong feelings for you. When I finally put it to him I had expected him to deny it, but I guess he needed someone to pour his heart out to." A warm smile stretched on her lips and I smiled nervously in return.

"Anyway, if I know Simon, Gibson and Chloe will be the last to know about this, so if you need someone to talk to I'll try to be objective, but he's my brother first and I guess I may be pretty biased unless he fucks you over."

I grinned at her honesty, but my mind went straight back to Gibson's warning. "*This business is so fucking tough... and it's riddled with people who either want to fuck you, fuck you over, or kick you the fuck out of the way.*"

Stevie picked up an oversized purse, slung it over her shoulder, and came around to my side of the counter. "Lunch basket is packed; drinks are in the cooler; bacon, patties, and pancakes, are on the warming setting in the oven. I'm not sure what his plans are for later so can you ask him to text me please?"

Placing a hand on my back, she leaned in and pecked me on the cheek. She grabbed my hand and squeezed, "Take your time, Piper. If Simon really wants something he's patient, and he's got a great heart."

Turning away from me she left the house and closed the door softly behind her.

CHAPTER TWELVE

Simon returned looking drop dead gorgeous in a white linen shirt with his sleeves rolled up, his inked muscular arms partly showing. Black jeans and expensive black, soft-leather shoes completed his rather immaculate appearance. *Damn he's got taste.*

Sliding his hand around my back he asked playfully, "Do you mind if I kidnap you for the whole weekend? I want to take you for a ride somewhere." As far as I was concerned he could have kidnapped me all year with no complaints. My only issue was the clothes I wore.

"Look at me," I said with a frown and gestured down at my attire, "I didn't bring another change because I thought I would be going home last night."

Casting his eyes slowly down my front his eyes stopped over my breasts and he swallowed roughly and quickly looked up at my face. "Fuck, that wasn't a good idea," he said and chuckled. "I've never wanted to take a breast in my mouth as much as I want to right now."

"What's stopping you?" My comment was out before I realized the implications of what I had said, and I blushed. Eyeing me warily, he reached up and stroked my left breast tenderly with the back of his fingers.

Simon's eyes immediately glanced up to meet mine and when I

didn't object he did it again before engulfing it in his huge hand and giving it a small squeeze.

My whole body shook with the small thrill I felt. Sure, I'd had my breast felt before but not in the way Simon did it so openly.

In the blink of an eye, he plucked me off the counter stool and carried me over to his couch and gently sat me down. Grabbing the hem of my tank top he shoved it up past my breasts to my neck and hissed in a breath at my bare chest.

"You're so fucking perfect, Piper," he crooned as his hands slid gingerly up the sides of my ribs and came to rest over my breasts. "Is this okay?" he asked me again, and I swallowed, nodded, and willed him in my head to do more.

"I need you to say it, baby," he told me, and I heard the restraint in his voice.

"Yes," I whispered nervously, and he gave me a half smile.

Letting go, he eyed me carefully, knelt in front of me and spread my legs at the knees.

My core pulsed as electricity seared through my veins and my panties became flooded with desire. Glancing down toward him I saw my belly vibrate from my heart beating rapidly inside me.

Kneeling up, he swiftly grabbed both sides of my tank and pulled it over my head. Lying me on my back he took a good long look at my upper body. "Look at you, baby. No tats, no belly piercing, my blank canvas... pure in every way."

My heart fluttered wildly as I watched lust fill his eyes and his tongue ran the length of his lips. Looking intently at him became an addiction. Sitting back on his knees he sighed. "You're so beautiful, sweetheart. I don't know what's wrong with me but I'm kinda scared to touch you in case I fuck this up."

"You won't," I replied on impulse. We both smiled at the same time and I guess I must have made a face after being so bold because he chuckled again.

"You gotta let me know what's cool; you hear, Piper?"

"I will," I said, growing in confidence the longer he sat there just looking at me.

When his hands began to skate smoothly over my bare legs, a tiny buzz radiated through me. It was a tremor of need, and the building anticipation of what may come next. My breath hitched as my senses came alive with his sensual attentive strokes.

Simon's breathing changed from the calm slow intakes of breath to more ragged, shallow, and occasionally deeper ones. Blowing slowly out of his nose, his breathing sounded urgent, heavy and shaky as he attempted to control his feelings.

I became hyper-focused on his touch when his middle finger scored a perfect feather-light trail from the middle of the waistline of my shorts, up over the valley of my breasts to my collarbone.

Goose bumps erupted from every pore and my scalp crept with the sensation. Next, he traced his fingers in a tentative motion across my neck, then closed his hand around it on one side.

Rising between my legs he leaned over me and held my neck firmly on both sides before he dropped his forehead to mine.

The intent in his stare made my heart skip a beat.

"You want more, Piper? You want me to keep going?" he asked, with a questioning stare. His eyes were heavy with lust.

"If you want," I replied, too shy to voice what I needed.

"Oh, I want... fuck do I *ever* want," he groaned as the intensity in his eyes reached a whole new level. "But this isn't about me, baby... I've had my turn of being where you are or where you're headed, and it has to be your call." My heart swelled with affection when I noted he was still committed to doing things at my pace even if his need was apparent.

"Now I'm gonna ask you one more time, Piper. Do I keep going or are we done here?"

"Not done," I said in a whisper, but with a serious tone. I shook my head in case my words weren't enough. Every fiber of my being was on edge, my anticipation so overwhelming I almost begged for more.

Simon had a highly addictive effect on me, and I knew since the moment he'd kissed me I wanted anything he was willing to give me, for however long he was willing to give it. The realization of this sounded so wrong in my head, but it felt so right when I was with him.

"Sure?"

"Positive," I said, and he chuckled again.

"That's what I needed to hear," he said with his sexy grin. My heart flipped over again, and I felt petrified and excited once more.

Lowering his lips to touch mine, the kiss that followed was nothing like any of the ones we'd had before. This kiss was all-consuming, breathtaking, and full of passion. Bruising my lips, it was packed full of desire.

"Oh," I moaned as his thumbs smoothed over my stomach, setting off tiny detonators of thrilling sensations running through my veins. I felt my knees relax open.

"Jesus Christ," Simon cussed under his breath and moved his lips from my mouth to my neck. Kissing sensually along my collar bone he then traveled lower until he engulfed my breast in his mouth. He swirled the other between his thumb and forefinger before paying the same attention to this one as well.

My breathing was shallow and rapid, my pulse erratic, as his passionate assault on my body made me feel like my bones were melting while my core pulsed more times than I'd ever imagined it could. For the first time in my life I felt empty inside and I ached like I had never known before.

Sitting back on his heels again, Simon feathered his fingertips all over my stomach and reached for my waistband. "This, okay?" he asked with a note of concern with his fingers on the button.

"Yes," I muttered, my voice cracking between a soft voice and a whisper. My mouth was dry, and I swallowed again.

I wondered if I hadn't sounded convincing when he didn't move and figured it was up to me. Reaching down, I popped the button on my jean shorts and pulled the zipper down. It never even occurred to me I was being too forward.

Watching me closely, Simon shook his head, his eyes never leaving my hands until I was done then he glanced back to me.

"Sweet Jesus, baby," He muttered. "Maybe we can fool around for a bit, but I don't want to fuck you yet, Piper. I don't want this to be like all the others."

If I hadn't been so sensitive, I may have taken his comment as a compliment, but for some reason what he had said had made me feel less than a woman. Immediately, my body stiffened again as embarrass-

ment took over. Simon flinched at my reaction, but I could see he
didn't understand what he'd done wrong.

He tried again. "What I mean is you matter. You're *all* that matters
in this, Piper. Your tender heart is very precious to me and I don't want
anything I do with you to be tainted by something you're not prepared
for or you'll later regret."

His new explanation settled my nerves and made me feel calm.
All the possibilities there were between us were instantly there
again. I got it he was afraid of the impact of his actions on me and
my heart clenched with affection that he was so willing to put
me first.

Simon pulled his shirt over his head and discarded it on the floor.
Next, he stood up, scooped me up, and sat with me straddled across
his lap. When he pulled me forward, my skin grazed his, and he
moaned.

"Oh damn that feels amazing." He let out a shaky breath, "Your
skin feels like satin, baby," he whispered into my ear as he cradled my
head with one hand.

In that moment I felt we were on the precipice of something
monumental happening between us—life changing even—yet strangely
I had never felt safer in my whole life. Tears sprang to my eyes,
touched by his tender care. I blinked them back.

Simon slid one hand down into the back of the denim and cupped
my ass.

"Thank you, Piper." His voice was both gruff and loaded with
emotion.

I lifted my head and looked at him.

"What for?" I asked, puzzled because we hadn't done much at all in
my eyes.

"Your trust. Your faith in me."

I placed my lips lightly to his and kissed him, softly. Simon deepened the kiss like he was claiming me. It would have knocked me off
my feet had I not been sitting down. The demanding force of it left me
breathless and his hands gripped my hips as wiggled my center directly
over his solid cock.

My heart thudded hard in my chest when Simon's other hand slid gently into the back of my jean shorts and his fingers stretched under my butt cheeks and slid to my warm, wet folds.

"Fuck, so wet, incredible," he muttered, tearing his mouth away from mine as his fingers glided over my slick warm entrance.

I had barely drawn breath before he spun me around on my back and his hand worked my jean shorts slowly over my butt and down my legs. He barely had one leg out before he spread the leg already in his hand widely and dipped his mouth to the top of my thigh.

Excited and nervous, I held my breath as his lips trailed over the soft skin on my inner thigh then stopped. Drawing a deep breath, he stared at me and sighed. "Fuck, this is difficult. I'm too fucking hard," he muttered and groaned again.

Heat instantly rose to my cheeks when he paused, giving me time to realize where we were at and how his face was almost touching my wet underwear. It felt much more intimate than I had imagined it would feel.

Probably more intimate than if we'd had sex. But even though I felt shy and unprepared, I took pleasure from knowing I had riled Simon up and he really wanted me.

Although inexperienced, I knew enough to know better than to tease a man like Simon, and figured if he was being honest, then so was I.

"Don't stop," I said, trying to behave like what was happening wasn't a big thing. The man of my dreams was inches from the most intimate part of my body and I knew my reaction was all important in letting him know I was ready to explore my sexuality.

"You've done this before?" He asked, his eyes narrowed to mine.

I shook my head, "I'm not totally innocent. A boy in school wanted me to have sex, but I said no. We did some other stuff and fooled around, but we didn't do this and we didn't have sex." I felt myself flush again and was greeted with a soft smile.

"You sucked his cock?" He asked pointedly, and I shrugged, embarrassed again in an instant. I chewed the side of my mouth and nodded again.

"Well, now I'm pissed and jealous of him that he got anywhere near you," he muttered without a hint of humor. "I needed to know, baby, so don't be embarrassed because I was wondering how you'd respond to this. Some chicks are weirded out by oral sex in the beginning."

"I kind of am... it's very intimate for a girl."

"I understand. You have played with yourself before, right? Had orgasms... come I mean? Shit. Ignore me, I'm fucking useless at tact," he offered and shook his head. "You're fucking twenty," he said, like that told him I masturbated. Of course I had. What female my age wouldn't be curious about her body and what it could do?

"Ever used a vibrator?"

"No. Please stop beating yourself up. To be honest, I'm stunned at your patience. I think you're amazing. What other guy would have had the patience you have shown me?" I asked.

"One that wants the ultimate prize," he blurted out.

Shoving him away, I sat up and hid myself. His comment suddenly making me feel dirty. "And there it is. The reason for all this molly-coddling."

"What the fuck did I do?" He asked, staring up in confusion with his brow bunched and with a hurt look on his face.

"I'm a prize? A prize what? Idiot? Poor naïve Piper can't possibly make it in the music business if her cherry's still intact?"

"Whoa, what the fuck?" he argued and climbed up to sit on the couch again with his hands held up in front of him "What the fuck happened? What's going on? Why are you flipping out on me?"

"You said you were taking your time to ensure you got the 'ultimate prize'," I stated using quote marks with my fingers.

"Yep, I did. What's wrong with that?"

"Ha. So you admit it. All this is just so you can what? Deflower me?"

"Good God, no," he chuckled like what I had said was absurd.

"I mean the prize as in having you for the long haul, Piper. I told you yesterday I'm not in this to tap you. If that was all I wanted, I'd have done it by now and you'd never have seen it coming... if you'll excuse the pun. But as my comment has turned you off and made you angry, I think this would be a good time to take a break. Let's both cool down and you can draw breath for a while. I'm never going to pressure you," he repeated.

Once again my eyes ticked over his face for the truth and my instincts told me he meant what he said.

"Fuck, I need you to believe me when I say being around you and not taking what I want is killing me. My balls were almost exploding in these pants as I sat there between your legs. The sweet smell of your wet pussy was so fucking tempting. *You* are so incredibly tempting, but this is at your pace, not mine, remember?"

My focus was on my hands and he took them in his. Pulling me to stand, he bent down to the floor, grabbed my tank top and pulled it over my head. His action, while caring, made me feel like a child again. Stepping to the side of him, I fed my foot back into my jean shorts and pulled them up.

"I'm so sorry, baby. Are you okay?" Simon asked with a deep concern in his tone.

"Sure," I answered, my voice lighter than I felt. I swallowed hard as I fought the growing lump in my throat. My voice didn't fool me, so I knew he would never believe that, but I was surprised when he went along with my answer.

"Good. Let's try to put this behind us and get back to my plans for the day." My head was suddenly bathed in confusion at the way he had appeared to brush off what happened between us. It felt as if he was done with me. If I wasn't putting out, I was getting dressed.

I folded my arms and swallowed again. "If you don't mind, I may just duck out and head home," I replied, determined not to cry in front of him. *I hate leaving like this, but I really need time to think.*

A flash of hurt flitted through Simon's eyes, but he didn't argue with me. "Want me to take you, or would you rather have a car?"

"There's no point in you wasting your day by driving back and forth. If you could just get me a driver that would be great."

For a minute he paused like he wanted to say something, but eventually he let out a soft sigh, scratched the back of his head and reluctantly pulled out his cell phone.

Wandering away from me and out toward the pool I heard him arrange my lift back to Santa Monica and I wanted to cry. Staring at his strong muscular back with his shoulders slumped, I immediately regretted my decision. My eyes drifted down to the ground near where he stood, and I noticed my clothing still lay where I'd discarded them.

At that very same moment he must have noticed as well because when he placed his cell back in his pocket he reached down and swiped them up off the floor. Neatly, he turned my crop pants the right way out and even from a distance I could see how sad my decision had made him.

Am I being immature by leaving? Will he think I'm running away? Will me going home put him off me? I felt bad for ruining his plans, but I felt it was the right decision.

So much had happened in twenty-four or so hours. I needed time to absorb everything I had learned since I had arrived at Simon's place.

I had no regrets about what we had done, but I was glad we had stopped, because if I ever crossed a line with Simon I had to be sure he wanted me for all the right reasons.

CHAPTER THIRTEEN

The journey home gave me plenty of time to think about everything Simon had told me. As hard as it was to leave him behind, to my mind it was the right thing to do.

It would have been easy to have stayed and given in to the new feelings coursing through me, but I respected myself more than that.

Perhaps if Gibson's warning about Simon to Chloe hadn't rung in my ears, I wouldn't have regarded Simon with as much suspicion, but it had only taken one comment for me to doubt the situation that had developed between us.

No matter what had taken place before I left, Simon and I had chemistry. No one had ever made me feel how I had when I was with him, but I had no regrets in calling a halt and taking the time to consider it all.

From the moment I arrived home, I thought about how fast Simon had made his move, yet how soft and gentle he had treated me in comparison to everything I'd read about him. On paper he was a prize douche bag, but his reputation and history with women was nothing like the man I saw in his own home.

Did I read the situation wrong? Unless I was mistaken, Simon's gaze held genuine warmth and attraction, but what did I know about that, given my past?

My mind wandered to his smile; his powerful, lean, yet muscular body; the way his eyes appeared to change color when he became heated; and I groaned aloud in frustration.

Then there were all the ways he kissed me: tentative and gentle, sensual and tender, and later more demanding, less controlled, and much more seductive and intoxicating. Seduction: were those different kinds of kisses all part of his player technique?

Fresh doubts and confusion plagued me for the whole of the weekend as new thoughts for analysis popped into my head, but actions spoke louder than words and not once since I left his place did he try to contact me.

If he were serious about getting to know me better wouldn't he have done this? *Hell, maybe he's moved on already.*

Perhaps I was a little piece of forbidden fruit because of Gibson, but after Saturday morning he had decided I wasn't worth the hassle. Who knew?

Debating his behavior, the time we spent together, and countering the negatives with his sister Stevie's account of how Simon had changed, exhausted me, and for the most part I thought Simon's behavior was genuine, but his mention of 'the prize' was very off-putting to say the least. Especially from someone with a reputation like his.

By Monday morning I felt far from rested. *What did I think would happen? Did I think he'd come running after me? Beg me to be with him? Of course not. Simon McLennan has never had to chase any woman... but he could have called if his intentions were real.*

On the way to work it seemed as if every tune on the radio reminded me of my weekend. "Without You" Avicii, and "Numb", by Linkin Park, were usually two of my favorite songs, but when I heard them in the context of my mood they didn't make me feel like they usually did.

As I neared the studio, my heart skittered chaotically at the thought of facing Jeff. Although the incident from Friday had been at the back of my mind, I had refused to deal with the fact I'd have to stand up to him again.

Thinking about this I turned into the parking lot of Gravity. Switching off the music my anxiety grew because right there in front of me Jeff was waiting at the entrance.

"Fuck," I muttered with a sense of dread in my heavy heart as I angrily gathered up my purse and notebook from the passenger seat beside me. *Keep calm. Don't panic. You got this. If he doesn't get out of the way, kick him in the balls.*

Adrenaline fueled my anger and with no further contact from Simon, my mood was even darker than I knew I was capable of being. *Don't let this douche intimidate you. You got this.*

Fortunately, I was opening my car door when Otto drove into the parking lot and into the space next to me. My gaze slid over to Jeff and saw him enter the doors of the studio. Relief washed through me.

"Good weekend? I hope you got plenty of rest, we got a lot of work to do today," he asked and advised me.

"Yeah, stayed home and rested for most of it." Which was true, but it was more restless than restful given all the emotional shit I digested.

Smiling his approval, he nodded, and gestured with his hand in the direction of the studio, "Shall we?" he asked and we both made our way inside.

The people present in the studio would never have guessed there was a huge rift between Jeff and I from the way we worked closely together. His hands were on fire and the angst I felt about Simon translated to the lyrics. It gave my performance of the songs extra emotional weight. I had never sung better.

Otto beamed from ear to ear and even Grunt banged his drum sticks together in applause in approval. "Dope," he muttered, meaning I rocked the tracks.

Once again Grunt was the person who put the biggest beaming

smile on my face. Being a man of few words, whenever he praised me he was the person who had the biggest impact on my confidence.

Every day I felt my range grow more solid thanks to the warm-up exercises Gibson had taught me. Before, I could usually sing most things, but he had taught me how to slide from one voice to another using my head, chest, and abdomen, while controlling my breathing.

It gave me a greater understanding that my voice, like any other instrument, had to be finely tuned.

During lunch I avoided Jeff by staying in the studio to listen to the other band recording and when Otto called Jeff back to talk to him as we were leaving at the end of the day, I hastily ran to my car and was driving out of the parking lot when I saw him coming out of the building in my peripheral vision.

Driving home, I had mixed feelings: relief at avoiding a confrontation with Jeff, and annoyance at Simon for his continued silence.

Checking my cell several times during the day, my disappointment grew when Simon hadn't made contact. *What did I expect?* Someone like him had never had to try with a woman.

My heart hurt, bruised with uncertainty and doubt and I wondered if he had decided I was too young and skittish to pursue me further. I sighed.

Shaking my low mood, I tried to focus on the satellite navigation guiding me home, but no matter how hard I tried, my mind continually flitted over our conversations from the weekend, like some broken down record.

In all the distraction I hadn't noticed Jeff had followed me, and it wasn't until I was entering the security gates that I caught his huge shiny bike and his unmistakable form as I swung into the parking garage from the other side of the closed iron gates. *Shit.*

First thing I did when I locked up my car was to inform the superintendent not to disclose information about me. I had no one who should be looking for me. Gibson, Chloe, Thomas, and Simon all knew where I was.

As far as Otto knew, I was staying at an apartment belonging to Thomas' friend and any correspondence was to go through Thomas as his office was given as my official address.

Although confident I was safe inside the complex, I wasn't sure how else to handle Jeff other than to threaten him with the police. *Could I really do that? What if that didn't work? What if it made matters worse?* Unwanted familiar feelings of being trapped from my time at home began to surface and I wasn't sure who to turn to.

If I called Gibson to confide in him, I knew I would have had to tell him the whole sorry story and I figured I'd get the whole 'I told you so' lecture or worse.

Also, knowing Gibson was fearless when he became protective, the last thing I wanted was his involvement, both from the perspective of it drawing more attention to our connection and his personal life.

As for Simon, it had begun to look as if he had dropped me like a hot potato when I hadn't put out like he'd hoped.

Contacting Thomas again was my only option and hoped that he could help. The dread I felt as I made the call bubbled up to my throat and made me dissolve in tears. Fears I had didn't completely vanish with Thomas, but he had concluded the call with the promise to pull his weight.

Thomas rang Otto and threatened to pull me from the contract with the studio if Otto didn't sack Jeff or get him off my back. But when Otto rang Jeff, he apparently told him all he had wanted to do was apologize for his behavior in the parking lot on the Friday before.

When Thomas told me this I felt relieved, but I was still unsure if I completely trusted Jeff's explanation. At least everyone knew what he'd done, and I was assured by both Thomas and Otto they'd keep a close eye on him.

Cooking spaghetti Bolognese, I sat down to eat and thought about how fortunate I was again. Not all women had the security of living in the lap of luxury and staying safe in their beds at night like I had.

My thoughts were interrupted by the intercom and I jumped high in my chair, startled by the unexpected buzzer. Anxiety gripped me as I stared at the intercom box on the wall. *Jeff fear gripped my stomach and tied it in knots even though no one could get at me here.*

The light continued to flash on the wall indicating the super's call and for a moment I was hesitant in answering, but curiosity outweighed my fears because I was safe in my apartment, so I wandered over to the button and answered.

"Simon McLennan is here in the hallway, Miss," I was informed. *Simon? Here?*

I was shocked, speechless for a moment, as my head turned, and I looked at my messy kitchen with dirty pots and pans in the sink. I groaned because I looked like an unorganized slob.

"What do you want me to tell him?" the doorman asked, interrupting my thoughts when I hadn't answered him.

"Oh, sorry," I replied and shook my head still struggling for ways to clean the apartment and make myself presentable. I needed a genie for that. Then I glanced at the plate of uneaten spaghetti bolognase. I could hardly eat that in front of him either for the same reasons of mess as the last time.

"Send him up," I replied knowing it took less than three minutes from the front lobby to my door. Grabbing the metal pots and pans I piled everything into the dishwasher, shoved my food down the waste disposal and ran into the bedroom while undressing.

My doorbell chimed as I pulled on a clean thong and I swiped my favorite Dior perfume from the dressing table, spraying it liberally as I snatched a small violet-colored off-the-shoulder sundress from my closet.

On the way to the door, I pulled the dress over my head. Bending my head over I flicked my hair down then back up as I straightened again. Then, taking a long deep breath, I pulled the heavy wooden door to the hallway open.

"Simon, what are you doing here?" I asked with a straight face and a hint of surprise in my voice as I tried to appear relaxed. Inside, my heart pounded in my chest so hard I felt slightly dizzy.

"I wanted to see you... to talk to you," he told me. "And I couldn't stay away any longer," he confessed as he stood with his hands on my wooden doorjamb in the hall.

Inviting him in, I stood to the side to let him walk past me.

"After you," he said, gesturing for me to walk ahead of him. I walked further into the room and turned to see him softly close the door.

"Is it okay for me to be here?"

"Isn't it a little late to ask that question?" I asked in a flat tone.

He snickered, and I found it hard to hold his gaze because his surprise visit had set off a riot of emotions I could hardly control. Everything from anger at his silence, to an air of anticipation gripped me.

"I suppose." He shrugged flashing me the same sexy grin that always melted me as he wandered over to the couch. "Your place looks amazing, Piper," he praised, tipping his chin at the room. I was pleased he approved because his taste was impeccable.

"Thanks, but it's Gibson and Chloe who deserve the credit... oh and the oversized cushions are all Melody," I said, pointing to the two incongruent orange elephant cushions in the otherwise navy-blue leather and cream décor.

"They complement the color scheme well."

I was dying to dispense with the pleasantries and get down to why he was here. "Did you come to check out my apartment or was there something else?" I asked in a clipped tone.

"Piper," he shook his head as he stared at me and smiled, "With you, there's always gonna be something else," he replied with a tease in his voice.

"Go on then, I'm listening." My outer shell of a body was passive whereas every cell on the inside was buzzed by his flirtatious answer.

Rubbing his hands together, for the first time I saw a hint of nerves and felt amazed because he was one of the most self-assured people I had ever met.

"Firstly, I want to apologize for how I behaved this weekend." He sighed. My chest ached because I felt his angst and wondered if he felt he'd made a terrible mistake. Glancing up, our eyes met, and the intensity of how he looked at me stole my breath.

"Piper, I should never have done what we did, but everything happened so fast... though not fast enough for me." Pausing, he rubbed his hands together again. Still locked in his gaze, I sat slowly on the arm of the couch nearest me and across from him.

"I meant everything I said, Piper. My prize comment was stupid... and it wasn't meant in the way you took it. I guess I'm not used to being thoughtful with my smart mouth around women."

His apology seemed sincere. I felt it in my gut.

"I've been thinking too, Simon, and maybe I overreacted. I guess I judged you by the reputation you have and maybe your age and experience."

"Piper, you're the one who's been hollering for everyone to see you for the adult you are, yet you're the very person quoting age and experience, not me. For the record I couldn't give a fuck what people think. Being a virgin isn't a prize to me; popping your cherry isn't some notch I have stashed somewhere I want to mark off."

I cringed at how blunt he was talking.

"What I'm trying to say is I know what you've been through. I was there when you told all those stories about Colin. I've never wanted to find and kill anyone as much as I did that dude for what he did to you and your mom, but I'm not Colin... and I neither want to hurt or control you, Piper, you deserve much more than that."

"Is that what this is about, Simon? You're worried you feel you have to save me from the wrong guys?" My question wasn't a challenge, but I had to know I wasn't someone he felt he had to protect because there was no one else.

No way would I let any man manipulate, hit, or control me, the way Colin had with my mom. "I know enough to know you're nothing like Colin, but now you've made me wonder if you pity me. Like you want me out of some misplaced duty to keep me safe."

"If you really knew anything about me you'd know what you just said was a heap of shit. I'm selfish, Piper. You can see that by how I live. I do what I want, when I want, with whom I want."

"And right now, you want me, huh?"

"Fuck. This isn't getting us anywhere. Right here, right now. I'm telling you what I feel for you is more than I've felt for any girl in the past. You're already in here, Piper," he said slapping his chest, "I love everything about you. That's not to say I'm in love with you. I guess I may get to that after the in-lust phase, but you fucking matter to me.

No one else apart from my family and the band have ever mattered to me."

CHAPTER FOURTEEN

*M*y eyes narrowed as I studied the seasoned womanizing rock star in front of me. Charismatic and sexy as sin, Simon, processed so much magnetism that women flocked to him like bees to honey, and he professed to have all these feelings or attraction for me.

Most women had been willing to throw caution to the wind for one night with him but knowing him for as long as I had, there were deeper feelings at play for me. Understanding he felt some of those same feelings for me was hard to imagine.

Either I accepted he was an honest man, or he was one hell of an actor, because the intense soul-searching look in his eyes felt intimate and true. It terrified me because he sounded genuine and believable.

"Do you know how difficult it is to get my head around this? Why me, Simon? Of all the women you could have, what is it about me you can't get past?"

"For all the reasons I already said the other day, and for how strong you are despite what you've been through. You're so fucking sweet and lively. Baby, your zest for life is inspiring. Besides that, I think you're sexy as fuck and I feel happy just to be in your company."

I shrugged, not knowing how to reply.

"Do you know how much you turned me on by blowing me out and hightailing it out of my house like that?" he smirked, sheepishly. "I can't explain it plainer than what I've said already. As for you, you just gotta let it happen if you want it, Piper."

My eyes ticked over his beautiful face and his gaze was unwaveringly intense as he stared back. Everything about surrendering to my feelings petrified me because I felt I could well have been staring at the man who would break my heart.

When I remained silent, he tried harder to convince me what he had said was the truth. "Look, I wouldn't have come all the way down here if I wasn't sure it's what I wanted. Trust me, I'm risking it all for the opportunity to see where this leads. If age, inexperience, and trust, are the only things holding you back, fuck those who'll judge us and trust me. I have enough experience for the both of us and I won't do you wrong."

"Alright, enough with the creepy old man routine," I replied snickering, "If this happens people are gonna think—"

"Fuck 'em, let them think what they want, who cares? We're not living our lives for them, we're living for us." I nodded. He was right they weren't walking in our shoes. "So you're in?"

"I guess but—" I thought about Gibson, their band, and the likely rift this may cause between Simon and Gibson.

"On your time, babe. Take all the time you need," he reaffirmed and waved me over beside him.

Fighting a sudden shyness, I tried to look confident as I unfolded my leg from the chair arm and wandered over and stood in front of him.

Placing his hands on my hips, he glanced up into my eyes and wiggled my hips back and forth. "Now this," he tugged the material of my dress gently between one finger and thumb, "This is stunning. It suits you," he said complimenting it, "And I missed you after you left this weekend," he added in a tender tone before he pulled me onto his lap.

Cradling my head, he placed it against his chest. A deep sigh of contentment escaped from his lungs and he swallowed hard as he stroked the skin on my shoulder with his thumb.

The affectionate gesture felt both soothing and sensual at the same time. I lifted my head, my eyes dropping to his lips, and without hesitation we both went in for a kiss.

Within seconds any inhibitions about being with Simon slid rapidly from my mind. My arms slid lazily around his neck, his slid tighter around my body as my fingers found their way into his hair.

A stifled moan passed from Simon's mouth into mine and the desire inside me from days before reignited. Kissing him back with all that I had, it was me who was losing control.

The solid bulge in his jeans felt like steel beneath me, pressing deliciously hard against my entrance in a way that wasn't enough. A soft whimper escaped my throat, and I wiggled my hips, creating friction between us. Like before, it was Simon who broke the kiss, and he spun me onto my back on my couch hovering above me.

"Damn," he rasped, his breathing labored as his arms vibrated slightly, showing his restraint. "You gotta understand this isn't easy for me," he ground out in a husky voice as his lust-filled eyes searched my face.

"Do it," I goaded. "Teach me."

My demand was met with a wicked smile, his eyes softening with affection. "You're not there yet," he stated.

"What do you mean I'm not there? I'm here, ready and willing, I stated, completely unabashed because lust and desire had taken over.

I was frustrated beyond measure at waiting to have more with him. "There can't be that many twenty year old virgins left in the music business now, can there?"

Shaking his head, he chuckled and shook his head thinking I was only half serious. "Piper, don't tempt me, baby," he said in a gravelly tone and his eyes darkened as he stared me out.

"Isn't that what I'm supposed to do?" As recently as the day before, I wasn't sure how, when, or if, I'd sleep with Simon. Less than an hour after having such doubts I felt if I didn't I'd die. He told me he really did want me and if I hadn't been ready to take such an important step, I would never have said it.

"We don't have to—"

"Yes. We do," I said, interrupting his protests. "That is if you're serious about wanting me?" I teased.

Standing, he scooped me up in his arms. A thrill of excitement shot through my body, making my heart stutter in my chest and my mind went blank. "Bedroom?" His one word question stole my breath with his sudden change of heart.

"First door on the right," I replied, and a buzz travelled through my veins and pulsed in my core. *Damn, this is it.*

Carelessly, he kicked the door open and strode toward my bed, setting me down gently. In one fluid movement, he grabbed the hem of my dress and pulled it over my head. My long hair flew loose and fell behind my shoulders as his eyes dropped to my firm breasts and my small white lacy thong.

Swallowing roughly, Simon licked his lips then he drew in a deep, deep breath. Looking up to my face, he eyed me with total intent as he bent his knees without breaking his stare. *Oh. My. God. This is really going to happen.*

A long pause stretched out and the air in the room became charged full of expectation, his hungry eyes left mine and travelled down over my mostly bare body. "So fucking pure... everywhere," he whispered, dropping his gaze to the thin patch of material covering my pussy.

Reaching down, Simon adjusted his cock in his pants and when he looked back up, he caught me watching him. Smirking he shrugged, "I'm so fucking hard for you, baby." I felt myself blush because I wanted to ask to see it.

Swallowing audibly, Simon put his palms over both breasts, thumbs bumping over each pebbled nipple, before his hands swept up to my neck. Placing his thumbs under me he cradled my head in his hands.

"You're so fucking special, Piper. I need you to know that before this goes any further. No matter what shit people say—and trust me there'll be all kinds of shit from cheating to... whatever—I'm the only one who can tell you the truth... and I will. Even if it hurts you. You gotta trust me to do that, baby, you hear?"

I nodded but didn't speak, remembering the stories Chloe told me about how the papers were willing to wreck what she and Gibson had for the sake of carrying a sensational headline.

Dipping his head, he kissed the sensitive spot on my neck, my collar bone, both shoulders, the hollow of my neck, then both breasts.

A shiver streaked down my spine and I shuddered. Pulling his head back to look at me, Simon gave me a small sensual smile for the effect it had.

Sliding his tongue slowly across one nipple and then the other, he closed in and engulfed the one on my left with his hot wet mouth.

A strangled gasp fell from my mouth and my head rolled back as pangs of ecstasy shot all the way through me. Glancing up to gauge my reaction he sucked again then shifted across to the other.

Delight spread through me in a wave as my hands rose to his hair. He wasn't gentle and the sensation of the attention he paid to each breast was so thrilling it almost made me come.

Tightening my grip on a fistful of his thick dark hair, I pulled his head up to look at mine. "More," I whispered huskily through my dry mouth with desperation unmistakable in my tone.

My demand was so out of character I had expected Simon to laugh. Instead I was met with his seriously dark, carnal gaze and we stared in silence.

"Take your clothes off," I demanded, and Simon's smile widened.

"Yes, Ma'am," he replied and pulled his t-shirt over his head. Standing up, he yanked the leather on his belt and the buckle jingled softly as he unfastened it. Popping the button in his jeans, he unzipped the fly and shoved his jeans down his legs. As before, Simon wore nothing underneath.

Stepping out of his pants he stood with his cock jutting toward me and smiled. "Better?"

How much I craved to hold his cock in my hand shocked me. Never in my life had I felt so forward to take what I wanted from a situation. "Come closer," I urged him.

Simon stood with his toes to the edge of the bed and I wrapped my fingers around his cock as far as I could and caressed it in my palm.

A small hiss escaped Simon's lips as I stood and gently moved my hand against the satin skin covering the solid flesh I knew would eventually satisfy both my curiosity and my desire. His reaction to my touch egged me on.

Sliding my other arm tentatively around his hip, I slid my inquisitive fingertips over his silky smooth skin, traced them over his hip and around to his sculpted abs. As soon as my fingers had connected with his warm firm body he shuddered.

"Fuck," he muttered as he huffed out a breath and I felt myself smile. Millions of tiny bumps erupted all over his body in an instant reaction of how I affected him. "Damn, I've never gone so slow at this before."

A feeling of power the likes of which I had never known before radiated through me, giving me confidence and it spurred me on to want more from him.

My eyes dropped from his torso to his groin and I traced my wandering hand to meet the other still holding his cock. I rolled it between both of my palms as Simon's stance grew wider giving me better access. I then gave him a few strokes while my other hand played with his balls.

A small dewy drop of pre-cum leaked from the head of his shaft and trailed down my finger. I used this and smoothed it over his tip. "Damn, baby, you're killing me," he muttered, showing great patience as he stood impassively allowing me to explore him.

A series of soft sighs and long moans passed from Simon's lips as his pelvis bucked forward every now and then like he was desperate to have more and I couldn't believe he was reacting like he was to my actions.

Eventually, Simon placed his hand over mine and stroked his cock in the way he wanted from me. Squeezing my fingers gently, he taught me the right amount of pressure to bear.

Concentrating on getting it right, I paid attention to what he was doing but when I looked up and saw his half-closed eyes and the way he was biting his lip, I knew his moans weren't done to be polite but were spontaneous and out of delight.

After some time, he let me go solo and readdressed his attention on me. With firmer hands than before he explored, his sweeping movements more deliberate, and targeted over erogenous zones in my body I had yet to discover myself.

"You, okay?" he asked, his breathing barely controlled by the way he breathed through his nose. They were ragged, fast, or stolen little breaths.

"No. I need more," I urged, completely unfiltered and wanton; my senses alive as my body clung on the edge of something bigger than I knew.

The words had barely passed my lips when my feet were kicked from under me and I landed flat on my back on my bed. Moving swiftly, he swept his hands under my knees, lifted them toward my chest and splayed them wide for his pleasure.

Staring down with intent to my thong he asked, "Like this? You want more?" I nodded, and his fingers trailed across the thin material covering my pussy and rubbed gently over my clit. I moaned as a thrill shot through me, leaving a small wave of vibration lingering in its wake.

Grabbing both sides of the thong he slipped it down my legs, barely managing to get one foot out before he assumed the same stance. "How's this?" he asked, his fingers sliding up my outer lips before he parted them to look at my pussy in more detail and a whimper left my lips.

"Damn, baby, look at you," he murmured with hot lust in his eyes as he gently explored my clit and entrance.

"Mm, feels incredible," I said, before the echo of an "Oh," got stuck in my throat. Arching my back, I lifted my butt for a firmer connection, but Simon pushed me flat against the mattress again.

"Easy, babe," he soothed, pushing my butt back on the bed with a flat hand over my stomach to keep me there as he explored my seam from back to front.

The sensation his fingers evoked in me was off the charts, especially when his middle finger teased and discovered my slick wet entrance.

In another swift move his hot tongue replaced his finger, and he lapped and sucked my pussy with such force I almost came. Staring unblinkingly, his eyes looked serious as he ate me out.

A long groan passed from Simon's mouth and traveled straight through me. "Fuck," he said, barely lifting his mouth away as he ground the cuss out before another hiss passed his lips.

My butt rose up to meet him at the lack of contact and this time he held it in the air with his hands as he licked at my clit, entrance and almost my butt. My whole body was on fire, yet I needed more.

"I want you," I murmured, my eyes staring straight down the middle of my stomach into his. He stopped instantly and stared with concern. "We can't. Not today, No condoms, baby," he muttered in frustration and placed his mouth back on my pussy.

"I don't care." And I truly didn't. Nothing was more important than Simon being inside me right then.

Simon sucked harder and within seconds a dizzy feeling engulfed me as my body tightened and immediately thousands of tiny lights burst behind my eyelids in a wave of ecstasy I had never experienced before.

From my toes to my head, every last nerve shook and quivered, as I became lost in the headiest orgasm of my life. I screamed, losing control as it all became too much. I fought to push Simon's head away, but he continued to lap at me like he'd die if he pulled away.

Immediately after I came, he crawled up beside me and kissed me hard, then he tenderly pulled me close to his chest. Waiting until my body recovered, we eventually settled down, and my breathing returned to normal.

Softly, he kissed my temple and stroked my hair. I looked up into his eyes. Tears sprang to my eyes because I felt overcome with emotion; hurt because he didn't do what I knew we both wanted.

"Shh, babe. I'm not having unprotected sex with you right out of the gate. Last thing I want is for you to regret any of this later. I'm really honored you trust me with this, but I'm not prepared to take risks with you for a few minutes pleasure."

"You're making me feel like I don't know my own mind," I pouted, hurt I'd been willing to go all the way and he'd called a halt to it.

"Look, I get you have all these feelings running through you and they can make you feel like it's what you need, but one of us has to be responsible for the consequences of them. I'm not gonna take advantage of you like that. When we get down to it I want to know you're protected."

It was hard to be mad when deep down I knew he was right. I was in the moment and acting on impulse and my heart squeezed that even in the heat of passion, Simon had still been willing to forgo his own pleasure to ensure we made the right decisions that kept me safe.

CHAPTER FIFTEEN

*W*aking with an empty ache in my stomach, I groaned and stretched until my toes trailed down a hairy leg. My eyes immediately shot open and my heart leapt to my mouth.

Simon lay facing me sound asleep and my heart flipped over in my chest. I was surprised he hadn't left. Oh. My. God. He stayed the night with me.

Stunningly handsome, he looked so peaceful in sleep, with his red shiny lips slightly parted, long dark lashes fanning his cheekbones and his soft, tan skin meeting his dark brown beard. His large hand lay palm down and was partially hidden by his pillow.

Wild feelings ran through my body when I thought back to what we had done, and my heart squeezed as my core clenched excitedly. Feelings of affection, desire, and lust filled my head and my chest felt tight because I never wanted to leave my bed. Even though he was right there, I was still struggling to accept he wanted only me.

Fighting off negative thoughts, I had decided to take the risk. Continuing to give him my trust, he'd have it unless there was overwhelming proof to the contrary.

It wasn't as if he hadn't already earned it from all the time we had spent at home in Colorado. I'd known him for over two years and from my perspective that was a long time for someone to hide their flaws.

"Are you watching me sleeping?" he murmured. His lips barely moved and his eyes remained closed. An instant smile graced my lips. *Is he always good natured in the morning?*

"I may have been," I admitted, and he cracked a slow sleepy smile and moved his hand from under his pillow to scoop me into his chest. He placed his other hand on my butt and tugged me into his side. I moved my head over his heart and listened to his steady heartbeat.

"You're so fucking delicious, you know that?" He muttered and kissed the top of my head.

"Delicious?" I asked, thinking it a strange choice of words.

"Yeah, exactly my taste," he clarified before letting out a deep sigh of contentment. My heart swelled with his admission and butterflies joined the ache in my belly.

"Do you know what time it is?" he asked, and I rolled away to grab hold of my cell on the nightstand.

I groaned and dropped my head on his chest again. "Almost 7am. I need to shower and get something to eat. I missed dinner last night."

"Didn't you have Italian?" he asked, straining his head back as he looked down to see my face.

Immediately I chuckled and suddenly felt stupid. I may have been able to hide the physical evidence but not the smell. "I almost did, except you showed up and I threw it away. Ribs, spaghetti Bolognese... what is it about messy food and being around you?"

"You didn't want me to lick it off your face, huh?" he teased, chuckling.

"Ah, it was stupid, eh?"

"Cute," he corrected. He flashed me an affectionate smile before he slapped my butt firmly and gave it a soft squeeze.

"All right, get up before I pin you to the bed. My poor balls are aching. I'm only human and although I'm determined to ignore your hot little body, it's confusing the fuck out of them," he said snickering as he gently rolled away from me.

Getting out of bed he stood naked, his huge, thick cock at full mast and he stretched his arms above his head. "How about we get cleaned up and head over the road to that little pancake shack before you leave for work?"

"Sounds like heaven," I replied, "I'll shower first, you'll be quicker than me. I have all this hair to wash," I suggested gesturing at my matted bed hair.

"I guess," he said, his eyes darkening when they dropped to focus on my breast poking out of the bedsheet. Bending, he pecked a small kiss on it, licked around the pebbled tip and gave it a sharp suck. A pang of delight shot through my body, but as quick as his lips were on me they were gone.

"Fuck," he muttered dragging himself away and grabbing his shaft in his hand. "Shower. Now," he mumbled as if there were conflicting thoughts going on inside and slumped back on the bed.

After washing myself in the shower, we swapped places and I left him to it as I went to get dressed. Once I had done this I headed back to the bathroom to brush my teeth and grab my hairdryer.

My feet stopped moving as soon as my eyes connected with the shower stall straight ahead of me. Simon stood naked and wet, in profile, less than five feet away from me.

Partially obscured behind the steamed-up window, he was supporting himself with one hand on the tiled wall, his head bowed under the jets of water rapidly pounding his shoulders from the showerhead.

My gaze dropped down his body and I noticed him working his cock at a punishing pace with his other hand. I swallowed roughly but didn't move or look away because he looked so appealing as he stood there.

When he suddenly threw his face up toward the cascading water, I was rooted to the spot, both mesmerized and terrified at the sheer power he used to take him over the edge. I'd never seen Simon look more serious, stunning, or sexy, as I had in that pose.

With a dry mouth, I watched with feelings of unadulterated desire coursing through my body. The sight of him fisting himself to release rocked through me.

My giddy heart flipped over in my chest, the pulse of it tingled lightly in my mouth as I struggled to control the rush of want that gripped my body and soul in that moment.

My thighs clenched in wonder of how I'd cope with being on the receiving end of that kind of power. *If watching him makes me feel this turned on, God alone knew how I'd feel when he gets inside me.*

My body startled when his knees suddenly buckled a little as his head slumped forward. A sharp audible gasp rushed from his mouth, followed by a soft groan of relief. He continued to work his hand at a much slower pace after he came, wringing the last pangs of pleasure from his quiet moment alone.

His whole body jerked rhythmically as he squeezed the last pulses from his release.

Eventually, his hand fell away and joined the other against the wall, then suddenly he turned in my direction, wiped the window and stared directly into my eyes. When he didn't look startled and instead flashed me his sexy smile, I knew he knew I'd been watching him.

Shock radiated through me and I instantly sympathized with all those rabbits caught in the headlamps of a speeding car because I had nowhere to run, so I waited for him to speak.

"Enjoying the view?" he asked in a low playful tone.

"Every minute of it," I replied, matching his cheeky question. He grinned wider and shook his head. "You know, Piper, I think once I've taken you and taught you what to do, you'll wear me out."

"Because you're getting old, or because you think I'll be sensational?" I goaded, and he chuckled again at my unexpected response. "Damn, girl, I may need to up my game by the time you're done with me," he smiled and wrung his hands together under the water once again.

Stepping out of the shower, he stepped forward and grabbed me against him, his wet hard body soaking the thin cotton dress I wore. "Fuck, you smell so fucking alluring." His eyes darkened even though he had only come seconds before, and I felt his cock grow stronger against my belly.

"From what I just saw, I may never be done with you," I replied, with such frank honesty I shocked myself, but I jutted my jaw up in defiance. Letting go, he moved away and grabbed a large white bath towel and wrapped it around his waist. I felt lonely at the loss of his touch.

Smiling warmly, he walked back toward me and took my cheeks in his hands. I swear he stared right through me for a few seconds and I held my breath at the weight of the desperate look he gave me. Pulling my face toward his, he kissed me roughly, pushed me away and shook his head.

"We need to leave *now*, or I won't be held responsible for the feelings I may unleash," he admitted with a sharp slap to my butt. My knees felt weak from the demanding way he spoke with his sudden move and I fought for breath as he brushed right past me.

Stepping inside the small, independently-owned pancake shack, I glanced around and felt relieved to find Simon and I were the only two patrons for breakfast. Sliding into a booth, the single server placed two cups of coffee in front of us and slid the menu across.

After placing our order, Simon signed a few autographs, and we hastily made arrangements between ourselves to have a takeout dinner at my place in the evening to avoid further recognition.

I devoured my pancakes and ordered more. They were the first truly leisurely sustenance I'd had without interruptions or anxiety playing into my food, but as we were leaving the diner, that changed when my cell rang and I saw it was Gibson.

When I looked at Simon I was immediately riddled by guilt but too alarmed by the early unexpected call not to answer.

"Hey, what's wrong?" I asked with a note of concern.

"Nothing's wrong, but I just wanted to touch base and give you the heads up about a possible spot supporting Layla Hartmann for a small tour next month. If you want it, I'm gonna talk to Thomas, but I wanted to ask you first 'cause I know Thomas will force the issue even if you don't feel ready."

I looked wide-eyed at Simon and gave a silent scream, while I ran on the spot, "Oh. My. God. Are you serious? Of course I want the gig." My heart swelled in my chest with the pounding it took.

Gibson told me the details and said he was forwarding the email she had sent him after he had played her a couple of my songs, but he swore he had introduced me as an up-and-coming artist he'd heard about.

"Nothing like a proud dad boasting about his baby to anyone who would listen," Chloe shouted into the phone, making me chuckle.

Gibson again reiterated that was not what he did. I thanked him for sticking his neck out telling others about me. Then he said they were flying down on Friday to see me because they, but mostly Melody, needed to see me.

On the way back over to the apartment and our cars, I filled Simon in on what Gibson had arranged and Simon made a face. I knew he thought it meant I would be seeing him.

Although I didn't want to keep Gibson in the dark, I figured I wasn't ready to share the news about Simon and me yet.

Apart from Jeff, my life couldn't have been better, but I wasn't going to force things with Simon and Gibson, in the event it blew up in my face.

Thomas was true to his word and Jeff was nothing but polite toward me all day at the studio. The harmonious atmosphere allowed my creativity to strive. We were racing through the album numbers and Otto was impressed with my level of technical knowledge for a 'newbie'.

Simon texted me around 4pm taking a raincheck on dinner at my place, as something urgent had come up, but said he'd try to make it back to my place later in the evening.

Fortunately, everything happens for a reason and his delay turned out to be a blessing in disguise. Otto also sprung dinner on me to meet with an image stylist and photographer, to plan the album cover artwork and look at my public image.

My professional future suddenly felt very real. Up to this point I had been doing what I had done for years—sing. Even as we were cutting the tracks for the album, I never once felt any pressure because I was mainly competing with myself to do better.

An introduction to the marketing and promotion teams, together with Gibson's call about being a supporting act, had made me more nervous about the reality of what I hoped to achieve.

My connections were still my secret, and I hoped they would stay that way until I had reviews of my first album at the very least.

I wasn't so naïve as to think people wouldn't ever know who the people behind me were, but I wanted as many people as possible to know I had synched the recording deal with Gravity on my own merit and not because I had used their names.

Supporting Layla Hartmann was different. Yes, obviously Gibson had spoken to her, but from his account once she had heard me sing it was she herself who suggested it.

All the praise I received during dinner had me pumped with enthusiasm and when I saw the concepts for the album cover, it became clear they believed in me because they were pushing their budgets to the max.

When Otto sprang it on me they had already cut the first single from the second day's recording, I almost fell over.

No one had spoken in terms of timelines for single tracks to be released. That was going to be taken care of as the album progressed, but I was obviously doing something right when they pushed the timeline up. It made sense to get people interested in some of the songs before the album began to be promoted.

I felt deeply humbled for their faith and support and swore to do what I could to ensure the album's success.

I could hardly wait to tell them I had been chosen to support Layla during her tour, but as I hadn't signed anything and had only briefly read the email, I knew a few days wouldn't make that much difference to their plans. After all, her tour was still around six weeks out.

Leaving the restaurant at 9:45 pm, I arrived home and shoved my key in my apartment door just before 10pm. I was exhausted, and I hadn't heard from Simon again.

Checking my phone one last time for a message I frowned, wondering why his sudden change of plans, but I was too tired to worry. Showering quickly, I remade my messy bed and climbed on in there.

Slipping between the sheets, I tightly gripped the pillow Simon had slept on, hugging it tight and inhaled his scent. It gave me a warm, calming feeling, and I passed right out until drool dripped from my mouth as my cell vibrated and pulled me from a deep, dreamless sleep. "Yeah," I croaked, not quite with it.

"Morning, baby," Simon's voice sounded slightly slurry, "Sorry about last night. Had to go represent the band in Chicago at some last-minute invite interview for MTV. I tried to call you a couple times but your phone was off during the day yesterday, and the evening event I was at had limited media... something or other to do with security," he informed me with a huge yawn.

"Anyway, I just got home, and I didn't want you to worry, but I'm gonna get my head down for a while and I'll catch up with you later. How does this evening sound to cash in the raincheck for take-out food?"

I wasn't sure why Simon had felt the need to explain himself, plans changed, and he had to work. He owed me nothing.

CHAPTER SIXTEEN

"We'll be done in another week to ten days at this rate," Otto looked delighted with the progress as he held his finger on the intercom button to deliver his assessment into the booth.

Grunt muttered I was 'the bomb' and even Jeff had settled down to do what he was paid for.

Wyatt was a sweetheart and did as he was asked, then the rest of the time he played on his phone. I felt as if something had shifted in the team after Thomas's call and everyone was finally on the same page.

Jeff didn't interact with me at all outside of the booth except during professional group meetings and I was happy to live with this.

With each day that passed, the material we recorded made the album feel stronger and every track we nailed had the best arrangement we could possibly have achieved.

When Otto mentioned a meeting to decide what the track order of the songs should be, I knew he was already thinking in terms of us wrapping it up.

Ambition didn't stop the wave of nerves that occasionally gripped me when I considered the time for the album to hit the airwaves.

Going to the studio was now an integral part of my routine and the conversations at the label were becoming more focused on the promotion schedule, so I decided to tell them about the opportunity presented to me by Layla Hartmann.

"How the fuck did Thomas pull that off?" Otto asked with wide eyes and a look of surprise shoving his brows to his hairline.

I shrugged nonchalantly and felt as if I wasn't lying if I didn't say anything. After all, the assumption was the producer's not mine.

"This is fucking epic. Epic! You know how many young female artists get this kind of a gig? Like none... well maybe Adele and what's her name? Paloma Faith. You see what I'm saying?" I did. "And Ellie Goulding for being chosen for the Fifty Shades track."

By supporting a household name, I appeared more established, and I wondered again if Gibson had pushed for this or if I really had got the gig on merit.

Whatever the real reason was, I'd shared the details, and it was up to me to make everyone involved see the authenticity in why I was chosen.

My cell began to vibrate in my purse and Otto glanced to it then to me. "I guess you're wanted somewhere. Sorry I've kept you later than I intended."

"No, it's fine. It's probably Thomas," I offered because I couldn't really mention anyone else. I felt a little guilty that Otto had put his faith in me and I had hidden a lot of my story for the best possible reasons.

Before I had signed up, there had been a background check to fill in. I did it to the best of my ability, leaving out Gibson's guardianship, but I had been honest about leaving the state I lived in due to fleeing with my mother from her abusive relationship.

Once Otto knew that his firm stopped searching. All they wanted to know was I had no convictions for drugs, or sexual or violent offences, and I didn't.

Digging into my purse I pulled out my cell and saw Simon had tried to contact me. "All right, if there's nothing else today, I'm going to head out," I said, already making my way to the door before he could think of anything. I had already called my voicemail and was waiting for it to connect.

Simon's dulcet tones immediately made my heart flip over in my chest, "Hey, baby, swinging by in about twenty minutes. You are home, right? Called for a Chinese takeout and it's gonna be delivered in about an hour and a half." I glanced at my watch and knew he had left the message about ten minutes previously. I climbed in my car. *If I hurry, I'll hopefully get there before him.*

The excitement and anticipation of spending another night with him made me feel giddy and nervous because I was sure a guy like Simon wouldn't make the same mistake twice in having no condoms.

As I came down the street, I saw Simon's car held up at the gates. My heart rate spiked ridiculously fast at the mere sight of his Mercedes.

Pulling up behind him, I reached out and hit the fob, opening the electronic gates. He entered, with me following, and I closed the gates directly behind me.

Once we had parked the cars in the underground garage, he came over and opened my car door for me to get out.

"Hello, gorgeous," he said, complimenting me with his usual sexy smile.

"Hey, handsome," I replied and stretched up on tiptoe to kiss him. Simon grabbed me by my hips and pushed me hard against my car, pressing himself into me and kissing me hungrily. As quick as he made his move, he stepped back and held my hand, "Damn, I missed you," he said, gruffly.

"So it would seem," I replied, staring at him in disbelief as I touched my bruised lips, while my face tingled from beard burn.

Snickering, he gave me a sheepish smile, "Sorry, baby, what can I say? I'm fucking smitten," he replied, and his words struck a chord because they were the very same ones his sister had said about how he felt about me.

Entering the elevator, he slid my purse from my shoulder and pushed me gently against the elevator car wall, kissing me as his hands slid first to my hair then my arms and eventually he gripped my butt. Breaking the kiss, he let his forehead drop to mine and he gave me a slow sexy smile.

"I hope the food gets here fast or we're both going to be a hundred pounds shortly, with all the food we keep missing," he told me and grinned. I knew exactly what he meant. The hunger we both felt had nothing to do with food, but we still had to eat.

We had barely entered my apartment when the buzzer sounded. I figured the food had arrived early and went to answer it, but it was the superintendent from the lobby to tell me that Gibson was on his way up and he was fuming about something.

I stood frozen, with the handset for the intercom system suspended in mid-air and stared speechless at Simon.

"What the fuck is it?" he said, noting my anxiety. He rose quickly from the chair and stalked in long strides across the room toward me.

"Gibson's here. He's coming up."

"He is?" he asked a little surprised, but instead of freaking out like I was he took off his shirt and laid it over the counter stool then sat back down on the couch in his t-shirt looking perfectly at home.

"No... no. You can't be here... oh, this is bad," I said, in a weak whiny tone not wanting to deal with the wrath of the man who in effect had saved me.

"Look. The day before yesterday you said you wanted this to be legit between us. We knew there'd be consequences. Bring it, I say, because you can't help who your heart wants and mine definitely knows that it wants you."

"I'm really touched, Simon, but can we please do this another day when I've gotten used to the idea?" I choked.

Shaking his head, he spread his arms the length of the back of the couch and crossed his ankle over his knee. "Baby, I'm not ducking and diving. I'm thirty-two years old. I'm not fucking hiding from Gibson. Sure, he's gonna be pissed and puff his chest an 'all but at the end of all of this, I'm still gonna be here and so are you. He'll learn we're not doing pretend roleplay and we're serious about doing this."

A sharp knock at the door made my legs buckle on the spot and Simon burst out laughing. I made a pleading motion and clasped my hands in prayer and he chuckled heartily. "Open the door, Piper," he said. Almost immediately, Gibson's voice demanded the same from the other side of it and I shook my head. *So much for this adulting thing. I'm out.*

When I didn't move, Simon got up from the couch, steered me toward it and gently sat me down. "Let me do the talking," he ordered then made his way to open the door. He had barely cracked it open when Gibson's huge hand grabbed tightly at his throat and walked him back into the room.

Turning his head to look at me, Gibson growled, "Bedroom now," he barked like I was eight years old and had been caught with my hand in the cookie jar. Simon snickered, and Gibson shook him by the throat. "Oh, you think this is fucking funny, huh? We'll see if you're still laughing when I've beaten the shit out of you," he warned.

Chloe arrived at the door and came rushing in. "Take your hand off his throat, Gibson. This is Piper's home. You can't come storming in here because you don't agree with what's going on," she reasoned. Gibson stared her down for a few seconds.

"And you're condoning this? You think this randy douche bag fucker here deserves our precious girl over there? You really want her tangled up with this sick fuck?"

"That sick fuck is one of your best friends, Gibson. Now take your hands off him, or I'm leaving and you won't be welcome at home tonight." Gibson glared at Chloe, glanced thunderously at me and stood his ground. "I mean it. Do you think violence is the way to stop what's happening? You think this is making Piper see things from your perspective when you're behaving no better than the guy who abused her mother?"

Gibson immediately dropped Simon, like his throat was on fire and stared in shock at Chloe. If Simon was afraid of him, he never showed it and wandered over to check I was okay, "It's okay, sweetheart, he's just a little passionate where you're concerned," he said, totally unfazed by the incident. Sitting down beside me, Simon slipped an arm around my waist.

"Fucking right I am, you dick. You couldn't leave her be, could you? Was that too much to ask?"

"Yeah, Gibson it was. It still is and if you think I'm not serious about Piper, you don't know me at all."

"Oh, I know you. I've seen what you're capable of or have you forgotten the times I was there?"

"Nope, but it hasn't been all one way either or are you forgetting the times when you were—"

Chloe sighed. "Enough. I'm tired of hearing you tell me what Simon is like when I have eyes of my own. I haven't been around you for all these years not to see what went on. Yeah, even you in the early days before me, Gibson, so I suggest you wind your neck back in and let's talk about this like the adults we are."

Gibson winced and turned to Chloe with a wounded look in his eyes at her outburst.

Simon shrugged. "Why do you feel the need to confront us about it? Surely what happens between me and Piper is our business? She's an adult, but the way you've both stormed in here it's like I'm a sixty year old pervert in an old gray trench coat and she's a fourteen year old with no common sense. Piper is a consenting adult and we're not interested in starting a war."

Gibson glanced over to Chloe, his eyes blazing with anger and he picked up from what she had said. "He's an asshole, Chloe. You've seen the way he uses women for sex. Other than being in the band, his other claim to fame is for fucking women."

Simon glanced down at me, obviously embarrassed to hear his friend's assessment of him and scratched the back of his head. "That was before—"

"And like Chloe said, you'd know all about that, right?" I threw back because I couldn't bear to see Simon having to defend himself like this.

As soon as my words were out I wanted to take them back when I saw how hurt Gibson was when I had defended Simon over him.

Whether he had barged in or not, I'd hurt Gibson and he didn't deserve it. All he'd ever done since the day I had met him was protect me, but I had to stand my ground or I feared he'd wade in every time he felt the need.

My heart squeezed tight because the last thing in the world I wanted to do was disrespect him.

Gibson gave me a hard stare. "You have no idea, baby girl—"

"Don't call me that," I snapped. "I'm no one's baby. Like Simon said, I'm a consenting adult."

"And if he said to jump out the window would you do it to be an adult?" Gibson roared.

"Oh, now that's just stupid talk," I replied. "Look," I said trying to calm the conversation down, "This is new for the both of us. I need your support, *we* need your support, not criticism."

Chloe gripped Gibson's forearm, and I saw the tension in his neck as he cracked it from side to side the way he always did if something frustrated him.

"Can I talk? Not holler. Talk? This is none of your business, but since you've made it so, I'm happy to explain what's been happening," Simon said in a soft tone.

"I can imagine what's been going on, so you can spare me the details," Gibson shot back.

"All right. Tell me what's been going on, Gibson?" I goaded. I stood up and folded my arms.

"Isn't it obvious?" he said, looking at Simon as he spoke through gritted teeth.

"Gibson, I've seen how you are when you're being protective. I've seen your passion when you do this, but all I feel right now is aggression... and it doesn't make me comfortable having you in my space while you are acting so hostile. However, I have known you long enough to know you would never hurt me, but I'm not all that confident about Simon's welfare."

Gibson looked shocked again and his eyes darted to Chloe. She nodded. "You're way out of line, honey." He sighed, running both hands through his hair and he sat down heavily on the couch across from us. Chloe sat beside him and placed a hand over his knee.

Silence fell between us and it was clear Gibson was taking a timeout to get his emotions in check. After a quiet minute, Chloe spoke.

"Maybe you should tell Piper how we found out about her and Simon?" she prompted, and Gibson's eyes flicked to Simon's then to mine.

"Where were you yesterday, Si?" he said, barely keeping the growl from his tone.

"You know where I was, Chicago. You were the one who rang and said I had to head up there because Lennox forgot and had gone to the Maldives.

"All right," he paused looking at me for a moment, then he took a deep breath, "And who was with you?"

Simon looked over to me and his eyes softened like he thought what he was about to say would hurt me. My heart stalled in fear of his reply.

Taking a deep breath, he looked at his hands and rubbed them together nervously, and his action was the same as the one he had done before when he poured out his feelings.

"Jess Barrington," he replied and twisted his lips. "But, Piper, I swear it was all up front. There wasn't anything in it but companionship. I needed a plus one for the event and we happened to be picked up at the airport by the TV company in the same courtesy car."

Gibson scoffed, "How convenient."

"It was," Simon agreed without emotion. "It prevented anyone from hitting on me all night. Besides, Jess is pretty serious about Monkon Graftus from Bar Queue Blues, and I flew straight back after the gig," he said. "I even spoke to Piper around 6:30 am when I arrived home," he offered.

The last part was true. He had called me early and had sounded a little tired, but his voice could have been due to alcohol consumption as well.

"I knew where he was, Gibson, and he called me like he said, not that it's any of your business," I added. Inside I was fighting an internal battle about the details Simon had left out of our conversation that Gibson had felt I needed to know.

Simon took my hand and gave it a small squeeze in a silent thank you, but I had defended him without all the facts. I prayed what I'd done was the right thing, and I hoped I wasn't falling into a trap like my mom had done all those years before.

CHAPTER SEVENTEEN

When I looked into Simon's eyes, I just knew nothing had happened between him and the woman Gibson brought up in conversation, so I shook the slightest doubt off when I saw the furious expression on Gibson's face as he looked at Simon.

"Can I say something?" I asked. I would have said it anyway, but I was trying to be polite and give Gibson his place. After all, he'd flown all the way to Santa Monica from Colorado to have my back.

"Shoot, darlin', but whatever it is I hope you're prepared for a comeback," Gibson replied, trying hard to speak to me in an even tone.

"You may think I know nothing about relationships. And the sexual part... I guess that's true. One thing I do know about is manipulation and lies, and my gut tells me Simon really does like me... and the thing is I really like him too. That's the bones of what is going on here."

Gibson shook his head, hung it low then glanced sideways to look at Chloe. She didn't blink or offer any kind of agreement.

"All right," I said as I thought of a different angle and threw my hands up in the air. "Here it is. If what I'm about to say is too much information for you I'm sorry, but since you're imagining the worst of Simon here goes."

Drawing in a sharp breath I held it for a few seconds then blew it out slowly in my attempt to hold my heart and nerves in check. Swallowing as I looked again at Gibson's face, I sighed.

"There's this guy at the studio, Jeff's his name. He's the guitar player on my album. Now he's what? Twenty-one, twenty-two... maybe three at the most. Chloe, you should see him, he's smokin' hot." I advised, pulling Chloe into the conversation and fanning myself for effect.

"Let me tell you, he's probably as good looking as you all," I said, wagging my hand at first Gibson and then Simon. "Oh and I'm sure he's left a long line of broken hearts in his wake already. Would you rather I dated him?"

Gibson lifted his eyebrow toward Chloe, "No one's saying you have to date anyone, but he sure is nearer your age. I mean you're bound to have more in common than you have with Simon."

"You think?" I sighed again because I couldn't believe Gibson was so stuck on the age thing. "I agree, we're the same age and he's very talented at what he does, so we have those things in common. I'm shy and he's quite an extrovert so we're opposite with that. What's the saying... opposites attract? Case in point here with Simon and me." I added and let the last comment sink in.

"Anyway, back to Jeff, he looks every inch the hot musician with his shoulder length sun-kissed blond hair, his golden tan, athletic build. I think you'd say he looks real SoCal surfer dude. Not forgetting his string of seductive chat-up lines and the hot as fuck shiny ride between his thighs."

"All right, I get the picture. He's got game, but do you have to cuss?" Gibson asked. I shrugged and continued.

"So you think I should prefer him to Simon, right?" Gibson shrugged, and I eyed Chloe for courage to confess what almost happened to me.

"Well what you don't know is the guy has terrorized me since day one at the studio." I went on to tell them the whole sorry story about the drugs and the party and when I was done I asked Gibson again, "So do you still think Jeff is a better fit for me than Simon?"

Gibson's fists clenched, his jaw ticked, and I could see I'd hit a nerve. Jeff had taken advantage of me and in a few sentences, I'd shifted his anger from Simon to Jeff.

"I had to call Thomas, to use Otto, the studio producer, to keep him in check. Jesus, Gibson, he even followed me home the other night. Thank God, Simon called me out to his place last weekend because I wouldn't have left the house in case the creep was lurking to pounce."

"So why don't I know any of this?" Gibson barked.

I waved a hand at him sitting in my living room. "This is the reason, Gibson. This adorable fucked-up protective caveman stunt you pull. I was scared you'd try to coax me back to Colorado or worse take your anger out on Jeff." My eyes softened when I saw how hurt he looked.

"I'm here in Santa Monica, a long way from home, and there's gonna be more 'Jeff's' out there waiting to fuck me, fuck me over, or kick me the fuck out of the way. Your words, Gibson, not mine. Only next time I'll be ready."

Gibson looked at Simon like he was about to say let's go find the bastard and I crouched in front of Gibson placing my hand on his forearm. "I really love you and Chloe. Melody is my sister for life, but you've got to let me make my own decisions. If Simon hurts me, then I accept I've been warned."

"I'm never gonna hurt you, baby," Simon muttered immediately.

"You say that now, Si, and I get that this may be a bit different from how you normally operate, but Piper's so young and with her background it isn't the same," Gibson said, and I knew he was talking from his experience with Chloe. But I wasn't Chloe and each of our experiences shapes us differently.

Simon sighed, like he was tired but knew Gibson's heart was in the right place. "Not in my eyes, Gibson. Yeah, she's got youth, but she's an incredible young woman and I've had strong feelings about her for a long time."

"And you pounced on her at the first opportunity. She's been here a little over a week for fuck's sake."

"He did no such thing. And not that it's any of your business, but we haven't slept together and that's not because I won't. Simon's the one who thinks we need to take it slow to make sure it's what I want," I snapped.

Gibson's eyes widened, his eyes darting to Simon like he was surprised, and he ran his hands through his hair. It was clear he hated the whole conversation.

My eyes softened again because as frustrating as the situation was, the man in front of me had sworn to my mom to protect me and I was eternally grateful for having someone who really did care about me the way Chloe and Gibson did.

"Look," I said huffing another breath. "Have any of you considered I may be the one to hurt Simon?"

Gibson's eyes connected with mine and he looked a little taken aback.

"Sure, Simon's a bit older, but maybe that's what I need. I don't really connect with people my age. I was so busy staying alive and getting to the end of each week intact, I barely had time to mix with kids my own age. Who's to say I won't walk away from Simon at some point? Don't you see, Gibson, we take chances with our hearts? No one knows what the future holds. All I know is right now I want Simon and he wants me. And I'd really like your blessing with this because I'd hate to have my relationship with your bandmate to be the elephant in the room every time you see one or other of us."

"I think on that note you need to apologize to both Piper and Simon and tell them why we're here," Chloe said, and I realized I had no clue how they had found out about us.

Staring at me, then at Simon, Gibson drew a long deep breath. He sighed and glanced directly at Simon. "The papers are running a story. You're the sugar daddy, Piper's the budding singer, the slant is the casting couch scenario, and there are photos of you two walking hand in hand across the road to that food shack directly opposite. There's also one very clear shot of your face driving through the gates in your car with Piper following behind. And you want to know the best part? I'm providing the secure accommodation for you to fuck this peach."

"Gibson, that's enough," Chloe snapped in disgust. She shook her head. I shook mine in disbelief and lastly Simon sighed heavily and collapsed into the back of the couch.

"The tabloid running the story contacted Gibson through the PR guys for his comment. Less than an hour later we were in the air on the way here," Chloe added.

Suddenly my throat burned with tears and despite my best attempts to swallow them down they fell down my face, bringing Simon to his feet. His eyes burned with concern as he pulled me up to stand and to his chest.

"That's it. I've tried to be fucking patient with you, Gibson, given what Piper means to you and Chloe, but I'm not gonna sit back and listen to you demean what Piper and I've got going on. You and me have known each other long enough to know what a tolerant person I am, but I'm so fucking close to losing my shit with you right now. You need to stop and think for a minute about the effect all of this is having on Piper... and maybe your wife."

Gibson looked furious and bit back. "The fact I am here and doing this should tell you how angry I am with you, Si. Piper wanted to do this her way, and I wasn't convinced she'd have the life skills to deal with all the shit that comes with this industry, but now that she's here I'm seriously pissed she hasn't had the space to grow without you charging in and fucking things up."

"That part was driven by Thomas, who called me to check on her after Doobie, or Jeff, messed with her. I wouldn't have gotten in touch so soon." Simon sighed and pulled me closer.

"What about her wishes for anonymity? It appears her story isn't gonna stay private now."

"So, I'll get an injunction against the tabloid bottom feeders," Simon threatened.

"For what? You were both seen holding hands for Christ's sake. They don't know Piper belongs to us so how are you going to explain the apartment?"

Simon scratched his beard then smoothed it down. "We say she's housesitting and she didn't know whose place it was. She was placed by an agency. I'm sure our guys can sort that part out."

"And how do you explain your part in all of this?"

"You asked me to pick up some personal stuff, and I took her to breakfast because she's a fan?"

My heart squeezed at my two protectors trying to find a way to keep my true connection to Gibson and Chloe private, but I'd been foolish to think I could. Besides, I always knew the day would come when people would find out, only I'd hoped it would have been after the album was made.

"No. I guess I'll just have to take a hit on staying anonymous." I shrugged. "At least I got the contract before anyone knew who you were," I replied. "Let them do their worst. It's gonna come out at some point anyway."

"No wait, Piper. What if it doesn't work out with Simon?" Gibson asked, and Simon scowled.

"Who says it's not going to? And anyway, look at Katy Perry and Taylor Swift. They've been connected to different guys almost weekly at some point and it hasn't done their careers any harm," I offered.

"You've been here a little over a week, Piper. You have no idea the pressures that will come to bear on your relationship when you start touring... when Simon starts touring again. Can you really cope with all that time apart? Accusations and photographs that show something so overwhelming it leaves you with doubts." His points were valid, and I twisted my lips, hating the thought of that. It's the one thing I hadn't really given much consideration, but some couples made it work.

"No, but like you said, Gibson, I'm twenty. I can only plan so much. There's no point in being anal about my privacy now my identity is known. I'm already publicly connected to Simon. I'm not ashamed of being with him. I feel proud that he wants to be with me, so I'm not going to hide it."

"You're not prepared for the shit stirring and conjecture they'll accuse the pair of you of. Or for the wrath of Simon's fans... and his old flames? They'll target you, say you got favors from the label and the Layla Hartmann tour. Piper, they'll credit your success to Simon."

"And they'd be wrong. Otto can vouch for that. He has no idea I lived with you or that I'm connected to you, yet. You somehow managed to keep me a secret when the story of Melody hit the press."

"That was damage limitation. I had connections, so the story about Melody was contained. What about Colin? You think he's not going to come after you when he thinks there's money to be had... when he thinks he can find your mom?"

I had considered this but I thought it could take years to really get my career going and I was prepared for it to take a long time, if at all. Not every artist hits the charts immediately. I had been ready for the long haul of supporting artists anywhere in the world so the chances of Colin even hearing of me were slim.

"I'm not the same girl who ran away from that tyrant. After all the therapy and preparation from Chloe and the team I'm stronger and I have you guys to call on if he turns up." At the back of my mind I knew he would more than likely find me at some point, but I never figured on it being this soon.

Gibson pulled me out of Simon's embrace and into his chest. Love radiated from his body to mine and I could feel the tension in his hard stance. Eventually he sighed, and it sounded like one of resignation.

"Hurt her again and I'll fucking kill you, Simon," he told him. His words were loaded with fierce determination. "You do whatever is necessary to protect her, whatever she needs to keep her safe."

Simon eyed Gibson with gratitude in the look he gave him and smiled. "Seriously, dude. I tried to fight these feelings, but when I could see she felt the same..." He sighed again, "Now I have her I'm not letting go. We don't give a fuck what anyone thinks, but we don't want to hurt you guys. We only want a chance to see where this takes us."

Gibson looked at Chloe and she raised her eyebrow and gave him a small smile, then we watched as he pursed his lips in thought. A few seconds later he nodded reluctantly. "I guess I'll have to accept this. Unfortunately, there's now the added pressures from external factors like the press. The only thing in our favor in this situation, is that we're not touring for the next six months so we can keep a close eye on Piper's situation and protect her as much as we can."

The 'we' was the all-important word in what Gibson said.

Squeezing his waist, I nuzzled into his chest. "Thanks, Gibson. You don't know what it means to have you and Chloe behind us," I said, feeling happy for the first time since they'd arrived.

I knew instinctively it had to have been Jeff who sold the story because he was the only person who knew about Simon and me apart from Stevie, Simon's sister, and she'd never have done anything to screw with his happiness.

"All right. Now that we know what's coming, it's time to get ahead of the race," Chloe offered, and for the following two hours we ate takeout Chinese food and planned the damage limitation to the new revelations we knew were going to cause a shitstorm for both Simon and me.

CHAPTER EIGHTEEN

*I*nstead of cowering away and waiting for the press to pounce, Simon decided we should pre-empt their story by leaving my apartment building together.

Gibson and Chloe had stayed overnight and remained out of sight because the superintendent for the building had rung to warn us questions from the press were being asked at the gate.

Simon squeezed my hand. "Relax, baby, let me do the talking. All I want you to do is smile, then we can be on our way. We're taking my ride for the foreseeable future," he advised me and for a moment I had to fight against the independence I wanted for the sake of feeling secure.

Driving up to the gate, I was more than a little shaken by the amount of reporters, photographers, and curious passers-by who had stopped to strain their necks, looking inside our car to see what all the fuss was about.

My heart pounded, and my legs bounced nervously. Simon leaned over and placed a hand on my knee. The shaking stopped immediately.

"Breathe, baby, I got you," he said in a slightly amused tone. At that particular moment he drew up to the gates and they slowly opened.

Instantly the car was swamped with paparazzi all vying for the best position.

"Simon, would you care to share your news with us?" one cheeky female reporter shouted, while another poked her phone in his face and I was almost certain she had the recording facility on.

"Is this Piper?" she asked, not really talking to Simon at all because she was staring straight past him at me. Without waiting for him to reply she continued, "Hi, Piper. Wow... Simon McLennan?" She said it like I wasn't worthy. "How does it feel to have a famous older man as your boyfriend? I bet you're very grateful he helped you snag a recording deal."

Inside my head, I heard a growl of frustration. I wanted more than anything to respond to her cocky cheap shot, but I did what Simon asked and smiled sweetly instead.

Simon turned his head away from me to look at her and I could only imagine the look he must have given her when I saw her visibly shrink and back away from the car.

"Good morning, everyone," Simon greeted with a gorgeous lazy grin as he looked from left to right. "It's another gorgeous Santa Monica day. Doesn't the sunshine make you feel glad to be alive?" He asked them while he slid his hand into mine, squeezed it, and turned to offer me a reassuring smile. For a moment it like there was no one else present but me.

His gesture sent a message to the world that said, 'Yes, she's with me', and to me it said, 'This is how you control a hungry mob of reporters'.

"We don't have anything to say to you all right now so if you wouldn't mind moving out of the way, we're gonna be late for an important appointment."

Hitting the electric window button, the tinted glass slid all the way up, effectively shutting them out. Simon's action abruptly and effectively brought their pursuit of us to a conclusion and sent them the message he was done.

Edging past them as camera bulbs flashed and camera shutters whirred and clicked—the noise penetrating the car—Simon turned and glanced briefly at me as he slowly made his way forward.

"You okay?" I gave him a grateful smile because the press gang had gotten nowhere. Stopping briefly to look down the street, Simon put his foot on the gas and steered us out onto the road.

Once he had made a little distance, he turned toward me again and gave me another easy smile. "You did great, baby," he cooed. "Anyone stops you and asks about us, all you gotta say is, 'You'd have to talk to Simon about that'."

"Music?" he asked, reaching over and turning on the radio. "Free Falling," by Tom Petty was playing. "I love this song," he said, turning it up then singing along. His relaxed attitude—bearing in mind what we'd just done—made me smile, but I couldn't relax because I knew I was facing Otto and the ten thousand questions I knew would play on Otto's mind.

Thankfully, everyone's car and Jeff's bike were already in place and I was the last to arrive. Whatever we had to say we only had to do it once since all were present. Simon parked, turned off the engine, slid out of the car and rounded the hood to open my door.

"You'll be fine. It'll be fine. No matter what they say, baby, you keep your game face and let none of your feelings out on display." I glanced nervously at him and nodded.

"Hey, I'm telling you, it's sweet. Just chill and in a few weeks someone else will be taking the heat," he told me. Simon's reassurance was great, but I wasn't sure I believed they would leave us alone. *What's the worst that could happen?* My overactive mind then gave me a long list of what could go wrong, but I wouldn't allow my thoughts to turn negative.

"Come on, baby, let's give them a show," he advised me, with a playful tone and a smile. Squeezing my hand, he led me toward the studio door and seconds later we were entering the mixing studio.

Jeff was in the booth and it looked like he was tuning his guitar from what I saw when he looked up. His face looked stunned when he saw Simon with me and when his jaw gaped and snapped shut I figured he'd almost swallowed his tongue that we were fronting this out together.

I didn't know him well, but with the face he pulled, I knew intuitively he had been the one who had contacted the press.

Grunt, bless him, was the most animated I'd ever seen him. Dropping his sticks, he scooted around his drum kit and out of the booth to hug Simon warmly then fist bumped him and muttered, "Respect." He held up his thumb, forefinger, and pinkie up in a rock salute and looked a little awestruck.

Simon thanked him. He knew Grunt by reputation and I'd never seen anyone so delighted for being given a bit of praise.

Grunt returned to the booth to take up his spot behind the drums and looked like he was going to burst while he waited to show off.

Turning back to me, Simon's hands slid around my waist and he pulled me into his chest. With his mouth close to my ear he whispered, "Mind if I stick around for a while? I want to hear how you're doing."

I shook my head, "Clear it with Otto," I told him, out of respect for my boss.

Simon and Gibson were so used to being welcome everywhere but I wanted him to remember it was Otto's domain and Simon should give him his place. He gave me one sharp nod indicating he would. "Go get 'em, Princess," he said, tipping his chin toward the booth with a cheeky smile and a wink.

"Don't call—" Before I could tell him not to call me Princess, he placed his finger across my lips.

I knew what he was doing. By heating my blood by using the nickname he knew that I'd be bristly with Jeff.

"Shh. Go do your thing and I'll sit right here. We gotta show them we're proud to be together."

"I am proud," I replied, pressing a small kiss to his lips, and I thought how surreal everything was again as I slipped my hand from his and entered into the soundproof booth. The lights dimmed on the production side and Otto gestured for Simon to take a seat next to him and turned his attention to me.

"Morning, Piper, can we start with the second number on the sheet today? I think that has the least changes we need to make." He set about flicking switches and sliding tone buttons and turned to look at me. Signaling with his hand in the air he brought it down as the red light lit up over the door indicating we were recording.

Jeff played the slow intro to the melancholic song, and I launched into a haunting melody that both tested my range and felt emotionally draining.

A couple of times I glanced at the window where Simon was watching and saw him scrutinizing both Jeff's musical ability and my performance.

Closing my eyes, I concentrated on reaching the highest note at the loudest part of the bridge and when I rocked it, I opened my eyes to see both Simon and Otto staring at each other, shaking their heads then grinning.

Simon turned to look at me, nodded slowly, and placed his hand over his heart. I took that as he was touched by my performance.

My heart swelled in my chest at how pleased I was for their approval and I instantly felt all the tension I held ease out of my muscles. Nailing the range was a huge relief but having Simon there to witness it meant everything to me.

When the last note on Jeff's guitar string died, Simon held my gaze and stood up shaking his head slowly like he couldn't believe what he'd heard and his smile grew wide. Breaking our eye contact he turned to Otto and had a pretty intense conversation about something.

As I was still inside the soundproof booth, I couldn't hear anything they said. Suddenly Otto smiled and nodded. Simon reached over and flicked the mic on Otto's side.

"Piper, baby, that was fucking dope. Every single hair on the back of my head stood on end. Otto agrees with me that the song stays cut for the album just like that. No tweaks necessary. I've seen power ballad singers try songs that have the kind of complex arrangement that one has, and they've never done a better job than you just did."

My heart pounded at his praise because I knew I had never sang the number better. Perhaps I had given a little extra because I had wanted to impress. Whatever the reason, I was happy with the result.

After the success of nailing the first song with no changes, the other two didn't go quite as smoothly, and one in particular was due to Jeff's mistakes.

Otto cut the number halfway through and Simon had a word then slid out of his seat and entered the booth.

"Dude, take a seat on the other side. You're drowning her out," he scolded and nodded toward Otto. Grabbing the spare electric Gibson guitar from its stand, Simon slipped the strap over his head.

Grinning widely at the shocked look on my face, he came close and whispered in my ears, "I've been hard since the moment you opened your mouth in here." His words made my core pulse, and he quickly stepped back and fingered the scales in a mini warm up, tweaking the tuning again.

"Ready, baby. Let's go one more time," he told me before hitting the rig pedal at his feet and nodding to Grunt. Immediately, Grunt being the awesome technician he was on percussions, kicked in and followed his lead.

To say I was a little shy and freaked was an understatement because I felt nothing I did would have done justice to their awesome set of skills, but in truth I was scared to sing on a track with someone as accomplished as Simon. "No one's recording this, let's see how this arrangement feels for you."

Without giving me any chance to back out he began to play the intro with Grunt, leaving me no option but to chime in as soon as the score dictated I should.

Nerves gave my voice a tentative sound in the beginning but worked well, bringing the right amount of vulnerability to the song lyrics. The overriding emotion in the words was anxiety, but by the bridge my vocals were settled and comfortable.

It wasn't like it was the first time I had sung while Simon had played, but it felt very different. Apart from those on the other side of the glass judging our professional performance, I knew they were also watching how we were around each other.

By the time I recorded the number, the arrangement was hardly recognizable as the same song, but it was one I had written so I was happy with the changes. Simon knew my song well and had put the new arrangement in his head taking the song to a whole new level.

The look of delight on Otto's face made me realize just how musically gifted Simon was. We even wrapped up early for the day because there were only two more songs left to record to finish the whole project.

Otto questioned why I had never mentioned Simon and was

impressed when I said I hadn't wanted anything or anyone to sway his decision, but I did admit to knowing Simon for a couple of years through mutual 'people', which also was the truth.

Jeff's suspicious eyes ticked from me, to Simon, to Otto, and back to me. Sitting next to Otto, he listened intently to everything being said but didn't contribute to the conversation. When I spoke in familiar terms about Simon, Jeff's eyes narrowed toward me.

It didn't take a genius to fathom what he thought. That Simon and I may have been together when I was still a minor, so I decided to bring that point up before he had any more ideas about contacting the press again.

Excusing myself, I headed off for the bathroom and as I came back a few minutes later, I heard Simon shooting a vague warning to Jeff. "Funny how people think they're smart, but they turn out to be the most stupid of fucks on the planet, huh, Jeff?"

"Sorry, Simon. I never knew you were tapping her," Jeff replied.

"What did you say?"

"I said…"

"I fucking heard you. That's my fucking woman you're talking about, not a groupie," he scolded.

"No offence, dude,"

"Mr. McLennan to you, dickhead," he spat. "Let me give you a cliff notes version of what's going to go down here from now on. You're going to listen carefully if you want to work in ANY capacity as a musician. You fuck with my girl, I'm gonna fuck with your future, got me? And for the record, I've never tapped Piper. We're very new as a couple, and she's got more class in her little finger than you'll ever have. She's amazing girl and she's going places. So… I'm a patient man and more than happy to wait."

Simon glanced over to me and straightened his back. "You must be starving after all that work today. Come on, babe, I think a bit of pampering is in order. What do you say to a soak in a luxurious bubble bath and some gourmet food?"

"Sounds like heaven," I replied, staring up into his gorgeous eyes like there was no one else in the room. He gave me a knowing smile as he slipped his hand into mine.

"And that's my cue, guys, we'll see you tomorrow," he chirped as he led me out the studio door.

~

"What was that about?" I asked. I knew full well, but I had wanted to know how Simon saw it.

"Nothing you need to concern yourself with. I think that dirtbag's got the message. It's one thing fucking with a young girl who he thinks he can take advantage of, but it would be quite another if I picked up the phone and cut off his main earning stream. The dude would find himself working in Target instead of living a lifestyle where he gets to stay in bed for half of the day when no one's recording."

"There's nothing wrong with working in Target," I said in defense.

"Agreed, but last time I looked they didn't hire musicians." He smirked, wickedly.

"You're not coming back with me tomorrow," I informed him, picking up from the sentence where he said he'd see them tomorrow. "Don't get me wrong, I was overwhelmed when you stayed and gave your input because it's ten times better for it."

I was also thankful he had been with me when the story broke about us, but I knew I had to stand on my own two feet and take on the wrath of the press if Simon and I were to have any chance of a future together.

"But, babe-"

"No. I need to do this. Please don't try to control me or pressure me into doing something I feel I need to manage alone. You know me well enough to know this by now. If you insist, it'll only push me away."

I watched his eyes narrow and scrutinize me as I told him what I needed.

"All my life I've been told how to behave by a man. Being deprived of basic decision-making skills was Colin's way of maintaining his hold over us. If you really care about me like you say you do, you'll under-stand how important it is that I show Jeff I am not afraid of anything he wants to throw at me. It's the only way he'll leave me alone. You can't be in Santa Monica all the time."

Simon kissed the top of my head and pulled me into his chest. He sighed heavily and turned me to walk toward the outer entrance door. I was so busy glancing up, waiting for him to agree that I almost fell over when he suddenly backed up and pulled me to the side.

"Shit. I knew they'd more than likely follow, but after five hours I'd have thought they would have had a break or found something better to chase."

Adrenaline coursed through my body when I thought about facing the press again, but I knew if I was going to make it then it would be something I'd have to contend with in my daily life. After all, I couldn't just be famous whenever I wanted to. All or nothing was how Gibson would have described it.

"What should we do?"

"That's up to you, baby. Either we can give them a show and hope they'll get fed up in a day or two or we get Otto to tell them we already left."

"Well unless that was through the skylight window they'd laugh at that excuse." I sighed. "I'm happy to deal if you are. The sooner we get it over with, the sooner we get home to eat."

"You're fucking awesome... and brave," he mumbled.

"Or plain stupid," I added, and he chuckled again.

Clasping my hand in his, he leaned in and pecked a small kiss to my temple. The look in his eyes said 'trust me, you've got this'. "Big smiles, sweetheart," he advised in a theatrical voice and led me chuckling purposely out of the door.

Facing around thirty-five photographers was pretty daunting, but I didn't want to create the impression I was some kind of bimbo, especially since Gibson's assessment of the original comment of Simon being my sugar daddy. Even the thought of that terminology made me cringe.

Squinting against the sun, I quickly dropped Simon's hand to fish into my oversized purse for my Armani sun specs and slipped them up my nose and over my ears. The tiny barrier created a modicum of privacy and let me watch them in return.

Seconds later, Simon's warm palm slid against mine again and he pulled me closer into his side.

"You okay, baby?" he asked, wrapping his other arm around me even though there were lots of people watching us.

"Not really, but unless I learn to face this I'm never gonna manage to control the press," I admitted.

"Good girl, you got this," he replied proudly, giving my hand a protective squeeze.

"Simon, when are you going to introduce us properly to your girl?" one shouted, but Simon ploughed through the group of mostly male reporters and led me over to his car. Opening the passenger door, he waited for me to get in, closed it, and wandered around the hood toward his side.

"Simon, we know you helped Piper with her record deal, but does she have any talent or..." his voice trailed away when I saw Simon's body stance change and I figured he was glaring at the reporter much in the same way as he had with Gibson when they were at odds the previous day.

"How long have you known Piper? We saw you with Jess Barrington on your arm only two days ago. Is this thing with Piper still casual? Piper, has Simon explained himself regarding the photographs of him with Jess Barrington?" asked another.

"For the record, I wasn't with Jess. We merely accompanied each other to the same event we had been invited to. As we were both alone and had flown in at the same time, we arranged to keep each other company."

"As for Piper," glancing around to look at me in the car, he gave me the most slow and sexy smile then turned back, "It could never be casual with Piper, look at her. Have you ever seen anyone more beautiful or appealing? I doubt any man in their right mind would see a princess like Piper as a casual arrangement. Speaking of which, this is where I take my leave and pay my gorgeous girl some attention."

Walking the rest of the way around to the car, he opened his door, slid behind the wheel, and closed the door softly. Reaching over, he lifted my hand and kissed it then glanced longingly into my eyes.

"Ready to go, baby?" He asked as he leaned in and planted a small kiss on my lips. Flashbulbs and cameras clicked in rapid succession as I tried not to freak out, but as if Simon knew how I felt, his hand tightened firmer around mine.

"Stay this cool around them and you'll have them eating right out of your hand," he whispered into my ear.

Glancing out through the windshield he shrugged, "Fuck it, let them look. I gotta have a better taste than that." Placing his hands on each side of my face, he drew me close and took what he wanted. And boy did he ever.

His kiss was loaded with intent and totally possessed me. Separating our lips as quickly, I sat slightly dizzy, body fully charged with expectation of what else he could do to blow my mind.

He pulled his head back just enough to catch my gaze and hold it. "All I want is for you to be safe, Princess. Anyone fucks with you and I'll tear them apart with my bare hands," he said with a gruff tone that let me know I should never doubt his words.

Immediately following his declaration, a warm glow filled my body from the inside out, all the way from my toes to my head. It should have been hard to believe he cared enough to feel this way, but in that moment, it was the easiest thing in the world for me.

"You got to give them just enough to let them think they won the hunt, when all they've done is walk into the trap you control," he advised, and when I turned to look at the salacious and smug grins of the reporters all standing staring back at us as if we were laboratory rats, I knew without doubt how right he was. I was in the best of hands with Simon.

"Thank you for being with me today and for protecting me the way you have. I found it very sexy how you dealt so confidently with the news hungry paparazzi and how you defended my honor," I said with a genuine smile.

"Glad you mentioned that honor... the way you sang today made me so fucking hard I was scared I was gonna sling that fucking guitar out of the way and ram you up against the nearest wall. Do you know how turned on I am when I hear you sing like that?" His comment made me chuckle because it was the very thing I had said to Gibson and he'd thought it was funny.

It may have sounded crude but unbeknown to Simon it was prob-

ably the best compliment he could ever have given me. It was definitely a boost to my confidence, especially as the press had been
hounding me earlier in the day about how I'd arrived at my recording
contract.

Firing up the car, Simon shifted the stick into drive and pulled us
slowly away from the waiting press. As soon as we'd cleared the pack
and turned into the open road, he slammed his foot on the gas and we
tore away from them at speed.

CHAPTER NINETEEN

Gibson and Chloe had gone by the time we arrived back at my apartment. I guessed it was weird for Gibson to see me with Simon, but knowing I didn't have another evening of awkward and challenging conversation made me sigh with relief.

As soon as I opened the door, the smell of garlic and fresh basil filled my nostrils and my stomach rumbled. "Thank God for Chloe," Simon offered in praise. She had obviously thought ahead and had some warm food and a beautiful healthy salad waiting and it was obvious Gibson had sent Jerry or Jonny, one of his bodyguards, to organize some supplies.

Wandering over to the oven, I saw it was on the 'keep warm' setting and opened the door. A mouthwatering lasagna with a crispy cheese topping was cooked to perfection. Simon came up behind me and slipped his arms around my waist, kissed my bare shoulder and rested his bearded chin on it, peering into the oven.

The way he held me brought an instant smile to my lips. "Fuck, that smells amazing, but I can't tell which smells better, the food or you." He sighed, and his warm breath fanned over my sensitive skin. "What's that you're wearing? It's been driving me insane all day," he asked.

"Only deodorant. I forgot to put any perfume on this morning before we left, but if you can smell me above this garlic odor, then the smell must be anything but alluring," I replied with a chuckle.

"Maybe we need to get you naked and into the shower then," he replied. Slamming the oven door shut, he spun me around to lean against the counter. Pressing his body against me, he slid his hand down and clasped my butt.

"You know how long I've been waiting to get you alone?" he asked, peppering small delicate kisses all over my neck. The unmistakable bulge at my belly made my body betray me and I wiggled my hips because I had found it increasingly impossible not to want more. His eyes burned with desire as his hands moved sensually over my butt.

"Since yesterday?" I asked, playfully.

"In the near past yes, before that... months," he whispered huskily as his teeth began to nibble at my ear. Suddenly he pushed away from me and grabbed my hand. Leading me around the other side of the counter he lifted me up and sat me on a stool. Walking back around to the other side of the counter he stared pointedly at me and sighed.

"Sit right there. Don't you dare move. We'll get nothing to eat... well you won't if I don't make some space between us," he told me as he turned and pulled the food out of the oven before I could speak. I was in awe as I watched him place the hot pottery dish on the granite counter and it had nothing to do with his skills in the kitchen.

His crude comment made me feel a little self-conscious and every word he had uttered turned my bones to Jell-O. I could never have imagined in my wildest dreams Simon McLennan would want me as much as he did.

Moving fluidly, he reached up into one cupboard and pulled out two glasses, then crouched down low opening and closing others until he found the flatware.

Placing two plates on the countertop he then pointed at drawers until I nodded at one. Opening it, he took out two place settings of the silverware, a large serving spoon and some salad tongs.

"Tell me something I don't know about you, Piper," he said and began to serve up the food. He didn't look at me. Being caught off guard by his demand, I sat quietly for a minute watching his strong muscular arms flex and relax as he added salad to both the plates.

"So you know my mom's ex-partner isn't my real dad? I've never met him, and I guess I never will." Simon stopped what he was doing and dropped the clear plastic tongs to the salad bowl slowly.

"I'm sorry," he offered, his voice sounding full of sympathy.

"Don't. I don't want you to ever feel sorry for me. For years I clung to the fact I had a real father and Colin wasn't my blood," I replied. "You have no idea how sane that kept me when that bastard verbally, physically, and psychologically abused my mom and me. But who knows, if I hadn't been subjected to his wrath I may never have discovered how much music means to me."

Simon gripped the edge of the counter and his knuckles blanched at the force he gripped the granite. "Whenever you've spoken about your mom's partner in the past, all I've wanted was a few minutes in a dark alley with maybe a set of spiked brass knuckles."

I chuckled at the image and Simon frowned, "I never thought of you as a mafioso."

He gave me a wry smirk, "No fucking kidding, Piper. I've never hated anyone in my life, yet I have so much venom running through my veins for that dude. If wants were wishes he'd be lying in a heap of his own shit, so debilitated he'd never be able to so much as look at another woman again, let alone pull the same domineering bullshit he used on you and your mom."

"Enough of him, tell me something about you now," I said because I didn't want to deal with the tight familiar feeling that had begun to settle in my chest when I thought of particular instances when Colin was particularly difficult toward us.

Placing the food in front of me, he put his plate next to mine and poured two bottles of water from the fridge into the glasses. Once he had given me mine, he sipped at his as he walked around the counter, sliding into the seat next to me.

Lifting his fork, he poked at his food, then shrugged. "I've not been the best man so far in my life, Piper." His comment was blunt and devoid of emotion.

"I think you're amazing," I replied.

Chuckling, he stared directly at me, "I wouldn't go that far." Taking a bite of his food, he wiped his mouth with his napkin. "How many guys have you been with?" I glanced up at him feeling a little shy at his pointed question.

"You already know the answer to that question."

"I meant fooled around with."

"One," I stated and felt totally out of my depth at my inexperience again.

"I can't say the same." His response confused me.

"You've been with men?" I joked.

Chuckling he shook his head. "No."

I frowned because I knew he was addressing how he had lived his life.

"What can you say?" I asked, not sure if I wanted the answer or not.

I watched him stab his fork at his food while he gathered his thoughts and I ate a forkful of mine.

"I guess I can say too many. You deserve my honesty, Piper.

"Then I believe that's more than I could ask for at this stage," I told him. My answer was rewarded when he gave me a small smile.

"Gibson's right. You're too shiny for me. All the experience I have has dulled my soul and you deserve better, Princess."

"I love Gibson with every bone in my body for what he's done for me, but I'll make my own choices and any mistakes are my own to make."

"Let's hope you never think being with me is a mistake. I totally get the way Gibson reacted to this, and he has every right to feel the way he does about me. Usually he's the most laid back, liberal person I know, but he's ferocious when it comes to protecting what's his. You being with me would be most father's nightmare."

"Right now, I guess he feels a little out of his depth with his promise to my mom and you being... you."

Simon chuckled, softly, "That's one way of putting it. What you mean is you being innocent and me being corrupt?"

I shrugged, "If you want to put it that way, perhaps, but I figure as there's no chance of you regaining your innocence, if you corrupt me a little then it wouldn't matter so much."

"Hmm," he hummed, "I could have a lot of fun after that invitation. A wicked smile made his eyes gleam and his flirtatious response turned me on in a heartbeat. I squeezed my thighs together to control the strong pulse that shot to my center. As lust rose inside him, his eyes grew heavier and the way he held my gaze was a little more intense.

"It means a lot to me to have his approval," he admitted, nodding to himself. His unexpected remark took me by surprise.

"Okay, tell me something else about you," he asked, moving the conversation forward.

Placing my fork on my plate I wiped my mouth and shrugged. "I'm scared."

A frown creased his brow, and he shoved his plate away and grabbed my hand in his. Caressing my knuckles, he looked at me with concern. "What are you scared of?"

"This. Us. I mean I want... of course I do, look at you... but what if I'm not enough? What if you get bored of me?" I knew I was babbling.

Simon placed his fingers over my lips silencing me, his other hand left mine as he brushed my hair away from my face.

Looking serious he stroked my cheek with a thumb. "I'm not going to tire of you, Princess. Trust me, you're more than enough for me." He dropped his hand from my lips and turned to his food.

"How can you say that? You can't..."

"Trust me, a man knows what he wants. I've been attracted to you since the first day I saw you. It wasn't only how you looked, but the way you are." Taking my hand he laced his fingers in mine and stared into my eyes. "You may not believe this... I'm so used to taking what I want, when I want, but I'm a little intimidated by this situation."

My eyes widened in disbelief at his admission. "Because of Gibson, you mean?"

"No, because of me. I'm scared if we get closer I'll do something to fuck it up. There's no getting away from how young you are, and I've never really thought about what it would be like to be a girlfriend of mine. When I hear myself say that, I know I sound like a huge selfish fuck, but I promised you honesty and I have to start as I mean to go on with that."

"How you treated women in the past?"

"No... yeah, maybe, but not just that. Stepping out with someone who is the focus of the world's media takes guts. Being subject to speculation and conjecture as well, because those reporters can be brutal and highly inaccurate at times. It won't be easy," he said, shaking his head.

"That's where Gibson and Chloe will help, they've been through all of that," I replied. "Since last weekend I can't tell you how many thoughts have run through my head. Every permutation of how this will play out. Either this could be it for me or I could be left with a shattered heart beyond repair, and yet the thought of being with you for even a short time outweighs the risks."

Simon squeezed my hand and tugged my stool turning me to face him. Shifting in his seat, he positioned his legs either side of mine and placed his hands on my hips.

"Trust me the risks are both ways and with so much at stake I think those risks are what's holding me back. This stuff with the press has forced me to look at what we're doing and has changed my point of view. Now that Gibson and the rest of the world know, I don't feel half as intimidated by our situation. I can't blame Gibson for wanting stability for you, given what you've been through."

"There's more to life than stability. From the outside looking in, life at home was full of stability. I had two parent figures, we had a place to live and food on the table, a bed to sleep in, but living on the inside was anything but stable. No one needs to take care of me anymore. I can make my own way. I'm not some 'Princess' with high expectations, Simon, I just want to be loved."

"And I already love you and I'm infatuated with you... mind and body."

We fell silent and I gave him a look of intent. "Are you taking me to bed?" I asked curtly and smiled.

"Is that what you want?"

"I do, but first I need to be straight with you."

Simon's eyes ticked over my face; his serious expression showed me how carefully he was listening.

"Taking my virginity does not tie you to me if this isn't what I want. Neither does it tie me to you. The last thing I want to take from our time together is either of us feeling resentful of the other, and I don't want you to stay with me out of some sense of duty because of Gibson."

Shaking his head again, he shut his eyes for a second then drew in a deep breath, "Damn that's concise. You think too much for someone so young."

Suddenly he stood up, scooped me up into his arms and headed down the hallway toward my bedroom. The purpose in his move sparked an instant adrenaline rush and my heart almost burst out of my chest at the expert confidence he handled me with.

Since the second he'd scooped me off the chair, I had been hyper-conscious of his nearness, the smell of his cologne and the way his arms squeezed me into his warm, hard chest.

Entering the bedroom, I half expected to be tossed on the bed, but he continued to make his way to the bathroom with me before he sat me down on top of the vanity. "It's so fucking hot we need to shower. I love living in California but sometimes the heat just pisses me off and makes me feel cranky. Add how frustrated I am, and it feels like a perfect storm going on inside my body right now." Spinning around, he reached into the shower and turned the faucet on, then walked back over to me.

"Lift," he ordered tugging at the hem of my top. As I held up my arms, he pulled my it up and over my head, then discarded it on the floor behind him. His Adam's apple bobbed on his neck as he fixed his hungry eyes on my black lacy bra. "Love this," he mumbled and slid his middle finger under one of the straps. Turning his gaze from it to me, I saw him swallow again before he leaned in and undid the clasp.

Straightening his stance, he peeled my bra away from me and as soon as his eyes settled on my breasts he licked his lips, dipped his head and planted a slow reverent kiss on each one.

Clearing his throat, he slid his hands under my arms and lifted me down off the vanity. As soon as I took my weight on my feet, I felt a hand trail down my back, stopping to rest on the curve of my ass.

My chest felt tight and I trembled slightly in anticipation of what he would do to me next. It wasn't the first time we'd been at this point and while I knew he was being considerate, the wait for the unknown was killing me.

CHAPTER TWENTY

Once I was naked, I found my courage and stripped him of his clothing like he'd done with mine. A sexy smirk played on his lips and his eyes widened then closed when my fingers closed around the satiny skin on his cock. My thumb grazed Simon's shiny tip, and he hissed, his eyes opening to stare intently into mine. "Fuck," he cussed quietly as his body tensed under my hands.

Standing naked together, my gaze dropped to look at his cock in my hand and I swallowed hard at the size and girth of it. It looked even bigger than before and I swallowed nervously.

"What's wrong?"

I wasn't going to lie. "This thing is huge," I offered, and he wrapped his hand around mine over it.

"It's not a thing, it's a cock," he snickered. He was thick and although my fingers surrounded him they didn't meet. Glancing up at his face, I noted his eyes were half-closed and his tongue ran the length of his lips.

Without talking, Simon moved his hand over mine and we stroked his cock back and forth. I instinctively knew he was teaching me the pace and the pressure he wanted me to use when I pleasured him this way.

With his other hand, he cupped the back of my head and pulled me closer. "You're so fucking beautiful, baby," he muttered as he shook his head like he couldn't believe I was in front of him.

His lips touched mine and at first it was a slow gentle kiss, but within seconds the passion burning between us made us both leave his cock as he grabbed my butt, pressing me tightly against him.

"Fuck, baby," he mumbled again and growled as he smashed his lips to mine. I clung to his back, my nails scoring his skin as we gave ourselves over to the sensations running through us. Suddenly, Simon pulled away heaving for breath.

"Shower," he whispered hurriedly into my ear then smacked my butt. I yelped as the stinging sensation radiated through my body and sent a ripple of desire all the way to my core. My pussy pulsed in desperation and I whimpered at the loss of contact when he moved away from me.

Stepping breathless into the shower, my heart pounded, and I gulped for air in an effort to steady my racing heartbeat.

Simon hugged me from behind, his front to my back; his hard length sliding up the crack of my butt before it settled against my lower back. Even in the shower I could tell I was wet between my legs and it had nothing to do with the water.

Reaching past me, Simon squirted some bodywash into his large palm in front of me and rubbed his hands together. Starting at my shoulders he smoothed the silky soap suds over my shoulders, down my arms and back up underneath them. He tickled my armpits making me giggle and my butt inadvertently thrust back against him.

Never missing a beat, Simon caught my hips and held me there, gyrating his hips against me. The feel of his stiff cock pressing hard against my butt made me desperate for more and little scared at the same time. Leaning forward he whispered in my ear, "Your ass is a peach, baby."

Continuing to wash me, he soaped from my collarbone and allowed his hands to slip over my breasts, his thumbs strumming my pebbled nipples gently. Leaning back, I closed my eyes and sank back against him, sagging a little as I got used to the feel of his hands on my skin.

"You like this?"

"Mm-hm," I said sounding a little shy once again.

"Say it," he demanded.

"I like it," I replied immediately.

"Good, because I'm going to be doing this pretty regularly with you, if that's okay?" he remarked.

"Is that a promise?"

"You can take it to the bank, baby," he said sounding amused, and he smiled against my neck as his hands slid lower.

When his fingers stroked the outer lips of my pussy, my body stiffened a little, not used to being touched in this way. "Relax, sweetheart, I got you," he coaxed, and I took another deep breath. Stroking the length of my seam his middle finger slid past my hard clit and down toward my entrance.

"How does this feel?"

"Good." The word was totally inadequate for how he made me feel. Buzzed, heady, horny, would have been better.

Turning me toward him, he lifted me up and wrapped my legs around him, leaned me against the wall and crushed his body to mine. His hard cock brushed my lips, but he repositioned it and it nestled along my entrance.

My hands trailed from his shoulders into his hair and my fingers gripped two handfuls. I tugged it back gently to look at him, "Oh, mm," he moaned. In small rhythmic movements he rocked his hips, his cock sliding between my thighs as he kneaded the soft flesh on my butt.

"Your ass feels amazing," he said, complimenting it, "and your pussy feels so fucking tempting," he said before he stopped talking and kissed me deeply again.

Breaking the kiss, he slid my front skin-to-skin against his until my feet reached the floor. "Come on, before I take you against these hard tiles," he mumbled and led me out of the cubicle and back into the open space of the bathroom. My heart thudded like crazy at the thought.

Grabbing a towel, I patted myself dry and saw Simon enjoying the view.

"You know what amazes me about you?"

I glanced in Simon's direction as he wrapped a towel low on his hips. I sighed heavily in awe as I took him in and he smiled, then I felt myself blush because my reaction was so spontaneous I wasn't prepared for how he affected me.

"What?" I asked skipping past my embarrassment of how he made me feel.

"I love that you're not body conscious. Even though your innocence radiates from every pore, you're not trying to hide yourself from me."

"I am... I'm fighting that feeling because I know it's not the first time you've seen a naked woman."

Simon grinned and chuckled softly. "Every woman is different, Piper. What can I say? Men are visual creatures. We love looking at tits, ass, and pussy." I felt heat flush my face. "But that's not what I see with you."

"Stop, you don't have to..."

"Yeah, I do. All those other women, that was what they were. Pretty faces, nice tits, firm ass, tight pussy, but that's all they were. I figure I should tell you that's all I thought about them before someone else does."

I lowered my eyes because I'd never heard anyone talk in such crude terms about women apart from in the movies.

He cupped my chin and raised my gaze to meet his again. "This is important, sweetheart. What I'm saying is you have no need to ever feel jealous of anyone I've been with in the past. In you I see things I've never noticed on any other women."

I frowned.

"You don't believe me? Did you know you have a tiny strawberry birthmark at the nape of your neck? I know you have a freckle on your left pinkie finger? I love this gorgeous tiny beauty queen nose you have and I love how your huge brown eyes turn me the fuck on every time you glance shyly at me. Do you need me to go on? When I touch your skin, my dick instantly reacts like there's some kind of invisible magnet. I'm so drawn to your body I ache all over. No other woman has had an effect like this on me since I was about eighteen."

He stopped and smirked, his sudden admission bringing us right back to the age thing and the difference between us.

"I don't care about the others. I can't allow myself to do that or I'll lose all confidence in what we're building here. All I care about is how you treat me."

It was the truth. I bore no malice toward the women he had been with before. Maybe that was due to ignorance or the fact that I never expected to be anything in Simon's world, but my philosophy had always been to try not to dwell on the things I could do nothing about.

CHAPTER TWENTY-ONE

Simon came toe to toe with me in my bathroom and lifted me up onto his torso. Wrapping my legs around his waist, he cupped my butt cheeks in his hands.

As he walked me to my bed, I could feel how wet my entrance was as it brushed against the fine hair trailing down from his belly button.

Stepping up to the bed, he bent forward and laid me down like I was made of bone china, but before he could do anything else I grabbed his hand and tugged him down beside me.

Turning onto his back he ran his fingers through his hair and I turned on my side and placed kisses on the hard, muscular lines that formed the taut six pack across his abdomen.

Smiling sexily up at me, his hand began to fan through my long dark hair and I felt like the luckiest girl in the world in that moment. He sighed, turning his head to look down at me in thought.

"What is it?"

"I'm an animal, Piper... or was. By now in the time I've spent with you in the shower I'd have fucked any other woman twice, yet, with you I feel I can't take this slow enough."

"See, that makes me feel like you'll tire of me."

"Never. I just want this to feel right for you. I have no desire to treat you like them."

"I'm not fragile, Simon."

Shaking his head in disbelief at my answer I saw him digest what I'd said. "All right, what do you want?" he asked turning his full focus on me.

"You," I replied, quickly.

Simon chuckled, "You need a minute to think about that?"

"Been thinking of nothing else all week," I replied honestly, and he grinned.

"Damn, you confuse the fuck out of me. You look like an angel then you come out with these straight-talking answers that most other women would make me work for," he replied. "I guess I've been testing you with some of the stuff that I've said, but I wanted you to be sure you knew what you were getting into. It's a difficult conversation to have, but I thought I should give it to you straight because I'd hate you to react to the shit they're going to throw at you for being with me."

"Bring it, I say. No one could ever hurt me with words nowadays, Simon. Let them do their worst. I've listened and nothing you have said has riled me because I knew you had a history with women, but before this goes all the way I only want to say one more thing. Treat me right because no matter how much I like you, if you do fuck me over there will never be a do-over."

"Noted," he said, his eyes serious. "Trust me, baby, it's the thing I fear the most. I'll never cheat on you. I can guarantee that but believe me now when I say the press and others will do everything they can to discredit us being together."

Taking his cock in my hand, I gave it a small squeeze and his head bobbed up to look at the firm grip I had on him. "That's all I needed to hear. I don't think you'd ever want to do me wrong, but I'm not a fool, so don't forget that."

Needing a change of direction, I gave into my urge because I couldn't resist tasting him, like he had done with me, so I scooted down and pressed my lips to his tip before he could blink.

Immediately, Simon gripped my wrist that held his cock and shook his head, "No, baby, you don't have—"

A long hiss interrupted his speech as I ignored him, taking his cock in my mouth. The salty taste was mingled with a faint hint of soap but I liked it. Lathing my tongue, I lapped up the pre-cum that leaked from the head of his cock.

"Fuck." The word came in a rush as his breathing became steady and his large warm palm came over to cradle my head. His hips undulated slightly as he gently pushed his cock a little deeper into my mouth.

"That's it, baby, just like that," he said in a soft encouraging tone before he thrust it a little deeper again. Glancing up his body, watching his reaction, and the look of pleasure on his face made my pussy pulse for more. The way he bit his lip in concentration and his lust-filled eyes focused on what I was doing was everything I could have hoped for.

A couple of minutes later his fingers wrapped around his cock and he pulled himself out of my mouth, grabbed me, and flipped me over. Lifting my legs, he pushed them up to my chest. The look of sheer intent in his eyes sent ripples of excitement coursing through me, causing every cell in my body to vibrate. The connection in our eyes deepened as he spread my knees wide.

"Look at you," he said, like he was seeing me for the first time. "So fucking beautiful. You have no idea how much I want this." His eyes shone with desire as he broke eye contact and dipped his head low.

When he inhaled deeply it reminded me of the first time he did this, and I almost closed my legs with embarrassment, but before I could dwell on his action he gave me one swift wet lick from my butt-hole to my clitoris. I trembled with the sudden thrill of it.

He smiled then chuckled, "Damn, how responsive was that?" he asked. I sighed a long breath and realized there was no part of my body he wasn't willing to explore.

Lavishing attention on me, his tongue expertly coaxed me to the edge of orgasm only for him to repeatedly slow my excitement down by gently blowing cool air on my hot swollen entrance. The tease was both delicious and frustrating.

After some time, he took my hand and traced my fingers along my soaked entrance, "Feel that? You know what that does to me?" he asked, glancing up at my face. I shook my head. "It makes me harder than you can imagine. Knowing I've made you this wet and it's all mine is the best feeling ever," he told me.

Losing my virginity had been something I'd worried about in the past. I wasn't a nun in that I'd been privy to conversations in the school canteen and during drama practice. Mostly they were stories where sex wasn't all it was cracked up to be. However, being with Simon and the thought of how experienced he was, I knew my experience would be different.

"Do you finger yourself?" he probed, his finger gently circling my entrance, and I stared back at him. Heat rose to my cheeks, and I shook my head, feeling inadequate again. "Never?" I shook my head again and closed my eyes, almost ashamed by my lack of carnal knowledge.

Slowly his middle finger moved up and swirled around my swollen clit. Sliding it down the slit he probed my entrance gently. "Relax," he whispered, and his finger slid in further. My entrance burned for a few seconds and he stayed still waiting for me to adjust. I only realized how tense I was when my muscles relaxed. I took a deep breath.

"More?" he asked. I nodded, and his finger slid in to the knuckle. I winced and bit my lip as he continued to make small circles until it felt good. He moved over me and kissed me slowly then more passionately. Losing myself I moaned into his mouth and my hips began to move against his finger. Simon began to anticipate my movements and gently finger-fucked me until it didn't feel like it was enough.

Pulling his finger out, he replaced it with two and repeated the slow process of gently stretching and preparing me for more. When I was comfortable with his fingers, he curved them upwards rubbing one particular spot and I instantly came.

A burst of flashing lights erupted behind my closed eyes as my whole body quivered and shook. I grabbed his wrist to stop him because the pleasure was so intense, but he pulled my hand away, pinned it to the bed and scooted down again, replacing his fingers with his mouth.

My brain felt as if it were melting from how hard I came, and I screamed loudly, losing control. Breaking away from my pussy, Simon chuckled as my head flopped to the side. "You okay?" he enquired with a frown.

"Damn, that was incredible." My body felt drained, my voice croaky. I swallowed noisily as I waited for Simon's next move.

"Condoms?"

I nodded at the nightstand. After the first time I wasn't going to be caught out again. I had braved it in Walgreens and bought some but when I went to put them in the nightstand there were boxes of them already there.

When I had found them there I was mortified because Gibson or Chloe had thought about these before the day I moved in.

"You bought these?" he asked and seemed impressed.

"No, they were here when I moved in."

He smirked, knowingly.

"What?" I asked.

"Jonny," he said and chuckled.

"Jonny?" Jonny was Gibson's lead security detail. My heart rhythm stuttered in shock at the thought Gibson had sent him to buy them.

"It's what he does." He shrugged and looked amused as he reached into the drawer and pulled a twelve pack out. "To think they were here before and I—"

"What do you mean?" My voice sounded tense.

"Before Gibson met Chloe, Jonny used to be so convinced Gibson was going to contract some deadly venereal disease or have an unplanned child. Jonny was obsessed about it. He put condoms in every nightstand of every hotel room or any apartment Gibson visited."

"You're kidding, right?"

"Nope. This has Jonny's signature all over it; used to drive Gibson crazy. And from what Gib said Jonny's move almost made Gib crash and burn the first time he went to get jiggy with Chloe on a hired boat and reached into the drawer to grab one. Chloe thought his seduction was all pre-planned," he replied chuckling.

"I'm glad Jonny's put them here," he admitted, checking the date on the box before he took two out and dropped one on the bed, "because as much as I want to go bareback with you, I have to put you first, Piper. Your career is just beginning. I'd hate anything to disrupt your shot at success."

Tearing the foil with his teeth, he pulled out the latex rubber and stretched it over his cock. My eyes were transfixed at how it strained against the thin clear protective sheath. Simon noted me watching and chuckled, "Attractive, huh?" he joked before hovering over me and bending his neck to kiss me again.

I had thought when Simon put the condom on that sex was imminent, but I was wrong. Once again he worked me up, paying attention to my neck, my collarbone, my breasts, peppering kisses all over my body until I couldn't stand it any longer and begged him to take me.

His talented fingertips drew small lazy circles over my clit until I thought I was going to go mad if he didn't do more. My core pulsed with every erogenous zone he hit, and my fists twisted the sheets as his teasing became almost unbearable.

"What do you want me to do?" he eventually whispered, his hot breath fanning my face. I shivered in anticipation again.

"You... inside, but I'm so nervous I'm shaking," I answered with complete honesty.

Simon felt my entrance and poked his finger inside, pulled it out and sucked it. A jolt of electricity passed through my body at his sexy dirty move. "Mm," he hummed, smiling, and he moved, positioning himself between my legs.

Placing his hands under my thighs, he pushed them once more to my chest then spread them wide. "Perfect," he said, his voice husky as he slid his hands under my calves and supported my lower limbs. He glanced at me quickly then down to his cock, lining it up with my entrance.

As soon as I felt the contact, I swallowed hard and my pulse raced as he nudged himself forward breaching my entrance. My breath hitched, and I suddenly tensed with the tight burning sensation I felt as he stretched me.

"Fuck," he hissed, softly smoothing my hair with one hand before placing it back under my leg. "Relax, baby, look at me. Do you trust me?" I nodded. "Then breathe," he instructed.

Repositioning himself he hovered over me and bent his head. "All right," he reassured me. The strain in his arms barely hid his frustration. Dipping down his chest brushed against mine then he lifted it clear and pressed his hot lips to mine.

Kissing me slow and tender at first, I felt my body relax and I sagged into the mattress when the need in me gave in to the hot, passionate kiss. Noting I was less tense, Simon nudged his cock forward and the stinging sensation as he stretched me burned in my core. Stiffening again, I took a sharp breath and held it.

"Relax, baby" he told me again and I let my breath go. "Sorry," I offered.

"Don't be," he smiled reassuringly again. "You're gonna take a deep breath with me now," he demanded and inhaled in through his nose. Copying his command, I did as he told me, then exhaled slowly. As I did, he held my eyes hostage in his and nudged himself forward, gliding deep inside me in one fluid move.

"Oh, fuck," he said through a breath then growled with pleasure when he looked into my eyes. "So fucking tight," he said, and I saw him struggle for breath. He breathed out a shuddery breath in his effort to control how being inside me made him feel. "Oh, my, God." he murmured as his eyes bore into mine when he started to move until gradually the pain had subsided.

Taking his lead from me, Simon began to glide in and out slowly, still stretching me up as my body adjusted to his size. The strain was clear in the tension from the restraint he showed. Suddenly the need in me took over, and I went from his cock feeling too big to needing him deeper.

My hands flew to his hair, his back, then his butt, as I ground myself against him. Simon broke the kiss and looked down at me, then flashed me a sexy grin. He growled in satisfaction, like he loved my response to him. "There." He said as he rocked into me at a steady rhythm, "You like this?"

I nodded, smiled back at him and for some strange reason I suddenly felt a huge lump of emotion growing in my throat. Tears sprang to my eyes and I was shocked when I started to cry.

He froze, looking alarmed. "Shit, am I still hurting you?" he asked, concerned. His muscles were tense as he held his body ridged above me.

I shook my head, "No it feels good, I don't know what the tears are about."

His eyes softened, "Doing this for the first time is a big deal, beautiful," he said as he dipped his head to kiss my tears and continued to rock me slowly. Lifting one hand, he smoothed my hair down and cupped my chin between his finger and thumb.

"Want to try on top?" he offered quietly, and I nodded, "Might be a good idea for you to set the pace for a bit." I knew instinctively why he asked it of me. Knowing my fear of being controlled I figured he was trying to remove another barrier between us. My heart squeezed at how perceptive he was to my feelings.

Rolling me over, he sat me astride him. I admit I felt less vulnerable than I had been when I was on my back. Placing his hands on my hips he gently guided me, undulating my pussy against his hips until I took over the rhythm.

As soon as my confidence grew, his hands cupped my butt, spread it in his hands and began to move me faster. Suddenly it felt so good I never wanted him to stop.

CHAPTER TWENTY-TWO

*W*aking up next to Simon inches from me, my heart immediately picked up its pace. I lay quietly staring at his gorgeous face. He truly was an exceptionally good-looking man.

Simon was just like Gibson in that sense, they stood out from all others. Being in a talented rock band they oozed sex appeal without having to utter a word. Simon's enticing sexuality and power radiated from him even as he slept.

I'm not sure how long I lay there staring at him but eventually I slid out of bed and headed for the shower.

My mind was a cluster of snapshots of the way Simon had looked at me as he took me for the first time, his eyes closing slowly as he sunk deep between my legs. Flashes in my mind of him on his back staring up at me with a look that said it all really meant something to him.

Other memories surfaced of how sensually his hands had felt on me as they explored every inch of my skin and even as I followed my daily routine of showering. My core pulsed with memories of how careful and gentle he had tried to be and how he had ultimately made me feel.

As I rinsed my hair and opened my eyes, I almost fell to the floor startled as Simon's gorgeous face grinned wickedly and he chuckled at my reaction from the other side of the cubicle. "I see you've started without me," he smirked as he opened the glass door and stepped in beside me.

Turning me away from the shower, his shoulders and back took the bulk of the water while he pulled my back to his front and wrapped his warm arms around my waist. I felt protected and desired as his hands slid across my flat abdomen and his hard cock nestled along my butt crease.

"Morning, Princess." The sexy gruff tone in his voice was still husky as he brushed my wet hair seductively to one side and began to lavish small kisses across my shoulder then unexpectedly licked my neck.

'The way he said 'Princess' no longer held the same annoying slant to it, but instead it felt right.

"G'morning," I replied, my tone a little breathless from the effect of his touch as I relaxed against him. The sensation of his warm embrace was intoxicating.

"Thank you for last night." The way I felt, I should have been thanking him. He continued to kiss my neck and nibble my ear as he lavished me with attention. My pussy pulsed at his touch, betraying the sore ache I felt there still.

Simon's wandering hand slid lower to cup my pussy, his large fingers gliding down both sides of my clit and he pinched them together trapping my clit in a delicious tease.

"Ah," I moaned with delight and he sucked at my neck spreading a rash of goosebumps all over my body.

I shivered slightly as my pebbled nipples ached for attention. Simon slid one foot between my feet and spread my legs further apart.

"Even with the water from the shower I can feel how turned on you are. You're soaked," he told me, "You sore?" he asked with a note of concern in his tone.

"A little," I admitted, and he dropped to his knees. "Good, you'll remember me all day," he advised me and chuckled. Pushing me out of the shower he smacked my ass leaving me dizzy and breathless.

"Get dressed and I'll shout you breakfast, Princess. If I keep you here any longer, you won't be able to walk very far or concentrate on those last songs for the album."

A slow smile spread on his face, probably from the lost look on my face from him pushing me away.

As soon as I wrapped a towel around myself and turned to leave, he grabbed his own cock and stroked himself slowly.

Glancing from me to his cock he looked up and shrugged, "What? I know you gotta be sore right now and if I don't take care of myself I'll probably nail you at the studio during your break today."

The sexy threat in his voice made my heart flutter wildly for a moment. I'd never heard him talk with such intent before. "You need some help with that?" I offered and nodded to his hand hoping he'd say yes.

"Get the fuck out of here and let me get it over with or you won't be eating breakfast today." I smirked and turned away from him, believing every word he said.

I thought the day I lost my virginity was perfect. Between Simon playing on a track for my album and the way he took care of me made me the happiest I'd ever felt inside. I felt lucky, like another step forward in my new beginnings.

My good fortune carried over into the studio as track after track was laid down smoothly and the album was completed four days ahead of my allotted studio time.

Oddly, I had mixed feelings, elation mingled with the sense of an anti-climax when we made the final cut because everyone said making an album was much more difficult than I had found it to be.

I felt sad not to be working directly with Otto anymore. His experience and insight helped incredibly. He was a very gifted producer; and with Grunt for that matter, who had turned out to be a real blessing. Talking about blessings, I was thankful I didn't have to face Jeff again.

Simon had wanted to take me out to dinner to celebrate, but with the album complete I felt a little homesick, especially when I knew it was Melody's week at home with Gibson and Chloe. If I was being honest, I was torn between spending time with Simon, and seeing Melody. I really had missed her.

"I'll fly you up there," Simon offered. I hesitated because I didn't want to face another confrontation with Gibson. My heart and my head were conflicted because the last thing I wanted to happen was for Gibson and Simon to have another spat about me. Nor did I feel it appropriate to thrust my relationship with Simon in Gibson's face.

"What do you say?" he prompted when I hadn't replied. Before I could answer he sighed. "Gibson, huh?" Pinching my lips together, I nodded. I felt terrible because I saw the disappointment in Simon's eyes.

"I don't..." I shrugged, "I guess I feel..."

"What? What do you feel? Embarrassed that you're with me?"

"Of course I'm not. I know he appeared to accept our relationship, albeit reluctantly, but I don't know how he's going to react in his own home."

"React to what? You think you have a neon sign above your head that says, 'Simon's fucking the shit out of me', or you're walking bow-legged?" His remark was cutting.

Apart from when Simon had spoken with Gibson about me, it was the first time I'd heard him sound angry. A note of fear crept into me that I'd never felt before around him. As I tried to shrug it off he continued.

"We dealt with this already, Piper. Maybe you felt Gibson's visit put you under pressure, but our news is out there, baby. We're either together or we're not. I'm way too long in the tooth to be dealing with half and half. I laid out my intentions to Gibson and if I'm not mistaken you had no hesitation of doing that too. So, what's the problem?" He shrugged, staring seriously at me.

Simon challenging me made me face exactly what I was worried about. "I'm trying, Simon. It's not like any of this has been planned. Around three weeks ago, I was in the middle of nowhere planning to come here, and since then I haven't had time to draw breath with all that has happened."

"So what are you saying? Do you want me to back off... after all that's gone down between us?" Panic set in and I shook my head. Of everything, losing Simon was the last thing I wanted. I sighed.

"It's the last thing I want. I thought you would know this."

"Then what the fuck is it?" he asked, running his hand through his hair in frustration.

"I guess it's like any young girl taking a guy home for the first time where the dad isn't convinced he's right for his little princess. Good lord, now I'm even calling myself a princess."

"Want my two cents worth? If you don't take this to Gibson and force him to make peace with it, you'll be skirting around his ass for the foreseeable future." A stony silence fell between us. Simon stood and pulled his car keys from his pocket.

"I know everything's happened too fast. I've been here... been a part of this. You think I wanted it to go the way it has? I get it... you need time. Come on, I'll take you home to Colorado, then I'll head out. Before we got together I was heading up to Chicago next week to party with Lennox. If you're going back to Colorado, there's no point in me hanging around California."

My heart sank into my stomach. The last thing I wanted was to leave him and I felt torn between meeting my obligations to Melody and staying in California with him.

Swallowing past a lump in my throat I felt tears burn. I barely managed to keep them at bay as we stepped out of the studio. I walked less than six inches from Simon, but it felt as if we were miles apart.

Two avid reporters lurked by the studio door hoping for a sensational scoop of some kind and an old balding photographer took several candid pictures as we both kept our heads bowed and walked briskly toward the car.

Even I felt the contrast in our public display compared to the image of bliss we'd previously portrayed.

Simon hit the car fob and walked purposely around the hood, opened my door and quickly closed it after I had sat inside.

Less willing to engage with the press, he walked around the wide trunk and entered the driver's door avoiding the questions they called out completely.

When he started the engine, "Naivety" by A Day To Remember

played on the radio and I sunk low in my seat as he drove out the car lot and onto the open road. The route to my apartment had only just begun to feel familiar, but the feeling in the car was uneasy between Simon and me.

I'd never been around Simon where the conversation didn't flow, and I hated the feeling that the closeness we had slipped away with one difference of opinion.

"How long will you be gone?" He suddenly asked. "Didn't Otto say your PR team were setting up some gigs and interviews soon?"

"We've got auditions for the band first, then they'll form a schedule of PR for me. I'll be gone three, maybe four days. You?" I asked, fighting my distress that he was going to party without me. *What did I expect? That a man like Simon would sit around and do nothing while I took off to do my thing? Yes... maybe I did, or maybe it just never crossed my mind he wouldn't wait around.*

I stared at how tightly Simon's hands gripped the steering wheel and noted his shoulders looked locked with tension and I instantly felt his frustration.

Wasn't I doing exactly what Gibson was? It wasn't very adult to shy away from supporting Simon and showing Gibson we were serious. I was also depriving Simon from the opportunity to manage his relationship with Gibson.

Worse than that, I was doing what I swore I wouldn't, by trying to avoid any confrontation that we may face by turning up at home together. The reality of my circumstances hit me like a brick to the chest and I sighed. Sometimes I pissed myself off by getting in my own way. "Come," I blurted.

Simon's head snapped around, and he looked directly at me. He eyed me with suspicion and for too long for someone driving. I felt panic rise to my chest because I had no idea how he'd respond. Dropping his gaze, he turned it back to the road. "Why the change of heart?"

"Because I'm trying to be brave? Or maybe it's because I can't avoid Gibson's reactions forever... but mostly because I don't want to spend my free time apart from you." I sighed. "I should be supporting us, not hiding what we have."

"Yeah?" he asked, holding back a small smile as he turned again to check out how serious I was.

"Yeah. I mean I've a lot to learn about relationships and I know you're trying to be patient with me, so I guess I need to remember that and meet you halfway."

"Do it for you, Piper. Not for me."

"I am doing it for me... and you," I added, and reached over, placing my hand on his thigh. Dropping his hand from the wheel he turned my hand palm up and laced his fingers in mine. Lifting them up to his mouth he pressed a kiss to my knuckles.

"Thank fuck for small mercies, because the thought of dropping you off and leaving you there has been eating away at my gut for the past five minutes. The best way to handle this is to meet Gibson head on." He said it with such conviction I never doubted he was right for a minute.

"Chloe's a great ally. She'll keep him calm... make him see sense," he sighed. "I get it with him, Piper. He thinks I'm only out to corrupt you, and as I keep saying, brutal honesty is the best I can offer. There have been many women in my past, but none have made me feel the way I do about you. Christ, I sound like a broken record but the way I feel about you, I'm serious when I tell you I hope you're the last."

At my place, Simon's eyes followed me diligently around the room as I grabbed some lingerie and clothing before stuffing them into my weekend case.

As I casually moved around the room, I tried to discuss how to approach Gibson about us arriving together, but when I suggested where he would sleep to spare Gibson's feelings out of my respect for him, Simon shut me down.

"No fucking way. You think Gibson would have slept in another room if he'd gone to Chloe's parents' place? Would he fuck. He'd rather have cut his own dick off," he said in frustration. "You're mine and I'm not waiting four fucking days to have you back in my bed. That's the equivalent of taking a sugar junkie into Krispy Kreme donuts and say you can choose one donut hole... no pun intended," he smirked.

"We'll play it by ear," I said, zipping the case closed and pulling it to the end of the bed. Before I could lift it, Simon sprang to his feet and lifted it like it was weightless off of the mattress and stuck it under his arm. "It has wheels, Simon," I said pointing them out.

"Playing by ear, are we? Then you'd do well to remember I'm pitch perfect. But, baby, that doesn't only apply to my music. You and I are in the same bed if I'm going." His firm demand made me swallow nervously.

Simon shook his head and laughed as he pulled me into his side. "Jesus, Princess, it'll be fine." I felt my face flush, and he chuckled heartily, kissed me on the temple and led me toward the door.

I didn't reply, but I knew my bravado wouldn't last until we got all the way to Colorado.

CHAPTER TWENTY-THREE

*M*y smile was wide as I heard the excitement in Chloe's voice when I told her I was on my way home. I told her Simon was bringing me and her conversation didn't drop a beat which was a positive sign in my view.

By the time we took off from Santa Monica, Melody was already in bed and Chloe had thought it best I sleep in the pool house because we weren't expected to land until 10pm.

I already knew Melody was a light sleeper; she woke up every time the alarm was reset on the house so that made perfect sense.

The sleeping arrangements suited me fine because it meant I didn't have to face Gibson until morning and that gave me time to adjust to being back home. If he wanted to challenge Simon being there at least it would be out of Melody's earshot.

Both Simon and I were dead on our feet by the time we arrived and after a quick shower we flopped into bed. It had been a very long day, but it wasn't too long for us not to enjoy each other's bodies.

Exhausted and sweating, we lay heaving for breath as Simon turned and swiped a few stray wet strands of hair from my forehead. "Damn, baby, you learn fast. I figure if I'm not careful you'll wear me out."

"I'll try," I replied, turning to grin at him and he scooped me into his side. I laid my head on his chest. Once I had made myself comfortable, I listened contentedly to the strong steady beat of his heart. The feel of his warm, smooth, satiny skin under my palm felt perfect and the smell of his scent engulfed me in a feeling of security I had never felt before. Stroking my back gently, he let out a long sigh.

"I can't explain how happy you make me feel, Princess," he whispered.

"Yeah?" I murmured, still finding it a little surreal I was all he wanted.

"You bet your sweet ass," he replied and bent his head to kiss my temple. Getting more comfortable, he nestled my head just under his chin, placed his large hand possessively over my butt cheek and held me firmly in place.

"Sleep, baby," he muttered, then he inhaled deeply and let out a long slow breath. I lay listening to the steady rhythm of his breaths after that until his heart beat slowed and his breathing got deeper. Eventually my eyes became so heavy I couldn't stay awake any longer.

A text alert woke me.

Chloe: You may want to get over here, honey, I think your rock star may need your support.

For a moment I was confused then I realized Simon was already out of bed and I was in the pool house on my own. The fresh mountain air had knocked me out and when I glanced at the time it was already 10:30 am.

Guilt rolled through me because I knew instinctively Simon had chosen to face Gibson on his own. Swiftly, I moved around the room, showering quickly to wash the smell of sex from my body.

I shrugged into some jeans and a sweater and headed over to the house. I stopped for a second and took a large gulp of cool mountain air before I went inside.

My heartbeat grew quicker with every step that I took, wondering what kind of reception I would receive when Gibson saw me because I knew in the cold light of day the comments he had made the last time I saw him would hardly be the last.

Pulling the slider open into the music room I padded down the hallway toward the kitchen, but I didn't get that far before I heard Gibson and Simon's voices raised in a heated discussion.

"You couldn't keep your hands to yourself, could you?"

"No, Gibson, I couldn't, but it's not how you think."

"And how is that?" Gibson bellowed.

"Newsflash, you're not the only one who wants to protect her."

Gibson scoffed, "So what? You're gonna tell me you're fucking her to protect her?"

"I'm not tapping her," Simon said, and my heart almost stopped. *He's denying we've slept together?* "I swear she's not the same as the others. I wouldn't use a girl like Piper. You think I'd risk all what we are to each other for a quick fuck? You know me better than that, dude. If that's all I wanted I would have done that with anyone else in a heartbeat. You know how many texts land on my phone every day? The constant offers from girls who would let me do anything to them I had a mind to do?" This was another part of the mystery about Simon I was yet to learn. I hated hearing this.

"And there it is. This is exactly why I don't want you around, Piper. She deserves the fucking world after all she's been through." Gibson sounded furious.

"She's entering an industry where there are so many sex hungry guys like we were waiting in the wings to pluck a gorgeous little peach like her."

Gibson's voice bit back loudly, "What do you mean were? I may have changed, but it's a weekly event for you to be linked with someone else."

"Yeah, and I told you the press made that up about Jess and me. I swear there's been no one else since Piper... no one for months before her."

Gibson scoffed but didn't speak.

"You don't believe me? Take a look online. You won't find any women on my arm. I've been extra careful lately and I haven't had sex in months. Clean living and a change in direction were long overdue for me and let me tell you, it's not been easy." Simon sighed, "Gibson what I'm saying is Piper is worth changing for."

"So you're a changed man, Si? Just like that?"

"No. I've explained how it is and you of all people should know how hard it is to change opinions. If you don't believe me maybe we should get Jess on the phone."

Silence fell between them and I thought I should show myself, but Simon spoke again before I could move. "You gonna tell me you'll take them all on, Gib? Why not trust me? I don't want to break her heart, I'm serious about her. Are you saying there's no one worse for her than me? Maybe someone who won't give a fuck about her feelings or be able to take care of her the way I want to?"

"Simon, I don't doubt at this minute how you feel. You forget I know you, so I know you can treat a girl right when it suits, it's what happens when you get bored. We've been here before." My heart stopped, hearing Gibson tell him that.

"No I haven't, Gibson. The only similarity is Amy's age to Piper's, and I was twenty-three back then." *Who's Amy?* I wondered.

"Have you forgotten the way her father beat you for how you treated her? Don't make me regret carrying your sorry wounded ass to the van and driving you to hospital." A shock of electricity ran through me that someone had hurt Simon in the past.

"Gibson, I'm really trying to give you your place right now with Piper, but let's do this. We've never really spoken about what happened since, so as we're being so fucking honest let's bring it all to the table. You weren't so fucking innocent in all that happened, Gib, or have you forgotten you fucked Amy as well?" Gibson fell silent for a few moments then his voice was much less volatile.

"No. I haven't forgotten. I had her first. She begged, remember?" Gibson said in a quieter voice.

"Then you asked me to take her off your hands," Simon added. I cringed at the distasteful conversation between them.

"I'm not proud of how that turned out, but she was there night after night and I had no attraction to her in the first place. It was me who placated her at first, but the chick freaked out when I said I wasn't interested and went out of her way to fuck anything around her that moved."

"Of all the guys, you were the one who kept the conversation going. You shouldn't have given her mixed messages, Si."

"Jesus, Gibson. I slept with her once and I did tell her there was no future beforehand. It wasn't my fault she became fixated on me and the reason I tried to placate her was because it became pretty apparent she had emotional issues. The reason her father beat my ass was because I was the name she couldn't stop talking about. I was doing you a favor."

"Maybe...at the beginning," Gibson said then left the conversation hanging.

Hearing how Simon blew some girl out made me feel a lot less settled about him, but from what he had said in his defense, it sounded as if Gibson wasn't a saint in the incident either. The way they both spoke, I got the idea neither Simon nor Gibson had any respect for the girls that they slept with before.

My guts twisted in my stomach and depression settled in my chest at how flippantly he and Gibson discussed what had happened in the past, but what affected me the most was the girl they mentioned was around my age back then and not how I imagined groupies to be. *Weren't they only out to fuck a rock star?*

Worst of all, of the thousands of women they had come into contact with over the years, this one had a name and that made her more memorable to Simon than the rest.

"You broke her heart, Simon. How long before you break Piper's? She's fucking precious to us and not nearly as strong as she appears to be."

"I never led Amy on and you need to start giving Piper more credit. She's not Amy and I'm not twenty-three anymore. Shit, you're not being fair because that incident was almost ten years ago."

"Yeah, and there's never been a steady girl since."

"Amy wasn't steady. You're not listening to me, and the reason I've not had a steady woman is because I never clicked with anyone the way I have with Piper." He sighed heavily. "Like it or not, me and you aren't that different, Gib. I knew you back then. Piper and I... we're doing this."

There was a pause in their conversation again and I thought I'd make my entrance, but Simon wasn't done.

"Let me ask you this. Say... for the sake of argument this doesn't work out between us. Who does she have to turn to? You think she's gonna confide in you? Chloe? Can't you see you're pushing her back to where she was right before her mom died? She'd have no one."

I'd heard enough, and I had a choice. Either I walked into the kitchen and stood united with Simon or I asked Gibson to put his finger on what it was about Simon that made him feel so determined to push us apart.

Chloe's flip-flops clapped noisily in the distance and I knew if I stood there much longer she'd find me. Tiptoeing back to the sliders I quickly opened and closed it more noisily to alert them of my presence.

"Morning, sweetheart, was the bed in the pool house okay?" I felt myself blush because Simon and I wrecked the bed—well the bed sheets at least—and I felt a wave of shyness at Simon being with me. *Get a grip, you're twenty for heaven's sake.* I glanced up at Chloe and tried to look her in the eyes.

"Yeah it was so comfortable. I passed right out when I got into bed last night after my shower," I lied.

Chloe saw right through me and smirked, then chuckled. "Gibson was having a meltdown because Simon came with you. I had to talk him down from the roof and make him stay in our room when he heard the plane land."

I glanced at the floor feeling more than a little awkward because although I was an adult and could do what I liked, most girls got to choose who knows when they enter into a relationship with a man or go all the way. However, because I was with Simon, I was robbed of my privacy or the privilege to choose who to tell.

"You may feel like it's none of my business, honey, but can I offer you some advice?" I hesitated and nodded, fully expecting a lecture about how to protect my heart against Simon.

"Gibson had a tough upbringing, but when he loves he loves hard.

Whether that's being in love or protecting those he cares about. You are so special to the both of us... all three of us. To little Melody you are her sister too."

Chloe flashed me a warm smile and placed her hand on my shoulder. She wasn't a 'touchy feely' person after what had happened to her, but I knew she loved me. I smiled affectionately in return. "Stay strong. If you really believe in this thing with Simon, then stand your ground. Gibson will learn to accept what you have, but please cut him some slack for having your best interests at heart."

Linking arms with me she led me into the kitchen. "Look what the wind blew in," she said, turning to give me a hug that caught me by surprise. "Breakfast?" she asked, pulling away from me and addressing everyone like nothing had been going on between both men.

I glanced at Simon who immediately got out of his chair and walked over to meet me. "Good morning, baby," he said, mindful that Gibson was in the room. Bending, he gave me a quick peck on the lips and pulled back. I was thankful when he didn't appear to push our relationship in Gibson's face.

Simon smoothed my hair down and cupped my chin. "Sleep well, sweetheart?" the look he gave me was a little intense and I saw Gibson glare from the side of my eye.

"Yeah, I was dead to the world. You should have woken me," I said, and narrowed my eyes. Simon chuckled and broke away from his embrace. "Nah, you were exhausted after the journey up here," he replied.

Ignoring his comment, I rounded the table to where Gibson sat and grabbed the butter toasted bagel from his plate. Taking a crunchy bite, I dropped it back in place, then I slung my arms around his neck and kissed him on the cheek. Gibson chuckled because it was a move he usually would have made and the mood in the room lightened instantly.

"Morning, Gibson. Tell me you're pleased to see me. It feels so good to be home with you guys. I can't wait to let you hear the demo of the album. Otto sent it to my phone this morning, but I haven't had the chance to listen to it. I thought the four of us could do that right after breakfast. I'm dying to share it with you to hear what you think."

Pushing back his chair, he pulled me in for one of his bear hugs and the love I felt for him made my heart swell.

"Can't wait, can we, darlin'? " he said to Chloe, "If you're singing on it, baby girl, I know I'm gonna love it, just as much as I love you." Turning his head, he glanced to Simon and gave a small sigh. "Si was just telling me how you killed the third to last track with a new arrangement when he jammed with you."

Without saying so, Gibson had offered a small peace offering when he mentioned Simon and it made me feel less apprehensive of spending time in the company of both of them.

"Yeah, he's a genius... you both are. If it weren't for the two of you, I'd never have had the confidence to push myself this way. Simon has also been a godsend in keeping Jeff in order and helping me to deal with the press. Apart from you, I don't think I could have had anyone better."

Simon smirked at me and looked down at the table while Gibson cracked a grin. "Piper, I'm trying to get my head around all this, but I ain't stupid. I saw what you did there, and even though you're right, there's no need to butter me up by saying I'd be the best man for the job." He shrugged, "Because I already know that."

CHAPTER TWENTY-FOUR

*P*ride shone in Gibson and Chloe's eyes when they heard the final cut. I wished I could have videoed the way Gibson rocked out to a couple of the numbers we had collaborated on because he was totally in his zone.

I knew he loved the drums, but to see him knock out the beat on a small table with his hands was something else.

I found myself giggling because he was singing a song about a woman loving her man and it was difficult not to see the funny side with his huge deep voice and his alpha vibe going on.

My heart almost burst with delight when I felt his warm hands surrounding me from behind.

Plucking me clean out the chair Gibson spun me around still singing the words of the song and I continued laughing.

"There ain't many men who can sing these words and stare out the punks with a straight face, baby girl. I'm comfortable enough in my own skin to sing anything and dare the fucker who'd challenge me about it to come forward. I've never met a guy who'd square up to me apart from Jonny."

Watching Chloe chuckle as he continued to spin me around, I

suddenly got the warmest feeling and knew exactly how it felt to be loved by a father.

Even if he wasn't my natural father and hadn't brought me up, Gibson had shown me more love, time, and attention in just over two years than my mother's partner ever had in seventeen years.

As Gibson sat down Simon caught my wrist when the slowest song of the album began to play. It was the neatest love song I'd ever heard, and I was excited to have been given it to sing. It was written by a world-famous artist and I couldn't believe my luck when we won the bid to record it.

Pulling me into his chest, Simon held his hand and mine to his chest and placed his other across the center of my back.

We were dancing waltz style; his body held some inches from mine, and I thought for a moment it was out of respect for Gibson until it came to the bridge when he pulled me sharply into his chest. Placing his cheek next to mine he sang softly, and it felt so romantic despite Gibson and Chloe being in the room.

Conscious Gibson and Chloe were probably watching, I tried hard to ignore what they may have taken from the scene and concentrated on how willing Simon was to show them his feelings for me. The least I could do was meet him halfway and invest in the moment with him.

When the song ended, Simon kissed my forehead and pulled his head back just enough to look into my eyes. "Baby, that song is so dope. You do realize it's gonna be played at almost every wedding in the states for the next fifty years, right?" I turned my head to look at Gibson and he nodded slowly in agreement.

"I hate to admit it but he's not wrong. The purity in your voice and those words don't make that a great song, it makes it a cut above." Gibson agreed. "From what I've heard Otto has done an amazing job in production and if I'm not mistaken you're gonna be so in demand you'll hardly have time to shit."

"Gibson, is that really necessary?" Chloe admonished.

Chuckling at Chloe's scolding, Gibson stood and swept her off her feet, "What? You keep telling me I need to let her be the adult she is, she's about to learn what it is to be told when to shit, where, and how much, because I can see a great future for our baby girl here, even if she went ahead and ignored my advice."

Stepping from Simon to Gibson, I flung my arms around his waist and cuddled in tight, then did the same to Chloe. "If it weren't for you, I wouldn't be here at all and the fact I've been given this chance at all is a privilege. Anything else is a bonus.

At 3:45 pm Melody burst in through the door, closely followed by Emma, Chloe's security. Melody was her responsibility even when she was at home with her birth mom. Emma did the school run with Jerry, Monday through Friday, and Gibson had hired a young female for Melody for all the other times.

"Where is she?" Melody screeched as her flat shoes pitter pattered down the tiled floor of the hallway and into the music room. Lunging at me, she hugged me so tight it hurt. Leaning back, she grinned widely and kissed the end of my nose. "I missed you so much," she gushed and hugged me tight again.

"I missed you too, Ladybug," I admitted and was surprised when she ran over and climbed up on Simon's knee.

"Can we go swimming? Mom said if I was good, you may take me swimming," she asked from her perched position on his lap. Her little face looked so bright with excitement I would never have turned her down.

"Sure, go get your bathing suit on and meet me by the pool house, but no trying to remove the cover until the adults are with you, got it?"

"Cross my heart; it's more than my life's worth with him around," she said, nudging her head and throwing her thumb in Gibson's direction. She'd obviously heard someone talking and mimicked their comment. Gibson grabbed her by her waist, spun her upside down and carried her on his shoulder with one hand.

"You're getting way too smart mouthed for a kid your age," he said, playfully.

"Is that so?" she said in a comeback

Chloe covered her mouth with her hand to hide her smile and

Gibson pretended to sound annoyed, "I see a paddle in your future, baby girl," he teased.

"Oh, you're taking me boating? Yippee," she shot back and dissolved in a fit of giggling when Gibson spun her into his arms and began to tickle her. No matter whether Gibson and I were having a little difficulty seeing eye to eye, watching him with Melody gave me huge insight. He was the same way with all the women in his life and no matter what happened with Simon and me, I knew Gibson's love was unconditional.

A swim with Melody was never only a swim. Within ten minutes of pulling off the protective cover to the pool designed to keep her from accidently drowning, we were blowing up inflatable slides, digging noodles out of the poolside storage boxes, and assembling polo nets to play ball.

Gibson and Simon were on one side of the net and Chloe, Melody, and I were on the other. Splashing, ducking, and cheating were Melody's main tactics and because I was on the same team as her, naturally we won, but I had to admit there was nothing like the heart of a child to pull everyone together.

By the time she went to bed, I'd read, glued, and glittered a project with her for her show and tell session at school. Then she sang three songs with me after showing me her latest skill of playing the scales on her new half-size guitar.

The girl definitely had Gibson's genes. Kissing her forehead, she hugged me tight once more and reminded me for the umpteenth time how much she loved me.

I was about to leave the room when Gibson and Chloe both came in to kiss her goodnight and I watched them interact with her from the doorway.

From Chloe's perspective it didn't matter who Melody's mother was, she was part of Gibson and that was all the excuse Chloe had needed to welcome Melody into the fold with open arms. I hoped

Melody would one day realize how fortunate she was to have such an amazing step-mom in her life.

"Piper, wait up, sweetheart," Gibson said as I began to head for the stairs. Chloe was still with Melody. Wandering up to me, he put his hand around my shoulder and squeezed me sideways into him.

"Thanks for coming back so soon. I was worried about how the little lady would cope now that you're gone. She told me a minute ago she knows you'll come back when you can now that you've been back once."

I sighed. My leaving had been hard on all of us as we'd grown so close. "It's not been easy, trust me. It's only been a short time and I've missed you all like crazy, but having Simon around has felt like a little bit of home, you know?"

Drawing a deep breath, he studied my face for a minute, his wise eyes reading how I felt about being with Simon. "He's really making you happy?" he asked with a note of concern.

"Who?" I joked refusing to allow another tense standoff.

"All right, I hear you. I'll back off and hope to hell the fucker's got his act together, 'cause God forbid..." He glanced at me and smirked awkwardly then shook his head, "I'm doing it again, huh?" he asked, not needing an answer.

"I know you love me. Simon knows you love me, but Simon and I will be whatever is meant. I'm prepared for a letdown and if it makes you feel any better no matter how I feel about any man, Simon included, they'll never put me down. I'd walk first."

"You are one tough little cookie." I took his comment as a compliment.

"And you're a pain in the ass," I replied, to use Simon's description of him when he annoyed him.

"I hear you. Jesus, between you, Chloe, and Melody, I have no chance of ruling my own domain."

"Now that's not true, Gibson, none of us have access to your webpage," I replied pretending I had no idea what he was talking about.

"I'll make you a deal, Piper. I'll get off your case if you promise you'll turn to Chloe if ever you're unhappy. The last thing I want is for you ever to feel there's no one you can seek advice from, or even only to vent."

I turned properly toward him and hugged him hard. "Thank you, Gibson. Simon really has been amazing to me and I'm not stupid enough to think this is going to be anything but a challenge for the both of us but knowing we have you and Chloe behind us means everything."

To me, the people in that pool today were the only ones that mattered in my life.

"Like you said before, Gibson, we're more than blood now and what affects you affects me, so I never want you to think the decisions I've made in my life have been taken lightly."

Chloe came out of Melody's room and Gibson immediately stepped back from me and hugged his wife to his side. "She settled?" he asked, and Chloe nodded.

"Yeah but not before she tried to talk me into some Luke Bryan concert tickets," she added with another small chuckle.

"She's definitely her father's daughter. As a kid I had a sixth sense for sniffing out an opportunity," he said, threw his head back and belly-laughed.

True to his word, Gibson didn't jibe Simon all evening after that. In fact the two men appeared to have buried the hatchet somewhere other than in each other's back. It made me feel good that they were able to continue with their friendship without our relationship driving a wedge between them.

Chloe took me over to Dignity, her safe-house facility, and we spoke to a new family: a young mother and three small children. I told her my story, and she thanked me before we left them to settle and headed back to the house.

The instant we walked within sight, Simon's eyes met mine and a sexy smile graced his lips. "There you are, I'm beat," he said, yawning, and I yawned in response then smiled. "God, I love that smile," he told me as he stood and scooped me into his side.

My smile grew wider, and I glanced at Gibson who was already out of his chair and on his way toward me. "Night, baby girl," he said holding his arms out, and I stepped away from Simon and into his arms.

~

The rest of the trip went better than I expected and true to his word Gibson tried hard to accept Simon and I were together, save the occasional jaw tick when Simon pulled me onto his lap and patted my butt.

I knew Simon wasn't doing it purposely to aggravate him; all he was doing was showing his affection and reacting naturally to being around me.

Poor little Melody cried buckets the day we left, and I felt like the worst sister in the world, but she brightened with hope when Chloe promised her a girlie weekend at my place as soon as I had finished my tour with Layla Hartmann.

"Glad you decided to bring me?" Simon asked as I sat facing him on the opposite seat on the plane.

"I am. You were right, I was being a pussy," I admitted and glanced up into his eyes.

"Say that again?"

"What?"

"Pussy?" His lips curled up into a smile. "Never heard you say it before." He chuckled to himself and I swatted him.

"I'm sure I've said It before," I blurted out through a giggle.

"Nope, but you have my permission to break out that pretty, potty mouth anytime, baby," he goaded playfully, and I tried not to blush as he moved over, slid into the seat beside me and wrapped his arms tightly around me.

"Jesus Christ, I just wanna eat you." He growled, "You're so fucking adorable when you're flustered, Princess." I readjusted myself and fought off my shyness by placing my head on his shoulder. He sighed. "Get some rest, hon, because when I get you home there won't be much sleeping going on."

CHAPTER TWENTY-FIVE

a week after returning to Santa Monica, my life became insanely busy. Simon and I had spent every waking moment getting to know more about each other at his place, then when I wasn't working we spent time at mine.

We spoke about the Amy thing I'd overheard in Colorado, but after he explained it, I accepted he felt bad but from what he told me nothing about the incident was down to him.

Maybe I should have been put off by his open conversations of the women he used to date and the antics he used to get up to, but from my perspective it was important to know exactly how his life had been before me.

With each admission I was a little more overawed, but he was insistent I had his complete honesty because like he told me, if I was aware I could prepare.

In the music business it was highly likely I'd come across some of the women he'd been with. If that were the case I knew I'd have to develop a pretty thick skin.

Each new revelation he disclosed about his past was frank but sensitively delivered and I knew he didn't want to hurt me by raking over old coals although there was more than one occasion where I had to remind myself why he was telling me it all.

Listening to how many women Simon had been connected to wasn't easy, but I knew what his lifestyle was before I came along and once I had the gist of the extent of his promiscuous past I could see why Gibson felt the way he did.

Meeting women linked to Simon was obviously the last thing I would have wished for, but I had to accept if I was going to hang with a man twelve years my senior, I could hardly be upset by his history.

At thirty-two years of age, I knew few people would be in a position where there were no skeletons in the closet, and a huge rock star such as Simon could have been expected to have many more. At least there had been no marriages, messy divorces, or children, to factor into the equation.

Instead of Simon putting me off him with all the stories of drunken debauchery and his dirty one-night-stands, it drew us closer.

This may have seemed strange to most people but the way we viewed it, him explaining would feel like less of a blow than hearing it elsewhere.

Knowing exactly how he functioned before me, gave me a clear understanding of how Simon viewed his life... especially on the road.

At work, my marketing and PR team really got to grips with shaping a firm 'Piper' branding. They focused on everything from the music similarities of other artists right down to the shoes I wore. Their aim was to ensure everything about me was instantly recognizable and associated with me.

Then there were the constant photo shoots. I'd never posed for so many pictures in my life. Taking advice on interview technique and presentation, what questions to answer and which to avoid, was exhausting.

However, by the time I was ready for my first television interview, I had much more self-awareness of how I presented myself and felt more confident.

When I came out of makeup to do my first live interview, I felt a ball of nerves, both with anxiety and excitement. My eyes scanned the vast open studio as I sought out Simon to gauge his reaction to my appearance.

I could hardly wait to see what he thought because when I had glanced at my reflection in the mirror I thought I looked sophisticated and womanly instead of the plain girl in my daily existence.

The instant he saw me he smiled before he eyed me speculatively and his jaw dropped. He looked stunned, and I smiled coyly expecting a flurry of compliments, but when his jaw snapped shut and he shook his head as he strode over toward me I knew he wasn't happy.

"Who the fuck did this to you?" he asked when he reached me. Holding me by my elbows he spun around to look for someone. Anger radiated through his hands and I had no understanding as to why. I'd only had a quick peek in the mirror but I had thought I looked great.

"Goddammnit, get all that shit off her face; she's fucking gorgeous as she is. What the fuck? She doesn't need that crap plastered all over her face to be noticed. Look at her. Did you use Crayola Crayons to get this look?"

Simon continued to give the makeup artist a dressing down and instead of me stepping out toward the studio to wait for the television presenter, my makeup was hastily redone with the minimum amount necessary for the television cameras and lights not to make me look pale and pasty.

On closer inspection, I had to admit once she had taken some off, it did look better.

"There's my beautiful woman," he praised.

"Don't you like me to look dressed up?" I asked, wondering briefly if Simon only wanted me because I looked much younger. I considered whether the novelty of me would wear off as I matured.

"Fuck no, Piper. You don't need all that shit on your face is what I'm saying. There was so much foundation and heavy eye make up on you a drag queen would have been proud."

I chuckled and felt relieved because when I thought about it, I had been very heavily made up. It had taken forever for the makeup artist to apply it and I had never seen anyone apply as many layers. I figured the makeup artist knew what she was doing and never questioned the over-the-top application she'd done.

"You really have to put your foot down with these image people, otherwise they'll start saying things like you're too fat, 'let's give you a little filler, honey', or plump your lips. Next thing you know your face looks like a puffed-up pillow and your speech is slurred. Promise me you won't get sucked into this shit."

After the interview, I met with Thomas who had also flown in, and we had fun holding open music auditions for my backing band. We wanted three guys and two girl backing singers but the standard of the candidates was so high we had trouble choosing who to pick.

Prior to the final choices, Thomas had me interview them too because they were the band who'd become my tribe and support me while I found my feet in the music industry.

Eventually we kept Wyatt from the studio as my piano player, selected a cool drummer named Austin, and a Scottish guy called Kerr who was an exceptional guitarist. Instead of two girls, we chose a sweet girl called Petra, and a neat looking guy, Isiah, who each had strong vocal ranges that blew us away.

They were all very grateful they'd been chosen, but in truth it was me who was indebted to them because I knew I'd be nothing in a live setting without them.

Thankfully, all of them appeared to be easy going people, and I bonded with them quickly, but there was an immediately infinity between me and Kerr. At two years older than me, he liked the same kinds of music, shared the same ideas, and was fun to be around.

Getting to know all of them was a blast and within weeks we were firm friends. They worked hard and were up to speed on the album picks and the occasional improvisations I made that let people know when I sang it was live and by the time I was ready to join Layla Hartmann they were as eager to get started as I was.

I liked that Kerr was European because he saw things from a different perspective and had come to the USA as a teen when his father, an oil worker, came to Texas to work as an engineer for one of the oil giants.

Witty as heck, he brought sunshine to my day, and we fell into an easy friendship from day one. Simon eyed him warily when he met him, and it made me chuckle.

With each day that passed we grew closer and within a few weeks I felt I'd known him all my life. I couldn't begin to explain how much he meant to me in such a short time.

I'd never had a friend I trusted enough to confide in before, yet I found myself telling him about my past. Usually I was a very private person, but somehow it had been important to me that he understood what had happened to me.

Perhaps it was a subconscious decision, in the event I did something unwittingly to screw up our friendship.

During the three weeks we were getting set up, we spent long hours rehearsing and working with the PR team in readiness for the schedule that lay ahead.

Simon came down to Santa Monica twice during the first week we rehearsed but became frustrated and restless when I couldn't spare any time for him.

Eventually Simon became impatient, probably due to always getting what he wanted before. He decided to go back to Los Angeles to hang out with some friends and I felt relieved.

All I did was apologize for not being able to see him. Guilty for not being able to spend time with him. Then even although I knew he was right to leave, I felt a sense of loss when he did.

I tried to accept that our lives would be this way if we continued to be together. I'd had back-to-back interviews while he visited, yet soon after he left, I found I had more time here and there where we could have spent time together—but he had gone.

Once our schedule started, I had very little time for anyone other than the musicians in my backing band and for the first time in my life I truly felt part of something much bigger, a place where it was accepted that I had to take the lead. Unlike when I was a teenager and snagged the main part in a play where others felt it was theirs by right, due to a sense of entitlement.

"Hey, beautiful, what's with the frown?" Kerr asked as he slumped into the band bus couch beside me and nudged our shoulders together.

"I know right? You'd think I'd be feeling elated at being taken from place to place to introduce myself to the public."

"And you're not?"

"Well, yeah I am, but I miss being with Simon and I'm a little homesick for my family." Kerr had no idea who my new family were, just that someone had stepped up as my guardian when my mom was dying.

Although we had grown close, my connection to the Barclays was the one thing I had kept to myself. One good thing about Simon and I being outed by the press was all the guys in the band already knew this before they had been taken on.

Even though I had been pretty open with him about my mom and Colin, I held back on telling him about the Barclays. I'd fought hard to keep that part of my life private and until I had put myself out there, I preferred not to tout my connection to Gibson about.

Kerr reached over and with his finger and thumb stretched my frown to a smile. I grinned widely at his attempt to cheer me up and he smiled warmly in return. "Sorry," I offered by way of an apology, rolling my head to the side to look at him.

My guitarist was possibly the best-looking boy I'd ever seen, with his gray-colored eyes, deep tan, and dark brown hair cut close to his head.

He looked more like a marine than a musician. There was something about Kerr that drew me in... something that made me feel I could always be myself and he'd accept me.

"That's more like it. When you smile, you light up the room... or the bus." He sniggered, and I blushed at his compliment. Completely ignoring any awkwardness I emitted, he stared at me with a quizzical look. "What can I do to cheer you up?" he asked, wiggling his brows mischievously.

I felt myself blush because our faces were close. He gave me a more scrutinizing look.

"I'm fine... missing Simon I guess."

His smile fell immediately, and he eyed me curiously, "That bad, huh?" He sighed and slowly leaned over, lifting a small wisp of hair that had fallen over my eye. Moving it to the side of my head he sighed again.

"Sorry, that was annoying me," he said, still staring back at me like what he'd done was nothing. It didn't feel like nothing to me. Everything from how close we were sitting, the familiarity in the way he interacted with me, and the natural way he moved my hair out of my eyes felt intimate... but not uncomfortable.

I looked away and took a deep breath because the air felt heavy between us. "Want to do something later when we stop?"

"Like what?" I asked, turning back to look at him again.

"I dunno. Ten-pin bowling with the rest of them, or we could catch a movie? Depends what there is to do when we get there." Both sounded great. I'd never done either.

"Sounds good, but I don't know how to play."

Kerr sat forward and turned toward me, his eyes wide with surprise. "You've never been bowling?"

"No, I guess I missed out on most fun things growing up," I admitted.

"Then we're gonna put that right, Miss Piper." He eyed me with a new determination, leaned over and held my hand for a second, "Tell me what you've never done that you would like to, and we'll try to find things during the road trips. You can make a bucket list of all the activities you'd like to do, and we'll make it happen."

My heart squeezed with affection because Kerr had become an important source of comfort to me during the previous few weeks and with every day that passed we got closer.

Traveling up the coast between San Francisco and Seattle, the weather was notably cooler. The fall colors painted the most amazing scenery that I knew I'd never tire of looking at.

Burnt amber and deep red along with twenty shades of brown and yellow leaves made me stare in wonder. During those precious moments of peace, I reflected on my past and allowed myself to feel the pain I hid inside.

My mom never got to experience the seasons with me and although I was very proud of what I had achieved, the one person I would have chosen above all others to share it with would never know I made it.

At other times Kerr and I sat slumped, side by side on the bus couch, either we talked, or I read while he had long private message conversations with his girlfriend on Facebook, while I did the same with Simon. It was nice to have someone I could share something exciting or funny Simon told me with.

As we moved further up the coast and the nearer we got to Seattle the more nervous I became. My stomach churned at the thought of meeting an iconic music legend such as Layla Hartmann.

Ms. Hartmann had been an A-list music act since before I was born. These days she did smaller tours in smaller venues, which were still terrifying in numbers to me. A few thousand crowd instead of the fifty thousand my boyfriend was used to, but he said those numbers were exactly the right size for someone like me starting out. *What if Layla doesn't like me? What if she changes her mind? What if I screw up on stage? What then?*

During a moment of insecurity, I voiced my concerns to Kerr then was immediately sorry I'd opened my mouth. Giving me a long-winded lecture about believing in myself, he told me to shake off any negativity I felt because I was wasting energy.

It wasn't that I didn't believe in myself, I did, but I wasn't as egotistical as to think no one would call me a talentless wonder who got her break through knowing Simon. Nudging me to listen when the Taylor Swift song, "Shake It Off", played on the radio, he made me smile and I grinned because for someone so new to me in my life, he was definitely in my corner.

When we finally arrived in Portland, it was still the early afternoon, and as we had slept for most of the morning I was full of energy. Kerr sat scrolling through his iPad and as I had listed 'Visit a funfair', as one of the activities on my new bucket list, he informed me we were within spitting distance of one at the hotel we were staying in.

It must have been fate that we arrived on the day we did because it was also the last day of the season at the park.

Palace Playland was a huge funfair by the beach. I was totally down for an afternoon of fun in the sun so after we had checked into our hotel, I couldn't wait to visit my first funfair.

From the moment we passed San Francisco, I had the opposite problem to being in Santa Monica and felt freezing cold all of the time.

For every few hundred miles north, I added an extra layer of clothing and by the time I stepped out for the funfair I looked fifty pounds heavier, dressed in a red tank top, red t-shirt, and a navy-blue sweater, under a silver-gray puffer jacket.

"You think you're gonna be warm enough?" Kerr's tone was laced with sarcasm as he tried to bite back a grin.

"It's freezing out here," I said shivering because he'd brought attention to the temperature again. He chuckled and pulled me into his side.

Before I could feel uncomfortable with his gesture, he began to walk toward the sidewalk. "Come on, let's get your adrenaline going and you'll soon forget the cold," he reassured me and raised his hand to flag down a cab.

If I thought being with Gibson and Chloe had breathed new life into me, it was nothing to how I felt when I sampled my first rollercoaster. Exhilarated and petrified weren't two emotions I had ever imagined went together, but I learned that pretty darn quickly.

My heart pounded wildly, and I found myself seeking out Kerr's hand as extra security during the two-minute ride that had felt never-ending as the suspended car we were strapped in flew over the brightly painted metal rails above our heads.

I wasn't ashamed to scream like the girl I was, and my throat and lungs burned by the time the ride eventually came to a standstill. Even though I had thought I was going to die at some points during the terrifying ride, it was one of the best moments of my life.

Kerr continued to test my limits because as an adrenaline junkie, the guy had none himself. But somehow, despite all the new feelings colliding inside of me, he had continued to give me the courage to try ride after ride.

The day was exactly what I had needed because I had been missing Simon badly, feeling homesick for my family over in Colorado, and nervous beyond belief about performing for the first time in front of a large live audience. Until that point I had done a few small malls, controlled studio performances, and recorded for shows yet to be aired.

After eating a junk food dinner and cotton candy, we fell laughing into a taxi cab for the short ride back to the hotel and I felt so thankful for having a friend like Kerr.

What Kerr had said was totally right because from the moment I entered the fairground to the moment I stepped out of the cab after we had arrived back I hadn't noticed the cold.

Once in the warmth of the cab I thawed out, but as soon as my feet hit the street a cold shiver ran down my spine and I shuddered.

"You're such a girl," Kerr teased and wrapped his strong arms around me, hugging me tight. A wave of comfort washed over me and I leaned into him, enjoying the warmth of his body. I sighed a little because it brought back a wave of sadness because Simon wasn't here with me.

Entering the foyer of the hotel, I was completely focused on Kerr who was cracking jokes again, but he ground to a halt, his body locking up tight and his laughter died in his throat. Glancing up at his face, his expression was frozen as he stared straight ahead.

Swallowing audibly, Kerr let his arms drop from around me and my eyes followed to where his were trained and excitement riddled my body as it flowed through my veins.

My heart almost leapt out of my chest when I saw Simon sitting directly in front of us pinning Kerr to the spot with an unpleasant stare. Simon didn't need to speak because the sour expression on his face told me he was less than impressed.

CHAPTER TWENTY-SIX

*S*urprised and delighted, I squealed at the sight of him and ran toward where he was sat. I launched myself onto his lap and I gave him an enthusiastic hug. The warm response I'd expected in return was missing and his body felt tense beneath me.

"Simon! I can't believe you're here. I didn't know you were coming, what a surprise."

"Obviously," he said, dryly. "Maybe I should have called ahead, huh?" The anger in his tone made me flinch and my eyes darted to Kerr.

"Ah no, buddy, you got it all wrong," Kerr quickly corrected Simon's assessment of what he thought was happening. By the time Kerr had finished speaking I had already cottoned on to the suggestion in my boyfriend's tone.

"Kerr has really looked after me today."

"I don't doubt it. Pity I turned up or he may have been taking great care of you all night as well... or has he been doing that anyway?"

His comment took my breath away. Shock turned my adrenaline-fuelled body stiff as my heartbeat pounded in my chest at his less than subtle suggestion. "What the fuck are you implying? Kerr's a good friend, Simon."

"A very close one from everything I witnessed just now."

"Seriously? Grow up," I challenged and shook my head. I had never seen this side of Simon.

"You looked pretty cozy from here." When he directed his comment toward us it felt degrading. After all, I had been through the last thing I'd ever do is cheat on someone.

"Really, Simon? You were the last person I'd have expected to be suspicious of me. Maybe it's something you'd think of doing when I'm not around. Is that why your mind worked overtime? After everything you've learned about me, how could you still think I would cheat on you?"

"Maybe not, but do you think it's okay to have some other guy hanging off your body when I'm not around?

"There's nothing between Kerr and I except friendship."

"Does he know that?" he spat, casting a warning glare at Kerr.

Kerr cleared his throat and shot back. "Don't you dare to judge us by your standards because apparently they're not very high."

"What was that?" he asked Kerr, cupping his ear like he was straining to hear him, then he stood and took a step closer. "Hm, what is it they say about being too defensive? Strikes me that this thing between you two is a close-to-more relationship," he stated.

"What the hell does that mean?" I challenged again, shaking my head in disbelief.

Tipping his chin in Kerr's direction he scoffed, his top lip lifting at one side as he snarled. "Work on getting emotionally close and wait for the opportunity to take advantage of any vulnerability you see. It's a classic move."

"Is that what you're doing, Kerr?" I asked Kerr, but I already knew full well it wasn't the case.

"Does it feel like that to you, Piper?" he asked, his shocked look matching the tinge of hurt in his voice.

"Answer the question," Simon ran his fingers through his hair and his eyes narrowed as he scrutinized Kerr more closely.

"Absolutely not." Kerr said in denial, shooting back an equally angry glare at Simon. I didn't doubt it. "What I'm doing is giving this girl some happy memories because God knows she hasn't had it easy so far."

Simon tossed his head back then looked at me as if to question my judgement about telling Kerr my private business. "She's got me for that," Simon answered dryly.

"She does... when you're around, but you weren't here," Kerr reminded him.

"So you thought you'd fill my shoes, huh?"

"Stop it, Simon. That isn't what Kerr did. To be frank with you, I had one of the best days of my life today, and you had to go and spoil it."

All conversation stopped, and Simon looked as if I'd slapped him. Kerr rubbed my upper arm then stepped back. "Look, all I wanted to do was give Piper some freedom from everything else that's been going on. Events have been pretty full on. She had a great time at a fairground. Would you have done something like that with her? Would your fans have allowed her to have an anonymous carefree day like she's had today?"

Glancing at Simon, I could see him consider what Kerr said, but Kerr didn't wait for him to answer.

"Sorry you're pissed, but if you have to be angry at anyone direct it toward yourself. You weren't here, and she got me instead. Who knows, Piper would probably have had an even better time with you than she did with me, but it is what it is. Now if you'll excuse me, I'm tired and hungry. Thank you for an awesome day, Piper, I'll see you tomorrow."

Without waiting for Simon to respond, Kerr headed over to the elevators and stepped inside when a car was already on the ground floor.

Turning to Simon I stared incredulously, "Wow... just... wow." I sighed, placing my hands on my hips, feeling helpless at what had gone down. I'd never seen Simon so keyed up about anything.

Simon glanced furtively around to ensure no one was watching and guided me by my elbow in the direction of the elevators.

I opened my mouth to speak, and he placed his fingers across my lips effectively silencing me until we entered the elevator car. My heart pounded as my temper grew.

"I can't believe you caused that scene just now. Kerr has been nothing but kind toward me," I hissed after the doors closed. And don't silence me."

"It's not controlling I'm protecting you from the press. It takes nothing for people to sell a story. Shout at me all you want but do it in private. Piper you might want to wake the fuck up. What man wouldn't be kind? Look at you?" he replied, gesturing at me with his hand.

Drawing in a long breath he let it out, stared back at me with a dark look in his eyes and shook his head in frustration.

"Look at me? What *is* this? Surely it can't be jealousy," I stated, "You're jealous of Kerr? For what? Showing me a good time? Would you rather I sat alone in the hotel room pining for you? You'd prefer me miserable when you're not around? You—"

Simon cut me off. "For Christ's sake, stop it. Stop." He ran his hand through his hair again and sighed. "You're right, I may have overreacted, but look at this from my perspective. I flew all the way over from Kansas this morning to spend the day with you and when I got here, they told me you'd gone out—*with him*. No one knew where you were and the guy on the desk wouldn't allow me to wait in your room. I had to check in to find somewhere to go because the crazies wouldn't stop asking for my autograph or taking my picture. I was in danger of being overrun with fans."

My chest ached and my eyes softened. Sympathy replaced rage. Simon came to surprise me, and it had backfired. Stretching his hand out, he pulled me closer and wrapped his arm around my waist.

Usually his hug was all the contact I needed to melt in his arms, but not this time. I remained tense because of how he'd challenged Kerr like he wanted to be more than my friend.

"How is that Kerr's fault, or mine for that matter? I'm sorry I wasn't here, but after the last few days where we've either been stuck on the bus or performing, I was thankful Kerr was thoughtful enough and wanted to spend time with me."

"You're sure that's what it is? Thoughtful? I've seen the way he looks at you; he fucking adores you."

"Not every man is trying to get in my panties, Simon. Perhaps you think like that, but it doesn't mean all men do."

"Don't be so naïve, baby. A man knows when another man is casing his woman."

"And that's what you think Kerr is doing? Casing me? You're wrong. Kerr has a gorgeous girlfriend back home. He's in love, Simon. I don't want to fight with you, but I can't live my life waiting for you to come from wherever you are to spend time with me. Are you going to do the same? Stay in your room when you're on the road?"

Simon blew out a breath he'd been holding. "Soon you won't have the luxury of going out without the media being all over you. What happens when the rumors and accusations start flying around? How are you going to deal with those?" He sighed and fell silent for a moment and the elevator arrived at my hotel room floor. Stepping out of it he stood facing me as the doors closed again.

"What about Kerr's girl? How do you think she'd feel? From what I saw when the two of you walked in, he wasn't behaving like a man who was concerned about how his girlfriend would view the two of you together."

Why had I not considered this? Why hadn't Kerr? I found it hard to believe Kerr was hitting on me. "We're close, very close, but it's purely platonic. We find comfort in spending time with each other on the road. Surely you out of everyone knows how lonely it can get?"

"Very close? You've known him what? A month at the most?"

"And I've only been with you for a few more weeks than that. Are we not close? Tell me, what is it you're trying to say here?"

Seeing pain in Simon's eyes almost killed me. The last thing I had ever wanted to do was to hurt him. I wouldn't have imagined being capable of that.

Simon was everything I wasn't, a rock god, and he said it himself, beautiful, rich, and famous women texted him daily and flung themselves at him wherever he went. If anyone should have had insecurities, it should have been me.

He nodded slowly and gazed into my eyes and rolled his shoulders back.

"What I'm saying is being your dependable friend is how it all starts. Then the *emotional* dependency grows until one night there's too much beer or tequila. From then on comes the drinking games and laughter and someone catches your eye. Fleeting glimpses become stolen glances until before you know it you've had a sloppy fuck and there's no going back from that."

"Wow, sounds like something you sure know a lot about," I stated, curtly. Simon shrugged with a wry smirk on his face and I knew it was something he'd done himself in the past.

I huffed and stared him out. "Are you warning me? Perhaps it's something at the back of your mind, Simon? I'm not as naïve as to think there won't be an abundance of women on your bus. Who's to say you're not warning me about the temptations in your own camp?"

"Trust me, I'm well aware of the temptations and the manipulations of the opposite sex. I'm not interested in anyone else. No matter how lonely the road gets." His jaw flexed with frustration and his piercing hazel eyes studied mine. "Look, you're young, you're inexperienced with guys. It would kill me if someone took advantage of you like that, and I want to protect you from it."

"Kerr is not taking liberties with me and you're starting to sound like Gibson."

Simon's breath hitched in his throat and his tongue poked at his cheek. I knew immediately he felt insulted. His body tightened, and he dropped his hand from my waist. "Let me ask you this; if you were the one sitting on that couch and you watched me walk in with a great looking woman my age how would that make you feel?"

"That's different?"

"Yeah?"

"Yeah."

"How?"

I sighed in defeat because I knew I'd immediately feel inferior to her, even though I was his girlfriend. "If you were with another woman, you'd have done something other than go to a fairground."

"Such as?"

"I don't know. Probably somewhere more sophisticated... a fancy dinner or something?"

"What are you trying to say, Piper? You're unsophisticated? Tell me because it sounds very much as if you think I'm too old to do the things Kerr is doing with you." I could have argued he was twisting my words but maybe he was right. Maybe I was. I swallowed as tears burned my throat.

"It's not that..."

"Save it." He snapped, sounding tired. "I accept you didn't see any harm in going out with him today. Hell, maybe he was being a genuinely nice dude, but I don't want you to fall into another trap like you did with that Doobie guy."

"I learned my lesson from that," I shot back in frustration, "And Kerr is nothing like Jeff. He makes me feel... comfortable."

"As long as that's all he makes you feel," Simon scolded, still struggling with his feelings. Threading his fingers through mine he clasped them tight, and I felt the desperation in his grasp.

I shook my head. "Damn, you really are jealous," I said, stunned at the insecurity in his statement.

"Damn straight I am. As you say, we're still new. I'm not the insecure type usually, but this feels different. I'm out of my depth because it's *you*... I can't explain, but I flew all this way because I was desperate to talk to you; to spend the day with my girl, and all we've done since the minute I saw you is talk about the guy who actually spent time with you." His comment made me feel guilty again.

Before I could dwell on this, he leaned in and kissed me hard. The passion in his kiss radiated between his soul and mine.

My heartbeat raced, and I squeezed my thighs together. Sliding his hands down over my ass he pulled my front flush against him.

Despite all the negative feelings running between us he was rock solid, his erection pressed hard against my belly.

With each second he kissed me, my anger dissolved until I couldn't think of anything but him and my only feeling was desire.

Breaking the kiss, he turned and hurriedly led me down the corridor. It was like he could hardly wait to get me alone, but I couldn't stop giggling when he cussed loudly when he had to enter the hotel suite keycard three times before the door unlocked.

We tumbled inside the door and he kicked it closed with his heel as his hands fought their way into my coat. Kissing me hungrily, he shoved it recklessly over my shoulders then his hands fumbled at the hem of my woolen sweater.

"You don't let men put their grubby hands on you, you hear me?" he ordered possessively as another agonized moan of need passed over his lips.

Breaking the kiss briefly, he tugged my sweater roughly over my head. "God, I've missed you so much, baby," he breathed shakily against my ear as he urgently stripped me out of my clothing. He kissed me again, urgent and fiercely, leaving me breathless. When he broke the kiss my lips felt swollen and bruised as I gasped for air.

Excitement made my body hum as his gaze turned carnal when his eyes took their fill of my body.

"Beautiful, sweetheart," he whispered, as his mouth seduced me by tracing tiny kisses from my neck to my ear. "You're so fucking delicious I want to eat you," he told me playfully, a hint of desperation in his tone.

Stepping back, he tipped his head to the side, brazenly regarding my body. Tracing his lips with his tongue, I watched a small smile break through and he shook his head again.

"I can't stop looking at you," he admitted and the heat of being perused so openly melted all other thoughts than my need of him.

"See this?" he asked, tracing his middle finger over my pale skin stained red with the desire burning within me. "This is everything to a man. Knowing I set you on fire makes me feel like a king, Princess."

Being with Simon made me feel weak, but in the most incredibly pleasurable way. Since we'd been together, there had always been something he did that made me feel unique.

I swallowed nervously because although we'd had sex many times in the previous few weeks, the way he was memorizing every line and curve took my breath away.

His fingertips traced the trail his eyes made over my body, tracing the curve of my breasts. His tender seductive touch made me moan and my skin reacted with goose bumps on the outside and fire blazing beneath.

Swallowing roughly, he licked his lips and his hungry eyes fell to my jeans. Kneeling in front of me, he whispered adoring words as his large hands made short work of the button and zipper there.

When he slid the rough material over my butt, his warm hands replaced the contact as they traced their path down my legs and I shivered as a jolt of electric delight traveled through me.

Once my jeans were on the floor, he lifted me possessively onto his waist, wrapping my legs behind him, holding me tight.

"Deep down I know you want me, Piper." It wasn't a question but a statement. "I can feel how much you want me when you look at me, but the thought of you with someone else makes me feel desperate—irrational. You're mine, you hear?"

My heart swelled in my chest until it felt tight at his incredible confession. It was everything I needed to hear.

Pressing his lips to mine, his kiss was everything from soft and gentle, to overwhelming and suffocating, and all the tension from the previous half hour suddenly ebbed into insignificance as Simon proceeded to claim every inch of my body as his.

CHAPTER TWENTY-SEVEN

a text alert came in as I wandered back into the room from my morning shower. Simon was naked, his towel having parted when he sat on the edge of the bed to check out his phone. Sliding his phone, he selected a number and made a call.

Whoever was on the other end must have started talking because he smiled, but there was something in the way he did it that instinctively told me he was listening to a woman. Don't ask me how I knew, I just did.

Hearing me come through the door his eyes flitted over to mine. His smile widened, and I knew that one was for me, then he dropped his gaze to the floor and continued to listen to the call.

"Hm, is that so?" he asked in a playful tone, "We'll see about that." I felt my body stiffen defensively, my gut twisting more in suspicion than curiosity.

All the work we'd done the previous night to regain the closeness we shared felt short-lived as my chest tightened in a feeling that was difficult to describe.

"I should get in tomorrow night around 8pm." For some reason he looked anxious for a moment as he listened intently to whatever was being said and a nervous chuckle escaped as he glanced toward me.

Instead of smiling again, his eyes lingered on me but his face looked serious as he chewed the inside of his cheek and continued to listen. Breaking eye contact, his face became solemn, and he ran his fingers through his hair.

He flopped back naked on the bed with his knees wide and his feet still on the floor. "Five to seven days?" he asked, his body relaxed in all his nakedness as he flashed a smile. He snickered again at whatever the caller had said. "Sounds like a plan. Anytime, sweetheart. I promised. I could do with a couple of days R'n'R in the sun." *Sweetheart? Anytime? What the hell?*

His affectionate comment toward someone else stung, and I instantly empathized with his position the previous night about Kerr, because despite hearing only snippets of their conversation out of context, it was enough to hurt me.

I tried to reassure myself I was being irrational, but from they had said, they had made arrangements to go somewhere together and I wondered if the invitation he was receiving meant I was starting to lose him.

My chest felt tight, my heart heaved, and I realized I no longer had a crush on Simon, I had fallen in love.

Insecurity swept through me and I questioned whether I'd been foolish to give my heart to someone with so much sex appeal, women literally threw themselves at him. Women who had far more to give and could steal him away in the blink of an eye.

Preoccupied by my last thought and struggling to calm my racing heart, I moved quietly around the room and dressed, pretending I wasn't interested in his call.

My heart stuttered and clenched when I realized the timeline for his trip clashed with my opening gig. As his conversation continued my insecurities grew and it felt as if Simon had even forgotten I was in the room.

"Don't worry. Whatever comes up, we'll deal with it together," he told her. "I'm sure I will be," he relied through a chuckle, in answer to something else said. By this point it took all I had not to turn and give him a questioning look, and I'd have given my two front teeth to have known who was on the other end of the line.

Sliding my feet into my panties, I pulled them up and then quickly grabbed a t-shirt and sweater from my suitcase. Slipping them over my head, I then pulled on a pair of jeans. Spinning around, I sat on a small chair by the window, putting on some socks and shoes.

I shot a quick glance to Simon who by this time had one foot resting up on the mattress, his leg bent at the knee, and was smiling like a deranged chimpanzee as he stared at the ceiling.

For someone so into me only a few hours before, it was as if I became invisible as soon as his call connected.

Once dressed I had no idea what else to do, but I wasn't going to sit there like some third wheel while he rudely flirted with someone else on his cell. To save face, I took out my cell, and I sent a text to Kerr.

Me: Coffee in the lounge downstairs, pretty please?
Kerr: Is your caveman still waving his club?

I smiled even in my bad situation because even though Kerr had been angry when he walked away the evening before, I knew he hadn't held Simon's outburst against me.

Me: Don't worry about him. He's not invited. I replied.
Silencing my cell, I slid it into my back pocket.

Swiping the keycard and my purse from the dresser, I headed to the door and let myself out without looking back or telling Simon where I was going. If his call had him so engrossed, I had no problem in entertaining myself. The last thing I'd let any man do was to make me clingy or needy.

Kerr was already sitting on one of the plush leather couches in the lounge bar scrolling through his tablet when I came into view. When he saw me coming, he stood up to greet me.

Glancing past me he drew me in for a hug. "I'm not going to get the shit kicked out of me for saying hello, am I?"

I scoffed, feeling embarrassed for how Simon had behaved toward him the previous evening and sat down heavily on the couch. Kerr sat down next to me and eyed me with concern. "Everything okay?"

I shrugged. "I guess so. I just had to get out of the room for a while," I said not wanting to voice anything until I was sure there was a real problem.

"That doesn't sound great since he only got here yesterday."

I shrugged again. *I know right?*

"What's wrong? Did he do something? Has he hurt you?" I narrowed my eyes as I stared at Kerr, annoyed that he would automatically think that of Simon. The one thing he definitely wasn't was violent. There had never been any vibe from him that had made me feel threatened or uncomfortable about my personal safety.

Searching the ceiling, I shook my head as a lump of emotion suddenly clogged my throat. *Don't you dare cry, Piper. Am I being oversensitive? Do men have open conversations with other women all the time and I don't know this? I don't even know how to react without sounding suspicious or jealous.*

"It's nothing."

"Then I'm sure it's something," Kerr countered. "If Mr. Hot Shot Rock Star is still in your bedroom and you're down here with me, it isn't nothing," Kerr countered.

I sighed. "I'm certain it'll sound stupid if I say it out loud," I argued.

"If you were upset enough to leave the room, then something has hurt your feelings. If you removed yourself from his presence because of him then it's not stupid." Kerr's concerned eyes searched my face, and I felt vindicated for stepping away.

I considered what he said for a few moments. "It sounds crazy but after we left you we argued... then we made up and... well..."

"You had angry dirty make-up sex," Kerr stated, turning to smile pleasantly at the waitress who had arrived with the coffee and pastries he had ordered. Mortified, I immediately blushed and wanted the floor to open up and swallow me whole. I stole a warning glance at Kerr that told him to shut up and he chuckled, "Aaa...dorable," he teased and pointed at how pink my cheeks were.

I huffed, "Do you want to know or not... and keep your voice down," the end of my sentence was quieter than the rest.

"Yes of course I do. Sorry, go on."

"When I came out of the shower this morning he got a text from someone and he immediately called her back. I'm sure it was a woman he was talking to... well, come to think of it, she did most of the talking and he listened, but it was almost like I had ceased to exist once she was on the line. I felt invisible."

"Invisible?"

"Yeah, like he laid flat out on the bed fresh from the shower and had this long conversation."

"You're this worked up because he made a phone call?"

"It wasn't that he made a phone call... it was how he was... how it made me feel. I was uncomfortable even being there," I explained, sounding exacerbated from the lack of how to describe it.

"Well, fuck, if you were with me I wouldn't be wasting my time talking to someone else on the phone." When I heard his reply, I had the slightest hesitation because of what Simon had said the evening before. I shook it off because Kerr was very straightforward, and I was sure what he said was only siding with me.

"There you are," Simon's low, clipped tone cut into our conversation. "I figured you came downstairs to find something to eat. You must be ravenous after last night." Simon glanced at Kerr, his eyes narrowing as he took him in sitting next to me.

The ravenous comment felt loaded with emphasis, and it made me feel uneasy because I didn't know if he meant because of all the sex we'd had or because neither of us had anything else to eat last night. I blushed at the thought he meant it terms of all we had done during the night.

Kerr glanced at me and quickly looked away like he was trying not to notice, and Simon took my hand and tugged me up off the couch. Leading me to the one across from Kerr he sat me on his lap and put his arms around me. I glanced at Kerr then to him.

"What time are you leaving today?"

"I think around midday," I replied and looked at Kerr for confirmation.

"Yeah, twelve-ish," he concurred. Simon huffed because I'd relied on Kerr and then looked at his wristwatch.

"We've got less than two hours left until then. Do you want to go to breakfast?" I was in no way precious in my temperament, but I was still smarting from the way he'd ignored me and turned to Kerr.

"Would you like to come to breakfast with us?" I offered, determined not to allow Simon to push Kerr to one side when I had asked him to meet me in the first place.

Glancing to Simon and then to me, Kerr shrugged. "Nah, I'm fine here. You go spend time with your man. I'll see you back on the bus." A growl escaped Simon's throat, and he flashed Kerr a dark warning glare.

Kerr scoffed and snickered back at him like he'd taken it as a joke. Then he reached forward and stuffed a pastry into his mouth. When neither made any further comment, Kerr lifted his cup and secretly smiled around the rim of it before sipping the hot coffee.

Pushing me to my feet, Simon stood up beside me and wrapped a strong arm around my shoulder. "Later, dude," he mumbled, stroking his thumb across my bare upper arm and he turned us to leave. I was annoyed at the thrill that ran through my body as his skin touched mine given how annoyed I felt.

"Later," Kerr replied, and I felt slightly impressed that even though Simon was a famous rock star, to Kerr he was a man first and a rock star second.

~

During breakfast, Simon was very attentive and made no mention of the call which had taken up so much of his time. I was dying to ask who he had been speaking with but my pride refused to allow me to do this, so I pretended not to care and quietly festered inside.

Kerr's comment from earlier about Simon making the call in the first place made me feel subdued and distracted, but Simon figured I was upset because we had to leave each other again.

It wasn't that I was afraid to challenge him, but I wasn't sure I'd like the answer he'd give me either, and part of me also held back from doing so because of the way he had jumped to conclusions about Kerr and me.

If the call turned out to be something innocent, I wouldn't have wanted to give him the satisfaction of throwing my day with Kerr back in my face again.

As we walked back to the bus, the atmosphere between us was stilted and even though he held my hand I felt a distance between us.

"Where are you off to now?" My open question should have given him an opportunity to clear the air and tell me his plans.

"I have to head down to the Bahamas to meet some people," he stated flatly, and when I glanced at him he didn't look at me as we arrived at the bus. He dropped his grip on my hand and my heart clenched at the loss of his touch.

Stuffing his hands deeply into his pockets he rocked on his heels and tried to look at me. He didn't inspire my confidence when he averted his gaze, my insecurities sent a jolt of electricity through me at his reply.

I was literally getting on a bus knowing that the next time I got off it I would be following my dream, the one thing that had kept me and my mom going all those years, and suddenly I didn't want to go. Something wasn't right between Simon and me.

Narrowing my eyes in suspicion I asked, "Is there anything wrong?" I offered this prompt to give him another opportunity to say what was on his mind. Shaking his head, he blew my question off, and my heart sank.

As strong as my feelings were for him, it appeared clear Simon was going to do what he wanted. My only hope was that he knew if he cheated on me there were no second chances, no matter who he was or how I felt about him.

The conversation felt guarded, I figured if I was supposed to know, he'd have spoken to me about it by now. His trip was either nothing, or he had chosen not to elaborate.

"Have a good time then," I said lamely. I felt weak for not calling him out, but I was being strong and I was determined not to cry.

My heart felt crushed by the heavy weight in my chest at the thought Simon was about to do what Gibson was afraid of. More importantly, I felt distressed by how casual his behavior with me was, if his intention was to leave me to spend time with another woman.

Stepping forward, Simon kissed me and it was loaded with passion and desperation. The bulge in his jeans pressed into my lower belly as he trapped me between his body and the cool metal panel of the tour bus.

When he drew back and looked at me, the adoration in his eyes as he stared lovingly into mine conflicted with everything else that had happened since the call and I wondered if his eyes hid any lies.

Fresh doubts swamped me, and I felt foolish to think I was different to all those other women he had been with. Maybe I was... for a while, but at the back of my mind the nagging uncertainty about keeping the interest of a man who had seen and done most things was always there. A lump grew in my throat and I swallowed hard.

"Hey." His voice was full of concern as he pulled back to look at me. "Eight days isn't that long," he said, reminding me how long it was until we saw each other again. *A lot can happen in eight days. Wars have been fought and won in that time. What about my first ever live performance? If I mean that much to him what's more important?*

Offering him a weak smile, I slid to the side and out of his arms. "I know. I guess I'd better get on the bus, I think they are only waiting for me."

Climbing the steps, I turned and looked down at him, my heart bursting with anxiety and fear at what I thought may potentially have been the last time he looked at me like he never wanted me to leave.

"Piper," he said with a sense of urgency. "Have fun, but don't forget what I said about life on the road." I knew he was warning me about Kerr. It was an unwarranted comment, and he had a cheek after what I suspected he was going to do.

Hearing his comment irked me. "I could say the same to you," I replied, my sassy side kicking in to warn him about his own behavior. Without gauging his reaction, I turned and climbed onto the bus without looking back.

Moments later, I glanced out of the window and he was gone. My gut clenched tight because he hadn't hung around to see me off and my imagination about where he was headed went into overdrive.

Tears welled in my eyes and I blinked rapidly in my attempt to prevent them from falling. *Why didn't I confront him about the call if it's made me feel so bad?*

Kerr sensed I wanted to be alone during the trip up to Seattle and spent the journey Skyping with his girlfriend in his cubby bunk. For most of the time I could hear his low rich tone murmuring, but not what he said, other than the occasional, 'Oh. My. God, baby' or 'You gotta be kidding me', floating through the air.

A few times I heard him laugh and it made me smile. Kerr made me smile. I sighed. This fact alone made me determined not to discard him as a friend just because Simon didn't like it.

CHAPTER TWENTY-EIGHT

*L*ate afternoon found us pulling into the secure area of the WaMu Theater in Seattle. If I had thought it looked big from the outside, it appeared huge on the inside. Stepping into the auditorium for the first time, I glanced around at the six-thousand-seven-hundred capacity seating and swallowed audibly as I scanned the vast empty-seated space.

"Holy shit," Petra muttered, glancing at Isiah who wore the same shocked face as she did.

"Damn," murmured Wyatt.

"This is going to be awesome," Kerr said to Austin who grinned back. I figured neither Kerr nor Austin had a nervous bone in their bodies because I was mentally freaking out inside.

The presence of the star of the gig, Layla, had been everywhere when we had passed through the foyer: with posters, life-size cut out cardboard statues, and other memorabilia heavily evident, and the crew had set up her expensive backdrop and technical equipment on stage.

Layla herself had yet to make herself available for her soundcheck, but her stage producer had met us at the stage door and after checking out the venue she escorted me onto the stage.

From the moment I saw the tall oriental beauty called Myleene, I knew she'd be ultra-efficient, "Michael?" she shouted out into the empty auditorium with an air of authority no one would question.

"Yeah?" A sharp hollow voice immediately echoed back from the balcony above. My eyes tracked the sound, and I saw the large mixing desk stationed right at the front of it, manned by a guy with long dark hair and a dark colored t-shirt.

"Piper's here. Can we get the sound levels done for her before Layla arrives please?"

I cleared my throat, totally unprepared to sing right off the bat. I had expected some introductions and conversation, a warm up and perhaps a drink of warm lemon and honey or something in preparation.

"Now?" I asked as my heart raced frantically, and I tried to hide the shock from my voice. *Talk about being thrown in at the deep end.*

"Sure, time's cracking on," she said glancing at her wristwatch. "Goodness knows how long Layla will keep everyone occupied once she gets here. She's such a perfectionist."

Swallowing hard, I shook my head, "Can I at least do a short warm up for my throat? I've been sitting on an air-conditioned bus for the past few hours."

Nodding, she shielded her eyes and looked out into the auditorium again. "Sandra? Can we get Piper some honey tea, sweetheart?"

"No problem," came the reply from a female voice I failed to find when my eyes scanned the stalls.

"Please sing three bridges from songs which challenge the vocal range. Michael will let you know when he has what he needs, then I'll come back and show you the dressing room. Call out to Michael when you are ready but don't take too long because when Layla appears you'll have missed your opportunity for the sound quality checks."

As Myleene strutted across the stage, the young runner, Sandra appeared with a beaker of steaming hot liquid. Passing it to me she smiled warmly.

"Honey and English Breakfast tea, is this okay?" she asked. Returning the smile, I thanked her and sipped tentatively at the scalding hot beverage.

Kerr had gone back to the bus and brought back the guitar he always carried with him. "What's the deal?"

"Soundcheck," I replied.

Kerr wandered over to a rig on the floor, took his guitar from the case, and unraveled and connected the electric wires to it, plugging the jack into his instrument.

"I'll accompany you. What do you want to sing?" I gave him the three bridges for the songs I had chosen to show my widest range then placed the cup on a stool at the side of the stage.

Taking off my cardigan, I warmed my voice up by singing sliding scales a few times into the garment to muffle the sound then spun around to look out to the auditorium again.

"Michael? I'm ready. This is Kerr, my guitarist. Do you want me to sing on my own or with him?"

"Both, we'll start with you accappella. Hold your hand up when you're ready to start," he instructed.

Taking my place in front of the microphone, I cleared my throat once again. Standing facing the mic it was the most nervous I had ever felt in my life and the place was empty.

My whole body buzzed in anticipation. Drawing in a deep breath, I sighed heavily, then lifted my hand to let him know I was about to sing.

Within five minutes Michael had my voice levels down then I did them again with Kerr accompanying me on guitar. When we were done Michael waved his arms then spoke into his mic.

"Awesome, you are going to rock this place, baby. Damn what a voice, those scale changes are as smooth as a knife gliding through warm butter."

Kerr grinned and nodded. Inhaling a sharp breath, I sighed with relief in return.

"Well, what do you know? Seems like I have some serious competition on my hands," the unmistakable Southern voice of Layla Hartmann interjected. "I love the tone of your voice, honey," she drawled. "As soon as I heard you, I just knew I had to have you for the tour. Gibson Barclay was right, you are the find of the century."

My eyes flicked to Kerr and his eyes widened in surprise. "Gibson? You mean Gibson Barclay? Fuck, Gibson Barclay heard you sing? I mean I know you're with Simon, but..." Glancing at Layla who obviously knew my connection to Gibson, I was nervous as to what she would say.

When she said nothing, it felt safe to reply. "Yeah," I replied and shrugged. I didn't expand or embellish the connection because it wasn't the time and I wasn't ready to talk about Gibson with him. I wanted the opportunity to perform under my own steam for a while and let people decide for themselves if they thought I deserved my place in the music industry.

"Of course, Simon must have introduced you, right? Well fuck, you're just full of surprises," he chuckled. I felt bad for not telling him, but I knew once I explained why, Kerr would forgive me.

Fortunately for me, Layla smoothed the way by discussing how the gig would go. Thankful for the distraction, I stood at the side of the stage and listened as she finalized her own soundcheck before she and Myleene went over all the markers on the stage of where to stand.

This was to maximize our visibility and ensure we didn't get tangled up in the junction of wires snaking over the stage floor.

Completing the checks and with a little over two hours left before the doors of the venue opened, we were shown to our dressing room. Petra was beyond excited and Isiah tried his best to calm her down.

Austin, our drummer, was as cool as a cucumber and sat disconnected from the buzz as he listened to loud music through his cell phone ear buds. I could hear the noise tinker but not enough to make out what the songs were.

As I sat and studied my set running order on my iPad, my cell rang. When I saw it was Gibson, I sought out some privacy and swiped to connect the call.

"Hey, baby girl. All set for the gig?" I nodded even though he couldn't see me and sat on a chair in the corridor tucking one leg beneath me.

"I think so. God, I bet you were never as nervous as me."

"Oh, I don't know about that. I wasn't always this cool," he replied, chuckling.

"I bet you were," I challenged. There was no way Gibson was ever

the nervous kind; he oozed natural leadership and was a true
alpha male.

"All right, maybe I was, but you're gonna rock this, sweetheart. Is Si
with you?"

The mention of his name made me swallow audibly. "No... h- he's
spending some time with friends," I replied and tried to sound as if I
didn't care. Admitting Simon wasn't around, I half expected a rant of
warning from him, but he fell silent for a moment.

"He isn't? Why the fuck not? If I had known, I'd have been there,
baby girl."

"Thomas is coming," I quickly offered to let him know I wasn't
doing this without support. He sighed.

"When are you seeing Simon again?"

I shrugged and felt helpless, "Not sure, last gig I think," I answered
honestly.

Gibson fell silent, and I had an ominous feeling. The pause in the
conversation gave me time to wonder if Gibson was thinking the worst
of Simon... like maybe I was.

Changing tack, Gibson quickly said, "Oh, by the way, I'm shooting
down to Chicago to see you next Thursday, baby girl. That's only six
more days. Chloe won't be with me because Melody has a 'mom and
daughter' thing at school and Kiran is working."

Kiran was Melody's birth mom and after a rocky beginning, Chloe
had managed the situation between Gibson and Melody with such
finesse that Kiran had no option but give up on her bitchy attitude
toward Chloe spending time with Melody. It was either that or Gibson
wouldn't have made her life as easy as he had.

Knowing Gibson took his role to support me seriously meant
everything. His timely call meant everything to me. With all the insecurities surrounding my past, trusting Simon after that call made the
gamble to be with him much greater.

My mind became preoccupied again by Simon until Gibson's voice
broke through my thoughts. "Break a leg tonight." Hearing his deep
velvety tone encouraging me with its hint of humor was exactly what I
had needed.

We said our goodbyes and when the call disconnected a lump grew in my throat. Suddenly I was homesick for the safety of Colorado. Since my mom had died, Gibson had done his best to ensure I never felt completely alone but with no one who mattered there on my opening night I did.

Hearing footsteps, I looked up and saw Thomas striding down the corridor toward me and he couldn't have timed his arrival better. When he smiled and held his arms out, I almost ran into them because although I had been striving for my independence, now that I had arrived at the foot of the music mountain I still had to climb, I felt much less invincible.

"All ready for the main event?" Of course the main event wasn't me, but Layla. Still, I knew what he meant.

"As ready as I'll ever be, but it's nerve wracking."

"Trust me, they are going to go nuts for you, sweetheart," He assured me as he put his arm around my shoulder and ushered me back into the dressing room. My heart swelled at his confidence in me and I prayed he was right.

Sandra knocked on the door, "Ten minutes until showtime," she cheerily informed us, and my heart immediately raced. "This is it," Kerr informed us, excitedly. I swallowed roughly as my eyes darted around to each member of my band.

Petra and Isiah stood and checked out their appearances in the dressing room mirror as Austin casually removed his buds and slid his iPhone back in his backpack. Kerr stood, smoothed his jeans down and wandered over to me. "All set?" he asked, checking out I was okay.

"Not really," I giggled, standing beside him. He stepped forward and hugged me, "You will be amazing as always." I thanked God for sending me Kerr as he stepped back, turned away from me and engaged Wyatt in conversation.

Taking my cell phone out of my pocket to leave it in the dressing room, I entered my password, my eyes eagerly searching for some news from Simon. I had been willing him to call all afternoon, but I knew he was traveling.

Pushing back the dark feelings that threatened to overshadow my mood, I was determined nothing would spoil my debut performance in front of a live, paying audience.

As if Kerr had felt my insecurity, he wrapped his arms around me in a natural gesture of comfort. "You were born to do this, Piper. You have to go out there and show them you deserve to be there because of what you can do, not who you know."

His words were all the motivation I had needed to shove all my personal shit to one side and focus on the job in hand—my music career.

A new sense of purpose filled every fiber of my body as I wandered behind Kerr toward the door and along the corridor toward the stage.

"Go get 'em," Thomas called after me. I smirked, suddenly trying to control the vibrations reverberating on every nerve ending I possessed.

Sweeping through the black curtain at the side of the stage, I took a deep breath and gathered my inner confidence as I stood quietly in the wings.

Before I had the opportunity to think of countering any doubts in my mind, the emcee announced my arrival on stage.

Running past me—Kerr, Austin, Isiah, Petra, and Wyatt, took their places on the stage and as soon as Wyatt hit the drums I forced myself out under the bright lights above me. I waved nervously as I took my place at the mic and tried hard not to focus too much on the crowd.

The polite ripple of applause I heard was still loud because there were so many fans out there, and it was the best I could have hoped for because I was relatively unknown.

Clearing my throat, I held the mic to my mouth and willed my hand to stop shaking.

"Hey, everyone. Are you ready to have a great time tonight?"

A subdued, "Yeah," came from the audience. I swallowed hard and tried again to control my racing heart as adrenaline threatened to overwhelm me.

Deciding it was pointless trying to win them over with conversation, I nodded to Kerr and he began to play the introduction to the first number in the set.

Taking a deep breath, I waited for my time to sing as the music vibes from my bandmates rose up through my feet.

When I began to perform, the first couple of lines of the song were a little shaky but once my heart settled down and I found my pace, the song I had chosen to open with just flowed.

Less than a minute after I had begun to sing, all eyes were on me. No one moved out of their seats and no one made a sound other than my bandmates.

No one could sing along because they'd never heard the song before, but they were paying attention. Briefly, I closed my eyes and threw a silent prayer up to my mom.

An instant feeling of calm washed over me. After that I remembered all the techniques she had spoken to me about and that I'd practiced with Gibson and Simon.

Pushing both men out of my mind, my sole focus was directed at showing the public why I deserved my spot on the stage.

With each song the applause grew louder, with every new number I appeared to affect the crowd more. Some even tried to join in at the bridge by the second verse of some numbers and by the end of our set, the fans were on their feet, cheering and clapping, whistling, and stamping their feet.

A sense of euphoria washed over me from their enthusiastic response to my set.

Drenched in sweat from the heat up on stage, my thin lightweight sleeveless shirt was soaked and stuck to my skin with sweat, but somehow knowing I had poured everything I had into my music, the blood, sweat, and tears from my past and present efforts only added to the whole experience.

As soon as we were finished, Kerr placed his shiny black Fender guitar back on a stand in front of the drum set and ran over toward me.

Wrapping his hands around my waist he lifted me off the stage floor and swung me around. Bouncing me up and down, he grinned from ear to ear before setting me back on my feet. I smiled breathlessly back at him, knowing for sure I wasn't alone in this experience after all—my band had experienced it with me.

Turning back to the audience one last time, I gave them a final wave before Kerr led me and the others back off the stage. Kerr made a goofy grin at me like he was wasted by the gig and it made me laugh out loud. His gray eyes glittered with happiness.

"Insane, right?" he asked as he placed his strong hands on my shoulders. The heat radiating from them seeped into my already hot, damp skin.

"In... cred... ible," he stated before I could reply, his breathing marked by short pants both from his excitement and exertion as his chest heaved up and down. "You were fucking dynamite out there," he added, turning to look at Austin for confirmation. Austin grinned and nodded more enthusiastically than I knew he was capable of.

"You were pure magic out there. The audience were captive and under your spell," Austin added, then shook his head this time. "I've always thought you were an amazing singer, but what you did out there was so enthralling, I almost forgot to play because I was focusing on your voice."

Glancing at Petra and Isiah, I could see they had both enjoyed the experience by the way they were excitedly hugging each other.

Petra broke the embrace and turned to look for me. "Dayum, girlie. If anyone had any doubts you were letting Simon McLennan fuck you to catch a break, you just put that rumor to bed, honey."

Petra's comment stunned me because she had voiced what I reckoned most women would have thought since the news broke about Simon and me.

No one had seen the years I practiced and the months of work that had gone into preparing with Gibson and Simon before I snagged my recording deal.

Unfortunately, the story about Simon and I had broken only days into our relationship and at approximately six short weeks in the past, it was still fresh in peoples' minds.

Even one of my band members had something to say about it. It appeared the finer details of what really went on didn't matter to most because people would think what they wanted.

I shrugged and sighed not wishing to feed into her comment, but the mention of Simon made my heart squeeze tight. His absence had taken the shine off my day and I wished he had been here to see it.

It had been another 'first' of mine, one which could have possibly been the most defining moment and significant experience I'd ever have in my lifetime.

Frustration and anger crept into my bones and I cussed the call he'd had which had been so damned important that he hadn't stuck around to support me.

During the day I had checked my cell incessantly after we had left, expecting to hear something from him.

Several thoughts had run through my mind: *Maybe I'd get a text confession of where he was going? A text or voicemail to tell me he'd made a mistake?* Each time I checked my cell, and he maintained radio silence, it left me more disappointed than the last.

"What's wrong?" Kerr asked intuitively. I shook my head because I didn't want to get into it. Not after we'd had such a high a few minutes before.

"It's nothing," I said shaking off the 'let down' feeling I had in my gut.

"Simon... that nothing?"

Feeling a wave of emotion threatening to bring me down, I turned without answering him and headed back to the dressing room. As I neared it, Myleene approached me. I was thankful for her interruption because I wasn't about to make any more excuses for Simon's absence.

"Layla would like a word with you before she goes on. If you'd care to follow me." Without waiting for me she headed for Layla's dressing room and I turned and quickly followed.

My heart rate gathered pace again as I walked silently behind her and as she opened the door, the beautiful artist I was supporting rose to her feet from a chair in front of a dressing table mirror.

"Piper, you were totally awesome out there. I can't believe that was your first ever live gig. The fans ate up every minute of your performance." I grinned, and my heart swelled against my ribcage. "You are going to go a long way, my darling," she gushed and my smile widened further.

"Thank you for giving me this opportunity," I offered with another grateful smile.

"No darling, thank you for agreeing to support me; although I fear next time I may be supporting you."

I blushed, shy at her humility. "You're too kind. I'm sure that won't ever happen," I replied with a small chuckle.

"Don't you believe it. It happens every day. Treat every performance as if it's your last. That way you'll respect the crowds who flock to see you and keep the fans you make." It was a great piece of advice.

Myleene interrupted us to give Layla her five-minute call, and I made my way back to my own dressing room, leaving her to get ready for her show; but I wasn't ready for the evening to be over.

It was only 9pm, but we never got the luxury of hanging around to watch Layla's performance. As Kansas was the next stop, we shipped straight out again on the bus.

Leaving the venue at the back via the loading dock, there was a four-foot drop to the ground. Kerr jumped down, waved at me with his hands up and helped me down. I fell into his arms when I lost my footing and he caught me tight to his chest. We both laughed and as our eyes met, we separated and climbed onto the bus.

Petra called after me as I climbed the steps. "Piper, I think this is yours," she said, holding out my cell phone.

"You're a lifesaver," I admitted because my phone held my whole life in it and I knew no one's phone number off by heart. I'd been so caught up in the excitement of going on stage before, I had forgotten to retrieve it from the dressing room counter to drop it into my purse.

As soon as I held my phone in my hand, it became the central focus for my attention. *I wonder if he's called.* The weight of the small gadget in my palm made it hard to ignore and an overwhelming urge to check again if Simon had called washed over me.

Knowing my night would be ruined if I checked and he hadn't called, I decided not to put myself in that position and quickly dropped it into my purse.

CHAPTER TWENTY-NINE

"'d like to propose a toast," said Kerr, holding up a Corona beer with a small wedge of lime still stuck in the neck of the bottle. "To our amazing leader, Piper. You knocked it out of the park tonight. Thank you for choosing us as your tribe," he added, grinning widely.

My heart swelled with pride and love for the group of people surrounding me, all invested to make sure I succeeded. Leaning in toward me Kerr hugged me tight, "So fucking proud of you," he told me with a slow smile. "Even though I've heard you sing hundreds of times now, I still get goosebumps. Your voice affects me like no other," he admitted.

When Kerr gave me validation of his approval, my throat constricted. *Simon should have been here.*

A mixture of emotions collided inside my head which included everything from elation to devastation as snapshots flashed in my mind: of my mom's dying face, the empty space outside the bus where Simon should have been as I turned to look out the bus that morning, and finally a happier one of how wildly the crowd had reacted to my performance.

When more fleeting thoughts ran through my mind about all the challenges I had faced, battled, and won, tears flowed down my cheeks unreservedly.

"What's the matter? What did I say?" Kerr asked as he eyed me with concern, placing one knee on the couch. He sat beside me, his leg tucked beneath him and he immediately pulled me into his chest. The comfort I drew from his embrace in that moment meant everything to me.

Petra and Isiah immediately stood and retreated to the back of the bus, leaving Austin and Wyatt staring awkwardly at us. "Would you guys mind giving Piper some space for a few?" Kerr asked, gesturing with his head for them to follow the others.

"Sure," Austin muttered. He and Wyatt shuffled off slowly and as I looked up, my teary eyes met with Wyatt's who had glanced over his shoulder. I offered a weak smile and he gave me a small one in return, but his eyes held his concern for me.

Once the other guys were out of earshot, Kerr pushed me away to arms-length to look at me. His questioning eyes burned into mine.

"All right, spill," he ordered.

I shook my head.

"I can't make you feel okay if I don't know what's wrong in the first place," he offered.

"I- it... it's not your job to do this."

When he continued to stare at me with concern, I sighed. "It's all a bit overwhelming," I stated. It was as clear a confession as I could voice.

Kerr sighed too like he hated seeing me upset and put my head back on his chest. "Singing? Performing? The live gig?" he probed.

"Not really that, it's more about my memories; people I care about not being here to share it all with," I admitted.

"Simon?" Kerr said in a flat tone. Taking in a deep breath, his lungs expanded his strong, broad chest beneath my cheeks, and I knew he was almost as annoyed as I was that Simon hadn't been there.

"Partly... and my mom," I blurted and burst into tears again.

"Hey," Kerr said, repositioning me so he could see my face again.

"Sorry. I guess I'm not as strong as I think I am."

"Piper, you are one of the strongest people I know. To have

achieved what you have after all you've been through is incredible. It's like no matter what shit life has thrown at you, you've managed to use your negative experiences and turn them into your amazing success."

I lifted my head to glance at him and shrugged in surprise, "Shit to sugar, huh?" I asked, giving him a wry smirk. "Thank you... sometimes I feel so alone, you know?"

"I do know. I've watched you battle your demons daily, listened to the way you talk about your mom. I can't imagine how you feel... and I have to be honest with you, Piper, Simon not being there tonight has totally pissed me off."

A knot immediately formed in my stomach at the tone in his voice and I felt Kerr's body tense. "I mean nothing should have been more important than seeing you perform tonight," he spat in frustration.

I swallowed roughly. I didn't want to believe Simon hadn't given a thought about what it would mean to me to have him there.

"It's hard to know what to think because looking at this in a realistic way, M3rCy and Simon have done what we did tonight, hundreds of times. The perspective is completely different."

"Bullshit, Piper," he countered, "I don't buy that and neither do you. Don't defend him. No matter how many times he's walked out on stage he has only ever had that one first time."

Thinking like Kerr only made me feel worse. I knew deep down he was right, but my tender heart didn't want to face the reality that I wasn't important enough to Simon for him to have been there.

Shaking my head, I pulled away from Kerr's embrace and stood up. "Come on, I'm not going to sit here and wallow in self-pity all night. I'm starving, and those pizzas smell incredible," I said, wiping my eyes as I gestured in the direction of the small galley where piles of pizza boxes had been waiting for us when we climbed on the bus.

It wasn't fair to create a bad vibe on the bus either, I had my bandmates to think about. Kerr stood and stuffed his hands deep in his pockets. Shaking his head, I knew he was annoyed when I wouldn't address it anymore, but he followed my lead and let the subject drop.

～

By 2am, I was drunk and emotionally in a much better place thanks to being introduced to Petra's Strawberry Daiquiri, and Tequila Sunrise cocktails.

No one was counting how much we had drunk and by the time I realized how inebriated I was my heart was numb.

I'd never played drinking games before or the game, Chubby Bunny; nor had I realized what a party girl Petra was. Watching a drunk girl stuffing thirty-one marshmallows in her mouth at one time was hysterical.

My sides positively ached from all the laughing I did and by the time I was ready for bed I was so merry my thoughts shrunk of anything other than the moment I was in.

"All right, I'm going to head into bed," I muttered when the mood changed, and Petra and Isiah began canoodling on the couch. Austin had already retired with some porn movie he had been recommended, and Wyatt was so drunk he'd fallen asleep where he sat.

Kerr stood up, "I'll walk you home," he offered with a chuckle because his cubby was the one next to mine. Simon's warning flashed through my head and the smile I had initially given him when he had spoken must have frozen on my face. *Kerr is not a cheater.*

Bracing myself for what he may do, I willed Kerr to prove Simon wrong and by the time I arrived at my cubby I felt as nervous as hell. Turning to Kerr, I placed my hand on his forearm and tried to behave as normally as I could around him.

"Thanks for all you've done to support me today, Kerr. I really appreciate your friendship," I stated.

Moving his hand around my shoulder, he pulled me close to his chest. I stiffened, wondering if, like Simon said, Kerr was about to make a pass.

"You're more than welcome, gorgeous," he informed me, his strong hands both swamping my small body as he engulfed me in a tight hug. Kissing the top of my head, he pushed me back effectively separating us and eyed me with curiosity.

"You going to be okay tomorrow?"

I nodded, swaying a little on my feet. Kerr chuckled.

"Yeah, it was a watershed moment today," I admitted. "Thank you for being so considerate and kind," I said a little slurry.

Kerr's hand swept around the back of my head and he pulled me close, placing a chaste kiss on the top of my head again before stepping away.

"Okay, honey, I need to get some shut eye. See you sometime in the morning... if you recover that quickly," he said, snickering.

Smirking, because I knew I must have looked a hot mess after all the alcohol, I turned and clumsily climbed into the cubby. I was about to pull my curtain divider closed when Kerr spoke again.

"Piper?" he murmured.

"Hmm," I asked, looking back out toward him.

"I think you're a fantastic girl and I was so proud of you today. Never stop being you for anyone else. Don't change who you are to fit anyone else's mold and keep kicking ass like I know you can." I smiled slowly but it turned into a wide grin the longer he stood there.

"Ditto... apart from the fantastic girl thing," I muttered back. My heart was instantly full of everything I knew I felt for him, but I had no other words to express what he meant to me as a friend at that point.

"For the record, Simon McLennan's a dick."

I heard what he said but spread out on the bed without getting undressed and shook my head. *Despite what you think Simon, you're dead wrong about Kerr.*

If Kerr was the player Simon had thought he was, he'd had every opportunity to make his move, and he hadn't. He was a true friend. Turning over, I punched my pillow and fought the tightening in my chest at the thought of Simon.

For a few minutes, I resisted another urge to check my phone, then decided if I was as important to him as he was to me, he'd have been at the gig.

～

Waves of nausea dragged me out of my sleep. The drone of the bus engine did nothing to settle the way my stomach rolled.

Edging up onto my elbows, I wondered where I was for a few seconds, then hazy memories of the games we played flooded back along with all the alcohol I had consumed.

Immediately, I edged my way out of the cubby, caught my foot on the drape and landed unceremoniously on my ass at the foot of the steps.

"Ouch," I winced, stumbling to my feet. I hurriedly staggered with my arms outstretched to balance me until I reached the toilet door.

Seconds later my nose wrinkled in revolt as I retched and vomited a rainbow of stale alcohol into the bowl. "You okay?" Kerr asked, sliding into the small restroom beside me and automatically gathering up my hair.

"No," I croaked. "I'm never drinking again; that Petra is the devil's spawn. I want her arrested for feeding me alcohol while I'm underage," I muttered before retching again. My throat stung from the effort of throwing up and Kerr chuckled.

"Fuck, what am I going to do with you?" Kerr asked in a playful tone. "Was this on your bucket list by any chance?"

"Leave me alone, I'm fine," I said and retched a dry heave again. "I'm sure I'll feel better once the contents of my stomach are safely deposited into this bowl."

"Ah, the 'feeling sorry for myself' phase," he stated. "It usually accompanies the 'I'm never drinking again' promise, which you'll break as soon as you've forgotten this time. I give it a couple of weeks."

"Who made you Professor of Puke?" I grumbled, wrapping the toilet tissue around my hand then wiping my mouth. I straightened up slowly in fear of a new wave of nausea. Turning to face him, he took his thumbs and wiped the mascara from under my eyes.

"There. You only look half dead now," he said, like he was my dad sending me off for a night on the town.

"Thanks, you're so good to me," I mumbled and wrapped my arms around his waist. It was then I realized he was naked apart from a pair of boxer briefs. I felt my face flush, but I tried not to act differently.

"I'm going to lie down again and hope the next time I wake this will all have been a dream."

Catching the handle, he opened the door, "Doubt that, Piper, we don't get many do-overs in life."

"Did you sleep in those?" he asked, noting I was still in the clothes I had changed into after the gig.

"May have," I stated and smirked, a little embarrassed.

"You're officially a lush," he declared. "You may want to take a shower and brush your teeth rather than go back to bed," he advised. "You can nap later. Going back to sleep now will only make you feel worse."

Hesitating outside my cubby, I nodded. "Sounds like a good idea," I admitted. "Go back to bed, I'm fine now. Thanks for caring for me," I said.

"Always, sweetheart," Kerr responded and climbed back into his bed. Hearing a deep sigh, I wondered what he thought of me and decided after what he'd just witnessed it couldn't have been good.

I also sighed because this had been the second time I had consumed too much alcohol—the first being with Simon—and the result had been the same.

I wondered how many more times it would take before I learned to hold it, and not reproduce it the following day.

CHAPTER THIRTY

*S*ix gigs, six days, and only one tiny text from Simon.

Simon: Do everything I know you can because you ARE everything.

If I'd received his text and he'd been around, it would have been the world. Instead, I had found it the day after my debut in Seattle. He'd sent it about two minutes before I had gone on stage.

Only two minutes before—that had felt like I wasn't on his mind and he'd almost forgotten. *Is he hedging his bets with me? Playing me along until he's bored with who he's with?*

At the very least, I had expected a response from him when on day four of the tour a picture emerged of Kerr and I 'hugging' in the loading bay after the first gig in Seattle. Of course it was nothing like what the picture suggested, but the caption had stung.

Piper acts her age and trades Playboy Simon McLennan for a much younger model.

After a love match lasting barely six weeks—a lifetime in terms of the relationships Simon McLennan has had in the past—has the Rock God been relegated into supporting act status in favor of Piper's hunky handsome band member, Kerr Logan? Sources close to the couple say they are "inseparable."

At the time of going to press neither McLennan, Piper, nor their representa-

tives, were available for comment, but with Simon's absence during the tour, one must assume the whirlwind romance with the much younger, gorgeous, and top drawer singer, Piper, has run its course.

On the music front, Piper has been touring with Layla Hartmann. Rumor has it, unknown Piper got close to McLennan who helped discover the talented young artist. Piper is now being hotly tipped as a next generation to rival the fabulous artist, P!nk.

When I had tried to contact Simon to deny the report, it was the first time I had reached out to him. He hadn't contacted me since his initial text, which I hadn't replied to, but the article had given me a valid reason to do so.

We were supposed to be together, yet as I called his number, I was plagued with anxiety because I had no idea where I stood. With Simon's lack of enthusiasm, I felt heartbroken and I wondered if I should have listened to the man who had never let me down.

As Simon's phone went to his answer service I closed the call out, not even bothering to leave a message. It was pointless if he wasn't concerned in the first place.

Unlike Simon, Gibson was quick to follow up, and I heard both relief and anxiety in his tone when I denied the rumor, but I had to confess I hadn't heard from Simon.

Gibson had figured the media were fishing but cussed under his breath about Simon and asked when I'd heard from him last.

I told him the night of my debut concert but didn't elaborate, and he appeared satisfied with my reply. Offering me reassurance and advice for dealing with the press, Gibson concluded the call, and I knew the first thing he'd do was contact Simon himself. I then wondered if Simon would contact me after he's spoken with Gibson.

$\sim$

Since the story had broken regarding Kerr and me, I had cried myself to sleep—both times in Kerr's arms, my head against his chest while he smoothed down my hair to soothe me. I never looked at Kerr as anything other than a brother and from what he told his girl, Louisa, it was the same for him.

Kerr had called her the morning the story broke and fortunately Louisa had been so gracious about the whole thing. She worked in advertising and was used to people spinning things to look a certain way.

Sitting shoulder to shoulder with me during a Skype call, Kerr declared how he felt about her and not once did Louisa eye me with suspicion.

"I've known you for seven years Kerr. In all that time I've felt blessed with what a caring and compassionate man you are. It's one of the things I love most about you. I don't feel threatened at all by you, Piper, for the reason I've just said. I. Know. Kerr."

Kerr smiled adoringly at the camera and it was clear he only had eyes for her. "Love you, baby," he cooed, and her smile grew wider.

Turning her attention to me she sighed, "Piper, I get your world is all glamor and people ditching people and getting with others. Kerr is part of that world where our relationship may be constantly questioned, but I'm not."

I wasn't sure what she meant, and I felt my brow crease.

She shrugged, "I'm a private girl and I have two options: either I become a suspicious, needy person who follows Kerr around, or I trust him. Honestly? I don't have to trust either of you, but I do. The one thing he promised me was if he met someone else he had feelings for he'd end it with me before anything happened."

My heart immediately squeezed for her. To think I was party to something that may have made her feel insecure, hurt me. "Thank you for trusting him and for trusting this story is a pack of lies," I told her.

"Don't think I'm a fool blinded by love, Piper. I have my own reasons for tolerating Kerr being close to you. I can see what he has with you, and it's a close friendship. Better he has that with you than be lonely, but I'd be a saint if I didn't say sometimes it makes me feel jealous. You get to spend time with him—time that I don't. I guess my trust in Kerr has to extend to you because you have opportunities with him I can do nothing about."

"Opportunities? You mean to cheat?" I asked, my voice rising in disbelief. "I'd nev—"

"I suppose," she said, cutting in as she shifted in her seat and my eyes darted to Kerr. He looked hurt.

"There is *no* opportunity, Louisa. I'm not interested in Kerr in that way and neither is he, in me. He loves you completely. The way he talks about you tells me that. Besides, if you knew my background you'd know I'd never go there. Even the hypothetical idea of this suggestion makes me feel sick."

Kerr sighed and leaned into the screen. "I want you to look into my eyes when I say this, Louisa. Piper is a gorgeous girl, I can't deny that, but she isn't you. You're all I want, babe. I'm yours." Kerr didn't take his eyes off the screen and Louisa leaned forward to touch it.

"I miss you, honey. Can't wait until tomorrow," she murmured quietly to him like I had ceased to be present. For a moment they stared silently at each other, then Louisa turned her attention back to me.

"Listen, fuck the media and their twisted lies. They take delight in splitting up genuine couples and we know that won't happen here. Let them say what they want. We can't stop them speculating. It'll be fun to see how they spin it when I turn up in Chicago tomorrow night," she said with determination in her tone.

My heart squeezed, "I'm sorry about the hugs," I said. I had been so caught up in my own needs and how innocent the contact was, it never really occurred to me how damaging it could have been for Kerr. "It was selfish of me to need them, but I never drew anything from them except comfort. But I do want to explain the picture. Kerr had helped me down from a loading bay as we left the venue in Seattle, that's all it was."

"Kerr hugs everyone, Piper, and I'd rather he hugged you than any other girl so long as it's only in a friendly way. I know how much he misses me." Her understanding blew me away.

Kerr was a stunning looking guy with an amazing personality. Simon was right. I doubted I could ever be as understanding if Simon hugged another woman and I had to deal with that.

"Piper's the sister I never had," he stated to Louisa. "It's so weird because I've never really felt comfortable in the company of women because they usually try to hit on me. You know how careful I am about that, babe. We've spoken about how much I hate it and I could never hurt you. This is like touring with my best mate. I don't get that vibe from this one," he said gesturing toward me with his thumb.

Relief washed through me because every contact I had ever had with Kerr had been spontaneous; and his reaction of hugging me was instinctive to comfort me through times when I hurt.

Innocent as we had felt we were, we had Louisa's feelings to think about, and my dependency on his support could have cost him his relationship. When the Skype call dropped, I shook my head as a wave of empathy struck me for Louisa and I burst into tears.

"Hey," Kerr said, his hands reaching for my shoulders to comfort me.

"Please, don't. That poor girl. I know you want to comfort me because I'm upset, but Simon was right. We know you are only reacting to my distress, but that girl feels as if she has no choice but to accept the story flying about us. It's hurt her, I can see that."

"We're solid, Piper. Louisa is a very level-headed girl."

"And she's being forced to behave like a doormat because of my behavior. Simon warned me about this and I ignored him. I waved his concern about how we looked together off and accused him of being jealous. He may have read us wrongly, but he knows a lot more about the gossip mill where the press is concerned and I know nothing. I'm so fucking flawed I can't see the woods for the trees."

Kerr looked down at his hands and rubbed them together, and for the first time I felt an awkwardness between us. His face looked solemn as he glanced up and his eyes met mine.

"So, I'm to change how I am... to stop the press spreading lies?"

"No, I'm saying we both need to think more. How we behave affects the people around us. Louisa said you hug everyone. I've never seen you do that with anyone apart from me. The only person who ever hugged me in my life before my new family was my mom." Kerr narrowed his eyes like he was angry at my admission.

I sighed, "Well, once before... at home, I had one brief boyfriend. Two months we were together. His hugs were... different." I sighed again as I thought how to best explain what I meant. "His hugs were linked to kisses and it was the only time he put his arms around me.

We messed around a bit, but his hugs were always an awkward, clumsy prelude to a kiss."

"I don't see what that has—"

"Let me finish. When the man that saved me from destitution hugged me, it was the first time in my life I felt completely safe and comfortable when a man touched me. I can't tell you what his protective hugs did for me as I absorbed the news about my mom... and then after her death. It was as if nothing could ever hurt me when I was with him."

"And that's how mine make you feel?"

I nodded. "They do, and I guess I've grown somewhat dependent on the hugs you've readily given me."

"I can't help wanting to comfort you. From all you've told me life has been so fucking difficult in the past. You're the bravest girl I've ever met, and when I see you hurting it wrecks me."

My heart clenched at his admission. "It's not your job to make me feel better. It's my job to grow stronger, become more resilient." Kerr considered my comment and nodded.

"Maybe so, but I care about you and my natural instinct is to want to make you feel better."

"Over Louisa's feelings?"

His eyes widened. "Of course not, but I guess I've been naïve and pretty thoughtless too."

Even with the mess of my personal life, I knew I could never allow anything to affect my performance. Fortunately, I had spent my whole life putting on a brave face, so I knew that wouldn't be an issue.

The following concert after the story broke turned out to be my best, and Thomas said the offers were coming thick and fast as word got around about how talented I was.

Everything I had envisioned for myself had come to fruition. I should have been floating with excitement, However, Simon's continued silence was breaking my heart.

Two concerts in two nights, one the day the story broke and one the day after, yet I saw nothing had prompted Simon to contact me. In the end I concluded either he hadn't seen it, or he didn't care.

Somehow after the fifth gig we performed, I managed to act as if nothing was bothering me, and after eating his food, Kerr retired to his cubby to spent a couple of hours talking to Louisa. Although it wasn't my intention to listen, I heard snippets of conversation.

When they spoke about the chat he and I had following the Skype call earlier that day, Louisa really had understood my position. Then she admitted to Kerr I was right in what I had told him. Louisa felt she had no option but to accept things as they were.

Climbing into my cubby, I realized how headstrong I had been about my independence and figured I had so much more to learn about how someone's selfish behavior impacted on another. In that moment I cried.

Swallowing rapidly, I tried to stem the salty tears burning my throat as I weakly fought against an agonizing wave of anger and grief that flooded though me. Giving in to my feelings, I silently sobbed into my pillow and cursed God for taking my mom when I needed her most.

CHAPTER THIRTY-ONE

*W*aking with a pounding headache, I fumbled for the buzzing cell vibrating somewhere in my bed. Eventually I found it and saw Chloe's number.

"Morning," I croaked and held my cell back to see the time. We had a day off when we got to Chicago.

"Are you okay, honey?"

"Sure. You?"

"Have you only just woken up?"

"Yeah," I said sleepily and stretched out as much as I could in the confined space of my bunk.

"Thomas hasn't spoken to you yet?"

My brow creased, and I shifted up on one elbow, propping my head up with my hand.

"No, why is there a problem?" I asked, suddenly more in tune with the concern in her voice.

Chloe sighed. "Have you heard anything from Simon?"

I swallowed roughly, my heart aching at the mere mention of his name.

"N- no, I haven't," I answered, ashamed by my admission.

Chloe's breath hitched, "I see."

"What do you see?" I snapped, frustrated because she wasn't getting to the point.

"When was the last time you spoke to him?"

I felt my face flush with embarrassment even though she was on the phone.

"Piper, honey, are you awake?" Kerr's voice sounded soft at the other side of the privacy drape to my cubby.

"Yeah, I'm speaking to Chloe at the moment," I offered and tried to focus back on the conversation.

"Is that Kerr with you?" she asked.

"He's outside my bunk," I stated quickly, in the event she got the wrong idea.

"Oh, I didn't mean it like that," she replied, and I shook my head at my paranoia.

I sighed heavily. I knew she didn't mean anything by it. "I know, I'm sorry. The article the other day has made us both defensive of the people we care about. Neither Kerr nor I want to give people the wrong idea."

"You're seeing Gibson tonight? I wish I could come but I have this thing with Mel—"

I smiled, "Its fine, Chloe. It's all good. I'm glad you're getting to spend time with Melody; she should always come first," I interjected.

"This isn't why I called. Look, there's no easy way to say this other than to say it outright." Her voice held a tinge of sadness.

"There are some pictures in the media today of Simon..." A shock of electricity shot through me and if I hadn't been lying down, I was almost certain I would have buckled at the knees. Dread flooded through me and I knew what she had to tell me was going to hurt me.

"Sparky Mitchell, the lead singer from STLO band who died two years ago?" she said like she was asking a question, "He was one of Simon's friends when they were younger."

"And?"

"We all know first-hand how things can get twisted by the press reporting but there are some pictures of him all over social media. In them Simon's lying on the deck of a yacht in the Caribbean with Sparky's widow and her two teenage kids. He was linked to her before, a month or so after Sparky's death, but they both denied there was anything going on between them."

I remembered the article in the press at the time. It happened when I first went to live in the Barclay's house and I'd overheard Simon deny there was anything in it.

Still, that knowledge didn't prevent my chest from tightening as I fought for breath, because knowing how Simon was in the past gave me cause to think the worst.

My heart pounded so hard my lips buzzed with its pace and I cussed at myself for being so trusting and innocent to the ways of men. "I see," was all I could manage as I choked back a sob.

"Don't. Please don't cry. I know you're upset. I've been where you are, remember? Every other week there was someone new linked to Gibson the moment I wasn't with him. The media was partly what Gibson was afraid of with Simon."

Partly being the operative word; the other part was how Simon had been a player for the longest time. The words leopards and spots came to mind, and I pushed that saying out of my mind, refusing to judge Simon guilty until I had all the facts.

"Gibson is flying down tonight. For what it's worth he hasn't been able to speak to Simon himself, but to say he is furious would be an understatement."

"I don't want to see Gibson if all he's going to do is lecture me with 'I told you so's," I snapped angrily through another sob. Swiping at the tears staining my face, I shook my head at my own stupidity. *Who did I think I was? How the heck did I believe for one minute I had what it took to capture and hold the attention of someone most women fantasized over?*

The bare truth of it all was I didn't want to face Gibson after the way I scolded him when all he had wanted to do was protect me against how I now felt. Digging deep, I fought for control of my feelings.

"Let's not tear ourselves up until we know the truth of the matter, honey," Chloe reasoned, offering me a fresh glimmer of hope. "You have to let Simon explain himself. Then you will be able to decide what to do."

"Can I call you back in a bit? I'm needed out in the galley." I lied through my teeth in a small shaky voice because I could feel my anxiety growing and I was seconds away from losing it. Chloe was hundreds of miles away and I didn't want her to hear the full impact of how hurt I was.

When I cancelled out the call I crumbled completely, my heart felt crushed. Soaking my pillow with fresh tears I heard muffled sobs long before I realized they were mine.

"You okay, Piper?" Kerr's caring voice came from the other side of the thin gray curtain again.

"You knew, didn't you?" I stated in a flat tone.

"You decent?" he asked, concerned.

"Mm-hm" I said, wiping away my tears with the sleeve of my cotton pajama top. Pulling back the drape my heart cracked when I saw the devastating look of sympathy in his eyes when he first saw my face.

"Petra showed me the pictures when I went to get breakfast a few minutes ago."

"It's bad isn't it?" I asked and sobbed into my hands.

"Hey, come here." Kerr ignored my question and tugged at my sleeve to entice me toward him.

"No, Kerr. This isn't your problem," I said, angry he felt the need to comfort me. "I got myself into this mess... it's my own fault for trusting him."

"We don't know what the deal is yet," he reminded me, and I figured like Chloe, he was trying to make me feel better. "I mean there was no truth in the stuff about us," he added.

"Let's look at the facts. Simon hasn't rung me. Not even after the shitty article about us. He couldn't get away from me quick enough when I got back on this bus. He wasn't even there when I turned around to look at him as I left. I've had one line of text in six days. Even that seemed like an afterthought because it arrived about two minutes before I went on stage... and there's been nothing since. Nada."

Kerr continued to try to pacify me, but I couldn't accept any of the explanations he touted and eventually he accepted the best thing he could do was allow me to wallow in my pain.

Thank God for the day off. Fury and frustration made my heart sink in my chest. Depression was something my mother had suffered with and until that night I had managed to keep my half-full glass attitude in check, but it had been much harder to do since Chloe's phone call.

Somehow, I couldn't bring myself to look at the pictures. I didn't need to see how it looked to know how I felt. I felt it would have destroyed every precious moment I had spent with him in the past and it would make everything he ever said to me lies.

My resilience was only so strong and from what had happened to me in the past there were only so many knock-backs I was prepared to take.

Kerr couldn't lift my mood. In the absence of my mom, the only person I wanted was Gibson. Even at that, I feared his lecture about how vigorously he had tried to protect me from Simon would piss me off more.

Then again, I had told him I was prepared for this to happen. It was one of the risks I had felt I had to take and it would appear the thought of being prepared and living out the reality of it wasn't as easy as I thought it would be.

The only constructive thing I could do was to pull myself together or risk Gibson turning on his band member. It was all a huge mess and the consequences of what I'd created were my own fault.

The least I could do was pretend to Gibson I had backed off. It was the only way forward I could see for him and Simon to remain bandmates and continue with M3rCy.

~

For some reason I felt relieved when we checked into our hotel in Chicago. I wasn't sure if it was due to me seeing Gibson a few hours later or being off of the bus. It had felt monotonous since the conversation with Louisa and Kerr.

The relationship between me and Kerr just wasn't the same. We were both being wary, and I hoped as time passed we'd find that natural affinity we had for liking the same things to bring our friendship closer again in the future.

During the night I had cried copious tears as I lay heartbroken about Simon. The way he had treated me was disgusting.

Gibson had gone with his gut and reacted the way he did when he'd found out about Simon and me because he wanted to protect me. Unfortunately, his gut was healthier than mine. I sighed, heavily. *How could I have been so wrong?*

From the moment I stepped off the bus that morning, I was determined to move forward with my life and after my period of wallowing in self-pity about Simon, I was certain he'd played me like all the others.

There was still a job to do, and as the leader of my band, I had to ensure they were happy. The best way to do that was to enlist Kerr's support and organize a team day out.

The man was full of ideas for what to do, but as Sears Tower had been one of my bucket list places everyone appeared as keen as me to visit it.

From the ground, Willis (Sears) Tower looked like any other skyscraper up close, but weaving our way around the crowds with our VIP status and entering the elevator that rocketed up to the top, gave me a sense of how spectacular it must have been when it first opened in the 1970s.

Stepping out on the top floor, I caught my breath when I looked at the panoramic view. My hungry eyes scanned left and right, and I was fascinated at how small most of the other buildings appeared below us.

It was different from being in an airplane. Speechless, I stood captivated as my mind built a memory for a sight that I knew would stay with me for the rest of my life.

"Let's see how brave you are," Kerr said, quickly grasping my hand. Less than a minute later I stood facing a glass bottomed platform with buildings so far below they looked like tiny boxes in the distance. I swallowed nervously but knew I hadn't taken many risks in my life that had happy outcomes and nodded.

"Yep, no problem I can do this," I said, sounding much braver than I felt as my feet reluctantly shuffled against the edge. Kerr chuckled, and I glanced up at him with a fearful look. "You're sure this is safe, right?"

"Safer than the risks most people take," he reassured me, and half tugged me onto the glass with him. Petra held her phone up to take a picture, and I immediately pulled my hand out of Kerr's like I had been burned and with that Kerr immediately put his arm around my shoulder and pulled me into his side.

"Don't," he snapped, clearly annoyed I had shunned him. I knew what he had done was spontaneous, but I didn't need yet another round of negative press.

"Anyone for pizza?" Austin asked a few minutes later, rubbing his stomach, "Can't come to Chicago and not have pizza," he advised. His comment gave me an easy way out of the potentially awkward conversation with Kerr.

"Sounds fantastic," I agreed, stepping off the platform and heading back toward the elevator. Austin, Wyatt, and I chatted excitedly about the view, while Isiah took another hundred pictures from his cell phone.

Meanwhile Petra and Kerr dropped back a way, and I knew instinctively they were talking about me.

As we entered the elevator to take us back to street level, the attendant was intent on cramming us all together and I found myself standing facing the front with a guy in his thirties standing to my side.

"Oh, God, you're that Piper, aren't you?" he asked in a surprised tone. I glanced in his direction and he smiled widely, "You're her, right?"

Heat rose to my cheeks as my shoulders hunched and I lowered my gaze, "I..." I shook my head, confused at how to answer. I wasn't famous, I had only done a little more than a handful of concerts, a few TV interviews, and a couple of malls.

Thankfully the elevator doors opened, and I pushed past Isiah to make space between the guy and me, "I'm not really hungry. I'm going to grab a cab and head back to the hotel. You guys have fun. I'm meeting someone from my family later, so I guess I'll be having dinner with him," I told them in a rush.

Kerr hurried after me, catching my forearm right before I made it out to the street. "You okay, Piper? Up there, I didn't really think about—"

Quickly, I explained I was a little paranoid about the press and when the guy in the elevator had recognized me it had freaked me out a little.

Once I convinced him I really did have a dinner date with my dad, Kerr looked relieved he had done nothing wrong and went off to join the others for a late lunch.

CHAPTER THIRTY-TWO

*E*xcitement and dread filled me in equal measure as I waited for Gibson to let me know when he had arrived. I didn't have to wait long before there was a knock on my hotel room door.

At first, I had figured it was the housekeeping staff but when I looked through the spyhole I saw Jonny, Gibson's bodyguard outside waiting for me.

When I opened the door, relief washed through me. Even Jonny was a welcome familiar face.

"All set, sweetheart?" he asked glancing toward the bank of elevators.

Grabbing my purse and jacket, I followed him out of the room. Instead of turning left toward the elevators, he led me down the corridor to a stairwell at the far end.

We didn't talk at all on the way down and I thought I'd go dizzy from all floor numbers we passed.

It was then that I realized why I had been placed on the seventh floor of the hotel and the rest of my band around twenty more floors above me.

Jonny weaved his way through a laundry room with me following closely, then he hit an exit bar on a door and I immediately saw a black Mercedes sports car waiting in the alleyway.

Jerry, Gibson's other security detail was the driver, but that was all I could see until Jonny opened the door and Gibson came into view.

A beaming smile spread over his face as he held out his hand, and my heart swelled with joy when I finally saw him.

"Look at you, baby girl," Gibson said, yanking me inside to sit next to him.

Stretching his arm along the seat behind me, he hurriedly grabbed me and gave me a tight squeeze of affection before tilting his head back to look at me.

"Been hearing great things about you, Piper," he admitted, and I flashed him a winning smile.

"Figure you're only around six months to a year before you get your own tour. I gotta hand it to you, darlin', you're far more ballsy than I gave you credit for. Layla told me you're a dream to work with. You're already riding high in her estimation."

"Thanks, it hasn't felt like that this last few days," I confessed.

"I take it there's been no word from Simon?" Gibson's body language stiffened as he instinctively knew I was referring to all the press coverage we'd had.

I shook my head because I couldn't bring myself to say the words and swallowed several times to keep my tears at bay.

"Fuck knows what he's playing at. He hasn't answered my calls either, Piper. Chloe's convinced he's shitting himself for the moment I get a hold of him."

"No, Gibson. I don't want you fighting my battles. You and Simon need to work together. I'm a big girl. If there's anything to be said I'll do the talking. You did warn me," I added before he had the opportunity to lecture me. "This is my own fault for trusting him." I shrugged as the man who had sworn to protect me gave me a grave look.

Running a hand through his hair in frustration, he shook it then eyed me seriously, "I don't know what the fuck to think because I saw the way he looked at you... the way he was around you. Piper, he did behave differently with you, then..." he shrugged and sighed. "Guess we'll learn soon enough when he surfaces."

Frustration radiated off Gibson as he talked about Simon because there wasn't much Gibson couldn't do about a situation when he put his mind to it. Except he couldn't save me from being hurt by Simon McLennan—not that he hadn't tried.

"I'm not gonna lie to you, I really thought he'd turned a corner with you. As much as I hated the thought of you two together, he didn't put a foot wrong until now." He sighed again and turned the window down in the car a tad, allowing the cool fresh air from outside to waft through the back of the saloon.

The heavy heart I'd struggled with since Simon left suddenly felt ten times heavier for airing how I felt to Gibson and hearing the hurt in his voice in return.

Whatever the reason Simon had stayed away, neither of us could think of any possible plausible excuse for the length of time he'd been away and his maintained silence.

It appeared Gibson had a personal list of his favorite 'hidden gem' restaurants everywhere. Since I had lived with them, I knew of several small backwater places in Colorado the Barclays used for private dinner parties.

The one he took me to for dinner in Chicago was, broadly speaking, the same type of small, Italian, family run affair. Except apart from Jonny and Jerry, we were the only two people dining.

Three hours at dinner wasn't nearly enough time for me because once Gibson had gotten past the subject of Simon, the evening was exactly what I had needed.

I'd forgotten how great a storyteller he was, and it was only when Jonny came to remind Gibson about the flight slot they had booked for the return to Gibson's ranch that the evening wound down to an end.

Dropping me back at the hotel, Jerry reversed into the alleyway again and Jonny got out with me to walk me back. Gibson kissed me on the cheek and hugged me tight.

"Try not to dwell on how Simon has treated you. Not all guys are the same. You could do much better anyway," he said with a wink. "Everything will work out, baby girl, and you will be right where you should be. Trust me, if it was meant to be, he'd be here with you now," he added. His jaw ticked again, and I could see he was barely holding back his temper.

Smiling innocently like his words hadn't impacted on me, I reached for the handle of the door Jonny held open and made my way out, hiding how wounded I felt by Gibson's remark. A wave of emotion swelled in my throat and suddenly I didn't want to hang around.

Turning, I made my way down the alley and had just reached the street when Jerry pulled alongside me and Gibson wound his window down. "Piper, you forgot this, darlin'," he called after me.

Spinning on my heels at the sound of his voice, I ran quickly back toward him and grabbed my purse. He pulled my head toward the window and kissed my cheek again. "See you a week from Sunday," he said, reminding me of my girl date with Chloe and Melody.

Hastily, I nodded and turned once again, heading inside the hotel. Taking the elevator this time, I arrived in my suite as the hotel room phone began to ring. "We have a message from Mr. McLennan for you. Would you please call suite fourteen-twenty-one?" the polite sounding receptionist enquired.

Simon? Suite? I cleared my throat, "Where?" I asked, my voice maybe an octave higher than usual.

"McLennan is in suite fourteen-twenty-one. Would you like me to connect you?"

"Connect me?" I was starting to sound like a parrot. "You mean he's here... in this hotel?"

"Yes, Ma'am. Would you like me to connect you?" the male reception caller asked patiently.

"No... no thank you," I said as my mind went into chaos.

"Would you like to leave a message?" he enquired, with a note of surprise in his Southern tone.

Heading over to the small wet bar with my heart beating so fast I could feel the pulsing in my mouth, I grabbed a bottle of water and twisted off the lid. Icy cold liquid passed over my lips and I took a long suck of it down. It felt like I was swallowing shards of glass.

"Ma'am?" the caller asked again when I hadn't replied.

"No... yes, tell him to go to hell. I have nothing to say to him, thank you," I replied and slammed down the handset.

For a few seconds my mind was numb, then came rage. It soared through me like wildfire. "What the fuck does he take me for? He thinks he can mug me off for someone else and come crawling back?

Does Simon think I'm that naïve? Hell will freeze over before he'll get into my bed again," I muttered aloud to myself after quickly discarding the thought.

How did I allow myself to get into such a mess? My music career was going incredibly well and my personal one was completely fucked.

Buzzing sounds came from my purse and I pulled out my vibrating cell. When I saw Gibson's face, I almost freaked because he had the most amazing intuition for calling at the most inopportune moments.

"Hey," I answered, trying to keep my voice even.

"Did he call you?" Gibson said ignoring all pleasantries.

"Who?" I asked knowing full well what this conversation was about.

"Simon... the fucker. He said he's at your hotel now," he replied. Gibson's anger radiated through his voice. "I'm coming back," he muttered, "Turn the fucking car around," he said, I presumed to Jerry who had been driving when they left.

"No, please, Gibson, it's fine. I'm fine. He's not coming here. I refused to take his call."

"And you think that'll stop him? He's in your hotel. I give him thirty minutes to find out what room you're in. You have no idea the lengths he will go to when he wants something. I'll be with you in ten."

The sound of the call dropping told me Gibson was done talking and he was on his way back, but before I could draw breath my cell rang again.

Simon's call was instantly recognizable from the ringtone of "Tell Me Something I Don't Know" by Selena Gomez I'd attached to his number.

I was inclined to answer and scream at him, but I figured maybe that would be what he'd expect, so I let it go to voicemail instead.

When a knock came at the door a few minutes later, I opened it thinking it was Gibson, only to find Simon standing before me. "Hey, Princess," he greeted as he flashed me his signature sexy as sin smile that would normally have made me melt on the spot.

The adrenaline coursing through my body at the shock from the sight of him should have fueled me with anger. Pictures of him with that woman and her teenage kids. I had felt humiliated. *He has a cheek coming to face me like this.*

"Are you fucking serious right now?" I asked in an incredulous tone.

A couple came out of one of the rooms a few doors down and glanced at us standing in the doorway as they passed. Simon shielded his face, but he wasn't quick enough.

"Oh. My. God, you're Simon McLennan," the girl said, giving him a salacious smile even though she hung on her boyfriend's arm.

"Keep moving, babe," Simon snapped, "I know who the fuck I am," he muttered and turned his back to the girl.

"Oy, you don't get to speak to my girl like that," her burly boyfriend replied through gritted teeth.

"Then get a stronger leash on her, buddy. She's hanging onto your arm and eye-fucking me," he informed him in an angry tone.

Before the guy could come back at him a noise at the bottom of the corridor saw Jonny step out, closely followed by Gibson.

"Fuck," Simon cussed and blew out a breath.

"Get the fuck away from her," Gibson bellowed down the hallway, "Piper, inside now." Both spectators from the other room stood with their jaws hanging open in shock and I wanted to disappear.

"Stop it, Gibson, I can handle this." I objected to my personal life being made a spectacle of.

"I told you to stay away from her," Gibson shouted as I grabbed Simon by the shirt sleeve and pulled him inside. Gibson followed quickly with Jonny, who closed the hotel room door with a bang.

"Jesus fucking Christ, will no one let me explain what went down?"

"Yeah, like we're all ears after your week in the Caribbean. Can't wait to hear you wiggle your way out of this one. You've played this poor girl and I'm so fucking angry right now I don't trust myself to get up close to you," Gibson added.

"Please, stop!" I said shouting above them. My heart raced as my chest tightened with the anxiety building inside.

All three men in the room stared at me and everything I felt inside must have been expressed on the outside because both Simon and Gibson immediately came to comfort me.

"Back off," Gibson told Simon as he pulled me in for a hug.

"For God's sake," Simon huffed, "If you'd just listen, I can explain. You're the last people who should take note of what it says in the press." Gibson growled, then nodded after a short pause.

"Personally, I think you're gonna have to pull an oversized rabbit out of your ass, make it fart glitter and shit gold to win me over," he said, grunting as he sat on the bed. He blew out a long breath and glanced at Jonny, "Can you believe the gall of this clown?"

Simon inhaled a deep breath and exhaled it nervously, "All right. Look, I've never spoken about this before, and I never intended on doing so either, but because of developments in the last couple of years and my relationship with Piper that position has changed. Before I tell you where I was, I have to say I was going to discuss this with Piper. I almost did then decided to wait until after she had finished her tour. I just didn't want anything to derail the high she was on."

"That was your first fail," Gibson interjected, prompting the stink eye from Simon.

"You want to hear this or not? Like it's any of your business anyway," Simon threw back in a defiant tone.

When a pause stretched in the conversation Simon tried again.

"We've all seen the pictures of me on the Mitchell's yacht in the press?"

All three men's heads bobbed in unison, including his own, and I wondered how the hell he had hoped to dig himself out of the hole he was in. Even Jonny was scowling.

"Piper... please bear in mind this is not how I wanted to do this," Simon stared intensely, his eyes pleading for understanding.

"This week was the Mitchells' twins' birthdays and years ago I made a promise to attend their thirteenth birthday."

"And that was more important than your girlfriend's debut gig?"

He sighed. "On this occasion, yes, because this was a promise I made a lifetime ago."

Gibson scoffed, "I've heard everything now. Since when did you care about anyone but yourself?" Shaking his head incredulously, Gibson folded his arms. "We're all ears, Si, and this better be good, because while you were off playing happy families your 'Princess' here was taking the biggest risk of her life and her so-called man was nowhere in sight to support her."

Simon glanced at me apologetically. "Believe me, the timing of everything sucked, but let's be fair when I say Piper and I had only been together for a couple of months," he said with a pleading look in his eyes gesturing toward me.

I flinched at his words, wondering what he could possibly say in the hope of redeeming himself.

"Do you think I didn't consider if there was any other way around this? Besides, it was Piper's time to shine whether I was there or not."

Simon looked at me silently begging with his dull hazel eyes that usually held a gleam of mischief and I felt the angst in his heart. My heart clenched because all I saw in his gaze was sadness, but for what reason? *Would he ever have told me where he went if those pictures hadn't been published?*

Turning his attention to Gibson he shrugged and sighed. "Look, I went over to Seattle with the idea of maybe telling her, but she'd gone out for the day and we spent half the evening arguing. There was no way I could have told her and left after that. I didn't have the time to explain it properly without leaving her with further questions. It could have destroyed her and left her distressed right before she had to get back on the tour bus."

Turning to address me, he shrugged helplessly. "You were performing for the first time that night, Piper."

Facing Gibson again he asked, "You really think I wanted to leave her alone on her opening night?"

Glancing back at me, he swallowed, roughly. "I know you said there was nothing between you and Kerr, but there's something between you two that feels... intimate, and I had to know if we were solid before I told you." Gibson looked at Simon and jerked his head back like what Simon had said was totally unexpected.

"Before you told me what?" I asked, my eyes darting between Simon and Gibson as my heart thumped erratically. The longer I looked at Simon the less strong I felt about walking away from what I thought we had.

"All right, let's hear you explain it all away." Gibson sounded resigned to some bullshit explanation, but instinct told me he had taken Simon seriously and that Simon had genuinely felt threatened by Kerr. He really had no need. I'll admit Kerr had held my attention, but not in the same way as I felt about Simon. It was friendship like I had never had before, that's all.

Simon bit his lip and glanced to Gibson then to Jonny. "I could do this better without a fucking audience."

Nodding toward the door Gibson looked at his bodyguard, "Can you wait outside?"

"I meant you as well," Simon added quickly to Gibson and my heart race spiked with anxiety because I knew how frustrated Gibson was. Instead of a comeback he remained calm.

"Not gonna happen, dude," Gibson responded and shook his head slowly.

As Jonny headed for the door, Gibson folded his arms over his chest and glanced from me to Simon. "We're waiting."

Inhaling deeply, I tried to calm my nerves. I desperately wanted to hear he hadn't cheated, but in my heart I felt the chances of a man like Simon staying faithful to me were slim to none.

Suddenly, I was reluctant to hear what he had to say because for as long as I didn't hear the words there was still hope.

CHAPTER THIRTY-THREE

Clearing his throat, Simon wandered over toward me and pulled me into his chest before I had the chance to move away from him.

"You're really gonna insist on being here for this, Gib?" He inhaled and sighed deeply, "Piper's an adult for fuck's sake, this is private between us," he ground out. I pulled away, walked over to the small couch and sat with my hands on my lap.

"Trust me, Piper. I never wanted to hurt you." Pain cut through me because the sentence implied whatever he said was going to do that anyway.

Glancing nervously toward Gibson, I pushed my palms under my thighs and sat on my hands.

"Get it over with, Simon. I want to know how you could be filling my head with possibilities and a week later be plastered all over the papers looking so fucking cozy with that woman."

I sounded so together... probably looked together too because I had kept my cool. Inside it couldn't have been further from the truth.

My heart ached, and I was a mess because although he was about to deliver a lethal blow to my heart, it still betrayed me and was melting inside.

Throwing his hands up in the air he cussed under his breath before his eyes settled on me.

"Jenna and Sparky Mitchell were riding high on Sparky's fame when I first ran into him again. Sparky came from my neck of the woods and lived a few towns over from me. Growing up we ran in mutual friend circles but we were never actually friends then; he was older... cooler, and Jenna had been his girl for a few years before I met them."

Simon fazed for a moment like he'd drifted off somewhere, then he took a deep breath and blew it out slowly. Shoving his hands in his pockets he shrugged and smoothed his beard.

"Anyway, right before I joined M3rCy, Sparky's band was racing up the charts and everything looked so fucking rosy for them, yet every time I saw the guy he looked so fucking miserable it bugged the fuck out of me."

Engaging Gibson he said, "You know what it was like, Gib, we were trying at every turn and this guy had what we were all hungry for, yet he didn't appear to appreciate where he was in the pecking order."

"Can you just cut to the chase and get the fuck on with the issue at hand. I don't want to hear your life story," Gibson snapped in a cutting tone.

Simon ran his hand through his hair then stuffed his hands in his pockets and chuckled nervously. He took a deep breath.

"Anyway, one night I ran into him at a mutual friend's party. Sparky was blind drunk and it wasn't pretty. Jenna looked heartbroken every time she glanced in his direction. I don't know why it bothered me, but it did. Who cared if a rock star got drunk and mugged off his wife?"

"Don't tell me you helped his wife to feel wanted?" Gibson taunted, making inverted commas with his fingers as he said 'helped', "Oh. My. God." He suddenly blurted, and I wondered what I'd missed.

"Yeah, I did help her... and him, but not in the way you think," Simon bit back, before glancing to me with hurt in his eyes. "Sorry, baby," he said to me by way of apology for what I suspected he had yet to say.

"Jenna confided in me that Sparky couldn't have kids, and although she had done everything she knew to convince him she didn't care, he knew it was a lie. It was about the only thing in the world she really did want... to be a mom I mean. What's the saying, 'You're only rich when you have something you can't buy'?"

Gibson slapped his legs and stood up. My heart missed a beat as I held my breath for the sentence I was sure was next, and Simon would say he was Jenna's kids father.

"So this wasn't the first time you had an affair with Jenna Mitchell?" I heard myself say quietly, swallowing back tears. My heart felt like it would burst out of my chest and a stabbing pain settled deep in my stomach.

Gibson's eyes narrowed like he might commit murder. Simon shook his head vigorously, "Stands to reason you'd both think the worst of me, but no. I've *never* had an affair with Jenna Mitchell. I'd swear on my sister's life I never touched her."

"Sure sounded to me like the next thing you had to tell us was that Jenna's kids were yours," Gibson told him.

Chewing the side of his cheek he shrugged. A desolate look cast over his face. "They are, but not like you think... I mean, I donated... fuck," he muttered as he stared at the floor and ran his hands through his hair again.

Both Gibson and I stood quiet. *He has two children?* I swallowed as my throat closed tight in distress and tried not to cry.

The only sound in the room was Gibson scratching the stubble on his chin, "Sparky's dead and what? You're playing daddy? You knew all of this and still you fucked with Piper's future?"

"No... never. I think the world of Piper. This thing with Jenna... it was something I promised them a long time ago and again shortly before Sparky died. They'd already told the kids when it would happen."

"Damnit, Simon you're not making sense," I barked.

"I didn't know any better. I mean, think about it...? I was nineteen when I offered to donate my sperm. At the time I thought I didn't want kids of my own and it was my way of leaving my mark on the world without the burden of responsibility. At that age no young guy thinks of the implications of doing something like that."

I could accept part of what he said. Who really understood the full implications of their actions at nineteen? My mom certainly didn't understand the implications about bringing up a child single-handed and then getting with Colin.

Deep down I struggled with rejecting Simon for having a good heart even if it wasn't an entirely selfless act. Confusion wrung out my feelings.

Is Simon with Jenna now? There was still the question of the pictures, and I wasn't sure how I felt knowing Simon had teenage children. It hurt me to think I wasn't much older than they were.

"What are you doing here, Si? You had enough of comforting the merry widow? Or did the picture force you back here because you knew I'd be gunning for blood?"

"Fuck. You need to stop. Both of you. This is hard enough without the judgments before you have the whole story. The day of Piper's first gig was the twins' thirteenth birthday. Since they were five years old they have known Sparky wasn't their biological father."

"I don't understand," Gibson said.

"Normally, a kid has to wait until they are eighteen to find out who the sperm donor is, but I had agreed they could know from the time they were thirteen. Jenna felt this way they still had time to come to terms with who I was while they were still at home. A lot of kids get emotionally stressed when they find their birth father. This was her way of protecting them from doing that because she had another five years to help them accept me before they went off to college or whatever."

"Makes sense," I mumbled, reluctantly. Gibson's wary eyes darted toward me.

"Obviously Sparky's untimely death made Ellis, their son, go off the rails quite a bit... he wasn't listening to Jenna and became angry about the whole situation. Jenna could see him slipping away and knew if she didn't handle him in the right way she'd lose his trust, so the original plan of going there with the purpose of introducing me got changed. I agreed to go and spend time with them on their birthday on the Mitchell's yacht because being at sea Ellis couldn't run off anywhere."

Gibson sat with a frown on his face and I wondered what he was thinking. The fact he'd stopped interjecting meant he was considering what Simon was telling us.

"That was the call I had to deal with that morning in Portland. Jenna was pre-empting me of all the comebacks Ellis may use, so when I spoke with the kids we'd be singing off the same hymn sheet as it were. I'm sorry I ignored you, but every time I looked at you I felt guilty as fuck for keeping it to myself."

"Father of the year," Gibson goaded, obviously wanting to protect me again.

"That's very unfair, Gibson. I supported you when Melody came into the picture," Simon snapped, and Gibson immediately winced. Simon had been fantastic listening to Gibson's fears and giving him words of advice.

"Anyway, Jenna asked if I would stay a few days and help the kids learn more about Sparky, you know, tell them stories about myself and their father from when he was young, to give them a sense of identity."

"That's where you've been... for a week?" Gibson began.

"Six days," Simon corrected, "Then as it was also the two-year anniversary since Sparky's death, Jenna wanted to take the kids to their place in the Bahamas, to have a small service of remembrance, just her, myself, and the kids, and to scatter his ashes in the place she felt as a family they were the happiest. Only she was worried about Ellis and how he'd react once she got him ashore."

"How did they take meeting you?" I asked, totally forgetting the pictures and what the newspapers had said. There was a young boy in distress who had only just met his biological father for the first time. As I'd never met my natural father, my concerns were focused on him.

Simon gave me a small smile, walked over and took my cheeks in his hands. "You're such a sweetheart. Only you would ask me that. Good. It went well. Much better than Jenna and I expected, and I think it gave Ellis closure. For the whole time I was down there we talked about their 'real father' and all the things he had taught them in life. I'm sorry, babe, truly I am."

Gibson sat speechless for once. He and Chloe had their own issues in regard to what Simon had to say. Simon wrapped his arms around me like Gibson had ceased to exist.

"I was going to tell you everything after the tour. We'd only been together such a short time. Is it reasonable, I'd hold on to something like that until you got to know me better?"

My eyes searched his face and his gaze grew intense. "You have no idea how much it killed me to walk away from you in Seattle. Now you know why, but that was only part of the reason. I know what you said about Kerr, but for the first time in my life I felt threatened, and it wasn't on looks or talent or anything like that. I was scared you'd found someone you related to better than me. As hard as it was, I figured we'd been full on since the moment we'd gotten together and being apart would test how you really felt. For the record it was the worst six days of my life."

Standing up, Gibson blew out a ragged breath. "Why have you never told me any of this? You've never mentioned Sparky apart from when you went to his funeral."

Loosening his arms, Simon stepped back and walked toward Gibson. Placing a hand on his shoulder, Simon shook his head. "I swore I'd never tell anyone the kids were mine. I'd never met them until the funeral, and only then until last week. Man, it felt weird because Ellis looks like my dad's older brother at that age."

Inhaling deeply, Gibson ran his hand through his hair, "I thought we had no secrets from each other?"

A smirk crossed Simon's face and he shrugged, "I almost told you once... the night you found out about Melody. Man, it was so hard to keep what I knew inside because it was then that I realized I was staring at my future. That sometime in the years to come I'd face the consequences of the decision I'd made."

Gibson stood and threw his hands around his back and pulled him in for a hug. "Jesus, dude, what a cluster fuck."

Breaking free of Gibson, Simon turned to me and stretched out a hand. Without hesitation I took it and he clasped his tightly around it.

"I'm sorry you found out like this, Piper. I'm sorry I couldn't make you my priority... how could I when I had made a promise and was faced with something like this?"

"You made the right decision to go. They were a consequence of something you did in your life before I knew you. Whether you had a relationship or not with them, I'm glad you took your responsibility seriously. If my dad had done that I may not have had the upbringing I had, and my mom would have had a much happier life."

Clearing his throat, Gibson said, "I'm sorry I jumped to conclusions and interfered it's just..."

"Don't. I'm so fucking glad Piper has you. She's a lucky girl to have you as a dad, trust me, Gib. I'm so impressed with how seriously you want to protect her."

"Yeah, but this was none of my business. I'm sorry, but you could have called."

"You think? If I had I'd have wanted to come straight home or told Piper on the phone." Simon chuckled, then his mouth turned downward. He shook his head in disgust, "Fucking press, they're the people who start wars you know? When I saw that report, it looked as shady as fuck."

"Yeah, but the one of me didn't look much better," I offered.

"One of you?" he asked. My heart quickened as my mind scrambled for how to explain. Gibson got there before me.

"They tried to make her out to be a player. Some fucker took a picture of Kerr helping Piper down from a loading bay when she almost fell. Photograph looked pretty damning and claimed she'd dumped you for a younger model." Gibson laughed at the irony.

Simon glanced at me, "Glad I didn't see it because I may have come back before I'd finished what I had to do," he admitted.

"Yeah, it hurt Louisa, Kerr's girlfriend, but she's amazing, Simon. She and Kerr are solid, but it made Kerr and I more sensitive about the people around us. Things are a little weird between us right now because neither of us wants to upset our other halves."

Simon slipped his arms around me. "Other halves, eh?" he looked thoughtful for a moment, "I really like that, Princess. So does that mean you're keeping me?" he asked with a raised eyebrow and a glimmer of hope in his eyes.

"Oh, fuck, well I guess that's my cue to leave," Gibson muttered, and I blushed, pulled away from Simon and took a tight squeezy hug from my amazing protector.

"Thank you for everything, Gibson," I mumbled as my heart clenched from the warmth I drew from his arms around me.

"Always," he ground out with ferocity and determination in his tone. He kissed the top of my head and separated from me and wandered toward the door. "Will we see you next week?" he asked, hesitating with his hand on the door handle.

"Of course. I can't wait to be back in Colorado," I confirmed.

Gibson opened the door and as he was about to leave, I ran over and hugged him again. "Thank you for caring about me," I whispered.

"Love you, baby girl. It's an honor to have you in our lives." I hugged him again and saw Jonny appear at the end of the corridor. Gibson strode toward him and they disappeared out of sight into the stairwell. Stepping back into the room, I closed the door and turned to look at Simon who had sat on the edge of the bed.

CHAPTER THIRTY-FOUR

"I'd have given anything for you to not find out about this that way." His normally bright hazel eyes were clouded with sadness. "I know we've got a lot to talk about and I'm sorry if I hurt you, Piper. The timing couldn't have been worse, but I couldn't do much about it. I gave Jenna my word years ago."

"I'm not going to lie to you, Simon. This is a huge revelation, they're only seven years younger than me. It's a lot to get my head around, but I knew when I got with you the likelihood of something I'd hate coming to light was a distinct possibility, but this..."

"If you think it's too much, I'd understand, because I know how it looks; but no one knows they're my kids. Both Ellis and Suranne most definitely don't want people to know. They both see Sparky as their real father and I totally get that."

"That day... in Seattle. You made me feel cheap, Simon. Lying on that bed flirting and joking when I had only just left your bed."

"I wasn't flirting, but yes I was joking, because my heart was beating out of my chest at the thought of facing those two kids. I mean look at me. Like Gibson said, I'm hardly 'father of the year' material now, am I? The last thing I wanted was for them to feel disappointed when they knew it was me."

"Disappointed? How could they ever be that?"

"Sparky was an incredible guy, a loving husband, and a fabulous father. Even though I wasn't ever going to play a part in their lives, putting myself out there to give them some closure was a massive risk. Ellis hasn't been entirely stable since Sparky died. Part of me wondered if he'd break the story or something."

"Why would that bother you? Giving his parents the gift of children was a pretty selfless thing to do."

"Before I got with you, I wouldn't have cared if people knew, but it would have bothered Jenna. Then I met you."

Eyeing him with a puzzled look, I waited for him to elaborate.

"Leaving you in Seattle was so damned hard. I'll admit how I behaved with Kerr was shitty, and I know you felt as if I'd ignored you. Deep down, I guess I wanted you to be pissed at me because it made it easier for me to go and do what I needed to do. I guess I felt stuck in my situation. If you hadn't been about to perform I'd have done things differently." I could see Simon was embarrassed thinking back on it.

"Trust me, I felt guilty as fuck not telling you what the call was about. If you'd asked me, I'd have been honest. You can't know how relieved I was when you didn't because the last thing I wanted was to blow up your world with a huge bombshell like this when it was almost at your feet."

"You know how that looked?"

"Indeed, and to be honest I couldn't get away from you quick enough when we were leaving Seattle."

A shock of electricity jolted my heart. Pain radiated through me to hear him say what I had feared I felt that day. "I noticed," I snapped in a clipped tone as a feeling of dread spread through me.

I made to move away from him, but he clutched me tightly to his chest. Immediately, my body grew stiff. "No, Piper, not because I was desperate to leave."

"Then why?" I whispered. My throat constricted as a lump grew there and my eyes stung with tears.

Releasing me just enough to look down at me, he sighed, his worried eyes matched the expression on his face. "Piper, you wreck me. The way you make me feel is unlike any other girl in my whole life."

"You have a strange way of showing it, if you couldn't wait to get away from me." I said and closed my eyes because I felt my defenses crumbling.

"I couldn't tell you then and this isn't the way I planned to tell you, but I guess it's the day for nothing going to plan. The night we spent together in Seattle was the most intimate of my life. I've never felt closer to anyone, and I found myself struggling with so many thoughts. It took me a while to figure out what was going on, but suddenly it hit me like a bullet to my chest and I realized I wasn't just into you, I loved you."

More confused than ever I shook my head. "You pushed me away because you love me?"

"No. I was scared to love you because I was sure once I told you about Ellis and Suranne it would all be too much for you."

"Do you see me running? Simon, if I've learned anything about life it's that families come in all kinds of colors of fucked-up. Don't you see? I don't know anyone who has a 'normal' two adults, two kids, nuclear family setting. Being with someone like you takes guts in the first place. We either embrace all of who we are and what we've done, or we're screwed. If two people love each other everything else has to swim around them."

"Swim?" A gamut of emotions flitted over his face from admiration to confusion.

"Yeah, baggage sinks people... drags them down. I don't want us to drown because of a decision you made when I was... a kid," I said, and we both stared at each other, then burst out laughing at my sponta-neous gaff.

"Fuck, when you say it like that I sound sick."

"No, you're not. We're both adults. I'm not a child anymore and from all I've been through, I know I could never be attracted to a man my own age. With the exception of Kerr, I don't believe they'd ever begin to understand what I'm about and frankly I don't have the time to explain myself. We are who we are, and we don't really get to choose who we love."

"So, you love me?" Simon asked with a look of expectation in his much brighter eyes, and a small smile curving his lips.

"Maybe," I replied, flashing him a coy smile.

"You're a fucking tease, you know that?"

"Only a tease, if I don't follow through," I countered.

Moving his hands around my body in a much more sensual way, his smile widened. "Ah, so I'm on to a promise here, then?" he asked in a playful tone.

"Obviously not, since you put me through hell, but I'll let you stick around and work on me," I replied, letting him know we had to work to push past this.

"Please, Princess. I'm sorry I hurt you and I'm willing to do whatever it takes to get us back to where we were." With a soft smile he held me tight and sighed with relief.

Waking in the night to a dull ache in my ribs, I opened my bleary eyes and realized I had been sleeping on my hand.

Simon was still awake, the soft light from the lamp on the nightstand bathed his beautiful face inches from mine. His eyes watched me intently.

"You're so fucking beautiful when you're asleep."

"Implying I'm mundane at best once my eyes are open," I teased.

"With that killer figure, this long dark hair and those big brown eyes that make my heart melt? No, Princess, you are stunning; twice as beautiful as when you're asleep."

"Wow, so smooth. Do you practice those lines?" I asked, giggling.

"Nope, they trip right off my tongue when I'm with you."

"Great answer."

"Yeah?"

"Yeah, definitely," I confirmed.

Lying on his back, he turned his head and looked at me. "Go on then", he said lifting the sheet and nodding at his morning wood.

"Huh?" I asked and chuckled.

"Reward me for being nice," he told me and wrapped his fist round his cock.

Giggling, I slapped his chest. "Don't be a pig," I said chiding him with a grin.

"You wouldn't have said that last night, if you'd have let me give you a good porking," he said through a laugh.

Moving quickly, I straddled his chest and his hands flew to my butt.

"You have a dirty mouth," I told him.

"Yeah, I do. Sit on my face and you can make that dirty as well," he replied. "Go on," he chuckled, and my eyes were riveted to his sensual smile. "You know I'm turning you on."

"You are?"

"Mm-hm otherwise your pussy wouldn't be leaving a wet patch over my heart right now," he replied, sliding one hand under my ass to run his fingers in my hot wet folds.

"No," I said groaning and rolling away from him. "You're not seducing me like this. I'm not jumping from one emotional state to another. You have to give me some time."

"Fuck," he choked out softly, "I'm sorry." Pulling me into his arms, he held me like he'd never let me go and whispered intimately into my ear. "Princess, I've fallen so fucking hard for you and I don't even want to fight it."

I lifted my head to look in his eyes and the honesty there almost made me cry. "Yeah?"

"Damn straight. In less than eight short weeks you've given me no option but to want more."

"More?"

"Yeah. You can't imagine how much I missed you when I was gone. Jenna said she never thought there was a woman alive who could pussy-whip me." He chuckled, "She also figured you had a magical vagina to make me pine after you the way I did."

"Very intuitive of her... I do." I stated flatly and moved my ear across his heart. A few heartbeats later we both burst out laughing.

"That was sassy as fuck... and funny," he said through a chuckle. "Come on, get some more sleep. I'm drained after staring down the barrel of your crazy adoptive father's shot gun."

We both laughed, and I remembered the ferocious look on Gibson's face when he arrived at the door earlier that night.

"You can't know what it means to me to have a man like him in my life," I told him in all seriousness.

"Oh, baby, I do. Don't forget I've seen him around Chloe. Before her, Gibson was a five-a-day man."

My brow creased, "He smoked?"

Simon laughed and the sound was infectious. He had a sexy laugh. "No, before Chloe, Gibson didn't have that protective instinct. To him a woman was anything with a heartbeat and a vagina."

"Eww, TMI. Remember who he is to me," I chided, "Besides, he'd say the same about you."

"He would... actually I believe he did to you; not in so many words, but I'm being blunt."

Lifting my hand, he clasped his fingers through mine and brought them to his lips.

"This may sound stupid, but the risk I took to be with you was ridiculous. Can you imagine if I had read the signals wrong?" A silence fell between us, then he sighed. "I'm glad I took that risk. Until I met you my life was trending, you know? Content being myself, having my own space, and partying when the mood took me. You made me grow up...take responsibility for myself. "

"This may sound strange coming from someone like me, but I'm no pushover, Simon. I'd hate to think anyone took me for granted. I won't be played."

"Who's playing? You have no idea how hard I fought this thing I felt inside. The right thing to do would have been to create some distance to gain perspective, but I was so into you it wasn't an option. At no other time in my thirty-two years have I had one foot on the gas and the other on the brake at the same time."

I turned my whole body into him and he did the same. My heart swelled when I felt the warmth of his skin against mine. "Don't hurt me, Simon. Hearing about those pictures in the newspaper almost ripped my heart out of my chest," I confessed.

"Never. Like I said before, the stuff with Ellis and Suranne was unfinished business from before I met you; but I have to be honest and say if they ever needed anything I'd be there for them."

My heart squeezed because he'd done something to help someone else and it was reassuring to hear he had stuck to his original agreement and not kicked them to the curb because I was on the scene.

"You have my respect for saying that. Let the press say what they want. Your hands are tied and now I know the circumstances about your time away, I don't care what anyone says."

Letting out a long sigh, Simon pulled me closer and tucked my head under his chin. Briefly, he dropped his mouth to my head and gave me a quick peck to my temple.

"Sleep, baby," he ordered and stroked his thumb over the smooth skin on my back until I fell asleep.

CHAPTER THIRTY-FIVE

*I*ncessant knocking woke me with a start. The room was in darkness. Simon had obviously turned the light out at some point.

I sat upright and peered past Simon's shape in the bed to see the shadow of feet breaking the light from the corridor under the door.

A strong hand slid around my waist and pulled me down in the bed, "Where are you going?" Simon mumbled.

"Someone's at the door," I replied and made to move again.

"Don't answer it. Stay here with me," he muttered and slid his other arm around me. No sooner had he began shifting in the bed to make himself comfortable than the knocking started again.

"Fuck," he groaned and rolled away from me. "Stay there, I'll get rid of the fucker," he said with a grunt clearing his throat as he padded toward the door.

By the time he got there my eyes had adjusted to watching his silhouette crossing the room. "What?" he barked, throwing the door wide open.

"I need to talk to Piper." I recognized Kerr's voice immediately, and there was a note of alarm in his voice I had never heard before.

Wrapping a sheet around me, I quickly made for the door and

Simon pulled it over, effectively protecting Kerr from seeing me. "Stop it, Simon," I said grabbing the door handle as I pulled it open again.

"What's wrong?" I asked.

Kerr glanced nervously at Simon. "Can we talk?"

"It's fine, what is it?"

"Austin has shared an article through Facebook. I thought you'd better take a look at it. Passing me the phone, I stared at the images on the page. There were four of them.

The first was of earlier in the day when Kerr had held my arm when I was leaving Sears Tower. In the second Gibson was leaning out the car window kissing me on the cheek as he held my hand. The third was of Simon and Gibson in the corridor with me behind them, and the last was of Gibson and I hugging as he left my hotel room.

"Fuck. That's enough. I've had it now," I stated, angrily.

"What's going on between you and Gibson?" Kerr asked.

"Seriously?" I asked in an indignant tone. I stopped and stared at Kerr, then remembered he didn't know the connection.

I sighed, "Come in." Holding the door open wide, I stepped back to let him enter.

"Yeah, come in, we didn't want to sleep anyway. We love being dragged from our bed because of shit-stirring rumors, don't we, Princess?"

"Stop it, Simon, and put some pants on. You look ridiculous strutting around trying to be a bad ass with your cock sticking out like that," I said, trying to hide how embarrassed I was.

Kerr chuckled and turned it into a cough when Simon drew daggers in his direction. "It wouldn't be the first time I've tucked it inside tonight," he bit back in a double entendre that I knew was for Kerr's benefit, but he was lying.

Pressing my lips into a line at Simon's childish jibe, I shook my head, but inside the feeling of warmth that he loved me so much he'd think any man was competition for my affections made my heart swell, even if I didn't show it.

Glancing to Kerr, I realized he was waiting for an explanation. "I'll explain in a minute," I said grabbing my phone.

When I checked out the time and saw it was 6:30 am, I knew the family would already be up. It was their week for Melody, and Gibson took his role as her father so seriously he insisted on being home when he could to take her to school.

Scrolling through my contacts I selected Gibson's number and waited for the call to connect.

"Who are you calling?" Simon asked.

"Gibson. There are no secrets when you two are who you are."

"Everything okay?" Gibson asked, barely keeping the anxiety from his tone.

Before I could explain, Jonny's voice interrupted in the background. "You gotta see this, Gibson," he said, with a note of urgency in his voice.

"Just a sec," Gibson said to me. "Fuckers," he cussed down the line and I knew immediately he'd seen the pictures.

I sighed and felt for Chloe. She was no stranger to constant opinion and conjecture about her husband.

"You've seen the pictures?" I don't know why I even asked the question because I already knew the answer. "They're obviously not going to leave this alone, so I think it's time to come clean and get them off our backs."

"Oh, baby girl, I'm down with that. I've hated not being able to take you anywhere," Gibson said flatly.

"Man, are they going to look stupid," I muttered as my eyes ran over the pictures on Kerr's tablet again. The headline was 'The Pied Piper.' I wasn't interested in reading the story as I'd already guessed its content.

Whoever took the pictures had obviously been stalking Simon because it was written by the same reporter as the one who'd covered the story on him and Jenna.

The photographs were obviously a collaborative effort and he had done a great job of tying up all the images to make it appear as if I was causing a shitstorm with the men in my life.

The article had made me look as if I was with Kerr one minute, Simon the next, then when Simon was pictured with Jenna and her kids, I had sought solace with Gibson. The look of genuine love on both Gibson's and Simon's faces toward me in the pictures took my breath away.

Did they really think the public would believe I was capable of wrecking what Gibson and Chloe had, and having two of the world's most famous rock stars vying for my attention? Anyone would have to be tripping on LSD or using crack to think I could have pulled this off.

What would have been a massive compliment to any other woman made me feel sick. This was drawing negative attention to my new dad, and Kerr was a dear friend.

The pictures also made Simon look like the player he once was and implied discord between him and Gibson. The press rumor mill was abhorrent because I only had eyes for Simon.

"Okay, baby girl, how do you want to play this?"

I realized I had fallen silent as I stared again at the pictures.

As it was my last show supporting Layla Hartmann and a Friday night, I figured that it would be better if we all came clean before I had time off. The last thing Simon and I needed after all the attention with Kerr and Jenna was this following us around.

"It's my last night of the tour tonight. Would it be possible to bring Chloe and Melody down? I'll ask Thomas to set up a press conference."

"I got you, baby girl. Don't worry, Piper. Do what you gotta do and we'll be there." Gibson sounded upbeat, a hint of excitement in his voice perhaps, and I knew he had never wanted to keep this secret. He was proud of me and now he'd get to tell the world of our connection.

Concluding the call, I glanced at Simon, and smirked. Still naked, he'd laid back on the bed, his head resting on the headboard, and I knew he wasn't going to get dressed any time soon, so I ignored him and turned to Kerr.

Sitting slowly on the edge of the bed I stared up at him. "I guess I owe you a big explanation." I didn't try to hide the guilt in my voice. "Gibson and Chloe are my new family. It's a long story and I'll explain it all to you one day, but Gibson was the man who agreed to be my guardian. Chloe and Gibson are like parents to me now."

Kerr's eyes almost fell out his head... for a moment I could see him fight for breath. "Fuck me, Gibson Barclay... then you..." he pointed to

Simon, "fuck, you've got massive cahoonas, taking on something belonging to Gibson Barclay, buddy," Kerr said with a chuckle.

Simon growled. "Piper's mine... no one else's; besides Gibson fine with how I feel about her."

"All right, enough about this. Kerr, I'm sorry I never told you before, but I was determined to make it on my own. If I found success I didn't want people looking at Simon and Gibson and thinking I had been pushed to the top of the pile because of them."

Nodding, Kerr eyed me with warmth, "You definitely have talent, honey, everyone can see that, plus you're mature and focused. I think when people find out about Gibson, you are going to get so much respect for not disclosing who he is to you."

"Right, meanwhile if this little pow-wow is finished, I'd still like to get some sleep with my woman. Nothing much we can do about the newspaper story, but we're all gonna need new rooms."

Swiping his phone from the table, he scrolled down his contacts. "Jennifer, can you book us into another hotel? The press is running a story about Piper, Gibson, and me; and send Dave over to move all our stuff from room seven-forty-seven and fourteen-twenty-one."

Wiggling down off the bed he stood up still buck naked and wandered over to the door. "Thanks for the heads up, dude, I'll take it from here," Simon advised him and it was apparent he wasn't ready to show much in the way of benevolence toward Kerr.

"Thanks, Kerr, you're a true friend. I promise we'll sit down after today and I'll explain and answer any questions you have."

Kerr walked toward the door, nodded to Simon, and stepped out into the corridor. Simon closed the door and pressed his hand on the wood to make sure it was firmly closed and turned to look at me.

Smiling like he'd won some secret bet with himself, he opened his arms as he walked back over to me. I sighed.

Despite how childishly he behaved toward Kerr, my heart squeezed with desire. His jealousy was cute, but I was determined not to pass over my friend because Simon felt jealous.

Creeping down the back stairs of a hotel because of Gibson was one thing, doing it for myself and Simon felt far more illicit and exciting.

Don't get me wrong, my body was tense and knots formed in my stomach, but being hurriedly led from one hotel and taken to another by the man of my dreams added a certain thrill to the experience for me.

Less than two hours later we should have been at breakfast, but instead we lay spooning under clean crisp cotton sheets in a room with a view.

Simon's heavy even breathing behind me felt blissful to listen to as his warm soft breaths fanned over my back. Despite all the controversy surrounding me, I'd never felt more at peace.

An unexpected wave of emotion swept over me and I felt my throat close tight. Staying confident about Simon staying true wasn't an easy choice to make. However, inside I knew I had to believe he would and I had to trust in what he said.

Oddly enough, I drew strength that Simon's feelings were bigger than he'd ever dealt with in the past because of the way Gibson had begrudgingly accepted we were together.

For another hour my mind went around in circles until I exhausted myself and eventually nodded off.

When Simon shifted away from me, it had felt like I'd only just fallen asleep. I was surprised to learn it was past 1pm.

My stomach rumbled in protest because I hadn't eaten anything since dinner with Gibson the evening before.

Reluctantly, I dragged my lethargic body into the shower. Refreshed and dressed, I sat opposite Simon as we ate lunch in our hotel room.

"You look fucking stunning in that dress," he said. I looked down at my attire. It was nothing special, a white cotton sun dress that showed a little cleavage but largely hid my figure.

"You look stunning in anything," I replied and dropped my fork to my plate. Placing my elbows on the table I stared into his beautiful hazel eyes framed by his long dark lashes. The only time I saw his eyes properly was when we were alone.

Usually they were hidden by large Armani sun shades in his attempt not to be noticed. As if that were at all possible. When Simon walked into a room, the guys suddenly turned to ashes and the women were suddenly dying of thirst.

"What are you looking at?" His sexy smile hinted to break free.

"Your eyes... they're the color of whiskey sometimes, hazel... or pale apple cider," I explained.

"Apple cider, really?"

"Yeah, you know what I mean. Sometimes they look hot and spicy, and at others the way you look at me, there's something sweet about them."

Simon chuckled, "Sweet... me? Not dark and dangerous?"

"Oh, yeah, there's that look as well, but only when Kerr's in the room," I answered honestly.

"I don't get you two..."

"You don't have to," I said, rubbing my hands on my cheeks. "I'm never going to have feelings for Kerr like the crazy euphoric ones I have in here for you," I replied, holding my hand over my heart. You need to learn to treat Kerr with respect as my friend and you need to trust me when I tell you the only thing between us is friendship.

Simon reached over and grabbed both wrists tight. "Sorry. I've never felt threatened by any man before. Maybe because no one mattered enough in the past, but I accept what you're saying and I'll give the guy a break."

"What about you? How are you feeling after the Jenna story and everything else?" I asked, fishing for more about his feelings.

"What about me?" He asked, his brow furrowed. I feel relieved you know what I did. I also feel reassured the kids don't resent me in any way and their happy to live with Sparky's memory. "And if you mean how do I feel when I look at you... when I'm with you?" He held his breath for a long moment then exhaled. When he let his breath go, I realized I'd been holding mine as I waited for his reply.

"Breathless. It's like I breathe in and forget to breathe out; then at other times, such as when you were asleep and I lay watching you, it felt as if I were suffocating."

I frowned, "Suffocating?" My voice sounded deflated, and I stared morbidly like I thought his next sentence would say he felt trapped.

"Yeah, like a sense of panic inside because I know if a time came where I wasn't with you my heart would be shredded. You can't breathe if your heart's not beating," he said in a gentle tone, gave me a slow smile and swallowed hard. "You make me feel young; like a giddy teenager and justified in being this way."

"Best answer in the world," I confessed and smiled widely. "I promise to keep trying to do that to you."

"Princess, I'm yours. You can do anything you want to me."

I rolled my eyes because I had no clue how to respond to that without us ending up on the floor, or the bed, or against a wall, so I shrugged nonchalantly like I wasn't fazed.

"I suppose I'll have to get my kink on, but as I have a gig where my 'Olds' are flying in and my boyfriend is going to be scrutinizing my every move on stage, I figure I'd better get my butt into gear and make ready to leave for the venue."

Simon stood, pulled my chair back and I stood up. He pecked me on the lips and my hand flew to his chest when I saw the wicked gleam in his eyes. "Oh no, you don't." I chuckled quickly as I did a body swerve and ran into the bathroom. Closing the bathroom door softly, I leaned against the cool wood and sighed.

Is this really my life? I knew exactly how Simon the felt when he looked at me from his description, because I felt the same way... and I had since the moment I saw him sitting in Gibson's sitting room... the only difference between us is at one time I *was* that giddy teenager.

CHAPTER THIRTY-SIX

*W*ho would have thought it would be *me* tearing down the stairwell of a hotel room to avoid the press? *This is insane.*

Despite the seriousness of the situation, I couldn't suppress the excitement I felt inside at being led to the street by the man of my dreams. The man of most women's dreams, yet he was *mine*.

"You, okay, Princess?" Simon asked, stalling for a moment to check I wasn't too distressed by the experience.

"Yeah," I laughed. "Somehow the thrill of doing something sneaky is really fun."

He stopped dead in his tracks, "Having sex right here on the landing would be much more fun and extra sneaky; the thrill of being caught would make you come in a heartbeat," he suggested in a seductive tone and trapped me between the stairwell wall and his body.

A wicked grin spread over his face and the glint of lust in his eyes told me he wasn't joking.

"Jesus, Simon, you should have been in big business. I've never known anyone who can smell an opportunity like you."

Leaning in, he inhaled the skin on my neck, "And a very fragrant opportunity as well if I may say so."

"Damn, cut the cheese and get me the fuck down to ground level, I have a job to do," I replied, pretending to be annoyed with his tease. The look he gave me was that of a wounded puppy and I laughed aloud on the stairs.

"Shh, someone will find us," he said, his eyes suddenly serious as he looked past me at the floors up above. The way he said it jolted me back to the reality of the situation because Simon didn't use body-guards often.

The risk of us being found together could have been dangerous for him if there happened to be a crazy fan around.

Turning back, he grabbed my hand and led me two flights further down into an underground car park.

The fob to a rental Mercedes was already in his hand and with two short beeps the blinkers flashed on a Black sports saloon in the bay nearest the exit. "Quick, get in," he ordered, and we both made for the car.

Fortunately, no one had followed us to the new hotel. It took me a moment to digest a car was in the new hotel car park and Simon knew exactly where it was. Then I remembered a knock on the door as I was in the bathroom.

The efficiency with which we were moved, and everything arranged told me this kind of escape was probably a well-rehearsed routine in the event any of the boys from M3rCy had a change in their plans.

Slumping back in my seat I hit the radio and "Run Like Hell" by Pink Floyd filled the car. Simon looked to me with huge round eyes and his sexy smile almost melted my bones. We both burst out laughing and he stretched out his hand and I took it in mine.

Lacing our fingers, he lifted the back of my hand to his lips. "Love you, baby. I can't wait to see you up there on stage tonight."

Butterflies rippled through my stomach at the thought of all the important people being at my gig. It felt like the previous few weeks had been practice concerts for the one where it mattered.

A pause in our conversation allowed me to reflect on the crazy past few years: the last at home under the cosh of Colin; my mom's short illness and death; and the following two and a bit in the nurturing care of Gibson, Chloe, and their extended entourage of Jonny, Jerry, and Emma. I even got the sister I had always wished for.

For some of my childhood I had thought all father figures were like Colin, and it was only when I entered school and got sucked up into the choir and drama classes, I was able to see how other kids interacted with their parents. It made me realize how dysfunctional my upbringing was.

Not once was I ever tempted to tell anyone how horrible he was for fear he'd target my mom. Abusers are great at using the people we love as a form of control.

"Ready to do this?" Simon's voice cut into my thoughts and I realized we'd arrived at the venue. "Last time we played this venue was about twelve years ago... maybe more. It was one of the first places M3rCy performed as an up-and-coming band.

My stomach flipped over knowing I was walking in the footsteps of giants like M3rCy, and an anxious feeling crept up inside. "Better knock it out of the park tonight then and not let the team down."

Pulling up at the tall iron-gated entrance, we saw a few reporters hanging around.

"You won't, baby. You got this," he said as his window glided down when we reached the security speaker on the wall.

"Looks like you've kissed and made up. Any comment, Simon?" one particularly tenacious reporter called out as he ran toward Simon's open window. He was a small, weedy looking guy, and I figured he was either very brave or very stupid to front Simon with his question the way he was doing.

"About what?" he asked, acting innocently.

"The reports linking you to Jenna Mitchell, the confrontation between you and Gibson... looks like Miss Piper here has made her choice," he said running off at the mouth.

Knowing the truth of the matter and seeing how salacious his eye contact with me was, taught me immediately to keep my mouth closed and let Simon do the talking.

"All right. Here's your exclusive," he said, grabbing the guy's phone from him that he was obviously using to record the conversation between them. Holding the screen close to his face Simon took a deep breath and exhaled.

"Firstly, Piper and I are solid. Period. Jenna and I are friends. Good friends. Sparky was my friend and even in death, I'd never fuck him over with his widow even if Piper and I weren't an item. Third point, Gibson Barclay is my band kin. We do not fuck each other over either. Gibson himself has something to say on this matter as does my girl, Piper, here. Watch this space because we aim to shed some light on where we're all at later this evening. Then you and the rest of your venomous cockroaches are going to look like the biggest asses you are."

Simon pressed the button on the speaker, "Piper," he barked. The CCTV camera swiveled around to the windshield of the car and the gates began to beep and buzz as they opened.

The old gray-haired guard wandered over to the window to greet us. "Hey there," Simon commented cheerily, "Got Piper here." The guard dipped his knees and eyed me warily before his face brightened.

"Damn, can I get your autograph?" he asked.

"Sure," Simon replied. The guard quickly grabbed a book from a small shelf inside his booth and handed it over to Simon with a pen.

Thick with pages, I immediately saw there were tons of autographs already in there from the people he'd met. Turning in his seat, Simon pushed the book toward me, "Here you go," he stated. Placing my hands on the book I hesitated.

"Think he meant you, Simon," I said with a chuckle.

"I'm not the one playing here tonight," he reminded me, and I felt myself blush a little. I'd signed plenty of autographs during the tour but never bypassed a world class rock star to make my mark before. Flicking open the book, my eyes flitted back to the guard who was curiously staring at me.

I wasn't totally convinced the guy wasn't going to be disappointed I'd ruined his book by writing in it, but I scribbled my name in a cursive script anyway and handed the book back to Simon. Snapping the book closed Simon handed it back.

The guy dipped his knees again and looked at me delighted as he nursed the book to his chest. "Thank you, lady. For the record I think you're amazing." His enthusiasm was unexpected, and I grinned before Simon drove over and parked in one of the spots.

"He never asked you to sign."

"Nah, he was too busy creaming his pants at the sight of you," he chuckled. "If he'd been any younger, I'd have put the guy on his back."

"I like older men, remember?" I said teasing, because the guy was sixty if he was a day.

"Ouch," Simon replied, clutching his chest like I'd wounded him, then answered my original thought. "To put you out of your misery, I signed one of his books a long time ago. He's been on security here for years. M3rCy played here quite a few times when we were first getting started, remember? How else do you think I knew my way here without directions and the guy didn't blink when I drew up there just now?"

"You don't need to sound so big-headed," I remarked, playfully. Shaking my head at his arrogance, I sat speechless until Simon grabbed the back of my head and smashed his lips against mine. Giving me another of his deep passionate kisses he drew back and smoothed down my hair.

Chuckling he said, "Look at you. Full of lust." Continuing to rest his hands at the sides of my face, his gorgeous bright eyes ticked back and forth as he stared at me like he wanted to say something else but didn't have the words.

When he took a deep breath, his hands fell away, and he gave me a simple wink. My heart lurched as a jolt of electricity shot through me and I shook my head at the thought he could make me swoon with the blink of one eye.

I sighed, lost in how I felt about him for a moment and it barely registered with me that he'd gotten out of the car until he swung my car door open and helped me out. "Let's go, baby, time to show them that awesome talent of yours.

～

Standing in the dark, seconds before I went on the stage, I was almost overcome with first night nerves all over again. It was normal for me to feel a little anxious before the start of every show, but this one was special.

As I built a more intimate relationship with God, I prayed I wouldn't screw up, and my eyes scanned every seat I could see from where I stood. I noted the venue was full.

Some performers say the sick feeling in their stomachs has never gone away no matter how many times they put themselves out there, but tonight was different. It was the first time the men who shaped my music career were here to witness what I had to give.

Even though it was highly expected, my legs still buckled when the emcee called my name. Kerr slapped my back and my breath hitched and although I knew it was my cue, my legs didn't move for a second.

The crowd roared their appreciation and suddenly I propelled myself out from the dark and into the light.

From the moment they saw me the racket they made intensified; a marked contrast to the first concert I had played only a week before, and I knew the word was spreading about me as an artist in my own right.

Drawing courage from their enthusiastic cheers, I stepped forward and grabbed the mic, feeding on their keen interest to hear me perform.

Once Austin cued the music, and the intro began to play, a wave of calm washed over me and I began to sway. Usually, I picked on a specific spot and sang to that for the first few lines, but instead I took the mic from the stand and wandered to one side.

The opening song, "Play the Melody", a power ballad, was designed to capture the naysayers and haters who would question my position in the music market.

The score was deep, intricate, and the range wide, all the elements set to test a singer, and separate karaoke singers from those who'd honed their voices to deliver a perfect sound as the song was intended to be sung.

From Contralto to Soprano my huge scale range reached the depths of a low female scale to the highest Soprano pitch giving me an insane ability to tackle any track the female voice could sing.

It was the first time during the tour I had attempted the song because my confidence was a little shaky about testing myself while still trying to capture my audience.

Until now I had been playing it safe but as this was my last night of the tour and it wouldn't reflect badly on Layla Hartmann, I took a calculated risk.

Watching the reaction of the fans was mesmerizing because their silence wasn't only out of politeness this time. From where I stood, I could tell by their expressions they were captivated by the words of the song.

When the last long note died in my throat, the audience exploded in rapturous applause and relief dripped through my veins like warm honey. The love in the room felt incredible.

Breathless, I moved center stage and looked over to the balcony box seat on my left where Simon, Gibson, Chloe, Melody, and Thomas sat, except they weren't sitting down, they were on their feet, Melody jumping excitedly, her little hands clapping like she'd wear them out.

A huge grin spread on my face at the sight of them and for some odd reason I felt shy. The lump that threatened to grow in my throat would have been catastrophic for me. There was no way could I have continued to sing if my emotions closed my airway, so I quickly looked away.

Nodding to Kerr he began the intro to a fast-paced song and for the following forty minutes left of my set I poured my heart and soul into my performance.

The wave of noise swelling out from the crowd choked me and the set ended on a high. They were calling for an encore and I was only there to support.

Bowing my thanks, I quickly left the stage with them clearly wanting more. Layla gripped my upper arm and stopped me before I reached my dressing room.

"Get back out there and give them one more song. I've been watching you on the monitor in my room, sweetheart. You are a musically gifted young woman. I'm happy for you to give the audience what they want."

Staring at her with wide eyes, I was humbled by how gracious and self-assured she was to allow me the privilege of something like that.

Not one to look a gift horse in the mouth, I nodded, and without having to speak to the backing band behind me they all turned and ran back to the stage.

Stepping back on stage, I no longer felt like someone who had to prove herself and I sang the encore number, the next song due to be released from my album like a boss.

Kerr told me I owned the stage when I sang it and by the time I walked off the stage that night I felt ready to take on the world.

CHAPTER THIRTY-SEVEN

*A*ustin led the others from the dressing room as they headed back to the hotel for the after-party Layla was throwing to wrap up the tour.

I'd hung back, waiting for Simon and my family Gibson had pulled together some media friendly people to break the news about my connection to him.

After a quick shower, I changed into a teal-green, figure-hugging dress and was reapplying my cherry lip-gloss when there was a knock on the door. "Yeah?" I asked.

Pushing open the door, Myleene grinned, "Your dad's here to see you," she informed me.

Briefly closing my eyes, I took a deep breath and couldn't believe Gibson had told her before we'd had a chance to announce it. "Thank you," I replied, and her head disappeared.

The door half-closed then opened again and my breath hitched in my throat as fear momentarily paralyzed me. Instead of seeing Gibson as I had expected, Colin stood there in his place.

Two years apart. Two years of counselling and confidence building were all the defenses I had against seventeen years of abuse at Colin's hands. No matter how mended I had thought I was, it was nothing

310

compared to the emotional anxiety and negative memories which suddenly flooded my brain.

All rational thoughts threatened to leave me; my weakening resolve to stand up to the abuser who stood in front of me was crumbling. *Never show fear. It was the first thing Chloe's team taught survivor's if they ever came face to face with their past.*

"What are you doing here?" I barked, having suddenly snapped out my shock. I swiped my cell from the dresser so fast I doubted it had registered with him. It felt heavy in my hand. *Oh God, my password is on. I need to get a message to Simon.*

"Think you were smart running away like that? Where is she?" he ground out through gritted teeth. His beady eyes narrowing, while his anger radiated toward me.

"She?" I asked incredulously, "You mean *my* mom?"

"Ah. Think you're tough now, do you, lady? Think you're smarter than me? You obviously forgot the fact I've been in this game since before you were born." Never. It had always been in the back of my mind he was road crew for bands.

Inside my bones had gone to Jell-O, but outwardly I tried to appear relaxed. In my head, I searched for ways to deal with the horrible monster from my past.

Seeing he was between me and the door, I knew it was pointless to even try to make a run for it. He was too fast... and strong.

Strolling over to the couch, I sat down and pulled my phone in front of me.

"Make a call and you're dead," he said in a threatening tone.

"Is that what you came for, to kill me?" I asked and pretended to scroll Facebook, so he could see. Opening Messenger, I noted Simon's message was the last one I had read, and I glanced up at Colin as if I were waiting for the answer.

"Money... I want money and your mom, or I'll ruin you."

"My mom is where you can never harm her again, and I'd rather watch you starve then give you anything."

I turned the sound off on my phone and quickly clicked the camera icon on the Inbox before taking what I hoped was a picture of Colin. Pressing send, I had barely cancelled out from Simon's message box when Colin swiped my phone from my hand and tossed it in the wastepaper basket by the side of the mirrored dresser.

"Get the fuck up," he muttered angrily, grabbing me by my wrist. Lifting my foot, I immediately kicked him hard between his legs with every ounce of strength in me.

While he rolled around the floor groaning and clutching his groin, I tore up off the couch and made for the door.

Before I reached the handle, his huge strong hand wrapped around my ankle and he pulled me down on the floor beside him.

Panic threatened to dull my thoughts, but I fought against the feeling and flailed my arms and legs continually as I tried to free myself and prevent him gaining a stronger grip on the rest of me.

Suddenly Simon burst through the door, closely followed by Gibson, "What the fuck?" he bellowed angrily and shoved Colin off of me. Lifting me like I was weightless, Simon stepped back to a safe space whereas Gibson dragged Colin to his feet and wrapped his hand around his throat. I'd never heard Gibson growl so loud in all my life.

"Go on, hit me," Colin goaded, "It'll be good for a few million when I sue you," he stated. "I don't know what this has to do with you anyway. This is between me, her mom, and my daughter," Colin argued.

"She's not yours, she's *mine*," Gibson snapped, loud enough for the whole corridor to hear.

"What the fuck is this? You fucking him... or you're fucking her mother?" he asked first me, then Gibson like he had no fear whatsoever.

Not being a small man, Gibson towered four or five inches above him and he made Colin look pathetic the way he held on to him.

Wriggling down from Simon's arms, I lunged at Colin and slapped him hard across his face. "Thank God my mom's not alive to see this. Thank God she never had to see your ugly ass again," I ranted.

Colin looked shell-shocked. "She's dead? What happened?"

"Nope. We're not talking about her. My mom's memory isn't going to be sullied by you. The way you treated us all, my childhood was horrific. You. Are. Not. A. Man. You are a weak bully whose only way of keeping a woman was to cripple her with fear. I thank God every day I got her out of there. At least she died free from you."

For a few moments it was as if we were all frozen in time. "Give me some money then and I'll leave you alone," he said, a note of desperation in his voice.

I was horrified at his indifference about my mom and my breath hitched. Simon immediately tightened his grip to help me feel a little safer. He kissed my temple tenderly.

"You think I'm really gonna do that?" Gibson chuckled. "What I should give you is a damn good hiding and a shallow grave in the Arizona desert," he snapped with dark intent in his eyes. "That may not be what you want, but even that would be an act of kindness. I should skin you alive and leave you for the buzzards, you shameless bastard."

"You want to press charges against this guy, sweetheart?" Gibson asked in all seriousness.

The fear in Colin's beady eyes as he stood flanked by Gibson, and Jonny who had joined him, was small payback for all the times he'd put that look on my mom's face.

I'd never thought about actually charging him. I was too afraid he'd run free and come back for us. It would have been like some kind of belated closure for my mom if he was stuck behind bars, but I had no tangible evidence.

Men like Colin were clever and manipulative, but they seldom paid for their treatment of women. When I didn't reply, Gibson continued.

"Tell you what we're gonna do here, Colin," Gibson said, in a tone that was so icy calm and controlled to how he would normally have reacted.

I swallowed hard because it was the tone I'd heard from Colin in the past. The one attached to the choice he would offer us which was no choice at all but to do as he asked. Manipulation dressed as choice.

"Jonny here is going to take you on a journey, Jerry as well in fact," Gibson said nodding at his two security details. "You're going to take a trip to the Chicago Police Department and you're going to confess to what you put Piper and her mom through for all those years."

Colin scoffed, "Oh, wow, you're so funny, my sides are splitting with laughter. Why in the hell would I do that? You've only got a strip of a girl's word for anything she may have said happened in my home. How do you even know she has told you the truth?" My heart sank because what he said was true.

Gibson grinned widely, but his eyes were wild as he glanced first at me, then at Simon, and eventually back to Colin.

"Ah, now we're getting to the crux of the matter. See, Piper here is a very clever girl, but you're right. Personally, she has no evidence from her time at home. However, what you don't know is Piper is mine now. Before Patricia died she gave Piper to me. I became Piper's guardian. You know what that word means right? *Guardian?*"

Simon glanced at me and placed my head on his chest, his strong hand protectively over my head. I was confused and frowned at Gibson because I had no idea what he was thinking.

"Let me enlighten you, dude. Guardian means protector. Pro- tect- or. This gives you a huge problem because as any of these guys will tell you I take my role as Piper's protector *very* seriously. As such, Piper's mom was determined to give me anything she had to help me protect her daughter even if she wasn't mentally strong enough to get away from you herself until years later."

The sly glimpse Colin gave Gibson intimated he thought Gibson was calling his bluff.

Gibson chuckled but it was without humor. "What you don't know is Piper came with an insurance package in the event you dared show your ugly mug around her one day. You see, when someone is kept suppressed in their own home, it gives them a lot of time for reflection... seven large volumes worth, and from what I've read they're full of times, dates, and detailed accounts of the abuse they suffered, written over an eight-year period from the time Piper was eight until she was sixteen."

"This is bullshit," he shot back angrily, but I saw real fear in his eyes for the very first time as he tried to shove Jerry out of the way and make for the dressing room door.

I jumped in fear because the sound of his raised voice still terrified me, even in a room full of men who would kill him before they'd let him get to me.

"Oh, I forgot. When Piper's mom was in counselling, she produced plenty more evidence, with photographic proof cataloging old injuries, consistent with the incidents she discussed in her confidential sessions."

Gibson's voice was flat... totally devoid of emotion and I knew *this* was the Gibson people should be afraid of. Not the volatile, passionate, opinionated advocate... but this.

My eyes flitted to Jonny and I noted the stance he held watching Gibson closely, perhaps to prevent him from making a move that would incriminate Gibson in anything, while Jerry's focus was solely on Colin.

If Colin were stupid and made any move toward Gibson, I was in no doubt Jonny and Jerry would take all and any necessary steps to stop Colin from harming a hair on Gibson's head and vice-versa.

There wasn't a single moment when I thought Gibson was in danger. He was more than a match for Colin, but something inside told me if Gibson made a move he'd cause Colin some permanent damage.

I trusted Gibson wasn't stupid enough to give him the satisfaction of laying hands on him. That would have made Colin a victim no matter what the circumstance.

"Time's up; are you going voluntarily or are we going to call the cops? Either way you're going down. Make it harder for Piper, and my lawyers will ensure you never see the outside of a jailhouse again in this lifetime."

Colin's Adam's apple bobbed in his throat and for the first time in my life I saw true fear in his spiteful dark eyes, but before he could reply, Gibson took one step to the side. Jonny twisted Colin's arm up his back in an arm lock and he was swiftly and effectively removed from the room.

Exhaling heavily, I hit a wall, then a wave of nausea made my stomach roll. I ran for the trash can and hurled the entire contents of my stomach.

"Fuck." Gibson cussed, a note of distress in his voice.

"Clear out, Gibson, she needs quiet." Simon interjected in an authoritative tone. I'd never heard him speak so forcefully to Gibson before. "You've done your job, I got this from here." The tone in Simon's voice left no room for argument and a growl tore from Gibson's throat, but he didn't protest.

Placing a hand on my back, Gibson leaned over and spoke to me. "Going to check on Chloe and Melody. I'll check back. You did great, baby girl," he advised as I attempted to wipe the putrid taste of vomit from my mouth with some tissue.

Seeing Gibson out the door, Simon closed it softly then grabbed a plastic bottle of water. Gently, he turned me to look at him and eyed me with concern.

Reaching over me, he tugged more tissue out of the box by the mirror and cracked open the lid on another bottle of water.

Soaking the tissue, he gently wiped under my eyes. Now that Gibson had taken care of the practicalities of Colin, Simon felt responsible for helping to make me feel whole again.

"You were terrific, Princess. I know that must have been terrifying for you. In my head I wanted to beat that fucker within an inch of his life, but I knew if we all got heavy-handed it would have been even more traumatic than it was. You understand what I'm saying? Someone had to stay on your level."

I did. "Thank you," I said, shakily and gave him a weak smile. Most girls would have expected their boyfriends to wade in balls-deep to offer physical protection like Gibson did, but Simon knew Gibson and his boys had that covered.

As hard as it was for him, Simon had done exactly the right thing to make me feel in control.

"Usually, Gibson pisses me off with his 'Big Bad Daddy' routine, but Gibson and I have an incredible bond and I actually admire how seriously he's taken on what he has with you. I've known him a long time and I let a lot slide, but when I speak up... and because I don't do it very often, Gibson usually listens."

"I knew what you were doing, Simon. The threat of violence when Colin was around was always only ever one sentence away. You here beside me with your calm manner has helped me more than you'll ever know." Every word I spoke was the truth. I would have fallen apart otherwise.

Soothing me, Simon's voice was soft and calm, praising me for all the great things I had achieved despite my history, and when he had finished, he flashed me his usual sexy smile. However, it didn't quite reach his eyes, and I didn't miss the pain held in them.

Seeing how difficult Simon had taken the incident with Colin, I reached up and grabbed his face on both sides. "I know what you're thinking, Simon," I said with conviction. "There's a look in your eyes that tells me you think you failed me because Colin got in here in the first place, when the truth is I owe you."

"You owe me?"

"If you hadn't been so quick in responding to my Messenger picture, God alone knows what could have happened in here." Every word I said was true. Gibson and his security may have been the muscle, but it was the quick thinking of Simon that prevented me from further harm.

"You know you have this innate ability to make me feel like the better man, Princess?"

"Not better... you just get me."

Sliding his arms around my waist, he nodded, narrowed his eyes, and placed a small kiss on the end of my nose. "I'd get you much better if you brushed your teeth; man, that sick smells putrid. What the fuck did you eat?" He chuckled, when I shoved him away, covering my mouth as I swung past him to do as suggested, instantly mortified by his comment.

"You think after all this you're ready to face the press?" Simon asked as he leaned his butt against the sink and folded his arms while I brushed my teeth and tongue.

"Yeah," I mumbled around the paste, "Piece of cake after the past half hour," I replied, slurping up some water from the palm of my hand and spitting it down the sink. Throwing the toothbrush from hospitality into the trashcan, I grabbed Simon's hand. "It's gotta be done, then maybe they'll leave us alone for a while," I hoped.

"All right, Princess, anything you say. Let's do this." Sounding more upbeat than he had at the start of our conversation, he took my hand in his, held it like he'd never let it go and led me to find the others.

CHAPTER THIRTY-EIGHT

*J*f I said the press were astounded when Gibson disclosed the true nature of my relationship within the family, it would be an understatement. Gasps and low murmurs spread through the small meeting room like wildfire.

Bluntly, he stated how much he and his bandmates had suffered at the hands of the press over the years and how irresponsible and careless they were with the truth.

Gibson then told them he would be making a statement and I would not be taking questions. He commanded the pack of reporters from the get-go.

"Rumors wreck lives." His salient comment was pointed, direct, and followed by a weighted silence as he quietly checked out every one of the reporters in front of him. *Goodness, if these are his friendly reporters, I'd hate to hear how he speaks to the rest.* I bit back a small smile at how focused the members of the press were.

Once Gibson had addressed his opinion about their shoddy research skills attached to the recent stories about all of us, he turned their attention on me.

Disclosing how he had offered to help me catch a break, he added this would be what any other father would do for their daughter if they believed they had talent.

There were a few raised eyebrows because I hadn't chosen to do this.

"Truth is, Piper has principles, bigger than any of you guys here. Not only did she reject a possible contract with Sly Records, but she also insisted we keep our connection on the down-low while she did it on her own. By the way, do you know Piper was offered an album with Gravity, forty-five minutes after she sent them her demo?"

Each of the reporters looked to the other as they mumbled amongst themselves.

"You know how forceful I can be when I want my own way, right?" he asked them. They nodded and a few chuckled. "Let me tell you how hard this young woman here fought for the right to sink or swim in her own boat." he told them, eyeing me as he shook his head and gave me a small smile.

"This young lady had other ideas, and let me tell you, she's damn well full of them." A ripple of laughter spread through the press pack. "Not only did she insist I back off, but if you all saw what I saw this evening, you'll know she was right to be confident she could make it on her own."

Low murmurs of agreement came from the group and I did what I could to prevent the scoff that hung on my lips. I thought it strange how human nature was and how they preferred to judge, sensational-ize, and target opinions with negative comments, but when proven wrong they found it difficult to admit their faults and apologize with the same enthusiasm.

"Our girl here is insanely talented. She's young, yet so mature... way beyond her years, and I've never met anyone more hard working. If I were any of you I'd be out there helping her spread the word about her voice, not focusing on what she does in her personal life. Being a public figure should be what she's known for, not what she does in her downtime."

My chest swelled with pride when Gibson praised me the way he did. It took a lot to impress him, music-wise.

Lifting a small jug of iced water sitting in front of him, Gibson poured himself a drink, took a large swig and placed his glass back down on the table before he continued.

"Piper is new to all this, yet you've given her the toughest run of propaganda since the minute she stepped out with Simon. He and I know better than anyone how hard it is to get space to breathe in this line of work. Believe me, this girl has had more press attention, directly or indirectly at the hands of you guys than any of us in M3rCy had in the beginning. Why? Simon, of course. Sure, he's got a past. Past. That means behind him. Piper is in front... ahead of him, and from what he tells me she has more than a fair chance of being his future."

"You approve of the relationship?" A female reporter threw out the question with a raised eyebrow. I recognized her from when Gibson brought her to our home to talk about Melody.

"One hundred percent. Like I said, Piper knows her own mind... Simon too... well... most of the time," he joked, and everyone chuckled.

Simon's hand squeezed mine under the table and I glanced to the side. His warm smile reached up to his eyes, and they locked with mine. My heart melted. As he licked his lips, he showed no hesitation when he leaned forward and pressed a chaste kiss on my own. His public display of affection meant the world to me.

"All right, there's not much else to say and I know Piper's little sister is busting to see her, so I'll leave you with one last comment. When our fans recognize us everywhere we go, we, as public figures accept them as part of the package when we're not officially working."

Gibson glanced at Simon then to me. Gesturing with his finger at all of us individually he nodded as if he were thinking to himself.

"However, you guys need to take better responsibility for what you report. In case you didn't know, we rock stars have deep pockets and much better legal teams than your daily rags and mags. You all would do well to remember this."

When his chair legs scraped back on the wooden floor, I looked up and saw Gibson was on his feet.

"Now if you'll excuse us all, I think you'd agree it's been a pretty big night for our beautiful Piper," he informed them, holding out his arm for me. Without releasing Simon's hand, I stood, stepped forward and took a hug from one of the two best men I had ever known, and Gibson kissed the top of my head.

"Next time you print a picture containing any of us three, my wife, or my other daughter, you'd better run it past my team or myself, Simon, or Piper, before you print it in the context of a story."

Weirdly, no one tried to squeeze in any questions and we filed out of the small room M3rCy's PA had snagged for the conference. None of us spoke until the door closed then Simon slung his arm around my shoulder.

"You doing okay?" he asked, concern clear in his tone. "Yeah, a little shaky still, but knowing he's not coming back helps." I said, about Colin.

"What say we show our faces and jump back on the plane to Breckenridge tonight?" Gibson suggested.

"Piper would you rather me take you home where you can have a few days peace and quiet by the beach? When you're rested I'll take you to Colorado when you had planned to go up there?" It sounded exactly what I needed but before I could reply, Simon addressed, Gibson. "Melody's with her mom next week until Saturday is she not, Gibson?"

I had expected Gibson to press the point about me going up there because he was worried about me being supported after Colin's appearance, but he nodded and shrugged.

"Whatever Piper wants. As long as she's happy." My heart clenched because both men left it to me to decide.

"Yeah, if you don't mind, Gibson, I'll go with Simon. I want to recharge my batteries before I see Mel if that's okay?"

From the moment of the press conference I had heard a shift in Gibson's language and the way he regarded Simon in respect of me. It was as if when he knew Colin wasn't a danger to me, he could relax a little and let me take responsibility for myself.

The way Gibson had spoken about Simon was as if he were part of the team and Simon would take care of me, even if Gibson hadn't voiced this.

Although I wasn't in a party mood, I was glad I had shown my face because I had wanted to thank my band for all their support since they'd come on board.

It had been a crazy couple of months and it was thanks to them I had an awesome team to help me put my best foot forward during my first small tour and performances.

Layla Hartmann gave me an end of tour bonus because in places where she'd been struggling to fill the venues, as word got out about me, her whole tour sold out. She said it was thanks to me, but most of the audience were hers first.

I passed most of the extras forward and onto the band, who were obviously delighted with their latest windfall.

During the party and a few glasses of wine later, I sang a duet with Melody to her favorite song, "No Tears Left To Cry," by Ariana Grande, and little Mel was totally badass.

I was so proud because it isn't the easiest song to do justice to, but the sweet kid has her father's timing and ear for music.

The lyrics were pretty on point for me as well because although I was still shaken, going forward my life was looking the best it had ever been.

I had a career I had made happen, an incredible boyfriend who despite his past felt perfect for me, and a second chance to be part of a family who had nothing but love for each other.

A small bump on my shoulder drew my attention from the group of partygoers I was talking to. "Wanna dance with me?" my gorgeous man asked as he gave me a coy look, pretending to be shy. The questioning look of expectation that followed made my heart flip over in my chest.

"Hmm. Oh, go on then," I said, like he'd had to coax me into it, when in truth any excuse was good for me to step into his arms.

Reaching down for my hand, he lifted it above my head, and twirled me romantically around. Placing one hand on the base of my spine and my other in his, lifting it to his chest, he swayed in time to the music with me.

Warmth radiated from his hard, muscular body into mine as he flashed me a mischievous, sexy smile. Licking his lips, he pressed them to mine.

Pulling his head back, he gave me a soul-searching look, and we danced quietly to "Say You Won't Let Go" by James Arthur. Simon heaved a long breath and exhaled.

"This song is perfect because I'm so into you," he murmured. I barely heard what he said above the music, but it still made my chest tighten when my heart swelled at his words. "Can we leave yet?" he asked as his gaze intensified.

I glanced around looking for Chloe and saw Gibson hugging Melody over his shoulder—she was sound asleep. "Sure, I think the family is about done for the night," I said causing Simon to look over his shoulder in the same direction as me and he sighed. "Thank God. Let's get out of here," he said, suddenly full of purpose.

~

The sound of birds chirping outside drew me out of my sleep as they competed with the constant whirr of the air conditioning. Stretching lazily, I turned to look at Simon who was sprawled flat out in the bed, naked, the white cotton sheet crumpled in a heap at his feet.

My chest filled with emotion, my throat constricted, and a swell of love engulfed every cell in my body for the man who slept beside me, oblivious I was objectifying him.

Taking in his beautiful closed eyes, his slightly parted mouth, the dark smooth beard on his chin, I loved it all: his skin, hair, teeth, strong hands; my eyes ticked over his strong lean body and I sighed.

"Are you checking out my dick?" he muttered, his eyes still closed.

"Not yet but give me long enough and I'll get to that," I stated honestly, "I was kind of saving that sight for last."

"Ah, spicy... the best bit, huh?" he asked, shifting on his side to pull me closer.

"How long have we been together now? Two months?" he asked.

Squinting in thought, I bit my lip to count the weeks then gave up, "Feels a lot longer than that," I stated, honestly.

Staring into my eyes, he fell quiet for a moment and our gaze intensified. *I love everything about this beautiful, gentle man.* I lay watching his eyes move like he had thoughts running through his head and wondered what he was thinking about.

Simon took a long deep breath and sighed. His gaze grew more serious and piercing. "I can't remember life before you, Princess."

"God, you're smooth," I teased with a chuckle, "And cheesy," I added, maybe because I felt scared at the depth of his feelings.

"Since I met you my life has been different." His comment made me reflect briefly on my own journey through the previous couple of years since I'd lost my beautiful mom. Incidents where Simon had helped me, the love I felt from the whole set-up at Dignity and the Barclays, and where my life path had led me.

"As in?" I asked.

"Cleaner. Better. Centered." Simon shrugged, and his hand moved to rest on my hip. "My sole focus in life is to please you." I must have looked shocked because he frowned. "I'm serious. Whatever you want, I want. Wherever you are, it's where I want to be. Whoever you're with, I automatically hate because I don't want to share you with anyone."

"You know you sound pussy-whipped?" I told him. "And clingy." I laughed softly.

"I'm in love, Piper. Never felt anything like it. I'm scared as fuck about what this means for us, but I never want it to end."

Excitement coursed through my body as his words stole my breath. My heart doubled its beat. Happiness vibrated within my chest with the thrill of his declaration.

Having someone special to love me the way Simon did was more than I'd ever dreamed of. *Simon McLennan loves me.*

"Me neither, I'm scared too," I confessed.

A frown creased his brow and he swiped some stray strands of my hair away from my forehead. "Tell me what you're scared of."

"This... how happy I am right now. How, when I'm happy there's always a downside just around the corner." I was thinking about my mom.

"A downside?"

"Yeah, like when I'll have to deal with a broken heart," I said.

Concern and hurt passed through his eyes and he shook his head. "Not by me... I promise. Never." The determination in his voice made me breathless.

I fell silent wondering how he could say any of this with so much certainty in his tone.

"You don't believe me?" His eyes suddenly dulled with worry. Searching his face, I could see in his heart he believed what he was saying, but who knew what would happen in the future?

"I'd marry you tomorrow, but that wouldn't be fair to you." My jaw dropped, and I almost choked, while my heart stuttered for a semblance of normal rhythm at his declaration and I jerked back from him.

Shaking my head in denial, my heart skipped another beat and I suddenly felt shy. A flush of embarrassment flooded through me.

Casually, I made a blasé joke about what he'd said because I was sure it was only said to reinforce how much he liked me. "No, you wouldn't," I chuckled, "but thank you for saying that."

He sighed and tightened his grip on my hip, "Baby, you have no clue how unsettled I feel about you. You say you love me, right? Think of how that feels, and I bet it pales in comparison to what's going on inside me."

Nothing could have prevented the beaming smile that spread on my face, "It's a lot to accept," I replied, my voice barely a whisper.

"You will, in time. I'm not going to overwhelm you, Princess, I've waited thirty-two years for a beautiful girl like you, a little longer won't chew me up. I'm not going to force what we have because I need you to be sure being mine is what you want... that I am what you need."

"I'm already yours, Simon," I said, my voice shaky with a sudden wave of emotion, "I don't think I'd ever find a better man," My eyes moved back and forth over his beautiful solemn face.

"Only time will tell, Princess. You have a huge career ahead of you, and we both know I have mine, so I'm willing to wait, to test it all out, but when you're ready if you want me, I'll still be here."

Tears sprang to my eyes as my heart swelled in response to his self-less comment and I knew Simon had a great deal of genuine thought to us being together.

Even though he felt I was 'The One' it took guts to put me first, even if that meant the risk of losing me. His statement said his love was unconditional, or he had faith in what we had.

"I hear what you're saying, and I'm so deeply touched you're willing to go at my pace. However, my mom waited for most of my life to take a risk that would finally make her happy. Unfortunately for her, she left it too late. I don't want to make the same mistake, Simon. It wouldn't matter how old I was or what I had achieved in life if I chose the wrong person or had no one to share that with."

Shifting up onto his elbow he gently rolled me onto my back. "You're certain you want to be with me now?" he asked, his eyes searching my face as his tone hinted of his excitement.

"If you'll have me... we don't have to get married, but maybe live between both places or something."

"Haven't we been doing that already?" he asked in a humorous tone, but his gorgeous hazel eyes were suspicious as he searched mine for any doubts.

"If you say I'm yours then I am," I said simply. My heart was full.

Dropping his forehead to mine, he smiled so wide I thought his face would split. Slowly his smile died, and his gaze intensified as his thoughts grew deeper. He sighed.

"Damn, I'm good." He chuckled. "Hands up. The time for total honesty has come. I was talking shit a few minutes ago." His eyes darkened but there was still a hint of playfulness in them. "Do you honestly think I'd stand aside for any other hairy-assed fucker who came sniffing around you? As you know Gibson has huge balls when his territory's threatened, but you ain't seen nothing if anyone fucks with my girl," he stated, frankly.

"Oh, my very own caveman, how original," I teased and laughed softly.

"Damn straight, maybe I better get that ring on your finger after all; we don't want to give them false hope," he mused. Scooping me up in his arms, he rolled onto his back, taking me with him.

"Is that a poor excuse for a proposal?"

"What would you say if I asked?"

"Hmm, I don't know. I guess I'd have to go with my gut if the moment presented itself."

Impulsively, Simon shoved me off of him, stood up off the bed, bodily lifted me and sat me at the edge of the bed with my feet on the floor. Buck naked, he dropped down on one knee in front of me.

"Marry me. I mean... Piper, what do you say? I have no elaborate romantic words or sparkly expensive ring that would do what I'm asking justice to you, but I'm here," he held out his hands to show me his body, "In all my naked glory... as are you; sensational look by the way."

Stopping for a moment, his eyes widened like he had only just realized what he was doing and he swallowed roughly.

A wave of emotion swept up from my throat, and tears sprang from my eyes. Quickly, I swiped them away as I stared back at the blurry image of the man I felt would shape my future.

My heart pounded wildly in my chest as I absorbed the enormity of the moment and I found I didn't need to think about my answer.

"Piper, Princess, would you do me the greatest honor of being my wife?"

For a few seconds I reminded myself of who he was and wondered if this was real. My breath hitched. The feeling of suffocation Simon had spoken of was inside my chest and it wasn't because I felt trapped, it was because the love I felt for him was so overwhelming I had forgotten how to breathe.

Emotion closed my throat so tight I couldn't speak at first. I stared totally mesmerized by the occasion then nodded. When Simon exhaled, I realized he had been holding his breath too.

"Yes," I said in a small shaky voice. Clearing my throat, I tried again, "Yes," I repeated. The second time my voice was far more decisive and committed. "With one condition."

His hesitant smile turned to a frown in a heartbeat. "Which is?"

"You stop calling me Princess." Simon chuckled and give me a wicked grin as he sat quietly for a moment taking me in.

Then he nodded. "Deal," he replied, jumping up off the floor. Shoving me back on the bed he climbed on top, surrounded me with his limbs and pressed his lips to mine.

Our kiss was charged with emotion and love and when he tore his lips away from mine, he stared at me with determination. "Thank you, My Queen," he said, and chuckled as I immediately swiped at his chest and rolled my eyes.

We both laughed harder before Simon tucked me into his chest and heaved another deep breath.

"Damn. I can't believe I just did that... and you said, yes. Fuck." He murmured then fell silent. I had thought for a second the enormity of his question was too quick, and he'd wanted to take it back when he sighed. "We're really going to do this, huh?" he asked playfully.

"Think we are," I confirmed, and felt relieved he wasn't changing his mind. We let a pause happen in our conversation and were content to lay absorbing the decision we'd made until I felt Simon's body stiffen like something was wrong. A chill ran down my spine and I glanced up at him.

"What? I questioned.

"Just wondering... who's telling Gibson?" A wicked smirk passed over his lips and I laughed.

"Hmm... usually the guy asks the father, doesn't he?" I replied and chuckled at the twisted facial expression he made.

"Ah, well, shit, I'll take it back... maybe we'll just live in sin for a while... or how good are you at keeping secrets?" he asked, stalling for a moment before we both stared at each other, pondered his question then chuckled again. Then I had another thought.

"Would this make you Gibson's son-in-law?"

Simon burst out laughing then continued laughing until there was no air left in his lungs. As I watched his body jerk hysterically, I knew he'd use the opportunity to his full advantage.

I also knew that whatever the future held for us, I was convinced with someone like my rock star, Simon, life would never be dull.

EPILOGUE

*T*hree years later.

"That should have come with a warning," Petra snapped like she was disgusted, nodding at the old string hammock nestled by the side of the pool house.

Kerr, his wife Louisa, and the rest of my band had been invited over for a last minute barbecue since Gibson, Chloe, and Melody, were down from Colorado for a few days.

Following Petra's gaze, a slow, smug smile crept over my lips. My heart instantly swelled with pride and love when I saw my husband Simon fast asleep in our old string hammock. On his bare chest lay our tiny precious newborn bundle of joy, Olivia.

Dressed only in a diaper, our Simon's new little princess was now my main competition for the love of my life's affections, and considering I was looking on, she appeared to be winning. Even in sleep, Simon's hand spread protectively across her back, holding her in place.

At only five days old, with her dad's dark-brown hair and hazel eyes, Olivia Patricia Chloe McLennan had already stolen Simon's heart, and mine. My eyes lingered as I thought of how amazing Simon had been since the moment she'd been born.

"Excuse me?" I asked, my voice rising with inflection, and I turned back to Petra with narrowed eyes. Pretending I was miffed, I raised an eyebrow and jabbed a hand on my hip like I was annoyed.

"Hot as fuck tattooed guys and tiny newborn babies," she muttered and sighed. "I know he's yours but my ovaries ache like hell looking at that scene over there."

Louisa chuckled after she too looked over at them and bashfully nodded in agreement. "A word of warning, please don't ever let him out with Olivia on their own. There's a good chance you'll never see either of them again, they'd be kidnapped in a heartbeat." She sniggered.

Austin's girl, Maria said nothing, and I wondered what she made of us. She was a new addition to the raucous clan. I felt for her because she still hadn't mastered the banter from the serious chat.

If anyone else apart from Petra and Louisa had made a leering remark like that about my man, I'd have been royally ticked, but Petra had Isiah, and Kerr had married Louisa a few months after Simon and I were married.

Ronnie Silvers bit back a grin and shook his head at Petra. Yes, Ronnie was as good as his word when he had said he'd buy my album and look me up. Since then he had turned out to be one of the best friends I ever had.

The people around the table were my little tribe and since marrying Kerr, Louisa had given up her job to travel around with us. She was found to be a brilliant marketing manager and I hired her as my personal PR and mouthpiece.

What was most exciting of all, was Louisa was also pregnant with a girl, and I was so over the moon for her and Kerr, but even more so for Olivia, because she'd have a friend.

When I first found out I was pregnant, I'm not going to lie, I was worried. The huge revelation about Jenna Mitchell and her twins had given me plenty to think about.

Hearing Simon say he thought he never wanted kids as a teenager, I had sworn to myself to be damned sure that had changed before I ever brought a child into the world. However, it was he who brought the subject up one night, saying we should think about planning for children because he was already in his thirties.

Little did he or I know when we spoke that night, there was no longer anything to decide. Olivia wasn't planned but when I saw Simon's reaction I knew he was honestly thrilled.

Receiving the news about parenthood shifted Simon's focus immediately and suddenly our security was his highest priority. As he had explained 'we had to take care of ourselves because we were responsible for another life'. It was cute how 'Gibson-like' he became about our safety.

As Olivia was five days old and we'd settled down at home, Simon had invited everyone over for the day because he said he wasn't having our home turned into Disneyworld with queues of people arriving at the door to play with Olivia.

Since the day Olivia had been born, Simon's parents, Lorna and Michael, had been staying next door with Stevie. I couldn't have wished for better in-laws and it felt weird to have another set of 'Olds' to think about.

Obviously, they were much older than Gibson and Chloe and more reserved, but Lorna's gentle ways and Michael's smart mouth were a fabulous combination and they had accepted me as a daughter from the moment we met.

Unfortunately, Olivia arrived the week Melody had important school tests in Colorado and after having a short discussion everyone agreed we didn't want our youngest family member to be left out of the Barclay's initial introductions to the newest member of the family.

Gibson and Chloe stayed home at our insistence and we Skype called daily until Chloe and Melody finally arrived on day four post Olivia's birth; the day before Gibson. Chloe cried when she held her granddaughter for the first time and my heart immediately ached for her.

Given the Barclay's history it must have been very difficult for her. Not that she showed it of course. I made a fuss of her new position and promised Chloe she'd be the most important female in Olivia's life after myself.

Fortunately, Melody interrupted the awkward moment and dragged me away by my hand to negotiate another hold for herself until Chloe tried to tamp her enthusiasm by reminding Melody baby Olivia wasn't a toy.

Melody pressed on regardless of Chloe's warning, gaining plenty of practice at being an aunt as we gathered to share our new baby girl with those closest to Simon and I.

It had taken us five full days to arrange for everyone we loved to get together in one place and they were all the most important people in our lives. But despite the small smiling crowd my heart still wasn't contented because a prior commitment of Gibson's had meant we'd had to wait until late in the day before he could join us.

My feeling of the scene being incomplete instantly vanished when Gibson suddenly appeared, with Jonny and Jerry carrying yet more fresh flowers and balloons.

With wide arms he grabbed me, stroked my back, and put his mouth close to my ear. "Very proud of you, Piper. Olivia is as gorgeous as her mom. Congratulations, sweetheart."

Glancing around the patio, I knew he was searching for Chloe and Melody. "Chloe, okay?" he asked, and I knew exactly what his concern was.

Nodding, I said, "She's doing okay." Shrugging, he scratched the back of his head in a gesture of helplessness, looked choked and hugged me again.

Breaking away from me he immediately went and sought his wife and daughter out. I watched them closely and my heart swelled to see Chloe's beaming smile when she saw him.

Chloe looked happy as she chatted with him and Melody. Eventually, she chuckled and nodded toward the pool house and I knew Gibson had asked where Simon was.

Looking over in the direction of Simon, Gibson spun on his heels and wandered slowly toward the hammock. Melody went to go after him, but Chloe caught her hand and distracted her. I suspected Chloe figured Gibson wanted a moment alone with my man.

Stopping when he reached the hammock, I had expected Gibson to wake Simon up. When he didn't, I was drawn toward him with a vibe that something was wrong.

Moving over beside him I stood shoulder to shoulder with Gibson, but he didn't look at me even though he knew I was there.

"You okay?" I asked in a soft tone.

"Yeah, I was only thinking."

"About?"

"Mel. I missed all of this. All her baby and toddler years... every-thing." He sighed, heavily. "All these important early days, this... skin to skin bonding stuff," his voice was thick with emotion and he shrugged helplessly again then cleared his throat. I'd never seen Gibson vulnerable before.

"Melody loves you so much, Gibson... and Chloe. What both you and Chloe have gone through..." my voice trailed away because I couldn't begin to imagine not having a child of my own or missing this part of Olivia's life.

Breathing in deeply, he exhaled and ran his fingers through his hair. He glanced at me with hurt in his eyes and gave me a small sad smile. "Shit we deal with makes us stronger, yeah?" he offered. I nodded.

"How is Chloe with this? I mean really?" I asked.

"Over the moon. We have a new baby in the family. She's stoked... as am I," he said, taking a moment to grin at me.

I sighed, "I'm taking a year off. The last two and a half have been grueling. I won't get this time again with Olivia," I informed him, decisively.

Simon stirred and opened his eyes, his hand immediately stroking the soft skin on our tiny sleeping daughter's back.

Clearing his throat, he grinned, "Ah, thank God you're here, Gramps."

"Oy, she's calling me Gibson," he corrected, and Simon laughed.

"We'll see," he smirked, "Gorgeous, isn't she?" Simon said proudly, "But for someone who looks so perfect, she behaves like she's pig ugly. If she's not hogging my wife's tits, she's shitting up a storm. She can turn the house into a sty in five minutes flat and nowhere in those instruction books did it say she was an entirely nocturnal creature."

Gibson chuckled and stuck his hands in his jeans pockets. I knew instinctively it was to help him resist overstepping and reaching out to pick her up off of Simon.

Simon's eyes Gibson's hands just like mine had, and he stretched lazily in the hammock again.

"Do me a favor, buddy. Can you grab hold of her in case I drop her getting out of this thing?"

Gibson's face brightened immediately, his hands swiftly leaving his pockets, and he slid one between Simon's chest and Olivia's belly effectively peeling her away from him.

"Damn she's sweaty," he chuckled, his eyes full of awe as he maneuvered her carefully over his shoulder.

"Jesus, take that rough shirt off if you're going to hold her like that," Simon instructed. My eyes flicked to Simon's and he immediately dropped his gaze which told me he'd heard our conversation.

Handing Olivia to me, Gibson did as Simon instructed and I handed my baby back. Expertly, Gibson placed her back over his shoulder, and as he cradled her tiny head, he inhaled her new baby scent.

"She's absolutely perfect," he said in his rich low tone, his thumb strumming over her back.

"Glad you think so, because as her Gramps you'll be in that position frequently when you and Grandma have her at weekends. I mean when Piper and I need alone time.

"Gramps? Are you fu..."

"Ah, not in front of the children," Simon interjected, cutting him off before Gibson cussed.

Nursing Olivia with slightly bended knees, I saw Gibson's heart melt. "This baby is a true blessing, but I'll put her straight from an early age on the name," Gibson said before he winced in pain.

Glancing at his chest it was clear Olivia had grabbed a fistful of chest hair close to his skin.

"Doubt that, Gibson, she's just like Melody and this one here," Simon said gesturing at me, "You'd do anything for them and you know it, so the sooner you stop fighting it the better." Chuckling heartily, Gibson began to head back in the direction of the others.

"That's right, Simon, and you'd do well to remember that. Upset any of my women or refer to me as Gramps and there will be hell to pay."

As I stood watching the banter between them, I couldn't help feeling grateful beyond words for all the Barclays had done, but the biggest joy they brought me was to know my daughter would grow up surrounded by these men in a world free from suppression.

Thanks to God, and Gibson, I'd never have to look over my shoulder again in fear. Colin had been sentenced to seven years and died in a prison fight less than three months later. None of us grieved for him.

Five years before, my mom and I had arrived in Colorado in the middle of the night, finally escaping a life of manipulations, control, and violence.

We thought we'd fled a tyrant and looked forward to building a better life. No one could have predicted then there was a greater blow to come.

On my knees at seventeen, my world turned upside down. But for the kindness and unlikely love of two generous people with the biggest hearts, I would most definitely have sunk.

In the beginning they gave me shelter and protection, held my hand when I cried and gave me time to grieve.

Gradually, through their consistent love and trust, I slowly learned to breathe again in a whole new life full of everything I could have wished for. Most importantly I learned who I was meant to be, and Gibson encouraged me to follow my dream.

As I looked at my beautiful loving family in front of me, I think I'm still dreaming. I would never forget what they've done for me and since the day I set out to chase my goal I had wanted to pay the Barclays, but they insisted their help was their gift to me.

However, the tables had turned, and I had a different wealth to them, and what better gift could I give them back than a new generation to love?

THE END

OTHER TITLES BY K.L. SHANDWICK

THE EVERYTHING TRILOGY

Enough Isn't Everything

Everything She Needs

Everything I Want

Love With Every Beat

just Jack

Everything Is Yours

LAST SCORE SERIES

Gibson's Legacy

Trusting Gibson

Gibson's Melody

READY FOR FLYNN SERIES

Ready For Flynn, Part 1

Ready For Flynn, Part 2

Ready For Flynn, Part 3

Flying Under The Radar

OTHER NOVELS

ABOUT THE AUTHOR

K. L. Shandwick lives on the outskirts of York, UK. She started writing after a challenge by a friend when she commented on a book she read. The result of this was 'The Everything Trilogy'. Her background has been mainly in the health and social care sector in the U.K. Her books tend to focus on the relationships of the main characters. Writing is a form of escapism for her and she is just as excited to find out where her characters take her as she is when she reads another author's work.

30655743R00195

Printed in Poland
by Amazon Fulfillment
Poland Sp. z o.o., Wrocław